I0646078

Jeremy Jessens

Fatal Force

The rights of Charles Boggett to be identified as the author
of this work has been asserted in accordance with the
Copyright. Designs and Patents Act 1988.
www.jjessens.co.uk

Registration © 272964 UK©CS

ISBN 978-0-9558546-0-6

All rights reserved. No part of this publication may be reproduced,
or stored in a retrieval system, or transmitted in any form
without written permission of the Author.

All characters in this publication are fictitious and any
resemblance to persons, living or dead is purely coincidental

Chapter 1

Steering his car off the main road, that ran from the western suburbs of St Petersburg to the city centre, Dennis Blackstoke drove onto a piece of wasteland with its cracked and broken concrete. Negotiating his car in a half circle and passing the many deep potholes that lay in abundance over the area, he finally brought his vehicle to a halt opposite a burger bar, which was one of a few shops that strung along the main road.

He was tired of travelling, for he had spent the last year working on a case that the department had given him and with little results to show for his labour, so he decided to take a rest and get something to eat.

His first stop had been Odessa to search for some of Russia's unsavoury characters that were trafficking drugs across Europe to England. The Russian authorities had asked the British government, to help them in a joint effort to get rid of the rotten trade for the last time.

Switching the engine off, he leaned back in his seat and watched the rain falling gently on the greasy smeared windscreen before making a move. Being in his early thirties and exceptionally fit, he quickly jumped from the car and sprinted across the road avoiding the deep puddles as he went towards the burger house. Then after paying for his pre- ordered meal, he returned to the car and slid silently into the driver's seat.

Not relishing the thought of going to Russia, but knowing he was the only one who could speak the language fluently in the department, he accepted the job with reluctant enthusiasm.

1

He made his way to Odessa and joined forces with an American by the name of Jack Pullman, who was also working on the same case, but had in fact had successfully infiltrated the crooks lair.

Once Dennis gathered his information he then passed it to his American friend in the hope they could catch the crooks much quicker, however; as things unfolded Dennis discovered more than drugs were at stake; indeed a far sinister operation was involved.

On completion of his work, he felt all his troubles were now behind him and left the remaining details to his friend Jack so the required arrests, could be made.

As he parked on that rugged piece of ground, he thought of the prospect of going home, now satisfied he had done all he could to make sure the crooks, would be locked away. Quietly listening to soft music from the car radio, he sat snugly in his seat enjoying the sanctuary of the moment and began thinking of his cottage in Cornwall and the renovation he needed to undertake when he returned. For this he hoped would be his last field job for a while, for he knew his boss had promoted him to a desk job.

So engrossed with his thoughts about his future and taking a bite from his burger, he never heard the police officer until the tap on the car window. Annoyed and irritated by the intrusion, he lowered the window before recognising it was a police officer trying to gain his attention.

'Sorry officer, have I parked in a restricted area?' Dennis said, amazed by the officer standing by his car.

Suddenly and without warning Dennis of his intentions, the officer swiftly drew his gun from its holster, and aiming it at Dennis's head and he squeezed the trigger.

Dennis's body jerked violently at the impact of the bullet hitting his head and slammed him back hard against the headrest. Blood pouring from the huge gaping wound, he released hold of the half-eaten burger and coke that fell to the floor mixing with his warm blood, which now spewed onto the carpet. The officer not bothering to check to see if Dennis was dead or not, casually returned his gun to its holster and began delving into the pockets of the dead man. Not finding what he required he looked round the area with cold chilling eyes, before turning away from the scene and walked quietly across the open space, gazing around to make sure no one had heard or saw what had taken place. Moving through the pile of bricks and concrete at the far end of the derelict area, he slumped into his car with a sickly grin across his face. Checking once again that nobody in the proximity had seen what had taken place; he started the engine and drove away from the scene.

Later that evening, after killing Dennis Blackstoke, the officer having changed from his uniform into his typical civilian clothes, drove through the quiet streets of the city towards the docks. Parking his car at the kerbside outside a block of flats, he left his car and walked into the entrance. Climbing several flights of stairs until arriving on the sixth floor, pausing briefly to check the passageway was clear for he did not want any body seeing him. He moved quietly along the corridor to the last door on the left.

Dennis's friend Jack Pullman stood gazing out of the window watching the small boats sailing back and forth in the harbour in the bright blue sunny evening. He had been in Russia longer than Dennis had and gained more information in solving the problem to the crooks intent. He had penetrated their lair successfully and established who the leaders were. Although Dennis's information had been practical, he nevertheless was on a different agenda in bringing crooks to justice. Now armed with the data he needed to find the right moment to dispatch it to his boss in Washington without the crook catching him. Hearing the knock on the door, but thinking it was Dennis coming to say goodbye, he moved expressively across the room to open it, and was surprised to see one of the crooks standing there in the doorway, who he had been working with.

'Oh it's you?' Jack announced with sarcasm. 'Good evening, I didn't expect to see you tonight; I thought the arrangements were to pick me up in the morning, have the orders changed?' Jack questioned turning his back on the crook to return to the window, where he had been watching the boats in the harbour.

'Yeah I was, but things have changed since I last spoke to you. I've been ordered to see you tonight instead,' the person grunted following Jack into the room. Then without warning and with precision he jumped on Jack, slapping a thin piece of cheese-wire round his throat and began pulling it tight. Jack unprepared for such an attempt and taken completely by surprise by the swiftness of the crook, tried desperately to free the wire from around his throat. He made a grab for the wire to free it from his throat, but was too slow, for the killer pushed his knee deep into his back while at the same time pulling the wire tighter. Jack choked bitterly; unable to breathe with the wire rapped round his throat he struggled in a frenzy trying to release it. Lashing out with his legs, he kicked the crook in the hope it might make his opponent fall and let go, but it was to no avail, it was too late. Gasping to breathe he became weaker and weaker, his legs buckled beneath his weight and slowly he slid towards the floor. Blood streamed down his chest from the lacerated wound as the wire dug deeper into his skin finally piercing his windpipe. Powerless to defend himself from the inevitable, his killer finally let go of him and Jack collapsed on the floor wriggling and twisted with convulsion. His voice croaking in a last attempt to breathe, he rolled over on his side and saw his killer with fading vision moving round his apartment. Then without uttering a sound, he closed his eyes and died in his pool of blood.

The crook as before with Dennis, checked to see if he was dead and then taking no further interest began searching the apartment, in a bid to find the required information on their organisation. He ripped open the bedroom clothes and cut through the mattress but found nothing. He then turned towards the drawers and dragged them from the cupboards, breaking them into small pieces in desperation but still with no results, then finally turning to Jack he tore at his clothes in disgust, while at the same time getting madder and madder at Jack for deceiving them, for Jack had hidden the data well.

Disturbed that he was not able to find the information, and not wanting the neighbours calling the real police, he fled the flat making his way back in which he entered the building, and escaped by car from the area.

Chapter 2

Tabor stepped from the rear of his car into a bright warm early sunlit afternoon, and noticed the small puffs of clouds that scattered high in the rich blue sky, drifting lazily on a westerly course.

He stood for a moment at his chauffeur's side viewing the area around him before making a move. To his right, stood an old burnt out farmhouse, only its brick walls remained standing, charred wood-ash lay scattered about showing what was left of the building. On his left, he saw the large barn where he had arranged to meet the dealer.

'I trust you are not going to say you have not got what I asked for,' he said in a calm gentle voice, as he walked towards the dealer in his spotlessly clean beige suit, that was made to fit his slim body. Around his neck, hung a light brown gold tie, which fitted perfectly with the rest of his attire. His glistening white shirt tucked neatly into his razor sharp crease trousers that ran down each leg ending slightly above his highly polished brown crocodile leather slip on shoes, which happened to be the fashion amongst the business class at that time. On his right index finger, a one-caret diamond ring sparkled as it caught the sunlight. He also wore gold-framed sunglasses with dark mirror lenses to shield his grey cold piecing eyes from the brightness of the day.

'Behind the barn,' the dealer grunted, 'in the back of the truck and ready for your inspection,' the person continued to say, pointing with his left thumb over his right shoulder in the direction to where he had parked his truck. They made their way side by side to the truck, the dealer conscious that Tabor was slightly taller and heavier than he was. He was aware if the need arose, Tabor could handle himself in the event of any unforeseen menace in which he may try to undertake.

Casually strolling towards the old Mercedes lorry with its forty-foot length trailer, which could carry up to 40 tonnes in weight if required.

Tabor noticed two of the dealer's men standing by the cab of the vehicle, both carrying Kalashnikov's rifles placed across their chests, nevertheless unconcerned by the threat he lifted the green tarpaulin sheet that hung loosely over the vehicle and revealed four long wooden crates. Inside the top crate a newly painted green metal cylinder shone, which gave it a menacing look. They had painted the end of the cylinder black for about 14 inches, and fitted additional boltholes to extend the cylinder by a further 18 inches if required. At the opposite end, two small propellers shielded by a casing to stop objects from infringing their movement when in operation.

'Excellent,' Tabor commented, 'they look admirable, I trust they work, you have had them tested I assume?'

'Absolutely,' the dealer said, 'there will be no problems I can assure you, you can trust me?' Tabor gave him a sideward glance, as he trusted no one, for in his language trust was a pretty tall order and they had to earn it over a long period, in fact, he only trusted a few men in his life.

'What about the others?' Tabor replied looking pleased at the objects but not showing the dealer how much, although he gave a slight evil grin.

'You are satisfied with them?' The other man added.

There was not much between them in build, though the dealer's feature was much rougher and had the characteristics to show for it. A scar ran down his left cheek from under the eye to his upper lip, implying he had been in many a brawl and showed the earmarks to prove it. He was not dressed near as smart as Tabor, for he was wearing old baggy dirty jeans and a green shirt that was to big for him; his scratched and muddy boots were of army issue and had seen better times.

'Yes you have done well so far; but how about the special ones I ordered?' Tabor said, not attempting to call him by his name. 'You will of course have the others ready in time?'

'I will have them all delivered at the place we arranged earlier,' the dealer added nervously.

'Excellent,' Tabor added feeling something could go wrong with the deal, as he had heard from his sources that this chap had squelched on numerous deals before this meeting. Nevertheless, for now he had no choice, for he was the only person who could get the goods he wanted, which put Tabor in a precarious position, nevertheless; he would deal ruthlessly with him if he tried to double-cross him. 'Right, I'll give you part payment now as I said I would and the rest when you deliver,' Tabor said, then waving his right arm to order his driver who was standing by his car to get a case from the boot. The driver doing as ordered handed over a black brief case to Tabor and took a couple of steps back, but remained at the ready in the event of trouble. 'Here is 500,000 American dollars which we arranged; the rest of the money be paid to you in Murmansk, when you have had the goods secretly loaded on board my ship, and the remainder stored in my warehouse. You can check the money if you wish?' Tabor announced.

'That won't be necessary,' Scar face assured him. 'You may recall that when we last spoke, I told you I would like to hit back at the enemy and see them squirm, so make them pay. They must not get away with what they did to your family, nor to all your friends,' Scar face hissed spitting out the words. 'I will enjoy reading the papers about the so-called civilized world's calamity for their hand in the murders. Washington in particular for condoning it and sitting back doing nothing to stop it happening,' the dealer remarked with venom in his voice.

'Fair enough,' Tabor stated. 'My ship will be in dock on Wednesday morning for what appears to be engine maintenance; I will be there Thursday evening at 7pm, so allowing for some hold-ups that will gives you 4 days to deliver. You know the score if discovered. I do not know you or anything about your activities, you understand.

'Yes Tabor, I'm perfectly aware of the consequences,' Scar face admitted,

'I promise there'll be no problems, so the sooner I get on my way the better,' the dealer said moving over towards his truck.

'Very well,' Tabor replied and then turning swiftly on his heels he walked slowly to where he had left his car and slithered into the back seat, and then ordered his chauffeur to drive unhurriedly away from the farm. They drove silently along the dirty road in which they previously came along earlier, then after reaching the main road they turned right onto the highway, and gathering speed headed towards his plane some seventy miles away.

'We will have to wait and see, if it goes according to plan,' he said to nobody in particular and then placing his arms round the back of his head he closed his eyes and thought to what the future may lay.

Chapter 3

'Mr and Mrs. Walker?' a man said as they walked out from the customs hall into the main terminal.

'Yes that is correct,' Mark replied.

'Good afternoon, and welcome to St Petersburg. My name is Fryderyk Leshin,' he said holding out a hand to shake them. 'I am your representative and guide for most of your vacation. So if I can help in anyway please ask and I will do my utmost to answer any of your questions to which you may put before me. Did you have an excellent flight? I see there were no delays; I must say it makes a change, for we frequently have some kind of hold-up or other,' he said speaking very quickly as they began to walk out of the terminal and towards the car park. 'My car is the black Mercedes over there,' he stated guiding them swiftly to where he had parked his car.

As Ann and Mark sat in the back seats, Leshin got behind the steering wheel and instantly started the engine. Moving the gearshift backwards and forwards, he struggled to find the first gear, and then finally succeeding they drove from the airport car park and headed towards the busy main road and towards their hotel. 'The hotels about 5km from here, it's also not far from the city centre, around 11km,' Leshin informed them as they sped along the highway towards the hotel.

Mark could not help noticing Leshin was very thin and not exactly, what he had imagined as a holiday representative. As his trousers had creases where he had not bothered to have had them pressed, his jacket was also on the large size in fact he estimated it was two sizes too big. Mark thought he would give the Russians some latitude to his attire, for it was conceivable the eastern block countries had not yet caught with the West's dress code.

Mark was aware he seemed edgy and nervous, his eyes kept on blinking as if he had some kind of irritant in them, and he kept looking round, to see if somebody was surveying him at what he was doing. He was not at all sure of himself. Mark would have put money on him he had never done this particular work before. Shrugging it from his thoughts, he put it down to the old days when the KGB ruled. It was not a very good start to the holiday and did not give him much reassurance it would be a good-break.

'We have booked you in the hotel Pulkouskaya, it is in a very quiet locality and being a four star hotel it is as good as any five star hotel we have in the area. I'm sure you will enjoy it. The weather conditions are supposed to be very good, warm and sunny; you have certainly picked the right time to visit us. I say again I hope you will like your stay,' Leshin said repeating himself and beginning to get on Marks nerve with his constant chatter; then at length and with some relief they arrived at the hotel. 'Here we are,' Leshin said.

'This is your hotel, I say again I hope it meets with your requirements, please inform me if you are not satisfied.'
Walking into the reception area Mark looked round the lounge area, while Leshin went to the checking desk. On entering the lounge, a sign in front of them showed where the dining room, swimming pool, casino and conference rooms were located. There were more facilities on the notice board but Leshin called him to the desk to sign the book, so wandering over Mark joined Leshin to do as required.

'I'm afraid I have to attend to some other commitments and don't want to be late for them, so if you don't mind will you excuse me. I will return later tonight when you have finished your dinner, we can then discuss the itinerary for tomorrow. Is that all right by you Mr. Walker?'

'Yes that is fine we will speak later,' Mark said as Leshin was already making a move to go.

11

'Until tonight then,' he said looking back over his shoulder as he departed quickly from the foyer. 'Well, he was in a dam hurry, could not get away fast enough,' Ann stated. 'So it seems,' Mark responded.

'Excuse me please,' the receptionist said, 'if you require a meal we have a fine restaurant and it caters for all types of meals. It will be open from 7pm to 10pm,' the receptionist informed them with a pleasant smile.

'Many thanks,' Mark responded and then left her to go in search of their room. 'Here's our room darling,' Ann said arriving at the door and inserting the key into the lock to open it.

'Look at this my love, not bad is it,' she announced leisurely and carrying on through to the bedroom.

'Yes my love, and what a lovely size this room is,' Mark added following behind her. 'You should be able to sleep in here alright,' he added nudging her towards the bed.

'Trust you to think of it,' she said continuing on to find the bathroom.

'Would you like a drink to celebrate this holiday? It's been sometime since having a break,' he said picking up the phone to dial the number that was on a coffee table which was positioned close to a black leather three-seated settee, that had been located opposite a large window, which overlooked the grand gardens.

When the waiter left, Mark poured the champagne into two glasses and passed one to his wife who now appeared from the bathroom.

'To us and happy holidays,' Mark said tapping her glass before taking a sip of champagne from his glass. 'Cheers and thanks for arranging this trip,' Mark remarked while taking a sip of the liquid from his glass.

After their celebration, they went in search of the dining room, and while there, they discussed the day's journey over dinner. Finishing their meal they left the restaurant with its fine crystal chandeliers hanging from the high ceiling and its pictures of grandeur on the walls to find Leshin, for he had assured them they would find him in the bar waiting.

'Hope we did not keep you waiting,' Mark said approaching Leshin who was leaning against the bar.

'No, not at all,' Leshin replied. 'Have you settled in your room?'

'Yes thank you. And I must say the meal was excellent,' Mark stated before Leshin could enquire about it.

'Considering they had to caterer for all tastes, it was very well presented,' Ann chirped.

'Everything was fine,' Mark added again sounding a bit tired for he did not want to indulge with Leshin for very long.

'May I offer you both a drink?'

'Thank you,' they said in unison.

When Leshin bought the drinks, they sat down on a big brown leather sofa and waited for him to tell them what was on the agenda for the couple of days that they would be in town.

'So what have you arranged tonight, Mr. Leshin?' Ann enquired.

'Oh please call me Fryderyk,' Leshin said in a calm voice.

'OK Fryderyk,' Ann responded.

'Nothing tonight for it's now too late, for nothing happens around here, so may I suggest you stay in the hotel, as it's not very wise to go out on your own, not that we have much trouble in this area, however it's just a precaution

'Fine,' said Ann. 'We can stay in the hotel and use their amenities,' she remarked.

'Tomorrow at 9am a trip has been laid on for you to explore the city; you can do some shopping if you desire, I've also arranged for you to see a show in the evening, I hope that is in order. The following day we'll take in some museums, and in the afternoon, you can do as you wish. Then on Sunday, we will fly to Murmansk, where we will have some lunch at a favourite café of mine, and then head for the boat. We need to be there for 3pm, as they want to sail by 4pm,' Leshin said. However, hearing Leshin mentioning a boat, Mark looked mystified as to what he had said. He then faced Leshin for further explanation but sensing he was not going to get it voluntarily, he said. 'Fryderyk what Boat? What are you talking about?'

'Oh dear, I am so sorry; I thought Mark was aware of the trip. I am so sorry Ann; I hope I have not spoilt the surprise that you had laid on for him. I think I had better leave the explaining to you Ann, as to what it is all about with the boat. Once again I must apologise for spoiling the surprise,' Leshin said with a grim face that showed how disturbed he was.

'That's ok Fryderyk, I will explain to Mark what has been arranged Ann said.

'Then I will say no more apart from good-night and will take my leave, I will see you both in the morning. Incidentally, the boats captain's name is, Krabava Babarika; he is a very experienced skipper and you will be in very good hands with him. Nevertheless should you need any further information just ask him, he will not mind. Then until to tomorrow and once again good night Ann, Mark,' Leshin said and stood up, pausing for a second as if to say something further but changing his mind he disappeared from the bar.

'Well Ann, I am waiting,' Mark said expecting a good explanation, 'what are you up to? What kind of boat is he talking about?'

'My darling, it's a surprise, so if I tell you now it will spoil what I have arranged, you will have to trust me and wait and see,' she said with a grin across her face and a twinkle in her eye. 'I think it is time to go to bed, for I expect it will be a long day tomorrow,' she added instantly getting up from the sofa and grabbing hold of his hand they left the lounge to retire to their room for the night.

The following two days as predicted, Leshin was waiting out side the hotel to take them to the city to see the sights. Then on the last day on their way back to the hotel, Mark turned and faced Leshin.

14

'What time are we booked on the flight tomorrow Fryderyk?' asked Mark.

'We need to be at the airport for 9.am,' he said as he stopped the car outside the hotel entrance hall, and then wishing them a good night's sleep he revved the engine and pulled away slowly from the hotel till he reached the road and accelerated fast towards the city.

At the check-in counter, the Walkers handed their bags in for the flight to Murmansk before continuing to the departure lounge.

'My dear you have been very, very crafty in keeping this all a secret,' he whispered kissing her cheek.

'No problem my love, just enjoy the trip,' she said softly to him with a radiant smile.

Chapter 4

Tabor sat at the far end of an old heavy wooden table, in an old disused office in a warehouse. Dents and scratches littered the table's surface that augmented the rest of the room. Two of his men Leshin and Pozvizd sat to the left of him. Tabor the tallest of the three looked at the two men, before starting to question them.

This time he was dressed in a grey suit, that like the other one fitted the contour of his body, a black tie was pinned to his white shirt by a gold staple in a shape of a submarine; his shiny black-laced shoes augmented his appearance that put the other two men to shame.

'Is there anything I need to know that you have not told me?' Tabor questioned slowly in a deliberate calm voice, and making it clear he was fully in charge of what he was doing and what he expected from the two.

Light filtered through the only small dusty window, casting a shadow of gloom across the room that made the two men feel uneasy as they sat waiting for their boss to give his orders. A single light bulb shone from the centre of the ceiling and gave a dull glow over the room, which enhanced the spider's cobwebs that spun along the walls and window. The room smelt mouldy through years of neglect and lack of use giving the two men additional discomfort in the bleak atmosphere.

'Leshin,' said Tabor at length. 'Have you completed everything you were instructed to do?'

'Yes Mr. Tabor, the only thing I have to say is the travel company you have me working for, have sent two couples. One of the couples who are the Walkers has come from England, and the other couple has come from Germany; both are to go on the boat tomorrow. You are aware the English are under the impression that it is a special kind of holiday, a trip out to sea for a couple of days. Evidently, the first of a kind and a surprise for Mr. Walker as it's his retirement. The Germans are booked in the Marriott and are going to make their own way to the boat. I never expected them so had not relied on it, for you never informed me. What do you suggest I do with the English couple? As they are at the hotel and expecting me to take them to the boat, if you like we could delay the mission until the English have return from this little trip. What do you suggest?'

'Don't worry I shall see to it they talk to anybody about where they have been,' the other guy replied facing Leshin with an evil grin on his face, that emphasised his rugged appearance, which showed that he had little or no compassion for anybody or anything. The authorities had released him from a Siberian jail for killing some chap, but they did not give him the death sentence in stead he served five years, although no one ever found out why he had killed the chap. He was one of Tabors henchmen and did whatever his boss ordered to do. Having very little hair on his head and his short stocky build with muscles that protruded through his tight fitting clothes, added to the menacing look he portrayed. A gold earring hung from his left ear that matched the heavy chain that round his neck.

He looked at Leshin with his green cold eyes while he rolled a cigar one handed through his grubby fingers. Then lighting it he took a long slow drag of the cigar inhaling the smoke before leisurely blowing it out and then finally he spoke to Leshin.

'I don't see it makes any difference with what I'll do with them; they won't get in the way. I'll bury them some place where they can't be found, so you can carry on as usual Leshin,' Pozvizd scoffed.

'No, no, no---! That is not the way Pozvizd; I think you have done far too much killing as of late since you killed those two

17

agents, and what a mess you made of that. No we will do it my way,' Tabor said sternly but with a calm deliberation to his voice.

'Let the Walkers and the Schmitt's go on board the boat, I can assure you we will give them a trip to remember. Leshin contact the travel firm; keep them informed where they are, for the moment that way no one will become suspicious of what is taking place. I cannot and will not let anything go wrong with my plans, do you both hear me!' Tabor barked. 'So Leshin, pick them up as instructed, Pozvizd you do what you are told, you will keep your head down and out of site until I say otherwise. So this is what you will do, Leshin take Pozvizd in my launch and meet the Zhuralev. Pozvizd you will stay on the boat until I say otherwise. Leshin after dropping him off go to Kiev, tell the travel company you have a problem with your folks, or make anything up, just keep them out of the way. Remember, the agent that thumped you will surely know who you are if he spots you, so get going.'

'As you say Mr. Tabor I will keep out of trouble, I swear,' Pozvizd stated.

'I do say so, so lets not hear of anymore killings, for if there is any killing to do I will tell you when, where and who,' Tabor remarked.

'Ok,' they said in unison and assuring their boss that nothing would go wrong, they fled the room.

'Ok its clear for you to come in, they have gone Sakhakov,' Tabor said as Sakhakov had already entered the room without saying a word and sat on a chair opposite Tabor.

'Sakhakov I want you to go on board the submarine with Pozvizd, keep an eye on him, if he tries anything stupid, well you have my permission to do as you think fit, but do not tell the others that I suggested to you to get rid of him,' Tabor said.

'What do you want me to do on board? Krabava won't want anymore passengers getting in his way, that I'm sure,' Sakhakov mentioned.

'Yes you are right, very well go as second mate on the radio and sonar; you can relieve Andrei as he could not possibly work day and night.'

'Right I'll catch the others, unless you have something further to add?' Sakhakov uttered before starting to make his way towards the door.

'No, not at the moment, I will give you a few days to make sure everything is working well. Krabava can send me a signal when he is satisfied everything is all right with the boat and then we can get down to business and load all the supplies for the long journey ahead,' Tabor said.

After Sakhakov left with his instruction, Tabor blew out a heavy sigh, for he was relieved that his plans were at last beginning to pull into shape. He bent down, reached into his bag, and pulled a bottle of vodka from it and then pouring some of the liquid into a mug he leaned back in the chair to reflect the past, and to what had brought him to take on such a challenge. His mind flashed back to the time when he arrived at his home, only to find his folks slaughtered in a brutal attack, along with the whole village. He discovered later that it was to do with drugs. He could see his mother nailed naked to a telegraph pole by her hands; whoever the killers were had removed her bloody breasts and placed them at the bottom of the pole soaking. She had attained further cuts and bruises all over her body; he recalled vomiting at the sight of seeing her in such away. He had laid her down on the ground and then went in search for his father, only to discover him in his garden along with his younger sister dead. She had been like the rest of the women raped and cut to pieces, her arms and legs lay scattered about as if they were part of a doll. With tears running down his face, he helped Krabava find his folks and buried them in the local cemetery. While the other villages lay sprawled on the ground in the village he had left them where they had fallen. Nevertheless, that had happened ten years ago and now in that

19

filthy warehouse his mind twirling in confusion, he knew he had to take revenge on those responsible, retribution was what he aimed to do and retribution was what he would get. After mulling over the past, he replaced the mug in the bag and picking it up he walked from that dirty room, down the short wooden steps into the main warehouse, stopping briefly to give his remaining cargo a final inspection before proceeding out of the building into the damp air with the atrocities still vividly on his mind. It would be long time before he could forget. Slumping into the rear seat of his car, he told his driver to move away from the area. His attention now fully on what lay ahead; he now needed time to focus on the agents, and whether they had discovered information that was detrimental to his plans.

Chapter 5

'Good morning Jeff, how was your holiday, catch any fish? I suppose you are going to tell me the big one got away,' Jeff's boss said laughing in a deep gravel voice thinking about Jeff catching fish, for he knew Jeff was not the best man in trying to catch fish.

Jim was a small man of 5 feet in height, and on the plump side with receding white hair that made him look more weathered than it actually was, as he had spent a lot of time in the sun and wind. He was very agile for his age of 60 years and reckoned he could give any of his team a good run for their money. He enjoyed a good social life dining with his wife and friends, and enjoyed each other's company spending every second they could together, for having no children he spent his energy doing things, which continually involved his wife.

'Oh very funny, always the same old gags Jim, can't you think of something better than that,' Jeff said standing on the other-side of the desk where his boss was sitting and in a light-hearted mood. For he could take a joke with the rest of them; what is more he could give it back when the need arose however, when there was work to be done he did not hesitate to get stuck into whatever it entailed. He had tackled some of the toughest rogues that the agency had sent his way, and had done the best way he knew how to accomplish the job at hand successfully to best of his ability. His 5 feet 11ins in height and 13 stone in weight kept him on his toes, although he never took anything for granted. His thick wavy dark brown hair reached just short of his shoulders and enhanced his sun-tanned face and blue eyes.

His job became predominantly dangerous so it was necessary for him to carry a gun, which he trusted, for his life depended on it. A standard 38 mm short barrel 6 shot light and comfortable to handle, as on more than one occasion it had saved his life.

His wife had died a couple of years ago in a hit and run road accident, but before the tragedy they had planed to have children and had discussed, he would then quit his present job and settle down in a more secure one. However, since that dreadful day, he had become a loner and chucked his energy into his work.

As he stood across the other side of his boss's plush dark mahogany desk waited for his boss Jim, to tell him why he had been called he looked around the office with its red wall-to-wall carpet and fine furniture.

Jim fiddled with a pen, twisting it round between his fingers while gazing at his agent Jeff for a short while, and wondered if he was the right person to send on this new assignment.

'What's the urgency Jim? Sounds important,' Jeff announced in his casual way.

'Jeff,' Jim said, pausing for a second before carrying on, 'the Russians have informed me that they had released a guy called Pozvizd from prison, who by all accounts had spent 5 years for killing some guy. It appears they could not pin a number one rap on him but did put him in jail for some time,' Jim said.

'So?' Jeff questioned a little puzzled by what was happening in Russia, 'still cannot see what it has to do with us?

'They would dearly have loved to put him to death, or give him at least a very longer sentence,' Jim continued saying while taking no notice of what Jeff had asked.

'Still don't see what it has to do with us with regards to a crummy Russian crook that has been released from one of their jails,' Jeff repeated, even though he was waiting for the crunch line, for he knew his boss would not have had him there to talk about a crummy crook, unless it was important.

'He's disappeared! What is more Jeff they are sure he is up to something really big, but as yet the Russians can't say what,' Jim remarked sitting back hard in his swivel chair.

Jeff sat heavily in a chair that was identical to the one his boss was sitting in and looked across the desk at his boss in anticipation of what was to come.

'I'll explain,' said Jim, 'you knew Jack didn't you?'

'Yeah of course I do, he is a good friend of mine, and we spent many occasions fishing together in the forest,' Jeff said.

'As you know he was our agent in Russia,' Jim announced solemnly, his voice dropping to a near whisper as if he was frightened he would be, over heard.

'Yeah he's a good, that's for sure, one of the best,' Jeff acknowledged.

'Was, what do you mean was? Jeff suddenly realising what Jim had said, this then started a bad niggling feeling inside him.

'Sorry to tell you Jeff, he was discovered in his apartment at the docks with his throat cut.

'What, wow---!' Jeff gasped in hearing the awful news. 'How how on earth did it happen? Do you know who did it?'

'That's not all,' Jim continued without answering him, 'the Brit's also lost an agent; only he was shot in the head on the other side of town in while sitting in his car having something to eat by all accounts. Bloody bad business I can tell you. There is more as well, a Class A Fox Trot submarine has gone missing,' Jim said watching his agent closely for a reaction to the news.

'What---! A submarine,' Jeff retorted. 'You mean to tell me the Russians have had a submarine nicked from under their bloody noses. Blinking hell, what was their security doing? Sleeping, I don't believe it. Was it a nuclear?' Jeff uttered with surprise at hearing the news.

'Thankfully no,' Jim said coolly while still thinking about the news at losing his agent Jack, for he was sure he would miss him within agency.

'Apparently the submarine belongs to a company called Travel-View; they deal in special kinds of holidays. The idea is to take people out to sea for a couple of days or so, so they could get a feel as to what the submariners went through. Mad but there you are, that's the Russians for you,' Jim added.

'So how do you suppose, this fellow Pozvizd is connected then Jim?' Jeff remarked.

'He had been shouting a lot of anti-American noises while in jail, mentioned he would deal with us once and for all, translated meaning us the Americans,' Jim said waving his arm in the air to proclaim his way of expressing his meaning.

'How about the submarine and where does it fit in?' Jeff questioned while trying to imagine somebody nicking a submarine from under the Russian noses, and instantly thinking what was taking place in Russia.

'We are not sure about that, but it's funny that it's disappeared at the same time that this Pozvizd fellow goes missing. Perhaps it's a coincidence, I'm not sure nevertheless, this is what was reported.' Jim then stood up and handed over a buff coloured folder to Jeff.

'I assume you want me to go there? What precisely do you want me to do when I'm there?' Jeff asked in his usual casual manner.

'I want you to go to St Petersburg and see what you can find out who killed Jack. Then go to Murmansk and see what information you can dig up with regards to that submarine, as I just said it might be nothing but check anyway; talk to the Russians try to get as much as you can from them, speak to whoever you can to resolve this mystery. To help you, there will be a British agent over there, work closely together if you please, do not go falling out for they are just as involved in this as we are. I have you booked in at the St Petersburg hotel. Let me know if you come across anything,

I say again you must be very careful, for if they went to the trouble of killing both agents they will not think twice at having a go at you. We believe that our man and the Brit met somebody and exchanged information although, we have no idea what or where. Do me a favour Jeff, when you arrive in St Petersburg and contact the Russians, try to get as much information as you can from them? Inform me of your progress and get it sorted; you are booked on the 3pm flight so you got time to pop home and pack your bags.' Jim finally said as he sat leaned hard against the back of his chair.

'Jim you don't let the grass grow under anybodies feet. Do you. Ok I'm on my way,' Jeff muttered, raising his arms in an action that showed that he understood everything and began to make a move towards the door.

'Jeff, please do not take any unnecessary risks,' Jim replied in an agitated voice.

'I didn't know you cared,' Jeff called back as he made a move to leave the room. 'Go on get out of here and stop giving me a hard time.'

'Incidentally what's the Brit; called?' Jeff questioned halfway out of the office.

'Charley, a Charley Blackstoke. 'For god sake Jeff will you take care, I can't keep emphasizing it enough, I mean it. It looks like those guys could be very treacherous. The Russians also stated that Pozvizd is a brutal killer and had several people before but they have been are unable to prove any of them to execute him or even put him away for life.'

'Do you know how long he served in jail and where?' Jeff said as he made another move to leave.

'Do you ever listen, I just mentioned it, you will find everything you want in that file your holding, so I suggest you read it on the flight, get acquainted with the details; he evidently went to one of those old Gulags that they still have. Nevertheless, he is out and

25

what's more he is hostile and no one knows where he is staying, so keep your head down low and your finger on the button. Keep me posted to what is happening,' Jim finally stated. 'Ok Jim,' Jeff added and left the office.

Making his way out of the building he headed for home, which was about a mile out of town and situated in a quieter part of the suburbs. On arriving at his house he prepared to get ready for the arduous trip to Russia, although not happy at the prospect of going to Russia he set about getting ready for he did not have much time.

He owned a four-bedroom detached brick house with the usual mod cons, and a large swimming pool that was located at the back of the house all of which was on two acres of prime land. He had put the house up for sale before his wife died, as they planed to move west but, that was the past and he now had dropped the sale, until he recovered from her death whenever, that would be.

When Jeff left the office, Jim leaned back against the headrest in his seat to light a cigar and reflected on the situation that he had put another one of his agents in grave danger. He thought of the possibilities of what could go wrong with the case, for he lacked vital information to help his agent. He dreaded the thought of what or could happen to Jeff, if things went wrong for him, for he was helpless on this side of the Atlantic.

Chapter 6

'Hello my name's Jeff Morgan; I understand you have a room reserved for me,' Jeff said walking up to the receptionist in the hotels foyer.

'I will confirm with the register,' the receptionist said in her broken English accent, and then began flicking through a book to check. Jeff's first thought was surely they would have had the information on hand but on reflection he supposed he was expecting too much, after all this was not the states.

He took the time to look around his surroundings as he leaned against the counter and saw a couple drinking in a corner of the lobby where a make shift bar was located. Another person was reading a newspaper or so it seemed by a large window that was near the main door that he entered. Jeff also wondered if he belonged to the old KGB, for old habits died hard in Russia. Well that was what his boss had told him.

'I'm sorry to keep you sir,' she whispered softly, 'yes we have you in room 210 and it is on the second floor. Would you like some assistance with your luggage?'

'Thanks but that will not be necessary, I don't have much and can manage thank you,' Jeff said with a smile, while taking hold of the key from her. Then was about to leave when he said.

'Oh yes there is one thing, I'm supposed to be meeting an Englishman here, can you inform him when he arrives that I am here. His name is Charley Blackstoke; I'll be in the lounge if he enquires,' Jeff said pointing towards the door that was near the steps that led to the upper floors of the hotel. He then turned away from the young assistant to search for his room. On finding the room and giving it a quick once over for unwanted listening devises, he made his way to the lounge for a long stiff drink.

Ordering a scotch from the barman, he sat on a stool at the bar and waited for the British agent to arrive. Tired from the long flight from the states, for it had been and tedious; he thought about his new partner and hoped they would get along together, for he was used to working alone.

He scanned the room from where he was sitting in the hope he would spot the agent when he arrived but, as yet no one showed that he could identify to the person he was to meet. However, he did not have long to wait, though it was not as he had expected for the Brit; turned out be a female. He could not believe his eyes as he faced her, noticing instantly her slim elegant figure. He gauged she was about 5 feet 8 inches in height and around 10 stone in weight, her short wavy black hair revealed her smooth tanned completion. She was wearing a light blue dress, which hung from her bare shoulders, and the low v cut neckline exposed her cleavage that began to make his plusher race as she glided towards him in her black high-heeled shoes.

'Hello,' Jeff said unable to take his eyes off her. 'Are you Charley by any chance,' he said stuttering in surprise. 'You look stunning not at all what I expected,' Jeff spluttered.

'What did you expect a monster?' Charley added coldly. 'No, not at all, it's just that I assumed you were going to be a fellow,' Jeff said spluttering and beginning to feel hot around the collar for he felt embarrassed at not thinking she would be cable of doing such work as an agent. 'Would care for a drink?'

'Please, make it a martini dry,' she added frostily

'Shall we sit over there by the window and away from prying eyes and ears?' Jeff said pointing in the direction where no one was sitting.

Once they settled at a table, he then ordered another drink before attempting to be further acquainted.

'You know you should not presume anything, it may get you into a lot of trouble one day,' she said with an annoyed look on her face. 'Are you against women?'

'No, not at all,' Jeff added, 'I'm so sorry; you caught me on the hop that's all, as I said, I expected you to be a fellow what with being in a place like this, and what with your name being Charley, I didn't think that's all. I must say you're very dazzling and as I said not what I was expecting, but I'm sure we'll get along swell.'

'Thank you for the complement,' Charley said acknowledging his remarks.

'But that's twice you have made me a compliment, do you always repeat yourself,' she said with a warm voice.
'No not at all, its just that I'm surprised that's all, I am sorry if I have made you feel uncomfortable. Anyway let me introduce myself, I'm Jeff Morgan and you may have gathered that the way I've been talking is I've not worked with women before,' Jeff said with a slight stutter, and then quickly dropping the subject, he decided to get down to the business to the reason why they were there.

'So what have you found Charley, anything?'

'I went to the morgue this morning and saw the deceased. You may not have known it but he was a good friend of mine.' 'Jack! I didn't know you knew him?'

'Jack---! Who the hell is he, I don't know Jack; I thought it was Dennis in the morgue.'

'Hang on a moment, what we talking about?' Jeff muttered.

'Jacks in the morgue and I'm here to check who killed him.'

'Well Jeff, he must be your man that I saw, for it certainly wasn't Dennis.'

'So where's Dennis?' Jeff added amazed that both men were not in the same place.

'When Dennis was killed outside a burger bar I took it that they brought him here for me to deal with; however it turned out to be your guy, so, at the moment I haven't a clue to where Dennis has been put?' Charley said pondering on whether Dennis liked his job. Which she thought was debatable.

'Jeff, Jack had his throat cut and was left in his apartment by the dockyard. I imagine there must have been a good connection between them for both of them to die,' Charley said looking across the table at him and hoping he could come up with an explanation.

'Your right there, so in the morning I will go to find Jacks apartment and see if or what clues can found to why he was killed,' Jeff remarked before taking a sip of his drink.

'Am I not included in your search mate, for two heads are better than one and that is why I was sent here,' Charley said with a smirk on her face.

'Well I can't argue with that. It's been a long day and it doesn't look as if our Russian friends are going to make any contact with us tonight, so I'm going to turn in and get some rest.' Then without saying another word concerning the assignment, he stood and said to her. 'Coming or are you going to stay there all night?' Arriving at their respective rooms, which was on the second floor she said to him.

'What number are you in?'

'210 and you're in?'

'208, I wonder who worked that one out, every convenient you think?' she uttered. 'Anyway, don't you get any ideas; remember we're both here to work?'

'Not a chance, you can rest in peace, but should you want me to get another room I'll arrange it tomorrow.'
Then as he started to place his key in the lock and was just about to open the door, Charley whispered in a quiet husky voice.

'You going to give an English girl an American kiss good night?' She whispered softly. Jeff instantly taken back and surprised by her sudden change in attitude, for one moment she was telling him

30

to keep his distance and the next making a pass on him to kiss her. No wonder men were confused over women.

He went over to her and put his arms round her slim waist and felt the warmth of her body penetrating through her dress, feeling hot and nervous and was about to kiss her when she voiced calmly.

'I have, or have had intruders, for I left a calling card in the top hinge of the door and it's been disturbed,' Charley said calmly. Jeff went rigid for a split second then at once released her, pulling his gun from its holster, he gripped the doors handle and with his left hand, and with his gun in his right he opened it very slowly. The room was in complete darkness for the staff had closed the curtains, this put him at a big disadvantage for he had the light from the corridor to his rear, which showed him clearly to a potential enemy inside the room making him very vulnerable. Yet he continued into the room, moving his left free hand to slide down the wall to find the light switch, on finding it he closed one eye before throwing the switch so when the light came on he would not be blinded by the sudden glare. Now holding his gun with both hands, he dropped to one knee, while at the same time scanning the room in a sweeping motion and prepared for the slightest sign of trouble, but he did not have to worry for there was no visible danger he could see in the room, it was completely quiet. Charley entered the room directly behind him and began to see if anything had been disturbed. 'Well,' she said taken down her guard at seeing nothing had been disturbed.

'Take a look in the bedroom Charley,' Jeff said, then at that instance noticed the curtain by the window move slightly. Placing his finger to his lips to show Charley to be silent, he whispered in a low tone. 'Did you leave a window open when you were in here last,' he said pointing towards the curtain that had moved, and at the same time carefully made his way towards the window but, as he approached the curtain a figure burst from behind it and made a mad dash for the door. Striking out furiously with his arms he knocked Jeff to one side pushing him off balance but, Jeff quickly gaining his stance dived for the intruder's ankles in a flying rugby tackle that sent them crashing to the floor. Slamming a fist into the villain's crutch, who yelled out loud with the sudden pain the intruder lashed back with a kick to Jeff's head, which made Jeff loose his grip on him. Then with such remarkable pace, the villain jumped to his feet, sped for the door, running along the corridor to where the stairs were and fled down them, and out of sight before Jeff and Charley could pursue him. Charley ran for the door although, in doing so collided with Jeff as he was stumbling to his feet and both crashed to the floor with arms and legs flying in all directions, finally Charley ending on top of him.

'Well that's cocked it,' he said sitting on the floor panting for breath and frustrated while trying to regain his composure. 'Not much good trying to catch the worm now. But he'll have a bloody good limp that's for sure,' Jeff uttered.

'How do you know it's a he?' Charley questioned.

'By the way I grabbed him,' Jeff said with a grin. 'I'll check the rest of the place,' she added getting to her feet and made for the bathroom and then to the bedroom, but seeing nothing had been disturbed she returned to the lounge where Jeff was still searching the room for any clues that the intruder may have left behind.

'No, nothings been touched as far as I can tell, we must have intervened before he could do anything,' Charley said.

'Yeah you could be right, I wonder what he was after and how did he get in?' said Jeff going back to the main door to examine it. 'He must have had a key for there was no sign of forced entry, where would he have got a key from?'

'You can have them made without much difficulty over here,' she added.

'Well there's nothing we can do now, so I think I'll retire for the night; if you want to keep the adjoining room open, your most welcome,' he said as he turned his back on her and started to leave but, got as far as the door when she called out to him.

'Ay fellow, I wonder what that kiss would have been like?'

Turning round to face her he gave her a smile, and then left without saying a word to go in his room, closing his door silently behind him. Then as he undressed to get into bed he began to think, what would have happened if he had accepted her invitation, pushing the thought from his mind he then started to wonder about the intruder in her room, and what could he have wanted to rob from her? Furthermore, how was he to know that she was staying in that particular room? Chewing it over in his mind, he finally drifted off to sleep.

Chapter 7

'Captain, the other guests have arrived,' the second officer Kazan shouted down the Conning tower hatch,

'Show them on board,' the Captain called back to Kazan.

Mark, Ann and with Leshin boarded the boat. Mark gasped seeing his wife Ann had organised such a trip on a submarine such as this one, for she had known, it had been a long-time since he had been on submarines. He noticed as he stepped on to the deck that the surface consisted of a hard rubber compound and had grooves along the whole length of the boat. In addition, its construction was in such a way to give the boat better speed under water.

They climbed through the hatchway, and entered the control room, although Leshin did not follow them.

'I will see you when you return, he shouted after them. 'Have a pleasant trip,' said Leshin with a nasty leer written on his face as he left the boat.

'Those stairs are a bit steep?' Ann remarked to no one in particular when she reached the last run.

'It is called a companionway madam,' the Captain said with amusement, 'you will get use to them. My name is Krabava Babarika and I welcome you on behalf of my crew and myself on board this boat, and the first voyage of its kind, in fact I believe in the world. I hope you will enjoy yourselves and find it interesting and to your liking. Please will you excuse me, as I need to get the boat underway? Kazan our second officer will escort you to your quarters and see to your needs, he will also show you round the boat and will explain everything to you. Ask him anything you like, I am sure he will be very happy to help you,' the skipper added before climbing the iron steps to the conning tower, and out into the fresh air to make sure the boat got underway safely. You could hear his voice bellowing out the instructions to the crew as the diesel engines started, and then settling down to a slight throb, which stirred life into the small boat. Mark was a little surprised, as they did not make the loud noise he had expected; nonetheless, the submarine shuddered and vibrated as the revs began to increase as they felt the boat moving away from the quayside as they began their journey. It was 4pm when the Zhuralev slipped its moorings, and turned towards the open channel with the crew pulling leavers and turning valves. The boats crew went about their tasks in a methodical way so the submarine could move smoothly. Leaving the harbour, they increased their speed to 8 knots moving majestically down stream to the mouth of the river and reached the dark black open cold waters of the Barents Sea.

It felt very strange for Mark, for it had been twenty years, since he had last sailed in submarines, but still he could feel the excitement that it gave and was now keen to see the engine room. For as an engineer he wanted to compare it with what he had dealt with years ago, for his job besides keeping an eye on the engines was maintaining the compressed air tanks that the boats had.

'Please will you follow me,' Kazan said.

Leaving the control room, he led them down a narrow passageway through the centre of the boat, which showed access to cabins on both sides.

'That's the galley on the right,' he pointed as they passed one of the rooms. 'Our chef does good food, he's the best,' Kazan chuckled as they continued through a small watertight door to another compartment.

'This is the bedroom where you will be sleeping while on board, or if you prefer you can call it the same as what we say, a bunkroom,' Kazan stated laughing and jesting with his hands, endorsing the fact about trying to sleep as they moved through the submarine. Progressing to the next and the last compartment, which was the forward torpedo room, except now converted into a lounge for the benefit of its passengers.

Another couple sat on a long soft bench, which stretched two-thirds of the left hand side of the room, while on the right, a small cocktail cabinet had been placed, with a small coffee table was situated in the middle of the room.

'Good day,' the two strangers said together standing to shake the Walkers hand as they entered the compartment.

'We're the Schmitt's. This is my wife Crystal and I am Hans,' he said putting his hand on her shoulder.

Hans was a small man of about 5 feet 2 inches with thin curly blonde hair and his bright blue eyes that emphasised his reddening face, which showed clearly in the subdued lighting of the boat.

'It is very good to meet you both and we looked forward to enjoying your company, we were told you would be joining us sometime today and I'm very glad, for this crew can't speak much German or English but I'm sure we'll get along fine in this closed confined space of this boat. The craft is not bad, well at least what I have seen so far, and as far as I can tell very effective.'

Mark glanced around the room and saw he was right about it being small, nevertheless; it was an ex-torpedo room so no one could expect anything different.

'Hans I understand you are from Hamburg?'

'Yes that's correct, we have a house on the outskirts of the city; it is in a quiet neighbour hood and with very little traffic, which is a blessing. So where do you come from Mark?' Hans responded, while quickly moving towards the drinks cabinet.

'We have a thatched cottage in Hampshire, which is not very far from Southampton.'

'Ah yes Southampton, I know it very well, a very nice place. I was there some ten years ago; I suppose it has not changed.'

Mark eyed him cautiously as he was trying to get a feel for the guy.

'What do you do for a living Hans?' Mark asked, watching Hans pour the wine into four glasses. Hans responded turning away from the drinks cabinet with a tray containing the four glasses of white wine.

'I work in finance for my troubles but now I have decided to take a calmer life and enjoy myself and spend more time with my lovely wife here. How about yourself Mark, what line of work are you into, anything exciting?' Hans said handing the Walkers the wine.

'Not very much I'm afraid, things got a bit uninteresting with my work, so I have done much the same as you Hans. I was a trouble-shooter in electrical and mechanical engineering amongst other things, although I must say it did have its moments but as I just mentioned there was not much doing so I decided to give it up and retire.

We like you are on a short break; well it was a surprise break really, for Ann booked it without me knowing anything about it,' Mark said while taking a sip of the wine, that Hans had given him. 'Have you had a chance to look round yet, Hans?'

'No we thought it would be appropriate to wait for you.'

'Thank you, that was good of you,' Ann said turning her attention to Crystal.

'Shall we start and investigate the boat? Ladies are you coming?' Hans asked.

'Not at the moment, we'll come along a little later for Crystal and I would like a little chat, if that is ok with you guys,' Ann retorted.

'Women, when they get together they can talk until the cows come home, is that not a saying in England,' Hans mentioned as they made a start to examine the boat.

Travelling through the bunkroom, where twelve beds were stacked in three tiers on either side of the passageway, each partitioned for privacy. They then carried on through to the next compartment where they came to the galley, where the chef was preparing their evening meal.

'Mark if you do not mind I would like to talk with the chef concerning Crystal's meal, I will catch up in a moment,' Hans said already making a move to enter the galley.

Mark did not worry about having Hans with him as he continued his way, as he really wanted to be on his own. On entering the control room, he found the radio operator by the name of Andrei, working in a small partitioned section of the room where he operated the sonar and radar equipment.

He was a small tubby chap with curly brown hair neatly combed back over his head. Dressed in his navy-overalls, he sat patiently listening in his headphones, and so involved with his work he never noticed Mark standing near him, which showed how qualified he was. Mark turned his attention back to the control room where directly in front of him was the main periscope, for this was the submarines life support. They had installed a second periscope although smaller behind it; later he found it was the attack periscope and left for affect. Kazan said they would not use the periscopes when they were on the surface. Nevertheless, Mark was already aware of this procedure, when he sailed in his submarine some years ago. Investigating past the scopes, he saw to his left some charts that were lying open on a table and placed for easy access for the skipper to read. Glancing quickly at the table as he passed, he noticed three charts, one of them was of the Barents Sea, another of the Arctic Ocean and the third consisted of the North Atlantic. In addition, a fourth with a route pencilled on the chart that showed part of the America coastline. Not giving it much attention at the time he carried through the next watertight door, passing the captain's cabin on his right, stopping briefly he noticed a smaller room to his left; which consisted of four bunks, which he presumed were for the crew to sleep in. Finally arriving at the engine room, and without pausing he went into the room and instantly saw two diesel engines before him, each fixed aligned on either side of the room, and beyond them were two electric motors for under-water propulsion, as he knew the diesels could not operate under-water without air to run on.

An old looking guy wearing brown greasy shaggy overalls was working on the left engine. His greasy black hair hung loose around his large ears, Mark estimated he was around five foot in height and some 15 stone in weight.

He turned and faced Mark, and with a huge grin that showed a mouth full of yellow teeth and a gold filling, which protruded on the right side of his mouth.

'Ay hi there' the engineer responded in a friendly manner.

'Hi there,' Mark announced on entering.

'My name is Yuri, are you from America?' he asked speaking in one breath while holding out his right filthy hand to shake Mark at the same time.

'No I'm English,' Mark answered shaking his hand with a firm grip. 'You speak very good English!' commented Mark. 'Where did you learn it so well?' Yuri rubbed his chin, then looking at an old rusty clock that hung by a metal bracket over the left engine. It had seen better days for the glass was badly cracked and made it difficult to read the face, however; Yuri did not seem to have much of a problem reading it.

'New York, he answered, 'I lived in Manhattan for five years,' he continued to say with an even wider grin.

'Where do you live now?' Mark questioned.

'St Petersburg, well between voyages,' he said responding freely to show how proud he was to tell Mark. 'I studied engineering there, then after passing my exams; I joined the navy, and served in submarines, have been in them since, so there's not much I don't know about them, I can tell you,' Yuri said with a friendly smile, for he loved to talk about his life. Seeing how forthcoming he was, Mark was just about to ask him more questions about where he lived in the states, when an officer entered and barked in a harsh and bullish voice some orders in Russian. Then turning to Mark, he stated.

'Mr Walker I am afraid I will have to ask you to leave the engine compartment as we are now underway and our engineer Yuri has much to do.' Somewhat bemused and startled by the officer's abruptness Mark left feeling cross at the way the first officer had behaved. Alarm bells began ringing in his head although he could not explain why, so doing as ordered he ambled back to where he had left the girls, knowing that something was amiss, except he was not able to come up with anything conclusive to what it could be. On entering the new lounge his eyes instantly focused on the bulkhead and noticed how they had assembled it. Ann sitting on the sofa watched her husband in disbelief at what he was looking at.

'You cannot sit still, can you?'

'Where's the Schmidt's Ann?' he asked calmly.'

'They went into the galley and as far as I know are still there, why?

Mark then told her about the charts and the first officer's abruptness,' emphasising his abruptness.

'The other thing is, why have they just bolted this bulkhead and not welded it,' he said, pointing at the bolts holding the wall in place, which concealed the torpedo's doors.

'I wouldn't have a clue,' she added. 'Aren't you a bit over active my dear? You're supposed to be on holiday, so let us join the others and enjoy the trip.'

'No,' Mark said. 'Something is not right about this boat, but I will endeavour to find out what before we leave,' he said shaking his head, and mumbling in a low voice that nobody understood.

'You're giving me the creeps Mark; she said worried at what her husband was suggesting.

'Come on Ann, let's join the others.'

'Hello again, come and have a drink with us,' Hans said in a jovial mood and again offering a glass of wine.

'This is our chef Rachko Hizzka, he has made us a special meal, hunters stew mixed with a touch of spice,' Crystal stated picking up a spoonful of the stew for Ann to taste.

'Certainly smells very good I must admit,' Mark added licking his lips and trying to forget what he had seen and heard.

'Have you two been in here all the time?' Ann asked.

'No,' crystal replied, 'I took a peep in the control room a little while ago. The Captains in there said he'll join us, as soon as he's got the boat going perfectly to his satisfaction.'

'Are you telling us that we have a problem,' answered Ann. 'No not at all,' remarked Hans, 'he's just making some fine adjustments to our course and trim of the boat that is all.' Then just as he finished speaking the Captain appeared in the doorway.

'I am sorry about the delay with being with you people, you must think I am very rude, I was needed to make some minor adjustments, but all is now fine. Our first officer has now taken over the controls, so I am all yours.

'How fast will we be travelling?' Ann enquired to the skipper.

'15 knots on the surface; although you will hardly feel us moving, as the sea is very calm, for there is little turbulence, we could go faster but I think it is unnecessary. Incidentally, please call me Krabava; it makes it so much friendlier, do you not agree. We will stay at this speed for the next four hours and on a course of 340° and then we will make another course change to 290° after dinner, then we will dive for the night.

You can watch through the periscope if you wish, and see what it looks like above us, as we will start at 50 feet before dropping down to 150 feet where we will stay until tomorrow morning. We will then return to the surface around 0800.hrs, so staying under the waves for the night will also give us all a better night's sleep, you won't even know you're in a submarine, for it will be so

41

stable. Anyway if the waves did increase in strength they won't throw us all over the place, which you can well imagine can be very uncomfortable.'

'Will we be doing the same speed under the waves?' Hans remarked.

'Oh no,' Krabava answered back endorsing the words with a force of wind that blew like a gale, 'I will reduce the boat to eight knots and change from diesel to electric motors as the diesels need oxygen to run on, but you need not worry, for we have plenty of oxygen on board to breathe.

As you already know, Rachko is our chef,' he said quickly changing the subject. 'He is a master at what he does, and the meal he has cooked for us, I am sure will be excellent.' Krabava said looking towards his chef in the confined space of the mess room. 'Will you open another bottle of champagne Rachko?'

'Krabava, are we allowed to look round all of the boat?' Only going into the engine room a little while ago, I tried to speak to the engineer Yuri, but alas he was very busy getting everything working, consequently I was unable to view what he was doing,' Mark stated, but did not add how the first officer behaved towards him.

'Of course, no problem,' the Captain answered with a warm grin. 'But the two far rooms are out of bounds as they are used to keep the stores in, and so there's nothing of interest apart from our supplies, plus I don't want you to see how much champagne we have here on board, as you'll want to take some of it home with you,' Krabava chuckled heartily. Then as the mood improved, and the drinks flowed, they began settling down to what they thought, would be a pleasant journey. Then when everyone, except the Walkers had left the room, Mark turned back to his wife to hold her hands.

'Darling what I'm going to say may alarm you, but you must not be frightened and show your concerns to anyone on board.'

'What is it Mark? For it's not like you to look to be so worried, have I made a mistake by bringing you here?' She said with a strained gaze in her deep brown eyes that showed she understood what he was about to say.

'Well, you remember I mentioned the charts and the one showing our route.'

'Yes darling, so what about them?'

'Well there was a line drawn from Murmansk to Iceland with no turning point to return to Murmansk.'

'Surely that doesn't mean we won't turn back. I cannot see what you are fretting about just because you sailed on these things before, does not mean that there is anything wrong; there could be a simple explanation. I think you are too excited and we should think about going to bed like the others,' she added standing to make a move to leave the room, but before she made a step for the door, she heard the sound of air escaping from the tanks, which made her jump with fright.

'What's that noise?' she stuttered with apprehension to what was happening to the boat.

'Do not be alarmed, it is air from the ballast tanks, which pushes the water out, so the boat can surface,' a man said standing in the doorway. 'We are going to surface.'

'Surfacing, why are we surfacing?' Ann questioned.

'Evidently we are picking up two more crewmen, it won't take long.
My name is Andrei,' he stated standing in the doorway. Mark straight away recognised him as the chap with the headphones. 'I'm the radio operator. I need to tell you, that you are in grave danger and you need to escape, get off this boat as soon as you can, for the skipper has no intention of letting you go,' Andrei cried in a low husky voice.

'Escape, why would we want to do that?' Ann gasped in utter horror to what this man had just mentioned.

'I can't explain right now, for I don't have the time, but they must not know who told you to get off this boat. We are all in danger; I will try to explain later if I get the chance,' Andrei whispered and then spinning on his heels he fled the room, leaving the Walker's dumfounded by what he had mentioned.

Chapter 8

Having arranged at the hotel to hire a car, Jeff and Charley drove to the city morgue, to see his dead colleague Jack. On arriving, they followed the attendant to the appropriate room, where they saw along one wall several rows of what looked like filing cabinets, but as the attendant opened one of them it became clear they were in fact fridges to hold bodies. Positioned the centre of the room was a large wooden oblong table to lay the unfortunate dead, so they could be investigated to what had happened to them. The attendant went over to one of the drawers, and opening it he reveal Jacks exposed body; Jeff could not help feeling sad about his friend's untimely death and was determined to find the culprit who killed him.

'My name is Pavel,' the attendant said after fully extending the drawer to its maximum distance.

Jeff nearly choked seeing Jack lying in front of him, but keeping his feelings from breaking apart, he quickly gained his composure when the attendant removed the sheet.

'Quite a cut, what did they say caused it?' Jeff asked.

'Don't look like a knife that's for sure,' Charley uttered, taking a closer look at the wound that killed him. Pavel then again looked at the wound.

'Cheese wire, I think is what the police said. I also heard it could have been the work of a thug called Pozvizd. Have you heard of him?'

'Pozvizd, yeah, I've heard of him,' Jeff replied to the attendant with a dry throat that affected his speech. 'Do you know if he's still in St Petersburg?' Jeff uttered in a husky voice, for he was having a problem with accepting his mate's death.

'Unlikely, I reckon he's long gone, I know I wouldn't hang around,' Pavel admitted as he watched the two of them.

'I'll kill him for this!' Jeff screamed and slamming his fist at the metal casing of the drawer in anger. He began trembling with the thought of Jack lying cold in the drawer, and with nobody to help him when he needed it most.

'He must have taken awhile to die,' Jeff heard Pavel saying as he offered more information about the way he died.

'What do you deduct from this,' Charley gestured.

'Not sure, but I bet my bottom dollar they took him by surprise, it would not have been Jack letting his guard down completely, my betting is he was so involved with what he was doing he forgot the golden rule of keeping an eye on his enemy. Besides, I reckon he was in much deeper than he realised. I guess the information that he had and whoever wanted it, wanted it badly enough to kill,' Jeff said with regret. 'Did the police find anything in his apartment Pavel?' Jeff asked the attendant, while still showing his remorse and being sick to the stomach with the appalling act.

'Not that I am aware of, the place was ransacked, however; you will have to talk to them, as they may have some answers that they have not released to me.'

'Ok, and thank you very much for your time and help, I have seen enough here, I will contact my boss, he can move his body back home to the States. Shall we go Charley?'

A little later that day at the police desk, Jeff spoke to the sergeant to find out what he knew and to get the keys to Jack's flat, while Charley remained in the car observing what was happening outside in the street.

'It's a mess,' announced the copper as Jeff began to make his way out of the station. Jumping into the car to get to Jack's apartment, they drove the short distance through the capitals winding narrow roads, towards the east side, in silence, until finally arriving at the docks and Jack's flat.

'Look at this place, it's a dump, how in heavens name do people live here?' Charley questioned slipping from the car to follow Jeff, but looking at the buildings adjacent to Jack's flat, to see who may be watching them. However, Jeff did not wait for her; he went at a fast gaunt to enter the block of flats. On entering the ground floor, he ran his finger down a list of names that were pinned on a notice board to ascertain where Jack's room was located. He began to ascend the concrete stairs with Charley soon following close behind his heels.

'Wow! Jesus-Christ, what a bloody smell,' she said holding her breath. 'Look at this excrement, its horrible,' she said spitting the words out between closed lips while holding her nose, and trying not to breathe the nasty fumes in the lobby.

'Yeah your right there mate,' Jeff remarked acknowledging her with the same disgust. 'We'll take the stairs, but be careful in the event of trouble.' On reaching the right floor and finding the door to Jacks room without any difficulty, Jeff slowly edged the door open and cautiously moved inside. 'The copper was right; it's really a bloody mess,' he said instantly noticing Jack's clothing scattered around the room and mingled with the bedding, that lay in a heap on the floor. Looking further, he saw the wooden wardrobe doors had been broken and shredded paper strewn across the apartment. 'It appears that whoever done this must have been in a frenzy and looking for something very important for them,' Jeff announced. 'Ok Charley, let's see if we can find anything useful?' They searched at what appeared to be a long time but in fact they had only spent about an hour and were just about to give up when Charley called him.

'Jeff take a look at this, it's a smart card from a digital camera.'

'Where did you find it,' Jeff asked.

'In his case, where he keeps his reading glasses, it was in the lining. It's a 1 gigabyte card, what do you make of it?' she queried.

'At the moment I can't think of anything, apart from the card having a few answers.'

'What's on your mind?' she questioned sadly looking round the apartment.

'Oh nothing much, I'm just trying to get my head round this, and wondering how much that evil guy Pozvizd might be involved with killing Jack and Dennis, plus how did he get to them so easy. A mystery that is for sure, but one thing is for certain, they're serious and mean business,' he muttered. 'Better get back to the hotel and see what the contents are on my laptop, first though I think we should eat.'

'Eat, it's beyond me how could you think of food and at a time like this,' she voiced with dismay.

'Easy babe, think of it, if anyone is watching us, what do you imagine they would think, that we have found something, while returning to the hotel, I reckon they'll be after us in a trice.'

'Yeah you've got a point,' she said twiddling the flexible card between her fingers, as they began to leave the flat with its excrement and filth splattered on the walls and stairs. Returning to the open air and car, Jeff quickly scanned the car to make certain it had not been tampered with, once satisfied it was ok, he slid behind the wheel, and starting the engine he pulled away from the curb, slowly at first, then gathering speed he drove round the block for reassurance that no one was observing them. Again contented at no one seeing them, they headed back to the police station to return the keys to the flat.

'I suggest we make it look as sociable as possible,' he told her as the waiter came over to show them to a table, when they entered a restaurant. Jeff ordered the same meal for both of them and then settled down to adjust to what they had discovered.

'Now we bide our time and keep our eyes peeled for anyone spying on us. Perhaps our Russian friends may help in the morning, that's of course if we see them.'

Charley looked straight at Jeff with tears forming in the corners of her eyes, as he spoke to her.

'Jeff, I have something to say to you, I've not had the opportunity to mention it,' Charley said interrupting him, and wondering whether it was the right time to talk about what she had to say concerning Jack and Dennis. 'As you may know Jack was in Odessa with Dennis, but what you probably don't know, is that several months ago they joined forces. Jack worked as an under-cover agent posing as one of the gang, while Dennis received info about the crooks and passed it to him, which in turn forwarded it to your headquarters.'

'I was involved by pretending to be married to Dennis, we went to Kiev at first; while Jack went somewhere else, never said where, but claimed he needed to do something for the mob. Then a few days later we met him back in Kiev and we noticed he looked very worried. He told us at the time he had to travel here to St Petersburg and that we should meet him at the hotel, where I met you. Anyway, Dennis told me to go on my own, for he needed to go to Murmansk to chase up another lead. That was the last time I saw them alive. I do not know who they met, or why they had been killed. Dennis did phone me to say he had something for Jack, although he didn't say what.'

'This adds some light to what's happening Charley,' Jeff said listening to her, but also cross with her for not mentioning this information before.

'So you believe Jack didn't know Dennis had been killed,' Jeff replied.

'Yes,' she said, 'I'm sure of that or he would not have been caught the way he had been. I am so sorry I have not said anything before now but I did not know who you were and whether you could be trusted and I didn't want to end like them,' She said finally, and then tried to change the subject to ease the situation between them. 'I must say Jeff; don't you think it's a bit strange the Russians have not shown up at the hotel? After all they knew we were coming,' Charley questioned.

'Well just a touch, considering I was told they were supposed to know where we are staying,' Jeff stated with a grim look across his face.

'I'm not so sure I want to trust them with what we've got,' Charley added facing him across the table.

'Yeah you're right about that, so we don't mention what we have found, and I think we should keep it to ourselves for awhile before telling our bosses.

As they ate their meal, Charley went very silent; tears appeared in the corner of her eyes but this time they began to roll down her cheeks, mixing with her make-up and it left long dark streaks that showed like railway lines.

'Are you going to let me in on your secret? I'm not stupid; I know there's something bothering you, so tell me.' Jeff said seeing how distressed she looked.

'Yes your right, I haven't been truly honest with you Jeff, but I couldn't find it in myself to tell you.'

'Well I'm a good listener; it's got to be serious. So what about telling me exactly what's on your mind.' She hesitated at first, and then her bottom lip started to tremble, her whole body shook with the thought at what he may say with holding her news. As the tears flowed down her face, she wiped them clear so as not to reveal to the other guest in the restaurant that there was a problem between them.

'It's about Dennis,' she spluttered in a faint voice, which Jeff could hardly hear.

'What about Dennis!' Jeff said studying the taught features off her face.

'Dennis was my brother---!' She blurted out his name in haste. Jeff was stunned, shocked and bewildered at hearing this news and was lost for words. He braced himself momentarily when he heard her tell him the news. He took hold of her hands to comfort her.

'I am so sorry Charley, I wasn't aware you were related, for nobody at the office had mentioned it.'

'That's because I told my boss not to tell anybody, so how could you know, I insisted it should be kept a total secret.'

'Of course Charley, I understand,' Jeff remarked not knowing what else to say or how to reassure her.

'In any case, it doesn't change a thing. I'm in this to the end; you or nobody else will deter me to find his killer. Surely you can appreciate that Jeff.'

'Yes I understand Charley, I'm also with you all the way, even so won't they know who you are, for surely you must have left something lying about, for you said you were pretending to be man and wife?'

'No we covered our tracks very well, I am positive nobody knows me,' she said at length pausing as she looked into his blue eyes.

After the meal they made their way slowly back to their hotel, where they could check the card that Charley had discovered. Retrieving the laptop from under the bed, he placed it on the bed and switched the set on to view the contents of the card, but stopped abruptly when he saw Charley removing her bra from under her white sweater.

'What are you doing?' Jeff questioned surprised in seeing what she was doing. 'What are you doing?' He repeated, but by this time, she had already removed the garment and was holding it in her hand. 'Why on earth, have you needed to remove that?' Jeff questioned, and now facing her, he was able to see straight through her sweater, which revealed the contour of her breasts.

'Sorry if I have embarrassed you mate, I hid the card in my bra, it's an unusual place I know but I'm convinced nobody would think of finding it there, it just came natural,' she added casually handing over the garment for him to remove the card.

Holding the bra with both hands, Jeff noticed the fancy stitching along the edge, cups of the bra, the top of the cups were made of lace, and you were able to see right through the garment, which revealed her firm breasts. The bottom part of the bra was made of solid material, which gave them added support; although he thought, they needed no firming. Also attached were two narrow straps that crossed over the shoulders and connected to the strap around her back by a thin single catch. She had made a small insert into the left cup and had placed the card in it carefully, as it was flexible and considered it a perfect place to hide.

He raised his eyebrows and focusing on her he realised even more how lovely she really looked standing there before him. Deep down inside him a pleasant feeling flowed through his veins, a feeling he had not experienced, since his wife had died, nevertheless, it only lasted in a trice and he was back to business, for there was a lot to do. With the laptop on his knees, he inserted the card in the computer, and waited for the contents of the card too load to the hard drive. Then casually glancing round as a precaution although he knew no one had entered the room, he continued to watch the screen to see what the card would reveal.

'Goddamn blast it!' Jeff swore bitterly.

'What's wrong?' Charley queried with the sudden outburst of bad language.

'Can't read the bloody card that's what's wrong,' he replied blaspheming constantly, 'the bloody computers not working,' he told her. 'I haven't a clue to what the problem is, and just when you want the thing, it's always the same. Any idea where I can get it fixed. Here of all places, bleeding hell---,' Jeff scorned for not being able to use the computer. Then removing the card from the laptop, he gave it as well as the bra back to her to put in a safe place.

'Put this back in you're hiding place, I must confess I would not have thought to look there, and I hope no one else does either,' he commented as his anger began to subside from the knowledge of the broken laptop and not seeing what the card had on it. Smiling at her as she stood standing staring at him, it took his mind away from the broken computer. 'Well there you go,' she said returning it to its hiding place.

'So,' Jeff said, 'I'm intrigued how you are going to get that garment back on without taking your top off,' he added grinning as he watched her facing him.

'You will have to stay and be intrigued, as it won't be going on; it's got to be cleaned. So what are you going to do now? I'm feeling rather dirty from that place, so I'm going to have a shower. Tell me Jeff, how do people live in places like where we just went? It was so run down, and that disgusting graffiti didn't help much either, it makes me shudder, thinking of the place.'

'I'm sure you have the same kind of places even in London,' he said.

'Yeah right, anyway why don't you go and see that bloke at the travel firm, what's it called. Oh yes, Travel-View.'

'Ok Charley, I won't be long, meanwhile don't open the door to anybody. I'll see if that travel agent knows where I can get the computer repaired as well, plus I'll see what he has to say about that missing submarine, as we have to investigate that while we are here,'

'The sooner the better my dear,' she called as she headed towards her room.

'I'll see you a little later,' he said closing the door behind him as he left.

Locking the door to her apartment as well as Jeff's, she sat on her bed ascertaining her next move. She needed time to think ahead, and still holding the bra, she grabbed hold of a needle and cotton and set about stitching the slit carefully with the card inside, once accomplished and satisfied with the repair, she threw it in the wash basket and made her way into the bathroom to run the water for a well-earned shower. As the water splashed on her face she began to wonder about Jeff, for she realised she had started to like him, but also knowing it should not happen, especially when you worked together as a partner, for things could get complicated. However, she decided she would take things a bit careful, for he may not respond in the same way.

When Jeff reached the hotels car park, as a precaution he gave the car a once over to make sure it had not been interfered with, satisfied that it had not been touched, he then drove the few blocks from the hotel to the travel agents. Having no difficulty in parking opposite the shop he locked the car and entered the shop.

'Hello my name is Jeff Morgan. I would like to see a Mr. Vkhin.

'Certainly sir I will tell him your here,' the receptionist said sliding off her chair to head for a door at the far end of the room. Although, heavily built, she walked gracefully with her long black hair, swaying from side to side with every movement she made. In a second, she came back holding a full smile on her round rosy face. 'He won't keep you,' she mentioned as she sat down in her chair instantly typing some kind of letter. While Jeff watched her type on an old word processor, the end door opened and Vkhin came through with a bright beam on his face. He was smartly dressed in a light blue suit, which gave the impression he was slimmer than he was. He stood in the doorway with his 6 feet tall body touching the top of the doorframe and seeing Jeff he called to him.

'How do you do Mr. Morgan,' he spoke with ease in a good English accent. 'I am sorry to keep you waiting, please come in.'

'No problem,' Jeff said as the proprietor showed him through the door and into his office.

Jeff witnessed that Vkhin kept a very clean tidy office, and saw on his right hand side, a big black leather sofa against the bright cream painted wall, to his left a chair was also made of the same material as the sofa and had been placed in front of a highly polished desk, where Vkhin sat. He pointed to a matching chair for Jeff to sit in, which was in front of the desk.

'Mr Morgan please sit down and make your self comfortable,' Vkhin said.

'Thank you,' Jeff acknowledged and sat down in the chair.

'Would you care for some tea, coffee, or perhaps something a little stronger?' Vkhin enquired.

'Thanks for asking but I'll decline,' Jeff responded.

'Now, how can I be of assistance to you Mr. Morgan?' the agent asked while removing a silver case from one of the drawers and taking a cigarette from the case. 'Would you care for one?

'No not for me, I don't smoke but thanks all the same for offering. I will come straight to the point Mr. Vkhin. You have a submarine and I've been told it has gone missing. Can you enlighten me, to what may have happened to it, and if there's a search to find it?' Jeff queried.

'Yes there is a search, but as yet nothing has been established. I think I had better start from the beginning to how this submarine came into existence.'

'It would help no end, and why it's disappeared,' Jeff replied in a calm voice.

'My profits had been sliding for sometime over the last few years and I was on my way to going bust. So about 3 years ago this chap by the name of Ofenka approached me with a business proposition, he claimed he wanted to invest some money and that my company appealed to him. Well after my lawyer checked his credentials, I made him a shareholder. Things began looking well for the business and it was starting to pick up with more people travelling around the world. He then came up with an idea about using a submarine as a holiday venture, he stated he would arrange the formalities and told me not to worry about a thing but carry on as usual with my side of the company, which I did. I knew he had the submarine completely refurbished and had new engines, plus he had other things installed that I did not understand, after all, he was the expert. He had officers and crew ready to sail when it was ready, although I did not see any of them so I cannot say anything about them, though I was told, some sailors were supposed to catch the boat at sea, somewhere. Apart from the occasional word, he didn't confer with me about the project in anyway whatsoever, in fact, he was quite secretive about the whole business.

'Did you not think it was a tiny bit strange, that this chap was spending a lot of cash and not telling you anything?' Jeff retorted thinking this guy was a touch naïve with the circumstances, to the fact this Ofenka chap walks in, and hands over a lot of cash.

'My salvation,' Vkhin said, 'as I stated I was getting desperate, he asked for nothing. As far as I know, he may have drowned with the others, including the Walker's; I must admit the disappearance is a mystery. The last thing he said to me was he was going to sail with the boat on its maiden voyage, and to welcome the Walkers on board.'

'The Walker's---, Mr. Vkhin, nobody mentioned to me about them missing, who are they and where do they come from?'

'Oh, Mr. and Mrs. Walker, is an English couple and were booked on the boat, it was some kind of anniversary or birthday present. That's all I know,' Vkhin said with a worried frown on his brow.

'Well thank you for your time, you have been most helpful, I shan't keep you any longer although should you get any further news you will let me know. I'm staying at the St Petersburg hotel at the moment,' Jeff said as he rose to his feet, and turning away from Vkhin, made his way towards the door and out of the building.

'I just remembered something,' Vkhin called after Jeff opened the door to leave. 'Ofenka spoke of two other guys, one was named Leshin, who he told me to employ, the other one, I only got part of his name, it sounded like it began with Poz. Ofenka never said to me why he used them.'

'So what did this Leshin do? Jeff asked facing him.

'As he was a holiday courier; it was he who escorted the Walker's when they arrived from England. But the moment the boat sailed, he said he needed to go to Kiev, said it was necessary to see his mother, for she had taken ill.'

'If that's the case with Leshin, what connection did this Poz Guy have with Ofenka?' Jeff inquired. 'Do you think his name could have been Pozvizd by any chance?'

'I have no idea,' the travel agent stated, 'but I will see what I can find out for you.'

'Well thanks again,' Jeff said acknowledging him and then ending the conversation left to go back to his car. After looking at the details that Vkhin gave, he headed for the computer shop that Vkhin had recommended. He began to ponder over the meeting with Vkhin, and thought to himself was the guy telling the truth or was he giving him the run around. On reflection, it seems to be a coincidence. He would need to check him out more closely.

Chapter 9

Pozvizd threw a right punch to his opponents face, but the sailor saw it coming and deflected the blow with his left arm, and returned at the same instance he threw a crashing fist into Pozvizd stomach, which made him bend sharply. Gasping for breath, he backed away a little, before springing back at the sailor, this time kicking him hard on the shin. The sailor cried with sudden pain and fell backwards giving Pozvizd another chance, for he now had the upper hand and pulled a white handled 8-inch knife from his belt. The polished chrome blade curved on its outer edge, while the inner edge was straight, narrow and jagged. The sailor's eyes opened wide with fear at seeing the weapon in Pozvizd's right hand, for he was unarmed and was no match with this guy who threatened him in the confined space of the rear torpedo room. He was helpless to fight back and knew he would die as his assailant was getting ready to lunge, but a voice roared behind Pozvizd and stopped him dead in his tracks.

'Drop the knife Pozvizd, or I'll shoot you where you stand,' the man said harshly. Pozvizd spun round to face the sound of the voice, and with an evil cold glare in his eyes, he watched the man intently with the gun who had it pointing at him.

'I said, drop the knife,' the voice bellowed again although this time he cocked the gun, emphasising what he meant, he said and raising the gun at shoulder height, he aimed it at Pozvizd head. 'Don't make me do it, I mean what I say.' Cautiously Pozvizd lowered his arm, which held the knife, and let the weapon drop to the deck. The knife echoed loudly through the room as it clattered on the deck. Nobody stirred; they stood frozen in silence waiting for Pozvizd to move.

'Very good,' the man said at length. 'Ok Pozvizd, move carefully along the passageway towards the control room and no funny business or I'll shoot you,' the man cried holding the gun at the ready. They then proceeded towards the control room, where the captain stood hunched across the chart table with Mianlia his 1st officer and Hans at his side. Pozvizd entered the room gingerly followed by Sakhakov who still held his gun at Pozvizd head. Mark quickly followed with Ann and Crystal into the room to see what the commotion was. The control room now crowded with the crew who were operating the equipment looked on in earnest and was wondering what had taken place.

The captain wild with anger, strained and irritated by the interruption, stood straight to wait for an explanation to this sudden intrusion.

'Stand where you are and give me an account to this affray!' the captain roared.

'I'm sorry sir, it was a bad miss understanding, we were having a game of cards and it got out of hand, it won't happen again sir. I'm so sorry I was very stupid,' Pozvizd declared as he stood facing the captain, for he was wondering what was going to happen to him.

'You are bloody right it was stupid,' the Captain replied sternly, showing his anger towards Pozvizd. 'It definitely will not happen again, I cannot condone such unbelievable behaviour. This incident is intolerable on such a small vessel, more so because we are 150 feet below the surface, it has been an immense lack of authority; I will place you under severe supervision until I can find alternative arrangements for you. I will deal with the other sailor later.'

'But Captain---,' Pozvizd blurted out and was about to try and say something further but as he took a step towards the captain. A loud bang from Sakhakov's gun rapidly followed, the sound vibrated round the small room as the shot bounced off the metal stone grey walls. The bullet hit Pozvizd in the upper stomach and pushed him a few paces back. Not believing being shot until he saw the blood starting to flow through his fingers, he gripped his stomach automatically as if his hands could stop the flow of blood and then with glazed eyes he stared at the others around him.

'Why, why! Surely that was not necessary, I was not going to do anything,' he stuttered as his voice became less perceptible to those near him, for his speech now slurred, the words becoming inaudible to those around him, it was all he could muster. Raggedly his legs began to buckle beneath him, and he dropped to his knees, his face and eyes distorted with pain from the bullet entering his body, he collapsed in a heap on the cold uninviting deck and rolling over on his left side became still.

Ann screamed with horror as she witnessed the killing and stood with the others beside her in astonishment, and powerless to act, for they and not really grasped the situation as they watched Pozvizd die.

'Did you have to kill him? You couldn't be sure he was going to attack the captain, you could have handed him over to the authorities when we docked.' Nevertheless, before the chief could answer her, a voice yelled from the sonar room.

'Contact bearing one five zero° distance 25 miles.' Undaunted by the shooting, the captain went into swift action.

'Action stations!' he called calmly and then pressed a button on the console to warn the crew. They responded by making off in all directions to their required positions as fast as they could, and in an unbelievable confined area.

'What is it Andrei?' the skipper said going into the radio room to see for himself.

'It's a big ship sir,' Andrei stated in a grated voice.

'Helm, take the boat to 50 feet, we'll go to periscope depth to see what ship it is.'

Ann trembled from the sound of the rumbling, which came from the ballast tanks as the air blew the water out. As the boat climbed to 50 feet, the sound from the escaping air tanks gave off an eerie sensation, in addition, the hydraulics created even more noise, which made Ann shiver with tension to what was going to happen.

Reaching their required depth, the captain then commanded.

'Up scope,' he commanded. Then taking hold of the scope to peer through the eyepiece, before it became fully extended he leaned on the handles, moving his position in a 360° circle to ascertain where the target might be.

'Down scope, surface,' he snapped. Once again, they endured the noises from the tanks as the sailors pushed the leavers and turned knobs to bring the boat to the surface.

Breaking through the waves, from beneath the ocean into a bright mid afternoon sun, the boat settled to a gentle rocking motion from the slight swell. As the first officer opened the hatch, a small amount of water dropped from the conning tower into the control room, making his coat wet as he climbed the companionway. Leaping up the companionway, he quickly followed onto the submarines deck by the captain. Then after a few minutes elapsed, Mianlia called down to the Walkers.

'Mr and Mrs. Walker, would you care to come and get some fresh air.'

'Come on my darling let's go, try and forget the incident with Pozvizd. I know its unfortunate but I'm sure everything will be all right now,' Mark said as they made their way out of the hot stuffy boat, quickly followed by Crystal and Hans, but Mark remembered as he went on deck what Andrei had said to him in the galley.

A big ship had come to a halt and moored alongside the submarine; Mark instantly noting that it was an old rusty cargo vessel.

'Hello,' Tabor called down to them as he leaned against the railings of the ship. 'Please, please come on board.'

An escort showed them the way to the lounge where a steward waited with a tray of drinks.

'Please be free to have a drink,' Tabor announced. Mark accepted the offer but was sceptical, as he could not think of a reason, why

61

Tabor brought them aboard his ship, but he had no choice but to accept Tabors offer.

'The killing of Pozvizd was most unfortunate and very bad, but nevertheless; I must say it was necessary, that I can assure you; perhaps later you will understand the reasons to why he was shot,' Tabor said calmly.

'My name is Tabor Pavelkko,' he said introducing himself, with a hand stretched out to shake. 'But please call me Tabor,' he said in a gentle voice, while waving a hand for the waiter to pour further drinks. Then after the waiter had accomplished it, he left the room, quietly closing the door behind him.

'Now to business,' Tabor finally announced. 'Hans and his wife Crystal you have already met, along with Captain Krabava, who I am sorry to say, will not be joining us, for he has a lot of work to do. This is Captain Pushkin of this ship, which is called the Oban,' Tabor said brushing his arm casually in the captain's direction, which he remained sitting in the corner of the lounge observing everything that was taking place.

'Of course, what you are not aware of, Hans is a finance expert and works for me; he makes the best judgments to what I need and how to spend the money.' Tabor grinned cunningly as he spoke, except Mark could find no reason in his humour, for he sensed something menacing was about to be revealed.

'I did mention I was in finance, although I'm afraid I neglected to let you know in what connection I had with the submarine,' Schmitt added turning to face Mark with a sickly grin written on his face.

'I am the founder of this project, and I am sorry to say you have become a member,' Tabor said, but stopped continuing to speak, for he saw Ann tapping on one of the windows.

'What's going on down there, on the submarines deck?' she cried. Mark along with the others moved towards the window, to see what she was talking about.

'Oh,' Tabor said still with an evil smile, 'Oh yes, they are loading torpedoes.'

'Torpedoes,' Mark uttered in surprise.

'Yes torpedoes, you see with everybody looking for us now, they may come in handy, who knows?' Tabor's smile had vanished and he was looking extremely serious. It's a preventive measure I need to take in the event our pursuers have ideas of their own.

'Now why would anyone want to harm us?' Mark questioned in disbelieve, that some one may even contemplate attacking them. 'Surely Tabor or whatever your name really is, what possible threat are we to anybody, we are supposed to be on holiday, for Christ sake, so Tabor, are you going to explain what this is all about.' Mark spat with anger, as his blood began to boil in his veins. 'What's going on?' Mark asked desperately, trying to get an answer from this evil man. 'First you shoot one of your own men, then you start loading torpedoes on that submarine, it seems to me, it's you who are after a fight, with whom I just can't imagine. I also want to know what you have in store for us, if nothing then let us go,' Mark said shaking with fury at Tabor and with the very thought of being a prisoner to this evil thug. For that is what he saw him as, and now proposing to keep them on that smelly submarine, along with his band of thugs.

'Once again I say to you, what's going on? I don't like this one bit,' Mark kept repeating, and feeling sick each time, he asked the question. Mark then faced his wife to see how she was responding to the wickedness of this man, and what he was conjuring up to do to them. He put his arms round her to give her support and felt her trembling with fear.

His mind flashed back to Ann arranging the holiday, and he felt guilty, for putting her in this position.

'For now it does not concern you Mr. Walker.' Mark heard Tabor's voice in the distance, for he was still thinking about his wife and how emotionally upset she was becoming.

Tabor made his way to the door, opening it he called to his waiter, who entered representing himself as a guard, cradling in his arms a Russian AK47 machine gun.

'Tell them to bring Pozvizd's body from the submarine, and ditch it overboard,' Tabor announced.

'Yes sir,' the guard said smartly while standing to attention, and then spinning on his heels he swiftly retreated to carry out the command. A deathly silence fell over the lounge, as Ann and Mark waited with anticipation of what next would take place, and then Ann whispered to Mark saying.

'What's going to happen to us?' A quiver in her voice told him exactly how she was feeling; her answer did not take very long in coming, as Tabor turned back from the door to face them.

'I'm afraid it's regrettable, we have to keep you with us for sometime, for we have to make a few changes to our programme. I foresee that killing you is not in my plans, unless of course you give us a reason to do such a thing. I am extremely sorry to keep you on the submarine; however, we will try to make you as comfortable as possible. As I just stated, no harm will befall you if you do exactly as asked. The voyage will be arduous; for there is along way to go and most of it will be under the waves, so I do hope you will collaborate with us and give the captain and his crew no problems while on board. I have instructed Captain Krabava to move you to another part of the boat; you will be bunked behind the wardroom, which is directly behind the control room, but forward of the engine department, which is in the stern of the boat. I am sure you are already familiar with the layout of the vessel but at least you will have some privacy. It will be a touch noisy, I am sorry we cannot offer better accommodation, however; as an ex, navy man and submariner I am positive you will soon adapt and find it secure. Again I am truly sorry for the inconvenience but I find it necessary at this stage to keep you.'

'Why do we have to go back on that boat?' Ann said expressing pain about the ordeal, she envisaged. She also noticed how her husband looked surprised at Tabor, knowing he had served on submarines. 'We as I can see it have no value to you or anybody else,' she stated with her voice sounding strained with having to stay with these evil thugs. 'We were just on holiday for a couple of days that's all, so whatever you have done we don't want to know, so let us go,' she cried.

'I only wish we could. We are aware of your arrangements but you are not totally accurate about being of no use,' Hans said intervening before Tabor could speak.

'We believe your husband has knowledge, which could be of extreme importance to us.'

As he spoke, Mark began to dislike the German more and more, and felt justified as his hatred grew towards him each time he opened his mouth. He knew he needed to find more at what they were up to, so he decided he wood have to endure this German's attitude further, for he was sure that eventually they would make a mistake and then he would be able to get his revenge on them. Therefore, with deliberation, he would go along with their scheme.

In the corner of the lounge, Pushkin with his drawn shallow cheeks sat taking notice of the events as they unfolded but said nothing to change things. He, like Tabor was tall, thin, but his big red nose stood beyond his ageing face, which seemed to make him older than his sixty years; his grey curly hair hung down over his pointed ears that emphasized his age. He wished he could retire, but he desperately needed the money, and as Tabor paid him handsomely for the use of his ship, although he was not keen on the cargo. His ship had become his home since the Serbs destroyed his natural home during the conflict with Croatia, so he made this his life.

He agreed to what was happening to the Walkers as he listened to Tabor and Schmitt, not that he could help them in any way.

'It is no point in saying anything further, you will stay and that is final,' Tabor barked abruptly. 'Captain Krabava will take care of you and will see no harm comes to you both,' Tabor said as he opened the door and shouted another command to a guard, which quickly entered to escort the Walkers back to the submarine now that the meeting had ended.

'Until we meet again Mr. and Mrs. Walker,' Tabor called behind them with a mocking grin, that increased as he spoke which revealed the wickedness in him that had grown over the last few years.

Climbing down the iron steps of the Oban, the Walkers made their way back to the submarine with the guard and his gun at the ready and aimed on Mark in the event he tried to do something unwise, like making a grab for it to try an escape. Not that it would do him any good, apart from getting himself killed.

Mark noticed as he descended the iron ladder that they were preparing to load on board the boat, apart from the usual stores, the last torpedo. This torpedo was as far has he could see, was very much different from the conventional types he had witnessed. The nose somehow seemed smaller but longer, its colour was a darker green than the others he had witnessed, and the propellers at the rear of the torpedo were dissimilar to what he had seen on other torpedoes that he had dealt with, when he was in the navy. This torpedo just did not match up; something was definitely a miss and did not seem right. He would need to get closer to it once he was back on the submarine, and as soon as possible.

Before entering the conning tower hatch again, the Walkers looked at the evening sunset, for all they knew it might be the last time they would ever see it. The sun glowed like a big massive ball of fire and as it blazed bright red and yellow in the vast space of blue sky, it began to sink low towards the horizon with a thin wisp of cloud running through the central point of the fireball. The very calm sea hardly moved as a gentle wind tucked at the waves; the

66

water was so still, it appeared as if it was a mirror, showing the reflection of the ship on the surface. So calm was the weather, you would not have thought, you were sailing in the Barents Sea.

Their observation soon ended by the nudge to Mark's back from the guard who still had his gun trained on him, so leaving the warm fresh air they re-entered the submarines control room and to an uncertain future. It would be the last they would see of light for a number of days, for everything had changed now they were back in the submarine. The guard descended the ladder behind the two of them and waited patiently for further orders.

Again, the captain was already calling out orders to prepare to sail, for he had been striding up and down in the control room waiting for them. Now all he wanted was Schmitt to arrive, and they then would be back on the move. Knowing the longer they stayed along side the Oban, the more at risk they were in being spotted by a passing ship or aircraft, so not wanting to get caught and ruin everything that Tabor and himself had worked for, he needed to get going.

'I'll take you to your new quarters,' Kazan said speaking in a not so friendly voice, for the captain had told his crew not to speak to them as freely as they had done in the past.'

They proceeded through a watertight door towards their allocated room, where they had been. Nevertheless, on passing, Mark glanced at the first officer on his way to his new room and saw he was studying what looked to be new charts, but regrettably, he was not able to see where they were heading and wondered where they would end up. As he entered the new cabin, he thought, what if the captain was under some kind of pressure from Tabor to take them on board, and why was his voice hostile, for they had not done anything to hinder him, and his boat.

'You are here,' the captain said entering the new compartment. Mark turned to face the captain and looked straight into his eyes, hoping he could read what his plans were for them.

67

'What's really going on? Are you going to enlighten us to what's so special about keeping us here on board this boat? In addition, how do we fit in with your plans? Furthermore what is it with the torpedoes you have on board?' Mark said hissing the words between clenched teeth.

'You owe us an explanation,' Ann exploded in a loud voice. 'What with that man you had killed and all, it's ghastly; tell us captain, you must know.'

'That is not entirely correct, I know little more than you both, as to why he needs your husband on this submarine, I have not the foggiest idea, however; as soon as I hear of something, I will indeed let you know. All I am able to say to you both now, is I have to sail on a specific course. As for the torpedoes, they are for our safety and security, for you must be aware there is a search underway to find us. I am afraid it is all I can add at this instant, but maybe Schmitt can help you with your questions, as I can hear him arriving. I'm sorry I will do my best to keep you informed of events, as and when they transpire if it is possible, so please in the meantime try and make yourselves as comfortable as you can, for I have now got to get this boat moving once again.'

The captain made to leave them but then pausing at the door, he turned round to face them and then added. 'Should you require anything that is in my power, let me know.' He then left them standing in their new surroundings baffled by the events that were unfolding before them.

'Well,' Ann remarked gritting her teeth that made her voice grate. 'What do you make of that?'

'I'm not at all sure Ann but I'll tell you this, I am going to do what I can to find out. I won't let them walk all over us.'

After the Walkers had left the ship and returned to the submarine, Schmitt faced his colleague Tabor.

'Did you find the memory card belonging to the camera?'

'No,' Tabor stated pouring another drink into his glass. 'Pozvizd said he had searched the apartment thoroughly but could not find anything.'

'Don't you find it a bit strange that the camera was all he discovered, and it only contained six pictures in its internal memory? Although I'm glad to say he had the sense and brought it straight to us, for if those agents got hold of it, they may have been able to identify us, and report it to Washington as to who we are.

'Yes Hans I take your point, and I agree with you, so now we have to make sure the two agents have not discovered anything that is detrimental to our course, which may give away to what we are planning. I will get in touch with Leshin, let me see what he can dig up, it is about time he earned his keep.'

'How do you suppose he's going to achieve that?' Hans remarked taking another bottle of vodka from the cabinet and began pouring its contents into a small tumbler. Taking it to his lips, he swallowed the liquid in one gulp while at the same time watched Tabor's reaction. 'You going to bring him back to St Petersburg?'

'No I think we will arrange it that the two agents go to him in Murmansk, I am sure they will enjoy the place, do you not agree?' Tabor added with a wide grin that showed his perfect white teeth. And with a scheming mind he began to chuckle, knowing what he had in store for the agents.

'Good so be it,' Schmitt said as he placed the empty glass on the cabinet. 'I'll leave it in your capable hands; it's time I made a move.' Then heading for the door he stopped with a second thought and spun round quickly to face Tabor.

'Will you make sure my wife gets to Hamburg safely, I would appreciate it, as I do not think she should be around in case of any adverse trouble?'

'I will see to it for you Hans,' Tabor said as he walked over to shake his hand, and then watched him make his way back to the Zhuralev.

'I'll be in touch in a few days, to see what progress has been made,' Schmitt called without waiting for a reply as he descended the iron steps to board the submarine.

Chapter 10

Casually chucking her bag on the bed, Charley walked to the partitioned door, which led from her room into Jeff's room. On opening, she looked inside but seeing he had not returned, she returned to take a well-earned shower, for she wanted to look her best for him when he returned, as she had started to like him very much. After sometime under the shower she heard the phone ringing in his room, and on the assumption it might be him needing her help, she scrambled from the shower and dashed into his room to pickup the phone. In haste and out of breath, for she was expecting to hear Jeff's voice on the other end of the phone line, but stopped suddenly surprised in hearing a stranger's voice. Stunned and taken aback, she listened to what the caller had to say when Jeff opened the door without knocking and having no idea she would be in his room or even on the phone. He stopped immediately on the spot and froze; utterly astounded by the way she stood with a finger placed to her lips, for she gestured to him not to make a sound by his sudden entrance. All Jeff could do was stand and wait until she had finished listening to whoever was speaking to her. Finally, she placed the phone on its cradle as the line went dead. Jeff stood motionless on the spot staring at her, as she stood completely naked before him, for her towel had dropped around her ankles. He saw small globules of water running from her black shinny hair onto her face and shoulders, they then continued onto her chest, travelling through her cleavage and finally dropping to the bedroom carpet. Further droplets flowed over the top of her full firm pert deep tanned breasts; they too ended on the floor. For what seemed an eternity, he stood facing her; unable to do anything about her situation, then at length he walked to her, bending down he picked up the towel which had fallen to the ground, when she had made a grab for the phone. Gently he smiled at her as he placed the towel around her exposed body, and then peering into her warm inviting eyes, he kissed her tenderly on her lips. She made no resistance as he pulled her closer to his body. Letting go of the towel, it fell silently back to the carpet but ignoring it; he reached for her soft lips again and kissed her until they could no longer breathe. Feeling the warmth from her wet body, he tentatively moved her towards the bed, where they embraced each other. Time meant nothing to them, as they embraced each other. He had forgotten everything he had learnt in his training as an agent. Then abruptly, he pulled away from her, realising what was happening to him, for his heart began to tell him one thing, while his brain spelt out danger. So not wanting to spoil their relationship, he stood up from the bed and walked away from her, thinking what might have taken place if he continued to do what they were doing.

'Who was it on the phone? When I came in,' Jeff asked at length, as he sat on the bed beside her, for work had once again raised its ugly head. So putting his thoughts of Charley to the back of his head, as he needed to concentrate wholly on what he needed to do in the future.

After kissing her, he realised he was falling in love, but also knowing he knew nothing about her, nevertheless he did not care, for it had been a long-time since being kissed by a woman, and it felt good.

'You know you looked rather eye-catching, when you were holding the phone,' he said grinning softly while picturing in his mind, her soft tanned naked body.

Eventually his eyes switched to the computer on the floor, where he had left it on entering the room. He reached down to pick it up and placing it on the bed, he plugged the laptop into the mains socket and switched it on. So engrossed with the laptop, he did not noticed her leave the room, but he did not have to wait very long before she returned, for holding the memory card in her hand which they had discovered earlier, she handed it to him.

While she was retrieving the card from her room, she managed to slip on a red pleated skirt and white jumper. Now sitting beside Jeff, she waited to see what information it had, hoping it would identify the crooks.

'Incidentally, the chap on the phone called himself Leshin. He claimed he was speaking from Murmansk, and had details to Jack and Dennis's death. He also suggested we should go to Murmansk, once there, we should ring him on this number and arrange a meeting,' she said handing Jeff a piece of paper with the phone number on it. 'What do you think we should do Jeff? Shall we go and see what he has to say?'

'Yes I suppose we should see what he has to say, although I'm a bit suspicious to why he's not phoned us before. Also how did he know we were staying here?'

'You think it's some kind of trick then?'

'Possibly yes, I wouldn't be surprised, for he was employed by Travel-View, it was them who told me about Leshin, and that he needed to go to Kiev see his parents about some problem or other. I was also told that Leshin was overseeing the boarding of the Walker's onto the submarine.' The thing is, what's he doing in Murmansk and how could he possibly have known about our mates deaths? Anyway, we don't have a choice but to go, although we'll need to be very vigilant in the event of it being a trap. For if the crooks, which killed our two agents and with so much ease, they won't hesitate to try and kill us.

They debated the problems further with what may arise when in Murmansk, as the card loaded its contents, the screen revealed twelve photos, which varied from several people to buildings and in particular an old corroding submarine.

'Interesting,' Charley said as she fixed her eyes on the picture of the submarine. 'What do you make of that?'

'No idea as yet, although it seems something rather dreadful is going to take place sometime in the future. Ok let's get these pictures to our respective bosses, so they can process them more fully, I dare say they will enlighten us to who the figures are and what may be happening.'

'I'm sure London will show some light on the case and may even be able to identify the figures,' Charley stated as she watched Jeff send the copies to their respective departments for further identification. Then after completing the process, they contemplated their next move.

'Well Charley there's nothing else we can do tonight, so I suggest we get something to eat and drink, we can discuss further about going to Murmansk over a meal, anyway I can think more clearly when I've got food inside me.'

'OK I agree with you there. But I think there is no doubt there seems to be a connection with the submarine, and the deaths of Jack and Dennis, but what? That is the question. What do you think Jeff?' Charley said with a heart-rending frown written across her face, for she visualised Dennis's body slumped in his car.

'Yes Charley I am afraid I agree with you,' he said looking at her in a strange way. 'Are you going to go to the restaurant like that?'

'No certainly not, just give me a couple of minutes and I will put something more suitable on,' she said scurrying to her room, only to return after a few minutes later, wearing navy blue slacks and a white blouse, in addition to them, she had put on a short jacket to match her slacks.

'How do I look?' she said with a smile. That began to make Jeff's heart pound. Then gripping his arm they made for the door to head for the restaurant. Jeff began thinking as they made their way to dinner, that he must be extremely cautious as to the way he felt about this lovely girl and where the relationship was heading, for he was certain, she felt the same way about him, nevertheless; it could put both them in a very precarious position at the wrong time. Additionally it was possible it could cloud his judgment, if not hers, and that would pronounce disaster. He was very aware she was an extremely attractive woman with all the curves in the right places, as they made for the restaurant. Her long black curly hair swayed from one side to the other as they made their way along the wide-open path beside the busy main road. He stole a glance at her as they walked along the pavement, and saw her bright green emerald eyes sparkling as the streetlights reflected on them. Her high cheekbones along with her full lips added to her beauty.

Arriving at the same restaurant, which they had visited the previous night, for it, was convenient as it was only a few minutes from the hotel. Once there, not waiting for the waiter they moved on through the tables with their clean white cloths draped over them, and sat at the same table by the window.

'Jeff I got a very uncanny sensation about what's going to happen once we get to Murmansk, and I'm afraid I don't like the look of it.'

'Maybe your right Charley, but you do not have to go.'

'I know Jeff, but I have too. I'm aware that we will have to tread very careful. I reckon we should go to the docks first and see what we can find about the submarine. Shall we do that before making contact with this Leshin guy?'

'Yeah, I agree with you. We may then have a better understanding as to what it's all about, for it's no good relying on the police, as you can't be sure who you can trust,' Jeff remarked with a grim look.

'Hello Jim,' Jeff said responding to the sound of his phone ringing in his pocket. He then continued to speak silently in the mouthpiece while Charley tried to listen to his conversation but was unable to catch the contents.

'It's a bit late ringing me! I forget, you never sleep, and of course, you are on a different time zone. I take it this is not a social call. The brit and me are having dinner, so what gives, yeah I can talk,' he said looking at her across the table. She watched him as his face showed strange expressions as he listened to his boss's voice on the other end of the phone line.

'When did this take place, how long ago?' Jeff garbled into the phone, hearing what his boss was saying.

'Anything else you can add,' he said before finishing the conversation and replacing his phone into his pocket. He then looked at Charley before telling her what he had heard.

'It appears that an ex-convict Pozvizd, who we believed killed our guys, was one of the men in those photos we sent. Further, more a Russian fishing boat had dragged him from the Barents Sea; evidently, he had been shot in the stomach. Well that's what my boss had just told me.'

'Good. That's one we shan't have to concern ourselves with,' Charley injected, 'any suggestion to why he had been killed and dumped into the sea?' She said charmingly inquiring with no compassion towards his death.

'Yes I agree with you, in the meantime we have to concern ourselves on keeping an eye on this Leshin bloke. If I remember correctly, that's the guy you spoke to on the phone. Although before we go, I reckon we should try and see if the police have any records on this chap Leshin, you never can tell what they may have found, we have lots to consider Charley?'

'Very well Jeff, but I think we're not going to accomplish anything further at this time of night,' she said standing up from the table, after finishing the meal. 'I'm tired and it's been an exhausting day, so shall we go to bed.'

'Bed, with you?' Jeff spluttered choking on the last drop wine from his glass.'

'Do you have someone else in mind; I didn't see you complaining a little time ago, when you saw me with nothing on, or is there another reason?' Charley questioned with a cheerful smile.

'No, no Charley, good God no,' he voiced hastily scrambling to his feet to join her.

On the way back to the hotel, the mood changed decidedly, so he decided to put everything about why they were there, for he was feeling very much better, and so with a pleasant beam across his face, they left arm in arm from the restaurant to head back to her room.

Chapter 11

Jim sat alone at his office desk, in the late afternoon studying the photos he received from Jeff. Some of them consisted of warehouses that were dotted about the Murmansk docks. One in particular took his attention, for its doors were wide open. He could clearly see inside the building, which revealed some wooden crates. He noticed they were long and sturdy in their appearance by the way they had been stacked. There were markings on the side of one of them, but it was too difficult for him to identify the characters clearly. Therefore, he ordered Matthew who was one of his team, to expand the photos in the hope he could get a better view of them, and tell him where they may be heading. He looked at another two photos, which showed six men sitting on a crate, to what it seemed they were toasting to some event.

'Boss, I have received a message from the Russians, they have told me they have dragged a dead body from the Barents's sea. They have identified it as one of their crooks who was called Pozvizd; you may recall Pozvizd was the chap who had been released from jail a little while ago,' Dave remarked on entering Jim's office, and who happened to be the youngest man on Jim's team.

Jim sprung to attention like a whip cracking in the afternoon air.

'Can't you damn well knock when entering, why on earth don't you ever knock, instead of just barging in?' Jim bellowed in anger, which made him all the more irritable to the sudden intrusion.

'Sorry boss but I thought this message was urgent and you should know.'

'Ok what else have you got that is important,' Jim replied apologising for his abruptness.

'Well, he'd been shot in the stomach by all accounts and had been in the water for some hours. The reds sent this photo, verifying that it's him, and they thought it may be of use to you,' Dave stated, as Jim handled the picture of Pozvizd. When Jim saw the photo, he instantly saw it was not a pretty sight, for it showed the body and his face contorted and screwed up from being in the water for too long.

'Did you thank them for this photo,' Jim said wanting to keep on the good side of the reds, but his patients was wearing thin, for it looked as if, they were dragging their feet over the death of his colleague.

'Yes I did,' Dave added.

'Very well, keep in touch with them and see what else you can find. In the meantime go tell Harvey and Jamie to pack, you had better pack as well; the three of you will be going to Murmansk to give Jeff some support. I reckon he's going to need help by what's happening over there.

'Do we need Jamie? Only if it's going to be dangerous, I wouldn't like to see her get hurt,' Dave responded, while showing his concern at how he felt for her welfare.

'That's true, but she is fluent with the Russian language, and that's going to be very useful for you guys, so yes she has to go, it'll be up to you to take care that nothing happens to her, now scoot off and ask her to see me, like now, if you please.'

'Jim, are you all right and not feeling ill by any chance? For saying please, you have gone and spoilt yourself, and just when I thought you were angry with me, are you turning over a new leaf and mending your ways? For I thought please, was not in your vocabulary,' Dave said smiling outwardly, as he started to depart from the office.

'Just do it,' Jim growled back at him as Dave left the office. However, deep inside he knew he liked him; in fact, he liked all of them, for they were a great bunch of guys, and the last thing he

79

wanted was no harm to come to any of them, especially what had happened to Jack. So deep with his thoughts, he never heard Jamie enter his office.

'You want me boss?' she enquired standing in front of his desk. She looked very pretty wearing a light green blouse and darker green waistcoat and with a tight fitting matching skirt, in all, it blended well with her green eyes. She was a slim woman, and it added a touch of class to her posture as she confronted her boss.

'You're needed to go with those other twits Dave and Harvey, to Murmansk, here's a photo of this guy,' Jim said handing her the picture of Pozvizd; taking it from him with her left hand, she revealed a fastidious cluster diamond ring on her index finger, that glinted in the bright lights of the office.

'Get some further copies and see what additional intelligence you can find on him, see who else he worked for and why he was bumped off. I don't need to tell you it could possibly get dangerous, so take very good care. I have told Dave you are to meet Jeff, work with him, and no heroes understand, tell those two blockheads the same and keep me well posted. Incidentally I would leave that rock your wearing behind, for if you value it and in the wake of things to where you're going, you won't have it long.'

Chapter 12

'Captain, the seabed's dropped to over a thousand,' Andrei declared while continuing to listen to the underwater sounds of the sea, in his headphones.

'Helm, take the boat down to 600 feet,' Krabava ordered, after hearing Andrei's statement.

The submarine slowly began its descent towards the ocean's floor, and then levelling at the depth the skipper commanded, it hovered as if waiting for further commands.

Then the radio operator cried out once more but this time with more zest in his voice.

'Contact 15 miles, and heading our way,' Andrei stated. This time the captain did not respond to the new information immediately, but waited for a second, thinking as he stood by the chart table. Looking briefly at the chart of the ocean on the table, he turned calmly round, and said silently to Kazan.

'Go and keep the Walker's company, we don't want them getting up to no good, a precaution you understand.' Kazan not replying to his skipper disappeared from the control room, but not before bumping into Hans Schmitt as he appeared.

'What's the fuss about?' Schmitt said speaking to no one in particular. Babarika busy at seeing to the question of the approaching ship ignored him and treated him with contempt, knowing eventually, they would have a show down, for he disliked Schmitt immensely.

'Sir, it's a large ship and it's heading our way, I reckon she must have spotted us,' Andrei reported.

'Very well,' the skipper stated without showing any emotion towards his crew. As the ship approached, they could hear the noise of its screws thrashing through the water pushing the sixty thousand tonnes of hard steel along.

'Periscope depth,' Krabava called out. 'Up scope,' he ordered reaching for the handles as it rose from its well, and then pushing his eyes into the lens for a better view, he turned in a 180° motion, to identify and make a fix on the ship, that was bearing down on them.

'5° to starboard, slow one third, dive to 300 feet,' he announced harshly but in a calm voice.

Krabava knew these waters well and that there was a hidden ledge near by, which if he found quickly it would give him cover from the above approaching vessel. Luck was on his side, as he found it where he thought it would be, and then very carefully so as not to be discovered he placed his boat under it. The ledge had a large overhang, which concealed his boat perfectly and safely from the oncoming ship above. He waited intently for the ship to pass over them, fearing that they maybe spotted. The vessel came ever closer with its asdic penetrating and vibrating through the water in a bid to discover them. The asdic sonar repeatedly hit the seabed and returned to the ship in a bitter attempt to find its target.

The crew looked at the cold grey ceiling of their boat, listening to the echo of the pinging from the asdic that approached; they became very quiet and subdued, as no one uttered a word, for they all felt vulnerable and feared if they made a noise it would alert the ship above.

Sweat ran down their bodies, as the tension increased in the hot smelly boat as they heard the pounding of the ship's throbbing engines clearly passing over them, for they were convinced that at any second the ship would discover them. In anticipation they waited for the inevitable to happen, nevertheless, as the ship reached them it passed over, and continued on its way with it's never ending churning of its screws, sounding like thunder in the depths below. The noise slowly it faded into the distance and off the scopes radar.

'That was close!' Schmitt muttered with a sigh of relief to the crew in the control room.

'It was to damn close for comfort, and it's a good job our captain knew what he was doing,' the first officer replied to Schmitt.

'Andrei what do you hear?' Babarika enquired, after hearing the conversation about him.

'Nothing sir, it's gone.'

'Good but keep alert. Helm slow ahead, steer west 230°.'
Slowly and gently, the skipper eased his submarine silently from its hiding place and turned on a new heading with relief.

'Surface the boat to periscope depth,' the skipper called feeling more relaxed now the threat had subsided.

As the scope broke through the oceans surface, Krabava again peered through the lens towards the horizon, to ascertain the ship had indeed disappeared, he then turned through the 380° angle, and seeing nothing, he ordered the helm to surface the boat. Then letting go of the handles, he faced his attention to Schmitt.

'We're going up, for the batteries and oxygen tanks need to be replenished as they are running low, besides I could do with some fresh air.'

'Fine, you're the skipper,' Hans replied shrugging his shoulders in a matter of fact attitude.

'Lookouts up top, keep your eyes peeled,' cried Krabava and immediately seeing the sailors jumping for the hatch cover to open it.

'Captain, are we aloud to go on deck for some fresh air, as it is rather stuffy in here. We are unlikely to go anywhere once on deck.' Mark said.

'Yes you may, but get down fast when ordered,' he barked.

'Yes of course,' Mark said. Then with his wife, they climbed the iron steps that would take them to the fresh evening air.

Slowly they walked to the stern of the boat and away from the conning tower so no one would hear them.

'Krabava, it was meant to be a compliment earlier, I'm sorry if you misunderstood me,' Schmitt said feeling guilty, or so it appeared as he tried to communicate with the skipper, for the last thing he wanted was a confrontation here with him at sea.

'Hans you haven't seen anything yet,' the skipper replied still with a sign of hostility in his voice. But barely as he was about to say any more, he heard the engines spluttering and coughing as if they were choking to death, and then finally he heard them grind to a halt. Babarika surprised, and then snorted with this sudden lack of power, pressed the mikes button hard.

'Engine room what's going on?' he said callously through the mike.

'Don't know as yet, but I'm working on it as fast as I can,' Yuri the engineer replied bitterly, and then a few moments later he called back through the mike to tell his skipper what the problem maybe.

'Christ what a time for the engines to break down.' Mianlia the 1st officer cringed with the knowledge they had a problem and were drifting idly with the seas current.

'Smell that lovely fresh air,' Ann retorted to Mark as she sniffed the fresh breeze that blew into her face.

'Strikingly fresh darling that I must admit, but it would be much better and sweeter in a different environment than that foul air we've been breathing down there in our cabin,' Mark said holding her hand while at the same time looking into her deep blue sparkling eyes.

'Still light Mianlia,' Babarika mentioned to his first officer, as he looked at the clear sky.

'Yeah, it will be a couple of hours or so yet, before it gets dark. Shouldn't we be entering the Atlantic soon?'

'It will be a while for we are only approaching the coast of Iceland.'

As Ann watched towards the horizon and saw how the sea met the sky, when suddenly, she said to her husband.

'What would be our chances in that?' pointing to the sea.

'Zero,' Mark claimed, 'you wouldn't live more than five minutes in it, why do you ask. Thinking of going for a swim?' He said gripping tightly of her hand. Then facing her, he pulled her body closer to him, hugging her gently and smiling in the hope it would help her feel better.

'Oh,' she stated, and then again returned her gaze to the water, to look at the horizon. 'If I am not mistaken, is that a ship on the horizon; I wonder if they have seen it?' She questioned, referring to their captor's.'

As Schmitt held on to the rail of the conning tower, he thought about his concerns of having any kind of battle, under or on the surface of the water, as he had never experienced anything of the kind before. So deciding not to interfere with the skipper's decisions in the future, he would stay quiet, although with a worried expression on his face, he asked.

'Aren't we taking a bit of a gamble on the surface in daylight?'

'Yes I am but as I mentioned we need to replenish the charge in the batteries as much as possible, it's a necessary precaution we need to undertake, you must appreciate that, for if I neglect to take the opportunity, and are discovered when below, it could put us in a very precarious position.' The skipper then began to explain to Schmitt about having a flat battery when submerged, but suddenly stopped talking when a voice roared from one of the lookouts.

'Ship on the port stern,' the sailor bellowed pointing in the direction for Krabava to see. Krabava quickly following the direction of the sailor's finger went into action, immediately.

'Blast,' he scorned with venom. 'Everybody below, and hurry, dive-dive-dive,' he cried aloud. Obeying at once the Walkers raced

85

along the decks hard rubber surface and flew through the hatch in a mad panic, and followed quickly by the last man who closed the cover spinning the wheel as fast as he was able to seal it, so no water could seep in. However barely before the hatch closed the skipper roared, for the crew to get to their stations.

'Take us down to 50 feet. Stop engines, rig for silent running,' Krabava said unremittingly to his crew as they continued to carry out his orders without question.

'What type of ship is it and what is it doing Sakhakov?' For Sakhakov had now relieved Andrei from operating the sonar.

'It's heading our way, it's a passenger ship, I guess it's on a cruise,' he answered back.

'Tell me when she's 5000 yards away.'

'Yes sir,' he said with a nervous voice, although he had served in the navy he had never experienced this kind of trouble before, it was to be a new ball game for him.

'Forward torpedo room, make ready tubes three and four,' Krabava called from the control rooms mike.

Once again and with great apprehension, they descended to the depths below the surface, and waited to see what would happen, if the oncoming ship came too close to them.

'Raise scope,' the skipper said, his voice altering in pitch as he sounded his authority. Looking through the eyepiece as it cut through the waves, he could see Sakhakov had been correct, for the ship's position was as he had stated; he noticed it was a passenger ship, in fact a liner, possibly on one of her Baltic cruises.

'Down scope, if she gets too close, we'll hit her with two torpedoes on the starboard side,' the skipper announced to his executive officer. 'Sakhakov, inform me if she sends a message of our position. No1 give me a range of 2000 yards.'

'Very well sir,' his No1 officer replied sharply.

'Sir, she's beginning to turn away,' the sonar operator sighed with relief as he informed his skipper, that the ship had started to move away from them.

'Up scope, yes your right it's turning and heading away from us. Well that's a smart move,' he said to his officers as he ordered the periscope down again.

'Yes a very smart move, why do you think she turned away?' Kazan asked to anyone who could give an answer, but nobody replied, for the men were mystified to the reason why the ship did not spot them.

'Go to 200 feet, we'll stay there for a while and see what happens, just in case the ship did get a message away and we didn't hear. We will run at 8 knots, so if you will helm.'

'Aye, aye sir 8 knots it is,' the response sharply came back.

'Must have taken us for a whale,' Mark added with amusement. Babarika ignoring his remark left the control room, and made his way to the engine department now the panic had abated.

'Yura what went wrong with the engines and have you found the problem?'

Yura was the engineer's nickname, for his real one was Yuri, but only Babarika the captain called him it. They had been like brothers since their school days, and had been through thick and thin no matter which of them got into trouble.

'Its ok captain, it turned out to be a cracked fuel pipe, but I've fixed it so we'll be alright from now on.'

'What made the pipe break Yuri? You know you cannot lie to me, you know that don't you Yuri, you will indeed tell me if that was all it was, that went wrong.' Looking down on the deck, Yuri picked up a piece of piping which he had removed earlier and had replaced it with a new piece.

'Captain this pipe had been pricked with a very narrow sharp pointed object like a pin, and I would say deliberately,' Yuri said with concern at the out come of finding the fault.

'Are you implying we have a saboteur on board?' the skipper asked with surprise at hearing his engineer revealing this information. Then with apprehension, he rubbed his chin with a dirty hand, thinking what his friend had said.

'Maybe skipper,' is all Yuri added.

'If it's the case we have to find and stop him Yuri, before he attempts anything else.'

'Yes I know you're right. But at the moment I haven't any idea as to who could have done it, for apart from the crew the only other person who came in here was Mr Walker but he had no opportunity to puncture the pipe, for I was talking to him all the time, besides he never moved towards that area.'

'Ok Yuri, nevertheless keep your eyes peeled, we cannot afford to let whoever it may be, to have a chance at sabotaging the boat.' Then turning his back on the engineer, he left Yuri to work, thinking hard as to who might be responsible for such an act, and how they actually could accomplished the task with so many crew members passing through the engine department. Apart from accomplishing what they did, what else could he or she do?

Chapter 13

When Jeff and Charley reached their hotel, which was located in the centre of Murmansk. He was about to suggest a coffee when her mobile rang.

'Hello Dale, what's up,' she said as she wandered round the room in search of listening devices. 'What did you say,' she continued speaking to her boss. 'Can you repeat that again? What, twenty-four! How could anyone get their hands on them? It's incredible,' she remarked stunned at hearing the news, and sitting down hard on the bed with astonishment. 'What---! For Christ sake! Who are they going to war with?' she blurted out.

After Charley stopped talking to her boss Dale, who was head of her department, she hung up, and solemnly laid the phone on the bed.

'Something really serious is a foot,' she said with apprehension written on her face.

'Like what?' Jeff said, noticing how worried she had become all of a sudden.

'Better brace yourself mate. Dale claims that twenty-two conventional, plus two nuke torpedoes had been stolen from a Russian navy base.'

All of a sudden, Jeff's face went ashen with hearing this latest news from Charley. 'We've been told to find them as fast as possible. And see where they're bound for and who may want to use such items,' she said glumly. 'We had better be quick before someone starts to create devastation to whom they maybe aiming for. My boss seems to think they're here in Murmansk. I don't mind telling you mate, the balloons gone up; everybody is running round like headless chickens, especially the reds, they're going crazy with the loss of them.

'Bleeding hell I should think so. So where do they think we're going to find them?' Jeff responded with a bitter taste in his mouth.

'The only place they have come up with, is somewhere along the docks. So I say we should start there; also that is where the submarine sailed from,' Charley said gazing at him from the bed.

Arriving at the docks gates a couple of hours later; they began looking round the area for some one to help them. As Jeff viewed the area with his sharp vision, he noticed an old man of some sixty years of age approaching their car.

'Hello, we are looking for someone who maybe able to help us with a few questions,' Jeff said to the guy as he came up to them.

'I'm the dock's attendant here. So what can I help you with,' he said grunting and pushing his head through the window of the car to get a closer look at them.

'Good afternoon, my name is Jeff Morgan and this is my colleague Charley Blackstoke.'

'So what can I do for you both?' said the thin scraggy unshaven dock attendant.

'We wonder if you can help us with some information, like a large consignment of wooden crates that had been delivered here recently.'

'Well I'll have to look it up on the ledger; you better come on into the office for me to check. Do you know who delivered them here?'

'No we're afraid not. But we would be very interested with any information as to the crates,' Charley offered.

On entering the hut, that was situated by the main gate, he flicked through the pages of his ledger, wetting his finger as he did so until stopping at a page, that had finger prints splashed across the whole area.

'Yes here we are, I thought I would recognise what you are looking for,' he said mumbling softly, 'yeah I thought as much, the wooden crates were loaded on to a ship called the Oban, twenty-four wooden boxes, plus some other stores.'

'Does your ledger say who owns the ship or where it's registered, and where it's bound for?' Jeff inquired to the old man.

'That I can, its registration is Argentina, and the owner is a fellow by the name of Pushkin. But my boss Tabor, he is a very big shot around these parts, and owns a lot of property, in addition to having a couple of aircraft. Some people say he owns the Kremlin.' Jeff glanced at Charley to see what kind of reaction she was giving to what this chap was saying about his boss Tabor.

'Could you recognise him,' Jeff asked pulling the photos from the inside pocket of his jacket, and held them in front of the old man to see.

'That's him, Tabor, the middle bloke on that photo, why is there a problem?' he asked holding the picture with his boss on it.

'Maybe,' Charley put in. 'Can you identify anyone else.'

'No I'm sorry, but I do know they stored the crates in shed 45, yeah that's it, shed 45, although I don't believe they are in there now.'

'Thank you very much, I will recommend you to the higher up,' Jeff said heading for the door and towards warehouse 45.

They wandered round the outside of the building, until arriving at a narrow metal door, where Charley said to Jeff.

'This one is open.'

Jeff gave it a slight nudge to open it; and without any resistance it sprang inwards, squeaking on its rusty hinges under his weight they crept inside. Crouching and sweeping the room with fast and accurate keen eyes and with guns at the ready in the event of trouble, only there was no one inside the building, so they began sifting through the contents of the warehouse. The place was full of lots of cardboard boxes and wooden crates. Jeff waved his arm at her to draw his attention to what he intended to do.

'You start at the other end of the building and see what you can find, while I'll search here amongst these wooden boxes.

'Jeff come and look at this,' she called after a while at looking round the boxes, and with great concern at what she may have found.

'What have you found Charley?'

'I can't be sure, but something's not quite right with this crate. Let's see if there's something we can prise open the lid,' she whispered to him for their voices echoed across the warehouse. After shoving a few items about, they found an iron bar, and then instantly began prising the lid from the crate. Splinters of wood flew into the air as the lid came free, then pushing it out of the way for a closer look inside, they saw with utter disbelief and horror the contents of the box. For staring at them from the crate, they witnessed a long gleaming green shiny cylinder rapped in straw for protection. It seemed unbelievable to them, that they had stumbled on such an item without a guard standing over it.

'Christ almighty,' Charley hissed in dismay at the sight of seeing the cylinder in the crate.

'Don't move.' The sound of a harsh voice brought them suddenly back to reality with a thump.

'How stupid could we be for not thinking that this place would not have had a security guard somewhere near by,' Charley said.

'Not a muscle or I will shoot you both dead, what are you two up to?' he continued to say.

'We are looking for information,' Jeff added carefully moving his head in the direction to where the voice was coming from.

'I said don't move. Who are you? The old man asked again, who seemed for Jeff to be in his sixties. He was wearing worn out dirty style army denim pants and old boots, as well as a filthy white shirt that matched his thinning wiry white hair. He waved an old

92

German Luger gun in a threatening manner in his right hand, which had seen better days.

'Careful,' the old man said, 'I mean it, I'll shoot you.' Then without warning, a loud thunderous bang echoed across the building, the sound bouncing from one wall to another. A bullet from Charlie's gun hit the old man, who screamed with pain as it smashed into his hand. Letting go of the weapon as he gripped his wounded hand, it fell to the floor with a loud clatter. Jeff seeing the old man was helpless, he leapt at him and pinned him to a wooden crate, as Charley came closer with her gun in her hand and aimed it at the guards head. Bending down slowly, Jeff retrieved the fallen firearm and stuck it into his belt, and then faced the old guy before speaking.

'Who are you and what are you doing here?' Jeff said in a hostile voice.

'I'm the security officer and I look after this place,' he muttered still clutching onto his injured hand.

'I asked you two, what are you doing snooping round this building?'

'You're now not in the position to ask questions mate, but for your benefit we've discovered that this crate here contains what looks like to be a bloody torpedo, what do you know about it?' Jeff said pulling the guard by the front of his shirt.'

'Come with us into that office. I think you have a lot of explaining to do, for we need answers, and quick. You've got to tell us what you have here and what we have run into, and how those crates got here?' Charley mentioned aggressively as she steered him up the wooden flight of stairs into the office, and forced him into a chair.

'Ok let's have it, or we'll call the police,' Jeff said, 'I'm sure they won't be as lenient as us, and I believe you could end up doing a long stretch in jail, or even be sent to one of their old fashioned gulags in the east.' Jeff responded in an angry voice,

93

while standing close to make sure the old man was unable to make a bolt for it.

'I'm sorry but there's not much to say, only this warehouse belongs to a Mr Tabor, he is my boss and pays my wages. The supplies belong to a guy called Scar Face, I've heard he's a gun runner and he'll kill me, if he finds out that I'm telling you all this, that's all I can tell you, I really don't know anything else, I swear.' As Jeff listened to him squirm, he pulled the photos from his pocket and showed them to the guard.

'Recognise any of these guys,' Jeff asked handing them over to the guard, hoping he may be able to recognise the guys who were in the pictures.

'That man in the middle is Tabor, he's the smart one, and I think he sailed on the Oban. The one on the left of him is a Mr Leshin, he is just a courier for Tabor, the other chap is Pozvizd, and he's a brutal thug and killer. I only saw them a couple of times as they used this place for their meetings,' the security guy stated with beads of sweat running down his face, showing just how scared he was of the agents.

'I think enough has been said; now drop the gun,' a voice roared from the doorway. 'Be very careful, no sudden moves you hear, for I will not hesitate to shoot the lot of you.' The sound of the threatening voice told Charley he meant every word. So obeying she did as she dropped her gun on the floor, but at the same time turning somewhat round to face her challenger. Her gun clattering onto the bare wooden floor added to the tension in the room. She saw four men standing in the open doorway, who stood behind the man holding a gun in his right hand and appeared to be the leader. As he stood facing them, she noticed a deep distinctive scar running down his face, starting from his left ear to his chin and sent a cold chilling sensation through her.

Turning his attention to face the security bloke, he aimed his gun at him, and then began to apologise.

'I'm so sorry my friend,' is all he said before squeezing the trigger. A crash of thunder exploded in the small room, and ripped into the warehouse as the leader's gun belched flame and smoke from its muzzle. The impact of the bullet thudded into the guard and sent him flying across the room, landing in the far corner with blood instantly oozing from a large hole in his chest. He looked at them, his face contorted with pain as the colour drained from him. He tried to speak, but no sound could be heard coming from his lips, his eyes glazed and glowed red as his blood ran across them, and then his face distorting with pain and with the astonishment of being shot, his life ebbed away from him, for the only word they could identify was.

'Why?'

'Yes why?' Charley said seeing the pour old guard with his head slumped to one side dead in the corner of the room. Mortified at what the thug had done, the two agents stared at what they had just witnessed.

'You two, sit in those chairs. We understand you've been asking too many questions about Mr Tabor and his operation, and that you are looking for him,' Scar Face hissed.

'So,' Jeff said in defiance. 'I've no doubt you are working for him,' Jeff said quietly trying to take the tension from the situation but also hoping not to provoke him into shooting them.

'I'm afraid you have missed him,' Scar Face said with a sickly grin, he will be out of town for sometime to come,' he continued while dialling a number on his mobile phone, and then, at last after a few rings he started to speak to another person on the end of the line.

'It's me, I have two nosey parkers at the warehouse, and they've been snooping round and seen what we have here. There names, oh yeah, they are.' He paused before asking. 'What's your name? He hissed at them. 'They are Morgan and Blackstoke, what do you want me to do with them? I could kill them now; I've had to kill the security officer for he was blabbing too much.' He stopped talking to listen to the voice on the other end of the line and then with a sigh he faced the agents.

'Pity, alright if you say so, I'll carry it out,' he said with a disappointed expression written on his face. 'You have been reprieved, well for a while anyway, I've been ordered not to kill you yet, but it'll keep.'

'Was killing the old man so important to you, he was just an old man doing a dull job?' Charley responded with a hostile glare.

'Well excuse me,' Scar Face replied spitting out the words. 'There are times I'm unable to control myself, especially when an idiot like him blabbed to you, like the way he did, he had it coming.

Come on, stand up, we're going to take a little ride, so don't try anything stupid as I won't hesitate to shoot you both.' Gingerly they moved towards the doorway and escorted by the cold-blooded killer, they made their way out of the room to the short flight of stairs, passing the crates they had opened a little earlier; they made their way from the building into the bright sunshine, where two black BMW cars were in the alleyway waiting for them.

'He sure likes killing people Charley, so don't give him an excuse to shoot you,' Jeff whispered to her very softly.

'Shut up,' one of the guards roared showing his black stained teeth and waving his revolver in the air. He then prodded Jeff in the ribs with his gun and said.

'You two, get in the second car,' as they began pushing the two in the back of the stretched car, while Scar Face went to the other car, and sat beside his driver. As soon as black teeth closed his door, they sped away along the side of the building onto the main road, turning right into a northerly direction they headed for the motorway.

While travelling at a steady pace along the main road heading towards the motorway, Black teeth sat awkwardly opposite Jeff with a gun in his hand and had it trained all the time in him in the event Jeff may make a strike for his gun. Jeff nicknamed his opponent Gun-Ho, not thinking of a better word, for he hated this man and his black teeth.

He began to get on Jeff's nerves as he flashed his cannon about and Jeff relished the thought of tearing it from him.

Driving along the highway, the car suddenly came to a screeching halt at a red light. Although, the other car carrying Scar Face missed the change and carried on not noticing what had happened.

'What's going on?' Gun-Ho asked the driver without taking his eyes away from Jeff.

'A police car, it's parked on the far corner of the junction. I can't take a chance in jumping the light,' the driver announced. 'Close though, just keep calm as he's looking our way,' the driver continued to say as they waited patiently for the lights to change green.

'Yeah you're right; don't need him to come after us. So you pair of sweeties keep real quiet and don't make a sound,' Gun-Ho growled gritting his teeth as he spoke.

The lights soon changed to green and they proceeded on their way, keeping to the speed limit for the copper had pulled out from his parking space and began to follow them.

'Stay real steady mate, he's not gaining on us, so don't make any daft moves,' Gun-Ho remarked as they approached the slip road to the M18 motorway. 'Now it's a real pity, for my boss wants to see you both alive, now I'll have to wait a little longer before killing you,' he said spitting the word kill.

'Good, he's turning in to a small lane on the left.' the other crook said who was sitting beside Gun-Ho and opposite Charley. They began gathering more speed in a bid to catch Scar Face that was ahead of them and out of sight.

Jeff being attentive, noticed Gun-Ho's eyes flickering towards Charley, as did his mate's, who was also taking a very keen interest in her as well. Jeff sneaking a glance towards her noticed she was undoing the top buttons of her blouse and began to fumble with her right breast and then removed it from the bra's cup. Jeff swiftly gazed back on Gun-Ho, who was now staring intently at Charley, to what she was doing. Taking full advantage and within a fraction of a second, Jeff pounced on the thug with precision and hit him squarely on the chin with his left fist, at the same time grabbing his gun hand and pinning it across his chest. Gun-Ho not slow to react, immediately tried to force Jeff's hand away from the gun, but in doing so, he squeezed the trigger and fired the gun at point blank range towards his partner. The bullet penetrated his partner's mouth, ripped through the tissue and continued travelling up into his brain and killing him instantly.

Jeff began to find it tough fighting with this guy in the confined space of the car and began to loose his grip on him, but then another shot exploded with a deafening roar, instantly killing Gun-Ho. Then as the car filled with smoke and the smell of cordite, it delayed Charley from turning the gun on the driver. But the driver acted quickly, noticing the threat as Gun-Ho had been killed, he fiercely slammed on the brakes bringing the car to a screeching halt, and then wrenching the door open, he dived out before the car came to a stop and fled for his life.

'Get him Jeff, don't let him get away,' Charley screamed as she jumped from the rear of the car as it came to a halt and climbed behind the steering wheel.

Jeff returned a little later to the car, puffing and panting, he then began to explain why the crook got away from his grasped.

'I'm afraid he's too good for me,' Jeff announced still trying to get his breath back.

'I thought you were supposed to be fit? You need to do more, old man,' she blurted out as she started the engine and then began turning the car round to head back to the way they had come.

'Scar Face isn't going to be very impressed with us by killing his men,' Jeff said, as he eyed her with a broad grin.

'What, what have you got to be smirking about?' she said, but knowing all the time, what he was thinking.

'Is it common for you to flash those boobs of yours to all and sundry?' Jeff queried.

'No I certainly do not, however; I thought it was necessary to do something to distract those thugs to stay alive.'

'Well it worked that's for sure,' Jeff said still looking at her with a large grin on his face.

'Where do we go now, master?' she said relieved at getting away from the hostile thugs and now able to have a joke with him.

'Let's make our way back to the docks; we can pick up our own car, if it's still there? Then we'll head for a town called Nickel.' Jeff said, remembering the town was near the Russian/Norwegian border.'

'How far is it?'

'It's about a 3 hour drive I guess, for its only 90 miles. We should reach it before nightfall, if we get our skates on. We can then get in touch with the others.'

Arriving back at the docks and without any further incidents they dropped the crooks car to change to their hire car, they then proceeded to move from the docks and towards Nickel.

'What's that up a head Jeff? She asked after driving for an hour and entering a wooded area.

'It's looks as if it's a road block; someone's placed a couple of cars across the road,' Jeff retorted and started braking hard to avoid the roadblock, but as he desperately tried to turn the car, another car came from behind some trees and prevented his retreat. Men jumped out of the woods and the cars, which block them from getting away. The crooks now had them surrounded and had taken the two agents completely by surprise. Dragging them from the car, Jeff realised that this time it would be curtains for them, for they surely would kill them.

'Nice stunt you pulled back there, except, did you really think you would escape as easily as that,' a man said with a nasty smear. 'My name is Leshin, perhaps you may remember I asked you to contact me, but now it's not so important anymore. Well lady, this time you won't be flashing your tits at me, you may have taken the others in, however, it will not wear with me,' he stated spitting in her face. 'Nobody will take any notice here,' he added seizing her by the arm and slinging her against his car.

'Keep a good eye on her,' Leshin barked to his colleague and then leaving them to get closer to Jeff, but stopping short of him as he stood in front of him. Then with a right fist, he swung a hard punch at Jeff. Hitting him in the stomach he knocked the air out of his lungs, which made Jeff bend over double with the impact. His legs giving way with the force of the blow he fell face down on the ground, while at the same time trying to protect his face against a further kicking, which he thought Leshin was going to deliver.

'Get them both in the cars, this time we'll keep them separate.' But as he began to push Charley into his car, she was able to look towards Jeff, as he tried to stand up from where he was slung to the ground. Then one of the thugs abruptly turned on Jeff and swinging his gun on him, he fired a single shot into Jeff's body.

'No. Noooo----!' Charley screamed with horror at them shooting her man and seeing him collapse on the grass verge holding his side. With the aid of the crook, which shot him, they rolled repeatedly until he fell into a deep dry ditch, which ran along side the road. Charley helpless to what had taken place could do nothing to help him, as they forced her into the car.

Leaving Jeff for dead, the thugs drove away from the scene to head for the narrow streets and alleyways of the city of Murmansk. Finally arriving at some big iron gates, they entered and pulled up in front of a large white stone house. Dragging Charley from the car, they pushed her into the house and slung her to the floor in a small room. Then slamming the door hard behind them they left her alone.

Slowly pulling herself together, she raised herself to her feet and looked about the room. Noticing it was some 12 feet square in size with no windows and only one door, and plane wooden floorboards and magnolia paint that peeled from the walls, made it a very unimpressive place to stay in. The room consisted of a small table and two chairs, plus a single bed.

She sat on one of the chairs by the table, and became aware the place smelt mouldy and damp, and realised it had not been used in a long time. She felt very dirty and was in a mess. She then started to wonder about what was to become of her; her thoughts brought back the recent incident with Jeff and where he was lying dead in that ditch. It was now, she realised she had fallen deeply in love with him, but only to lose him. After this assignment, she had hoped to take him to see her parents and stay in her cottage in Dorset. She continued to think about her mother and knew she would be petrified to what was happening to her.

The sound of a key rattling in the doors lock brought her back to reality and when it opened, it revealed a fat woman wheeling a trolley into the room.

'I have some food and drink, also your case with your clothes, you can change into them, if you so wish; there is also soap and towel to freshen up.'

'Where am I?' Is all Charley could ask before a couple of thugs entered carrying a mattress, some blankets and a pillow, and then slinging them onto the floor, they departed without a saying word.

'Across the hall is the bathroom, ask me when you need it,' the old woman said following the two men out of the room and locking the door behind her.

Carefully so as not to be seen, Charley went through her case searching for the bra with the card in it. Finding it, she gently pulled it to the top of the bag so she was able to detect the card that it was exactly where she had left it.

'Good,' she whispered and placing it deep in to the bag again. Putting on a gold coloured dressing gown, she went over to the door and banged heavily on it to draw attention to the old woman.

'Anybody there, I need a shower open up please,' she called and instantly heard the clanging of keys sounding in the lock to open it. As the door swung open, the old fat woman stood directly in the doorway blocking her from getting out of the room.

'Follow me and don't try to run for it, as all the outside doors are locked, there is no escape.'

Charley thought the old girl was a bundle of fun as she took her to the shower room, but was very glad she could have the opportunity to freshen up.

Once she had finished, she returned with her escort back to the room and could at least cope with what may be in store for her, and she now waited in anticipation for what was to come; it did not take long in coming.

'Good day Miss Blackstoke. I trust you have had a comfortable rest,' Leshin said walking into the room without knocking. 'As you know, I am Leshin and in case you had forgotten, we spoke on the phone at the hotel. It's a pity you didn't call me, it would have saved all this mess, what with your boyfriend getting killed, perhaps we may have stopped it happening, sad business that, I am so sorry but that's what happens when you try and make a run for it.'

'You are evil,' were the only words Charley could muster. 'Where is his body? I want to see him.'

'Oh Miss Blackstoke don't be in such a hurry. In due course my dear I will let you see him,' Leshin said taunting her in the hope she would break and give him the information he needed.

'First I want to know what you have found out about us.'

'Go to hell,' Charley growled through clenched teeth and going through the past events in her mind with her brother and now Jeff. She wiped away the tears in her eyes, for she could not comprehend it all, it seemed impossible, a dream, and then coming back to realism, she heard his voice booming in her head.

'Do you understand what I'm saying?'

'Yes I hear you, I've got nothing to say, you went through my things and found nothing, that's because I have nothing of yours,' she added realising they were not aware of London and Washington knowing about the photos; however, she was not going to enlighten them.

'I haven't a clue as to what you're after and I've got nothing of yours,' she repeated.

'Well if that's the way you want to play it, we'll see what Tabor has to say,' he said slapping her hard across the face with the back of his right hand. 'Get your things together; we are going for a drive.' He then motioned to his couple of thugs to escort her back to the car that was waiting out side. Then shoving her in the back seat as if she was a rag doll, they began to drive away from the house, for where she had no idea, as Leshin had not said anything to where they were taking her.

'I'm going to be kind to you my dear and take you back to where your dearly loved is lying, so you can take a last look at your lover resting in the ditch in peace,' Leshin said with the pleasure of teasing her.

When they arrived at the scene, where they had shot Jeff, she was again hustled from the car and stood by the rear door waiting for Leshin to escort her to the ditch.

'Take a good long look and see, he's in the ditch over there,' he stated pointing in the direction towards the ditch.

Slowly she walked towards the ditch feeling revolted to what she was about to see. However, when she arrived at the edge and looked down there was nobody in the ditch. Her first thought was, were they taunting her and had they removed him, or perhaps he was alive and got away. She stood on the edge of the ditch pondering a little longer, fearing the goons might come over; she turned and unhurriedly moved back towards the car, swearing at Leshin as she approached him.

'Ok now, are you satisfied you've seen him, may he rest in peace,' Leshin added again laughing aloud. 'Now get back in the car we've got to get going.'

'You are a nasty madman; do you really think you are going to get away with what you've done? They'll find you, and when they do I'll be glad to be at your trial and see you executed.'

'I am afraid it will not happen. Although personally I would be delighted to send you to the same paradise as your lover, but regrettably I have instructions for you to meet Tabor, why I have not a clue.'

'Why did you phone me at the hotel?'

'Oh yes, it was a pity you did not contact me, for as I had said earlier, this needless killing of your lover may never have happened. I needed to get you here but unfittingly once again you evaded me, yeah a pity.'

'Was it also you in my bedroom?'

'Yes it was and a bit close for comfort to, for you nearly caught me in your room, when you returned earlier than expected and before I could find anything of our plans about New York.' Abruptly he stopped speaking to her, realising he had said too much. Had she noticed it, he thought maybe, maybe not, he would now have to tell Tabor he had mentioned New York.

Chapter 14

'Bring her round to 160°,' Johnson the cruisers skipper ordered to his helmsman.

'Ay, ay, sir 160° it is,' the helmsman replied and instantly began spinning the wheel round fast to bring the ship on its new course. The ship creaked and groaned as the rudder took the strain from the pressure of water that pushed against the massive steel hull.

'Howard, general quarters,' the skipper ordered politely but sternly.

'Very well sir,' Howard the No1 officer said responding quickly but wondering at the same time what was up, for he had not read the message his captain had received.

'No1, bring the ship to full speed and tell the officers I want them to join me in the wardroom,' he said as he slid his bulky 6 foot of a body from his seat from the bridge that over looked the bows. Leaving the bridge, he made his way for the wardroom to meet his fellow officers without giving Howard any further orders. This was to be his last voyage on this ship; and with an unblemished record promised his next command would be a carrier.

'I expect you are wondering why, I have called this meeting,' he said speaking softly as he stood in front of them. 'Today I received this communication from command headquarters, they have informed me,' he said pausing to get a feel from his men. 'We have been ordered to seek a rogue submarine.' He paused again letting his men digest to what he had said, and then he continued to inform them. 'The Russians have had no luck in finding this submarine, but believe it entered the North Atlantic. We have been given the task to apprehend and if need be destroy it.

'Destroy it sir?' one of the younger officers stated with surprise.

'Yes that is what we have been ordered to do,' Johnson said without blinking an eyelid.

'Do you know what class it is?' the chief radar asked.

'Yes I can tell you that, it's a Russian Fox Trot, an old diesel, so it should not be very hard to find, although I cannot think why the Russians have not been able to trace it.'

'Sir, is it armed?' another officer asked.

'Not as far as I'm aware off, though the reds have admitted they are missing at least 42 torpedoes.' The officers looked at each other with utter surprise before turning their attention back to the Captain with utter amazement, as he faced them standing rigid as a rock.

'Anyone else got anything to add,' the skipper said waiting for someone to speak, then seeing there was no response, he continued. 'Thank you gentlemen; now back to your duties, I know I can rely on all of you.'

'Sir, how long shall we stay at general quarters?' Howard said concerned at how long his men would be effective at action stations, without knowing what was happening.

'Oh yes, you can tell them to stand down but be at the ready instantly when called for,' Johnson said sitting back in his chair on the bridge, to wait for future developments.

'Yes sir right away,' Howard said, but deep down he hoped they did not find the submarine.

'Sonar to bridge, have detected a surface vessel some 50 miles off the starboard bow.'

'Send her a signal and ask what her name and destination is,' the skipper replied.

'Sir, message from admiralty,' the radio operator stated to his captain holding a piece of paper and then stood back a couple of feet waiting for a reply.

'Read it please,' Johnson said to him, for he was looking through a pair of binoculars, trying to seek out the vessel the sonar man announced a little earlier.

'It states sir, "intercept ship called Oban, believe to be carrying illegal arms, detain if proved and wait for assistance." Message ends sir.' Johnson took hold of the paper and looked at the message for himself, in the event it had been misinterpreted and then facing his radio officer he replied.

'Thank you and acknowledge it.'

'Yes sir,' the radio operator said quickly coming to attention and then swiftly turning he vanished from the bridge.'

'Radio did you get a response from that ship?' Johnson asked shortly after the radioman had left him.

'Its just coming through sir,' was the quick reply.

'Sir, her name is the Oban.'

'The Oban,' the captain repeated, his body stiffening at hearing the answer.

'Tell the Oban to stop, as we are required to search her. No1 steer a course to intercept. No2, tell major Franks to meet me on the bridge.'

'You need to see me?' a deep growl of a voice came from behind the captain,' as the major entered the bridge.

'Yes major, it will be necessary to have some of your men at the ready, as we will have to board a Russian cargo ship.'

'Board a ship, a Russian ship?' What! What are we to find on this ship captain?'

'Possibly some arms, torpedoes and submarine parts by all accounts.'

'And what do we do with them, if we find any?' the major responded.

'We have instructions to impound her and wait for the USS Cruiser and Granada Bay, plus a Russian destroyer that is heading to assist us. When our ships arrive they will escort the Oban to meet with the Russian destroyer, where they will take her to Murmansk.'

'Very well captain,' the major said, and then turning sharply, he left the captain on his bridge too make the necessary arrangements for boarding a ship.

'Sir, if the Oban has arms on board, would she not have got rid of them by now?' Howard asked with a slight hesitation in his voice.

'Maybe, maybe not, we'll see very soon, for she should be coming into sight,' he said searching the ocean with his binoculars and then instantly recognising the Oban on the horizon waiting for them.

'Well I reckon this is going to be a waste of time,' the skipper added to his No1 officer.

'You think there will be nothing to find, as it's a big ship and lots of places to hide contraband,' his first officer stated.

'That's as maybe but, whether he has or not, we will soon find out, although, I've got a nasty feeling about that ship,' the skipper said stroking his white bushy beard, while giving the Oban a once over.

As the Texas came near to the Oban, the Captain called to the other captain to identify himself.

'Hello, I am Captain Johnson of the USS Texas and have authority to search your vessel for unauthorised weapons, and therefore duty bound to come on board your ship.'

'Ay Captain Johnson, my name's Pushkin. You are most welcome to come over with your men, for I have nothing to hide,' Pushkin responded with slight hesitation. 'Captain Johnson, would you care for some refreshments, while your men look round my ship,' Pushkin said uneasily with what was taking place on his ship.

'Thank you,' Johnson replied shaking hands with his counter part.

'Please take a seat, whisky Captain,' Pushkin offered as he moved towards the drinks cabinet.

'Thank you. I must apologise for this unfortunate interruption, but I have my orders, I am sure you will appreciate it and see the discomfort it puts me in.'

'Yes I realise it, I would have done no different,' Pushkin responded with a smile as he handed over a glass of whisky to Johnson.

'No, I first served for twenty years in the Russian navy and mastered a carrier; I must admit that ship was a touch different to this one. Have been on this old tub since, it's been some ten years now. Its ok, it is a living, how about yourself?'

'I have been on five ships, all frigates, apart from this one, this one is going to be my last, as I have been promised to serve a year or so on a carrier, before leaving the service,' he stated as the marines carried out their business on board the Oban. 'Apart from the carrier, have you always sailed merchant ships?' Johnson questioned.

An 18 year-old marine, began working his way along an aisle with boxes, which were stacked to the ceiling. His attention drawn to a box with unusual Russian markings stencilled on one side, and that someone had tampered with them to try to remove them. He decided to investigate further he began to try and translate the letters, but so engrossed with what he was doing, he never heard the person approaching from behind him, until he felt a sharp instrument plunge into his back and under his ribs into his heart. His assailant placed his free hand over the marine's mouth, so he could not utter a sound as his life ebbed away from of him. The killer held onto the marine as he withdrew the knife and putting the marine on his shoulders, he carried him to the small paint room that was located in the corner and at the far end of the hold. Leaving the young soldier there on the floor, he returned to where he killed him, to clean away any evidence of the attack. Once accomplished, he returned to the dead body and sprinkled fuel over the marine and the paint room, and then lighting a match he held it close to the inflammable vapours until it ignited.

'Cancel the search,' Johnson ordered, 'there is nothing to report on the ship with regard to any contraband,' he said shocked at hearing the accident of the young marine.

'May I then continue to sail Captain?' Pushkin asked.

'Oh, oh yes, yes of course, I am sorry to detain you, you can be on your way.'

'Thank you sir, God speed you, and please will you accept my apologies for what has happened here,' Pushkin said sadly, as Johnson moved to return to his ship.

Pushkin silently listened to the powerful engines of his ship as they thundered into life and began moving away from Johnson's ship.

'Tabor will you come to the bridge,' Pushkin called into his mike as he watched the Texas depart.

'You want to see me,' Tabor asked approaching Pushkin on the bridge.

'I know it was your handy work in killing that marine, must I remind you of the consequences it may have with your mission. I bet you never thought of the consequences if the yanks find out. What on earth were you thinking?'

'It had to be, I am afraid he found the supplies, I was not going to let him mess it all up, anyway I think they will buy the story we told them.'

'I do hope your right,' Pushkin said showing Tabor how worried he was about the whole affair, for he was not convinced the Americans would let the affair drop.

'Do you realise Tabor, if the yanks ever get a whiff of us pulling a stunt like that on them, and that we are also connected with the Zhuralev, they'll be on us like a ton of bricks, and I know doubt sink us for sure,' Pushkin said with dismay, at being involved with this evil bloke.

'Don't be so depressed, they won't find out, for as soon as we get back to Murmansk, we'll have the cargo removed and safely hidden,' Tabor added with a sickly looking smile written on his face.

Chapter 15

'He's alive!' Jeff heard as he began to regain consciousness and could just about make out shadows that were in front of him, for his vision was still very blurred from lying in the ditch.

'I know that voice anywhere,' Jeff mumbled quietly from his bed as he was still reacting to the punishment he had taken.

'Its Jamie, don't talk now you need to conserve your strength, Dave and Harvey are here and will come and see you in a tick.'

'Where is Charley?' Jeff stated trying to raise himself on his elbows to get out of bed.

'I said you must not move as you have to rest. Do you hear me?' Jamie said noticing him cringing with pain that made his eyes flicker. She leaned closer over Jeff to check his condition and tucked the blankets back under him to make him comfortable. 'Who is Charley?' Jamie asked surprised at hearing he was working with another person and that she had not heard. 'I'll tell you this mate; I'll give him a piece of my mind, in leaving you to die by the side of the road.'

'It's not a he, but a she. I think she must have been kidnapped, after I was shot and ended up in that ditch,' Jeff said recalling what had taken place.

'Well I never, I thought you wanted to stay single forever, but what a time to start courting,' Jamie added grinning down at him.

'Where am I?' Jeff asked as his vision started to clear with every second that passed and he began to focus on seeing his colleague Jamie at his bedside.

'You're in hospital in a town in Finland, which is close to the Russian border. The town's called Svanvil.'

'How did I get here?' he said confused and bewildered to what had happened to him.

'You're very lucky my old mate, a couple saw you trying to crawl by the side of the road and in a bad way by all accounts. They at first took you to the clinic on the other side of the border, but they didn't have the amenities to attend to you, so they brought you to this hospital. Anyway, you are in safe hands now, so take a rest, I will be back in a few minutes but I'm glad to see you're looking a lot better. I told Dave and Harvey you were much to evil to die,' Jamie said as she adjusted his bedcovers.

'Very astute of you, you were always the funny one,' Jeff said as she moved away from his bed and turned towards the door.

'How's it going mate,' Dave said as Jeff woke from a deep sleep. Through bleary eyes, Jeff could see his two other colleagues, Harvey and Jamie standing at his bedside with a stern expression on their faces.

'What is going on? Who will be kind enough to give me some good news,' Jeff said cringing with the pain in his side.

'What we want to know, who is this young lady called Charley? That you have been screaming out loud all damn night and keeping the whole town awake,' Harvey remarked smiling at him and noticing how much better, he looked from the battering he received.

'I'm sorry. She is an English agent I met in St Petersburg and before you say anything, I like her and I want to know what's happened to her and if she's still alive,' he said, and then gripping his wound he started to get out of bed, only failing to accomplish it.

'Calm down mate, do you realise, you've made the Russian police very unhappy, for wherever you've been, they've found dead bodies laying around, a habit I think you should consider giving up before someone decides to try again on you, and this time make you one of them,' Jamie mentioned, while tucking his blanket back under him.

'Jeff you take a good rest and get back on your feet, as Dave and I will see where your girl has gone. Jamie will stay with you to help you back to recovery. We'll see you soon,' Harvey remarked as he turned away from him to walk out of the ward and before Jeff could make any kind of protest.

'Where do we start Dave?' Harvey said.

'We will need to retrace Jeff's steps from where he was left for dead and then I guess, head on towards the docks,' Dave replied.

'Can I be of assistance?' A guard asked as Dave and Harvey stopped at the dock gates, where Jeff mentioned he saw the consignment of contraband.

'Yeah you might say that, who might you be? Dave questioned.

'I'm the yard attendant and in charge of this place, it's also my job knowing who's about.'

Dave then explained in brief as to what they wanted to know from the Guard and about Jeff and Charley being there sometime ago, plus how their enquiries led them to the warehouse where Scar Face and his bunch of cronies had captured them.

'Everybody is throwing questions at me these days, what is going on I do not understand,' the guard said scratching his groin.

'Like who's asking?' Harvey queried.

'Well all kinds of folks really, this place has never been so popular,' the old man said. Then began to explain what had taken place over the last few days.

'Do you recognise any of these men?' Dave asked pulling a photo from his inside pocket that he had taken from Jeff and placed it under the attendant's nose.

'Yeah I can, that chap in the middle of the other guys is my boss, Mr Tabor. He owns everything around these parts, but I told the other guy that, when he showed me it a few days ago,' the guard said to the agents.

'Has he been here of late?' Harvey asked.

'Who my boss,'

'Yes your boss Tabor,' Harvey remarked in a much harsher voice.

'As I keep saying, no he has not, and before you ask anymore questions I know nothing about him apart from the fact he has access to an airfield where he keeps his planes.

'Where is this airfield, situated?' Harvey asked.

'You take a right turn out of here and head for the M18 to Severomorsk, it's about 30 minutes from here, some 19kms,' the old guard stated waving his arm in the direction the agents needed to go.

Thanking him and giving him a reward for his effort, the two agents left him at the gate and made a move in the direction he had mentioned.

'What do you make of him? You thinking like I am?' Dave said questioningly as they drove along the route that Jeff had said to follow.

'I reckon he's ok and nothing to worry about, he's only doing his job,' Harvey said.

'I somehow don't like the look of it though, what with this Tabor having planes, boats and submarines, it's as if he's building himself an army, it's puzzling that's for sure.'

'You bet. Do you reckon we should ask for back up?' Harvey muttered.

'No not yet, anyway Jim could not lay it on, besides we don't have enough info to warrant it.'

As they arrived at the town of Severomorsk, they took a right turn off the M18 and proceeded for a further quarter of a mile until they came to the airfield where the old gate man had said. Then turning right, they drove pass a broken barrier onto the airfield and finally stopped their car on a large smooth asphalt car park.

'Harvey you stay here, while I'll go into that office over there on our left and see what info I can find,' Dave said as he turned the engine off and opened the door, but stopped short to look around the area in case anyone was in sight.

Once David disappeared out of sight, Harvey got out of the car and proceeded without hesitating and walked towards a building on the other side of the car park, where he spotted a man dressed in blue overalls.

'Good day comrade, it's a nice day,' Harvey said to the mechanic in dirty blue overhauls at the corner of a hanger.

'Yes it is, but who are you and what are you doing here?' he asked walking away from the hanger and towards an airplane that was on the grass near by.

'I'm glad you asked,' replied Harvey, 'I'm checking for Mr Tabor, that all his friends had left safely.'

'As far as I know yeah, but he would have known that. I didn't get your name,' the mechanic said with a suspicious tone in his voice.

'The only information you need to know, is that I'm one of Tabors guards. So how many passengers got on the flight?' Harvey asked him again, only this time more abruptly, while at the same time keeping his fingers crossed the guy did not ask him any further question, to who he actually was.

'Let me think,' the mechanic said. 'Ah yes I remember, there were two females, 4 guys, plus a crew of two, yeah that was all who got on the plane.'

'What about their destination,' Harvey said continuing to push his luck with his questioning and still hoping the guy would come through with the answers.

'Tuapaat, but of course you would have known that.'

'Are you sure? For I was informed it might have changed,' Harvey continued addressing him.

'Listen mate, I've worked on that aircraft for the last couple of years, and I can read log books, so I know I'm right it's going to Tuapaat.'

'Okay, thanks friend, I'm sorry to put you through the grill. I'll tell Tabor, he will be very grateful for what you have told me when I inform him of the work you have done,' Harvey said then turning away from the man, he strolled back to the car.

'Where have you been? I thought I said for you to stay with the car,' Dave said with a worried frown on his face.

'I was mate, but when I saw one of the guys here I had to talk to him, he was quite informative as well.' Harvey then explained briefly to him what the mechanic had said, unknowingly that a group of men was approaching them.

'How about you,' Harvey said looking out of the driver's side window and then saw some men approaching, but by this time, it was too late to do anything about it.

'Don't look round now, for we have attracted a crowd and I'm not so convinced they are here for a social chat,' Harvey said.

'What's your business here? A fellow said in a hostile voice, accompanied with a dozen other men who surrounded the car to stop them escaping. 'I don't think you have anything to do with Mr Tabor, for he would have notified me of your coming here,' he stated, pulling a gun from his inside coat pocket. 'Search them,' the leader ordered a couple of his associates who were close to the agents and preventing them from making a run for it.

'I suggest you start talking fast to what your business is, if I were you, for you would make it a lot easier on yourselves. If you don't, you just might end up in a whole lot of trouble,' the delegate declared pointing his gun in a threatening manner towards the agents.

'Right, you two start walking in the direction of that building.'

'It seems to me, they are at a lost and have no idea as to what they should do with us,' Dave whispered to his mate.

117

'No talking, I said,' the so-called leader shouted!

'Yeah you could be right, for if they're going to kill us, wouldn't they have done it before now? Harvey muttered silently.'

'If you don't do as I say I'll smash this gun over your skull,' the gang leader spat between clenched teeth and then pushed the agents harder towards the office with the gun barrel prodding into Harvey's back. 'In there,' the leader ordered, then pushed them both into a small room that measured some 12 feet square in size. There were no windows in the room apart from a narrow window above the doorframe. The only furniture visible was a solid glass table in the centre of the room.

'What do we do Dave? Reckon we got ourselves in a bit of a fix,' Harvey said wandering round the room with a gloomy look on his face.

'Maybe, we will have to wait and see to what develops; they obviously need to get confirmation as to what they should do with us,' Dave added as he walked around the room to confirm, that there was no way out of their predicament.

'Can't hear any noise outside, must have gone to see what they should do with us, I guess,' Harvey said. Then looking at the top of the door he nudged his mate in the ribs and said. 'Look at the top of the door mate, where that window is, lets see if we can get up there and see what's happening on the other side,' he added dragging the glass table over towards the door. 'I hope this takes my weight? Give me a hand Dave,' Harvey uttered trying not to make noise that would attract the attention of the guys on the other side of the door.

'What can you see mate?' Dave asked.

'Nothing it's clear, can't see nobody about at the moment,' he stated having a clear view through the window, at the door leading to the outside. 'I guess they all think we won't escape,' Harvey said dropping from the table and pulling some gum from his left side pocket and started rolling it in a ball with his hands, until it became soft enough to work with.

'What have you got?' his pal asked watching him squeeze the substance into the keyhole and placing more round the lock.

'Stand back old chap,' Harvey chirped smiling as he struck a match to a short piece of paper, that he had stuck to the soft gum. It flared a little and then a low thump sounded followed by some blue smoke.

'Come on mate, there's no time to lose, let's get out of here,' Harvey cried giving the door a slight push and making a run from the building. Without looking back, they raced for the car, sprinting as fast as their legs would carry them. Harvey dived behind the steering wheel while at the same time making a grab for the ignition key that he had placed on the sun visor earlier. Hurriedly and worried the car would not start, he inserted the ignition key into the start position and turned it. He need not have been concerned, for the engine roared into life. He instantly slammed his foot down hard on the accelerator for them to get out of the airport. The rear wheels spun on the tarmac desperately trying to make a firm grip with the sudden burst of energy that the engine delivered and then under a huge cloud of smoke, squealing and straining, the car sped off at a tremendous pace towards the entrance they had entered earlier.

'Which way do we need to go Dave? Left or right,' Harvey shouted above the noise of the engine as they approached the airport's entrance, for he was not taking any notice of the direction they were travelling in, as he looking through the rear view mirror and seeing men running for their cars to pursue them.

'Go right, we'll head for the city centre and try and lose them in the narrow streets,' Dave barked above the din while giving directions. They sped along the busy main road, which ran adjacent to the airport at a manic pace and at the same time taking note as to how far the thugs were behind them.

'They mean business to get us mate,' Dave shouted again above the roar of the engine, for the car had gained even more speed and was heading towards a set of traffic lights.

'Go left, forget the lights,' Dave cried not caring about whether there was traffic coming from their right. Harvey pulled hard on the steering wheel and jumping the red lights, they turned left with the car screaming round the corner on two wheels and nearly overturning it, nevertheless, Harvey quickly managed to straighten the car and put it back on four wheels as they continued at a breath taking pace to flee their pursuers. But with every second, the thugs came closer as their cars were more powerful and it seemed a matter of time before they would catch the agents.

'For Christ sake can't this thing go any faster?' Dave bellowed aloud.

'No I'm doing what I can,' Harvey screamed back at his mate while jamming the hand brake on at the same time.

'What in heavens name are you up to?' Dave cried out in response to the car skidding round in a half circle with its rear wheels locked. Holding onto whatever he could as the tyres ripped at the road surface, Harvey spun the steering wheel to the right, so the car turned at 180° and nearly rolling the car on its side he then accelerated back towards the crooks and aiming straight for the thugs, but at the last moment, he veered away avoiding a collision.

'Take the next right Harvey,' Dave roared excited by the fast way Harvey drove the car.

'It's a bit narrow,' he blurted but doing as his mate had said turned down the narrow street, which they had previously passed. The thugs in trying not to lose the agents tried to follow them along the same street, but the first of the cars failed to turn and ploughed into a wall on the corner of the street, leaving debris flying over a wide area.

'That's brilliant mate,' Dave said seeing what the crooks had done and partly blocking the road.

'You mad or something, you're not satisfied with just a narrow street, you have to pick a one-way street, and further more we're going in the wrong direction,' Dave roared as he kept glancing behind them to keep an eye on their pursuers, to ascertain if they had opened the road.

'It's a damn good job there's no traffic coming towards us, as we would have a bit of a problem, don't you think? Now take the next left turn, see if we can confuse them to which way we're heading.' They shot through the narrow streets of Severomorsk at an almighty high speed, turning one-way and then another, until they lost sight of the thugs that was at one time head on their heels after them.

'Go second right, right again, now pull up behind that van over there on the right.'

'What you mad!' Harvey barked and worried that the thugs would easily find them.

'Trust me mate, when have I ever let you down?' Harvey added grinning with exhilaration of belting through the town. 'Look, there they go,' Dave motioned with a hand as he watched the end of the road waiting for the thugs to go screaming past the turning.

'Whew that was too close for comfort, come on mate let's get moving, they'll be back and fast.' The agents carefully started to retrace their steps the way they had come. And rejoining the main road they continued on pass the airport and dropped onto the M18 motorway back to Murmansk

'So far so good, there's no sign of them, reckon we gave them the slip,' Harvey murmured, as they sped along the M18 towards the docks.

'Dave is your phone working?' Harvey said stopping the car outside the building that they had left earlier that day.

'Let's see if we can get a signal,' Dave muttered reaching for his mobile phone, which he had left in the car, when the thugs had searched them.

121

'Jamie, its Harvey and Dave, are you still at the hospital? Good, stay where you are as we're on our way back and won't be long, see you shortly.' 'We're to meet them at the hospital,' Harvey said replacing the phone in his inside pocket.

'Did Jamie know we're at the docks? Dave said looking at Harvey.

'No you heard, I never told her where we were, anyway it doesn't matter.'

'Do you think Jeff told Jamie about where he had been shot?' Dave mentioned as they sped along towards the hospital.

'Harvey, Dave, Jamie shouted running over to meet them as they pulled into the hospital car park. 'Are you both ok?'

'Yeah we're both fine,' Harvey said grinning as he switched off the ignition and proceeded to get out off the car to greet her.

'What's the score?' Jeff called as he limbered up behind her to hear what his mates had to say.

'We had a little trouble with some of the locals, but nothing we couldn't handle, although; we did find out it looks as if your girl's been taken to Greenland,' Harvey said.

'Greenland---,' Jeff uttered in surprise through closed teeth.

'Got any ideas to how long ago that was and why?' Jamie added before Jeff could utter.

'Got the impression from a mechanic I spoke to, that it was early this morning,' Harvey said solemnly.

'Why on earth, would they take her to Greenland? Did the guy say where in Greenland? It's a mighty big and barren place,' Jeff said urging them to reveal more information.

'A place called Tuapaat,' Harvey said.

'Never heard of the place, but never mind, let's make a start and get there,' Jeff said hanging on to his side and looking very anxious at the same time that Charley could be in real trouble. 'But at least she's still alive,' he added trying to convince the others it was not as bad as it sounded.

122

As soon as Jeff heard the news about Charley, they instantly prepared to leave the hospital. After thanking the staff, they soon left the small town behind them and taking the main highway, they pressed on with its series of sharp bends, which did not help them as it reduced their speed. Then adding to their frustration when turning off the highway onto a single-track road, they encountered a large farm tractor, which they were unable to pass for some distance.

'Dave get in touch with Jim on my mobile phone, tell him we are in need of transport to get to Greenland. Tell him we are in a hurry; also, see if he can arrange for us to have some supplies and weapons. You can never tell what we are going to encounter if we run into this mob, at least we will have some added protection.

'I forgot to ask you in all the excitement Jeff, how are you doing? I must say you are looking a great deal better than you were a little while ago,' Harvey said.

'Ok you guys, we've got a bit of discussing to do, at how we are going to apprehend the thugs, when we catch them. I also hope they will reveal where their leader is, so let's get down to it,' Jeff said ignoring Harvey's comments concerning his well-being. 'First the so called leader, by the name of Tabor, is he the same person as Ofenka, if not who is Ofenka? What roll does he play in this exercise, as the travel agent informed me he had organised the whole reconstruction of the submarine. Secondly what roll does the submarine play? As far as I am aware, it is carrying no ballistic missiles on board, and can't deliver any threat of any kind to any of our ships? Thirdly, why are they keeping the passengers on the boat?' Jeff questioned while looking and waiting for some kind of import from his friends to his questions.

When they finally arrived at the airport, they headed for a small shack that was the so-called terminal; to wait for the aircraft.

'Here it comes,' Dave said pointing at the plane landing above Jeff's consistent chatter. Once the twin-engine jet aircraft came to

123

a stop by the shack and took on more fuel, they were off to what they imagined to be their final destination and a conclusion to the task of apprehending the thugs and releasing Charley from her captures.

'At last, we are on the last leg of the journey,' Jamie acknowledged as the aircraft quickly climbed to 30,000 feet.

'I wonder why they should want to keep Charley and take her to Greenland, it baffles me,' Jeff said.

'I must admit it has got me puzzled as well,' Dave replied as he looked out of the aircrafts window and saw the green grass of the hills far below fading away in the distance. 'I'll tell you this mates, it's good to have friends at a time like this,' he remarked as they began to descend to land at Tuapaat's airport.

'Yeah you're right, anyhow the next step is where did they go from here?' Jamie chirped. 'I do hope we are not on a false errand, for Jim will get awfully mad at what we're costing the department.'

'Me to,' admitted Jeff, 'but all I'm concerned about right now is getting my hands on those thugs and teaching them a lesson they'll never forget, as well as getting this whole mess cleared up once and for all.'

Stepping out of the plane onto a waterlogged tarmac when they landed, they stood for a while to get their bearings. For although it had been raining heavy it now had subsided and turned into a fine light mist that hung low across the airport, reducing their visibility in seeing the inhospitable place. Jeff began to head for the main building, when he noticed a guy in overalls standing by another aircraft with Russian markings on its fuselage.

'Excuse me I don't suppose you can tell me where this plane came from?'

'Sorry fellow I can't, but that elderly looking woman that's standing by the building over there, maybe able to help you as she got off it.'

'Thanks mate,' Jeff said leaving the mechanic and started to stride casually over to meet the woman in question.

'Hello,' he began politely, 'I understand you got off that aircraft.'

'What about it,' she answered back coldly.

'I'm sorry miss, let me introduce myself. My name's Jeff Morgan,' but on hearing his name she suddenly froze rigid.

'I thought,' she began, then stopping all of a sudden in fear, she gave the impression she knew him.

'Ok madam, I can see you know who I am, so how many got off that aircraft; furthermore did a young lady by the name of Charley Blackstoke get off as well,' Jeff asked in a voice that gained an octave and sounding harsher and sterner with every word he uttered. By now the three other agents had arrived at his side and making their presence even more hostile for her.

'I'll say again lady, but if I get no response, I'll call the cops and we'll see what they might have to say.'

'All right, all right I'll tell you, but no cops, I was only acting on orders, for once you join that bunch there's no leaving alive, you follow me.'

'Go on,' Jeff responded coldly.

'Yes, the girl got off that plane with six men, they have as far as I know charted a boat and are going to rendezvous with the submarine I believe you are hunting for. I tell you this; I had nothing to do with it all, honest.'

'Shall I call the cops?' Harvey said with a large evil grin written on his face, which made it more threatening for the woman.

'No I don't think so, not yet, she'll not be going very far in this place; anyhow I may want to speak with her later, so my dear don't leave here if you know what's good for you.

Ok chaps let us get a boat,' Jeff added hastily turning his attention away from the old lady to make his way with the others to the waterfront in search for the right type of boat that would take them out to sea. But as he strode along the quayside all he could see

125

nothing apart from fishing vessels that were not suitable for his needs.

'What's that over there Jeff, looks like a fast launch to me,' Dave added beginning to walk faster to reach it.

'Excuse me,' Jeff said to a plump rugged looking woman, who was sitting on the side of a large but fast looking boat. 'Is this your boat madam?'

'Who's asking,' she said with a voice like a man speaking with a bad cold.

'My name's Morgan and these guys are my colleagues; we are American agents and would like to charter your boat for a few hours.'

'Why do you want it?' she questioned looking at them with a very stern and wiry expression, and not sure, what they were up too.

'We are led to believe another boat left here sometime ago, carrying some men and a woman, we would like to find out where they went and wondered if you could help us.'

She ran a dirty hand through her greasy knotted hair and thought for a few moments.

'Yeah come to think of it, I did see some odd-looking guys with a woman leaving here about a couple of hours ago. I take it, it's going to be dangerous, so if you want my service I will want to be paid in American dollars, also if my boat gets wrote off I want it replaced, that's my terms, take it or leave it, do you agree?'

'Fair enough,' Jeff said.

'How far have we got to go out to sea?' she said opening the throttles to full power as they made their way out of the harbour. Jeff then explained briefly, at what had taken place with his girl and the problems they were facing concerning the submarine. He then introduced her to his other colleagues, who were holding on with difficulty to the motion of the boat, as it sped across the waves, while at the same time keeping his eyes on the horizon for the crooks, but it was to no avail as there was nothing to see. but the fast expanse of water.

No one spoke for a while, as they all felt it was too late and that they may even be going in the wrong direction.

The owner eventually shut the boats powerful engines off and let it slowly drift with the current, for they had travelled some 15 miles out to sea and with nothing to show for it.

'Well we seem to be out of luck mates,' Dave said acknowledging the quietness, which had descended over the boat. For they were now showing signs of fatigue, as they had been running around the country side and with little sleep for the last 24 hours.

Once more, he made an attempt with the binoculars and focused in what seemed to be a useless effort to see something, he then yelled with joy.

'Ay guys, look there's a boat in the distance.'

'Can you identify what it is?' Jamie cried.

'It looks like the one we are looking for, lady you take a look and see if it's the one you saw earlier,' Jeff remarked handing her the glasses.

The owner of the boat took the binoculars from Jeff and peered across the water, while the others watched in anticipation.

'That's her, I know that boat anywhere, but what do we do now?' she said with an uneasy sound to her voice.

'Harvey, will you get the fishing rods out from below and pretend you are fishing. Dave, open up the engine cover, so when they pass they'll also think we have a problem with the engines and are trying to fix them. We'll then try tailing them to land at a safe distance and when they enter the harbour we'll get them,' Jeff stated. 'Jamie will you call the coastguard, for I fear we are going to need their help,' Jeff added as an after thought, guessing the crooks may try something different.

'Keep our distance from them and watch for any sudden moves they might make,' Jeff said as the crooks cruised by at a safe distance.

'Ok, they're far enough ahead now, so let's begin to follow them back,' Jeff announced above the roar of the engines as they sprang into life.

'What do you reckon they are doing, tailing us?' One of the crooks asked Leshin, 'or do you think it's just a coincidence,' the crook continued to say.

'I'm not sure, why don't we turn back on them and see what they do,' Leshin said studying the agent's boat carefully.

'Jeff they're turning back in our direction, what shall we do take them on?'

'No Harvey we can't match their fire power, just lay low and look as if you are still looking at that engine but, be at the ready. We'll try and surprise them as they come along side us.'

As both boats began closing on each other and unknowing to Leshin, the agents had weapons and were ready to respond to his assault, as he continued to approach them at a steady pace. The agents kept out of sight below the wooden rail of the powerboat and waited tensely for the attack, as the expanse of water between them became narrower.

'We'll take them on our port side at the last moment; it's going to be close, so stand by,' Leshin stated. Then as they came into range, he ordered his men, to open fire on Jeff and his team, thinking that it would be a walkover.

Jeff yelled at the top of his voice, above the ever-increasing noise of gunfire, for the crooks were now firing continuously at them. The bullets rained overhead and smashed into the cabins roof and windows, sending splinters of wood and glass on them, while other fragments of timber flew out across the water. The owner who was steering the boat crouched down as low as possible for the hail of bullets shattered the windscreen, showering her with particles of glass. Not impressed by what the crooks were doing to her boat, she joined the affray using her own automatic rifle that she carried in the cockpit for just such an event. Blasting off a deadly burst of bullets towards the crooks, it not only took the agents by surprise, but the crooks also, for neither side gave it a thought she held such a weapon.

'Steer to the left,' Jeff cried out to her as the boats were about to pass each other, but instead they collided tearing wood from both boats as they slid down each other's sides.

The agents let rip with another intense volley of fire as the boats passed. They heard a scream from one of the crooks hit by a bullet. Therefore, Jeff taking a chance at being over run by the crooks continued to keep the pressure on them, until they had passed.

Leshin then ordered them to turn again for another assault but this time to slow down even more.

'We'll board them when we get along side them this time and finish them off,' he said with a sickly grin.

'Lady, get the boat going as fast as you can, we'll try lead them nearer to the shore,' Jeff called aloud above the noise of the gunfire.

'Jeff what's that in the distance?' Jamie said pointing over the starboard side.

'It's the navy and just in the nick of time,' Jeff called back to her and showing it in his speech how relieved, he was at seeing the patrol boat approaching them. As the gunboat closed in on them, the crooks instantly noticed it as well and broke away from the fight. Veering to port and away from the coast guard, but found to their surprise they were heading towards a second gunboat, which was also closing fast in on them. Then the sound of a crack followed by a shell landing just ahead of the crooks, but ignoring it, they turned right to try to avoid the oncoming danger. More shots followed with the shells splashing closer to the crooks boat and missing them by a few feet.

'Heave too, or we'll sink you,' a command rang out over the water from a loud speaker of the first gunboat that had now decreased the gap between the crooks. Leshin ignored his command, hoping to gain an advantage over the water for he knew, his boat had more speed than theirs and so decided to make a bid for freedom, however; another shell burst at their stern, hitting the drive shaft and putting his boat out of action.

'Christ almighty, that was a bit close. What would have happened, if the navy had not arrived when they did? It does not bare thinking about,' Dave said to no one in particular.

'At last we have some of the evil bunch, maybe they will lead us to the rest of their gang, after we have interviewed them,' Jeff added.

Jeff brought the captain up to speed, concerning the circumstances of the shooting and informed him about the submarine and its approximate location.

'You must understand Mr. Morgan I am in no position, to go on a witch hunt after a submarine, whoever it may belong to, I would need far more information and that would only come from my superiors,' the captain said making it plain, he was only interested getting these crooks in jail to shooting at Jeff and his team. Not arguing with the officer knowing he had to settle with what he had stated, and in no mood for a confrontation, as he was very exhausted. Therefore, along with his team they eventually made their way to the hotel that had been pre-booked for them.

Chapter 16

The Zhuralev had surfaced sufficiently so as the seawater just flowed across its deck, although the conning tower protruded further from the water it still made it a difficult target for any pursuer to spot them.

When Leshin brought his motor launch along side the submarine, he was able to transfer Charley safely to it.

'Captain Krabava,' Leshin called from his boat. 'Mr Tabor has ordered me to deliver another passenger for you,' Leshin said calling his boss Mr Tabor, for he was frightened of him. Like all who worked for him, although Leshin considered him the main runner in what Tabor wanted, he was no way going to change his orders, for he did not want to get on the wrong side of his boss, as his reputation was brutal.

'What is he thinking of, that we are a damn cruise liner, I suppose you better bring him over then; I'll have a few words with our friend Tabor, when we next meet.'

'I think you should take a look Captain, only it's not a man, but a woman, I would also suggest you keep a good eye on her, as she is a British agent. We caught her with an American agent, unfortunately for him, he had a distasteful accident, if you follow my meaning,' Leshin added looking at Charley with his usual sickly grin written across his face.

'Is anybody tracking you?' the captain asked and changing the subject, alarmed someone may have followed and discover them.

'I've got enough problems as it is, I don't need anymore with anyone breathing down my neck.'

'You will be fine, they haven't found us and as far as I'm concerned they won't,' Leshin said as he escorted Charley from the launch onto the submarine.

'Please, go down the hatch, I will be with you in a minute, Mianlia the 1st officer will take care of you and will see you are made comfortable along with the others on board,' Krabava said.

'Mianlia,' Krabava called from the conning tower.

'Yes captain,' Mianlia responded, clicking his heels in acknowledgement to his captain.

'Take care of our new passenger.'

'Yes sir, very well sir. You will follow me madam,' he said politely to Charley, already making his way to the Walkers cabin.
The captain then turned his attention back to Leshin.

'Cigarette captain,' Leshin said offering a cigarette for the captain to take one.

'Thank you,' the captain responded, and lighting the cigarette he took a long drag on it, and then slowly blew the smoke out from between his lips and watched it drift into the late morning sunlight. Then he smiled, feeling somewhat relieved he could get back to sailing again, hoping there would be no more interruptions, for there was a long way to go, before their journeys end.

'Krabava, when do you expect to meet Mr Tabor?' Leshin said.

'I have no idea; all I am interested is we don't run into our navy. Fortunately they are not looking round these parts.'

'I have my ears close to the radio; my contacts will inform me in the event they make a move to travel further south and if they do I will try and contact you.'

'That's good to hear Leshin,' Krabava said, 'but I won't be hanging about this place so I bid you good day.' Then without hesitating he turned his back on Leshin and wandered towards the hatch opening, throwing the cigarette-butt over the side, he started to climb down the iron ladder into the control room, giving orders for his men to set sail.

'Cast off the ropes, conning to control prepare to get under way,' he called to his men on deck, not bothering to notice the launch departing from the submarines side.

'Lookouts keep your eyes peeled,' the skipper ordered, not waiting for a reply he finally descended the hatch into the control room and moved towards the Walker's cabin.

'Madam what do we call you,' Krabava asked interrupting the conversation between Ann and Charley.

'My name is Charley Blackstoke,' she said turning to confront the captain.

'I understand you are an agent for the British? Am I correct in this assumption,' the captain remarked politely.

'I'm afraid that's for you to assume skipper, you are the skipper of this boat I presume?' she politely said, for at the moment there was no need to be hostile towards him.

'Yes I am and I presume the Walker's are taking very good care of you,' he announced, sensing that at the moment he was not going to get any information from her, and then not waiting for a response he quickly turned on his heels and left the room.

'Where did she spring from?' Kazan the 2nd officer enquired seeing his captain had returned to the control room.

'I have not the faintest idea and at the moment I don't care Kazan, nevertheless, I will endeavour to contact Tabor and find out what the hell is going on, so if you please, get in touch with him, but keep the message as short as possible.'

When Charley arrived, Ann could see by the way she was looking that she was in no position to answer any questions, and therefore decided they would talk later.

'Mark have you got any idea as to where we are?' Ann said softly to him so as not to wake their new roommate.

'I imagine by the sound of Leshin's voice when Charley boarded the boat that we are somewhere off the coast of Greenland. But since then we have turned on a southerly course and are now

133

heading towards the States; plus he's also in a big hurry,' Mark claimed feeling the submarines speed increase as they travelled on the surface with her decks awash.

When Hans entered the control room and saw Krabava looking at the charts, he slowly so as not to interfere with any of the sailors who were operating the boat wandered over to him.

'I've just been speaking to Tabor with regards to the woman Blackstoke, it's quite a story; she gave Leshin a good run for his money by all accounts and said we will need to keep a good tab on her, as she could be a problem. I recommend that we will throw them overboard, if they give us a hard time.'

'That seems to be your answer to everything, doesn't it Hans,' Krabava muttered irritably raising his eyes away from the charts, to take a glance at Hans.

'I know how you feel captain Krabava, but as you are aware there is a lot at stake here, and we can't afford to take any unnecessary risks, as it is, this Walker guy could be a load of trouble for us as well.'

'So what's so important with this woman and why put her on board with us if she has undue intentions of stopping our mission?' Krabava questioned.

Hans smiled with a nasty smirk, which he often applied, before replying to a question.

'Not for me to suggest, but I can guess, if you follow my meaning.

'No I don't follow your meaning, so what gives,' Krabava expressed.

'Never mind, we will be rid of her when we rendezvous with Tabor.'

'I hope so, but it could be a while, if our navy has anything to do with it, so if you do not mind, I have things to check,' the captain finally said to him. 'Mianlia, take your rest now and then Kazan will go after you, I will call you if you are required.'

134

Some hours later, Charley awoke from her deep sleep, feeling disorientated with her new surroundings in which she found herself in.

'Ah, you are awake my dear, have a cup of tea, it will make you feel much better,' Ann said handing a mug to her. 'We are the Walker's. This is my husband Mark,' Ann said in a calm voice, while at the same time pointing where he was sitting. My name is Ann, can I offer anything else.

'Oh yes I remember. You were the people who booked a holiday on a submarine.'

'Yes that's correct, and what a holiday it's turned out to be,' Mark stated and surprised that Charley knew about them.

'So this is the famous submarine,' Charley added in horror. 'Jesus Christ---, so that's what they're up too.'

'What do you mean?' Mark questioned.

Charley then began explaining on how she arrived in this new predicament with the thugs shooting her feller Jeff.

'Charley, things won't get much better here either,' Mark proclaimed softly so as nobody else would hear him. 'I know we are heading towards the coast of America Charley, for I saw the chart containing their route,' Mark said.

'Have you any clues to where we might be heading?'

'The only thing I could make out on my way here was Leshin mentioning something about New York. I didn't get the full conversation as he stopped abruptly, when he stated the capital, so apart from that, I haven't anything else to offer, I'm sorry.'

The conversation between them became hard, for the boat began to roll heavily as the waves increased in size and pounded the boat. They had to concentrate holding on tightly as the motion from the boat continually plunged beneath the waves and then rose again in the heavy seas.

'Con to control, prepare to dive,' came the command from Mianlia.

'Look outs below, dive the boat.' Mianlia then descended the ladder into the control room while at the same time closing the hatch firmly behind him and then making sure the air hissed from the valves that operated the ballast tanks. Shuddering and shaking the boat in full swing began its plunge beneath the waves; once more Yuri stopped his diesel engines, so he could engage the electric motors for them to operate the propulsion of the boat.

'That's better,' Hans admitted.

'Take her down to 200 feet,' the first officer ordered.

Down they plunged at a sharp angle until reaching the given depth and then levelled onto an even keel.

Apart from the sound of the sonar, which the radioman Andrei was watching intently, a silence engulfed the submarine.

'Why do you think we dived in such a hurry?' Charley asked Mark.

'Routine that's all. I expect they didn't like the idea of us being thrown round as well; also, they may need to save on their diesel, as I guess we've got a long way to go, before refuelling.

Now that we can talk, I think its beginning to make sense, as to what they are trying to do. The problem is, what are they going to do with us and how are we going to stop them and save ourselves,' Mark whispered while at the same time rubbing his chin, as if that would make him think any better. 'I may be able to do something with those torpedoes, but of course there is no guarantee they won't harm you two if I get caught, and that's assuming I succeed.'

'Do you really think they are going to let us off this tub alive?' Charley replied showing her concern they would never get away from the boat alive.

'I don't really know,' Mark said looking towards his wife and seeing she was more than ever troubled to what may happen to them, and fearing she may never get home again.

'We can't just let them kill us without doing something,' Ann responded.

'I know darling, but please do not worry, we will get out safely somehow I know,' Mark said revealing his frustration at not being able to do anything, and helpless to think of how to improve their situation.

'Captain to the control room,' they heard Kazan's voice ring through the control room's mike.

'What's up,' Krabava said instantly arriving at Kazan's side.

'We have a contact, bearing 320°, but it's too far to ascertain what type of ship it is, sir.'

'How far away is it?' Krabava said to Andrei.

'It's some 75 miles away sir. Its speed is around 27 knots.'

'Moving quite fast isn't she. Slow to 10 knots and rig for silent running,' the skipper ordered, having taken command over his boat.

'Sir it's a Frigate,' shouted Andrei the sonar-man.

'Has it detected us?'

'I don't think so sir not as far as I can tell, as she's not coming our way.'

'Very well, stop engines,' the skipper commanded. 'We will wait till she passes; it's a nuisance I know, for we can't afford any delays, but it's necessary the ship does not find us, so we will all have to be extra silent.

'Something's up sir, she has begun to ping with her asdic,' Andrei blurted out.

'I reckon she's on to us skipper,' Mianlia mentioned.

'You could be right, I can't see any reason to why she should suddenly start her asdic, unless she believes we are here. Sonar what's her bearing now?' Krabava called from his chart table.

'The ships on a bearing of 341°, sir,' he answered back in a clear and calm voice.' Krabava bent over the chart table and studied it to ascertain how long the ships would take to reach them.

'Damn it,' he muttered under his breath, 'if we stay here he'll find us for sure. Take us down to 300 feet, slow ahead on both engines and come round to 300°,' Krabava said in a steady voice, while looking at the dials on the instrument panel.

As the submarine slowly reduced power and turned on its new course, it finally levelled on an even keel at the depth given by the skipper.

They waited silently, expecting the inevitable, for the ship was still approaching and it had now increased her speed.

'Splashes in the water---,' Andrei screamed while at the same time removing his headphones in case the explosions burst his eardrums.

When the warship dropped its first depth charge it drifted silently down towards the submarine and detonated a few yards from it. The might of the explosion cracked through the water, and hit the submarine with such force that it tossed the submarine violently about with its shock waves. More depth charges soon followed in quick succession, as the charges dropped from the warship, which was aiming to destroy them. There seemed to be no end to the explosions from above as they rained down. The sound as each explosion detonated it deafened the men in the submarine, for them it seemed to go on forever. The submarine rolled and pitched in oblique angles under the extreme force from each blast that exploded and put enormous pressure on the hull.

The Frigate continued to drop further charges in an attempt to either bring the submarine to the surface or sink it; the Captain of the ship thought the latter would be preferable.

'We have sprung a leak in the forward torpedo room,' a cry rang aloud by a sailor. 'Three pipes have broken and are leaking badly,' the voice vibrated nervously from the crewmember.

'Kazan go and see what you can do,' the skipper called above the din of the explosions.

'Yes sir,' he said moving quickly from the control room and bumping into Mark who had left the women in their cabin, to investigate the shouting from the men in the torpedo room.

As Kazan entered the torpedo room, he immediately saw water pouring from cracked pipes that ran across the roof of the room.

'Shut that bloody door!' Mark yelled above the racket. 'If this lot blows, the bloody boat will be destroyed and along with us in it.'

'Walker what brings you here to help us?' Kazan said surprised at the man holding onto one of the leaking pipes and yelling at the top of his voice.

'Give me a hand Kazan to stop this bloody leak or we won't have to worry about that Frigate, or any other ships come to that,' he stated as they both worked frantically in an attempt at getting the problem under control. Finally working on each leak in turn, they sealed them to stop any further water from entering the boat.

'It's a pity you are working for the other side Kazan, for we work very well together; it's such a pity.'

'That's only because we are in the same boat,' he replied with a slight beam across his oily face.

As the explosions died down, they could hear the ships screws pounding the water as they faded away.

'What do you think Skipper,' Mianlia asked, 'has she given up?'

'No I shouldn't think so for one moment,' Krabava replied leaning against the periscope. 'That ship will do its best in sinking us, or track us till she gets back up,' he said noticing Mark and Kazan returning from the forward torpedo room, now that they had repaired the pipes and everything was back under control.

'The repair is fixed,' Mark said to Krabava.

'Kazan, you didn't inform me Walker was with you.'

'There was no time to tell you; I didn't think it mattered, as long as we got the job accomplished and I can tell you this, he did a good job at that.'

'Okay captain, now that we have fixed the leaks it's up to you, so if you are the skipper they say you are, start by getting us out of this mess alive,' Mark said addressing the captain with a deep hostile voice. 'So are you up for it?' Mark repeated, believing the skipper might not be up to the challenge. However, Krabava knew very well Mark was right and had to think fast, if they wanted to survive from the cold depths of the ocean.

After what seemed to be eternity, he looked away from the scope and added.

'We don't have any choice but sink her.'

'Take on a Frigate Skipper?' Mianlia gasped taken back by his captain's statement. 'How are we going to do that, can we do it?'

'If we don't as Walker has suggested, we are dead, it's as simple as that, for that ship along with reinforcements, will pick us off for sure. As it has a fix on our position and what with all the noise we have been making it's a cinch he'll have us, and that'll be curtains for us,' Krabava mumbled while rubbing his eyes and then noticing the strain on his crews faces and that they have had enough of the bombs.

'Trust me, I won't let you down,' he remarked thinking what a good bunch of lads they are, and now relied on him to give them encouragement to deal with this aggressor. He then murmured silently as he looked at Mianlia, who was watching every move he made, as if he had lost his mind by trying to destroy a Frigate.

'Action stations,' Krabava called sharply aloud, he then pressed a button to sound the alarm, bringing his crew to take up their respective positions.

'Go to battle stations; send our passengers to their room. Check the trim, start engines, blow ballast tanks and then come round to 341° at full speed if you please,' Krabava commanded in one swift aggressive but decisive voice. As the submarine gained speed, it glided to just under the surface, situating itself at periscope depth. Then without any further questions to the outcome to what the skipper was thinking and how he was going to implement this dangerous act, in putting all their lives at risk they set about their tasks.

The skipper pushed his eyes closer into the lens of the scope to view exactly where the Frigate was to them and to ascertain what class of ship he was dealing with. Then with a slight smile on his face, he saw the Frigate returning to finish them, but now he had a plan as to how he would kill his enemy. 'Gentlemen, it's what we have been waiting for, the American is going to try and kill us,' the skipper stated and then began laughing as they all heard the pounding of the Frigate's screws hurrying towards them, churning their way through the water, approaching nearer and nearer. The thunder reaching to a frenzied pitch as it got louder and louder with every twist that they made.

As the Frigate closed, the danger was becoming imminent and it was now too late for Krabava to back away from; He had now to engage and destroy his enemy or die.

'Come round on the same course as the ship, down scope,' he said in a composed voice. 'If you're wondering what I'm going to do, I'm going to put our stern to the Frigate,' he commented to his officers around him, for he had judged the distance between them precisely in the eyepiece, to ascertain his strike.

'When the Frigate gets within 2,000 yards, we will release one of the mines. He will have to turn one way or the other to avoid the mine, he won't have a choice and then we will discharge two torpedoes from our stern tubes. Whichever way he turns the result will be the same, we'll have him in a trap and nowhere to manoeuvre to escape our torpedoes,' Krabava added with beads of sweat running down his face. 'Rear torpedo room, make ready both tubes,' he ordered, his voice sounding much harsher than previously after giving the order to his men. You could sense the stress he was under, for the decision lay heavily on his shoulders. He knew only to well he must not fail; they would not get another chance. 'Steady as she goes, keep the boat on the ship's course,' he uttered.

'Will it work; is he going to fall for it?' Kazan said with apprehension as to what the outcome would be.

'If it doesn't we will soon know,' Mianlia answered to him instead of the skipper.

'Up scope,' the skipper ordered once more. More hissing came from the tubes well as it pushed the periscope towards the surface. The skipper grabbed its handles as it reached its full length to watch the ship approach and expectantly waited for the right moment to strike.

'Release the mine now,' he yelled. The mine sprung loose from its holding and gently drifted up and away from the rear of the submarine; breaking through the surface it rolled repeatedly over as the waves tossed it about. Again, the captain checked to see what the ship's captain would do as the mine now lay directly in its path.

'She's going to starboard---!' he screamed.

'Steer 5° to port. Rear torpedo room stand by for firing,' Krabava said speaking softly but with assertiveness into the mike. 'Loose all torpedoes, now---!' The submarine shuddered as the torpedoes left their respective tubes, as the compressed air pushed them from their confinement to head for the target they had been programmed.

The helmsman began altering the trim to keep the submarine on an even keel so as not to drift off course. 'Down scope and dive to 200 feet, change course to 320°, engine room full power,' Krabava barked in one short breath.

The submarine responded quickly to actions of the crew, returned to the deep black depths of the ocean, and levelled as the skipper had ordered. Everybody on board the small boat waited with extreme anxiety for the impact which they hoped would soon follow; however, they did not have to wait long, for they heard two tremendous explosions quickly followed by the shock waves which reached them within seconds causing the submarine to bounce in different directions. They hung on to whatever was nearby as the boat bounced around by the blasts from the ship.

'Take her back to 50 feet,' Krabava ordered as the turbulence subsided. Raising the periscope as he surfaced his boat, for he needed to see what damage his torpedoes had inflicted on the American ship. Peering through the lens he witnessed the carnage of the Frigate, engulfed in a ball of fire from stem to stern, acrid smoke billowed towards the darkening sky. The ship was already starting to list badly to its port, and slowly it began to sink by the bow. Explosions erupted from within the ship and lifted its main gun from its mountings, the magnitude from the force of the explosions ripped the gun barrel from its mountings and threw it high into the air, and then it came back crashing into the sea, killing some of the crew who had managed to jump from the burning ship. Then another ear splitting crash came from beneath the ship as a huge sheet of metal spun into the air, only to fall back onto some of the seamen, who desperately tried to swim away from the path of the sinking ship, their lives becoming extinct in a fraction of a second.

Krabava overwhelmed by the magnitude of the event continued to watch the sailors in desperation to escape the stricken vessel and save themselves from the burning inferno, only to end in the freezing water and engulfed by the burning oil. The episode did not take very long, as the ship finally rolled over on its side and slid in slow motion beneath the waves. The cold water began extinguishing the flames as it met the burning ship, steam belched from air pockets that had formed below the decks and had trapped below the waterline. Air bubbles sprang out from the hold of the ship and surged for the sky only to burst on the surface, sending a spray of water in all directions. Finally, Krabava witnessed the doomed ship with its lethal weapons drift out of sight and to the bottom of the deep Ocean.

As Krabava looked at the men in the water, he knew they would not last very long; they would perish very quickly from the extreme cold North Atlantic Ocean.

'Down scope,' Krabava said as he walked away from the periscope with his head low, for he was truly disturbed at what he had just witnessed. 'Head on a course of 160° he ordered in a quiet subdued voice, and then left them to go to his cabin.

Once in his quarters he stumbled over to his chair and slumped in it feeling very tired. His mind could not focus on anything, other than that what he had done.

'Can I come in?' Yuri said standing in the doorway.

'Yes, Yuri come in and join me in a drink,' he said pulling a drawer open to reach for a bottle of Vodka and two glasses.

'Do you think I did the right thing by sinking that American warship?' Krabava stated. Yuri mystified by what his captain had just asked him was mystified, for he had never asked him or anyone about his reasons regarding his actions before.

'You never witnessed the slaughter of our friends in our village, or even saw my wife and child killed.

My wife like Tabor's were strung up by their arms to a poll, with their bodies slashed open and legs amputated, and my child was at the base with a bayonet through her chest.'

'No I never did see it; you remember I was at sea. But you should not keep dwelling on it, you can't repair the past, captain,' he said with an aching heart for his friend.

'Perhaps you're right, nevertheless; our loss can never be replaced and so they will have to pay.' He paused to take a sip of the alcohol and carrying it to his bunk he laid down and stretched his aching body on it. 'You know Yuri we've got a good crew and have put their training to the test by destroying the enemy.'

'You could not wish for better,' Yuri added as he poured more vodka into the captain's glass.

144

'It won't be the last, and it's going to be a tough ride in the days to follow,' Krabava stated with a slurred voice and gulped more of the liquid from the glass. 'Have you any idea, why the Americans killed everybody that day Yuri,' Krabava said returning to the subject of his village. 'They thought they had discovered a gang from Kazakhstan, who were supposed to be holding up in the village. However; they were given the wrong information but not before they had sent in their special forces in the dead of night, and slaughtered every living soul in a bloody frenzy attack, butchering and taking anything they could get their hands on.' Krabava's body shuddered at mentioning what had taken place. Yuri could see tears running down his face as he recalled the event. His world destroyed, all he had was his dreams. His life would never be the same without his wife and family; he knew he had to come to terms with the disaster. Since then he only dreamt of getting revenge on the perpetrators and now finally it had arrived. 'Tabor lost everyone as well you know, that's why we have to do what we have set out to do, you can understand that can't you? We spent our whole lives in the village playing as kids, until we were called to do the national service.' He paused again to take another gulp of the fiery liquid before continuing. 'It's our turn now to take revenge, for I hold the Americans most accountable for the destruction and death, so it's imperative I succeed, or go to my grave in the attempt,' Krabava said with a voice that was inaudible. Yuri then stood over his captain and noticing his skipper was nearly asleep, he placed a blanket over him to make him comfortable, before leaving the cabin.

'Where the hell have you been and what's going on?' Ann questioned Mark with tears in her eyes as he re-entered the room. Going over to her, he hugged her to bolster her spirit for he saw how distressed she was by the events that had taken place.

'I am sorry my dear I have not been here with you, but they needed a hand, to prevent this tub from sinking, I also had a word with Kazan, to see what the chances are if he could persuade the captain to let us off.'

'Do you think that will happen?'

'Frankly my dear no, even Kazan can't understand it, why he has to keep us on board.'

'Mark now that things have settled down, I could do with something to eat, will you come with me?'

'Why of course,' Mark said grabbing hold of her hand and helping her to her feet, to make their way out of the room to the make shift dining room, and watched Rachko the cook rustle up some food.

'Charley has been telling me what she had been through, and what had happened to her brother, as he was killed along with his American colleague. She said that until recently she had been working with a fellow by the name of Jeff Morgan, who the killers had shot as well. She also stated she had fallen for him, but doesn't know what had happened to his body, for when she was aloud back to where he was shot, but he was not there in the ditch, now she has no idea if he's alive.'

'Where is she now?' Mark asked.

'I have not a clue, although she said something about going to the toilet but I must say she has been gone a long time,' Ann responded.

'If that's the case I reckon we should go and look for her.' But as Mark made a move, she came through the doorway with a huge smile on her face.

'What are you grinning about?' Ann said angrily for leaving her on her own in the cabin for so long.

'I am trying to make the best of a rotten situation that we have found ourselves in, that's all.'

'What's that supposed to mean,' Mark replied. 'You got Ann worried.'

'Sorry but I was in need of being by myself for a while.'

'You could have told Ann,' Mark snorted showing how annoyed he was at her selfishness.

'I apologise to you both, for you have been very kind to me, I should have stated what I was going to do. I'm ok now and think we should seriously consider about getting off this tin-can they call a submarine.'

'I agree with you there, what with them sinking that ship, which will surely bring the American navy on us,' Ann replied.

'But how do you propose about getting away?' Mark said still unable to forgive her for leaving Ann without saying anything. 'There is no chance I can see at present, so we'll have to bide our time. When I visited the forward torpedo room earlier, I had a good look at the torpedoes and noticed they were the conventional ones, which would needed to be fired from the tubes, so whatever they have in mind; they'll have to get fairly close to their target. The terrifying thing is that two of them are nukes, but I'm relieved to say they will have to be calibrated, before they can use them,' Mark said trying his best not to get the girls unduly worried.

'Are they expecting you to do it Mark?' Charley said, surprised the weapons were not already calibrated and ready for use.

'I'm not sure, but if they do it won't be yet, but I'll bet they'll keep you two as hostages, so I'll have to fix them.' Charley whistled silently through her teeth at the very thought of it, knowing that she and Jeff had discovered other torpedoes in that warehouse.

'How can we stop them from using them?' Ann said with a sullen look on her face, for she was terrified at the prospects of the future.

'I'll try and delay them somehow,' Mark said responding in a quiet voice so as the crew would not hear what he was saying. He then faced them with a straight face to show the girls it was not as bad as it sounded.

When Krabava returned to the control room having slept for some time he noticed, Hans bending over the chart table.

'Oh good captain you have come to join me,' he said to Krabava who had wondered over to see what he was looking at.

'It appears we have gained another problem.'

'Oh! What's it this time Hans,' Krabava said finding it hard to contain his disgust at the German, although he had nothing to do with the incident with the slaughter of his family nevertheless, it was Tabor who introduced him to Krabava saying, he would be working with them on their project.

'I'll show you, look at the chart, it maintains we should have at least 5000 feet of water beneath our keel, but see here,' he said pointing at a position on the chart. 'Our sounding implies we have only 800 feet below us, don't you think that's strange, what do you think?' The captain studied the spot where Schmitt had shown him.

'Sakhakov, what's the reading under us?'

'We still have 800 feet of water sir.'

'Why wasn't I informed before now?' Krabava boomed loud across the control room and annoyed at the lack of information he had received from his officers.

'I am sorry sir, but I was not sure we were entering a rise in the seabed, or it was just a high mound we were going over,' Sakhakov replied.

'Very well, so where are we, and are we still on course?'

'According to the compass, yes for it's still reading 160°,' the helmsman said hoping he would not be blamed for being in the wrong area, for he had never seen the skipper so angry.

'Sir the seabed is rising a little more, but it should be by now getting deeper, that don't make sense,' Sakhakov said watching his scope.

Hans Schmitt had now moved to where the helmsman sat to make further observation as to what was taking place.

'That's correct,' Schmitt said to the captain. 'So what does it mean?'

'It appears, we're not in the right location to where we think we are supposed to be,' Mianlia informed them.

'Go to periscope depth,' Krabava said responding to what Mianlia had stated.

'You reckon that's wise to surface?' Schmitt alleged. 'We're not sure if there are any ships lurking about, and waiting for us to do such a thing.'

'Do not question my decisions; we need to find out where we are and if our compass is reading wrong, and if that's the case then we need to fix it and fast. It's a chance we will have to take but a necessary one,' he said scornfully then instantly pressing the button to sound the horn, so his crew would go to their stations.

As the skipper peered through the scopes lens again, he still could not identify their location, for the sky, overcast with a heavy mist lay low across the smooth calm sea.

'There's a low mist out there that's making the area difficult to see, so if we cannot see, then it would be difficult for anybody else to spot us either, so we'll use it to our advantage. We've no choice but to surface, so Mianlia if you will, take her up with the decks half awash.' Then turning to face Kazan he said. 'What's the reading on the compasses?'

'20° NE captain,' Kazan stated, while rechecking the compass as if he had misread it the first time.

'Kazan, go top side with the stand-by compass and try to confirm where we are. You had better take two men with you as lookouts; we'll stay at this position until we can ascertain where we are. Yuri stop engines,' Krabava called through the mike as Kazan began climbing the metal runs of the ladder, to make his way out on deck with the spare compass. After a short time on deck, Kazan returned to the control room and stated.

'Krabava the spare compass is working fine, and I've sent another crewman on deck to confirm a further reading, so we can carry on with our journey, well at least until we find out what happened to the main one.'

'Very well, we have no choice, but to use the standby compass, though it leaves us vulnerable and in a dangerous situation, and a good target should anyone spot us on the surface. So we will have to work fast and get the main one repaired, so get it working and calibrate it as fast as you can, I will deal with what has happened later here,' Krabava said realising only to well they were a dead duck drifting on the surface. However, his choices were very limited, for at present it was down to Kazan to have it fixed before there enemy finds them and destroys them.

Chapter 17

Once the Captain of the Norwegian frigate rescued Captain Johnson and his men from the hostile waters of the North Atlantic, they arrived in Bergen and taken to hospital for a thorough check to make sure that they were fit from their ordeal.

'My condolence for the lost of your men captain, it's a terrible tragedy. Everyone is putting all possible resources into pursuing the perpetrator,' the captain of the rescue ship said to Johnson while being seen to by a nurse.

'Many thanks for rescuing us all Captain, I don't think they could have lasted much longer out there,' he said shaking hands in acknowledgement to the other Captain, knowing they would hunt for this terrible enemy and destroy him.

'Transport has been arranged to take you and your men back home to the States but first we need to ask you a few questions, it's for our records you understand,' the Norwegian said holding a pen and pad in his lap, to write down what actually took place.
Johnson then explained what had happened and how he could not evade the submarines attack.

'Well goodbye Commander,' the Norwegian said satisfied the last survivor past his health check and began to board the plane for America and Washington DC.

'I am sorry to bother you sir, but would you mind belting up, as we are about to descend into Washington airport,' the pilot said feeling unsure at talking to the ships captain.

'Yes, yes of course,' Johnson said and then began to buckle the belt round his waist as instructed and waited for the aircraft to land. The plane smoothly landed and ran along the runway coming to a halt at the allocated point that the control tower instructed.

'Frank,' Commander Scott said introducing himself with a smile as Johnson came down the steps of the aircraft. 'I am so sorry to hear of the tragedy and your loss that you have sustained. I am sure they must have meant a lot to you,' he stated as they climbed into the back seat of a car, that was waiting to take them from the airport to the city, where Scott wanted to interview Johnson further with regards to the sinking of his ship.

Scott ushered Johnson into a large but cosy room, covered with a very expensive cream colour carpet and a beige leather sofa, which situated in the centre of the room. In front of the sofa, a large smoked glass coffee table with chrome legs positioned to place items for easy access. As he entered the room and to his right at the far end, he noticed a drinks cabinet made from dark mahogany wood, located under a big window.

Jeff's boss Jim Edwards, plus four other high-ranking officers had already taken to their seats and was waiting for Johnson to arrive.

'Frank please take a seat, take the weight off your feet,' said Johnson's Commander pointing to the sofa.

'Care for a drink Frank?' Scott asked.

'Please, bourbon if you have it.'

While they waited, for the waiter to pour the drinks, Scott picked up a file and opening it to the first page, so he was ready to get down to the mercilessness action the enemy had bestowed on them.

'I have some of your report; it appears that this raider you encountered had a big edge on you. I envisaged we are dealing with a very professional sailor, I also fear it will not be easy for us to catch him, would I be right in this assumption Captain?' Scott said.

'I hope your wrong commander, for he has to be caught, before he strikes again,' Jim responded.

'The dilemma is where do we go from here, we have all types of ships deployed and searching, but as yet to no avail as that submarine has just vanished,' Commander Scot added.

'We are not sure, but the information we have received from the Russians to date is, it seems possible that a connection between the submarine and a chap called Ofenko is involved. We have a voice on tape that has been sent to us and it states this Ofenko has gave us an ultimatum, however; our intelligence along with the Russians, has come up with the scenario he is using another name as a cover from his real one. Several names look likely, but we are still working to find the right one. Here is the tape I received a few days ago; perhaps it may pour some light on the crisis,' Scot said inserting the tape into the player and then pressing the play button.

'My name is Ofenko,' the voice began to say amongst the background crackle and buzz. 'First I must apologise for the unfortunate sinking of your frigate and with the loss of so many lives, most regrettable, but it was a sensual move, which adds to the importance to our mission. Therefore, I will come straight to the point, so here are my demands, you will undertake to call off your ships, and for you will not find the Zhuralev that, I can assure you. Second, you will place in a Swiss bank of my choice that I will give to you at a later date the sum of money in gold to the tune of $100.000.000. You have one week to arrange this, if this is not accomplished by the time I shall give you, America will have a disaster of untold proportion inflicted on it.' The voice ended giving them an account number and the name of the bank, where they should deposit the gold.

'Anyone got any suggestions as to where we should go from here?' Scot said to the group of men in the room, who were looking astonished at the information they heard.

'Who is this Ofenko?' A tall officer with thick greyish hair and dressed in a light blue suit enquired.

'I think I can add some light,' Jim put in, 'I've been thinking and I believe he is the same person as a man called Tabor, and according to our information he's also the mastermind behind this crazy scheme, and by all accounts he was on a ship called the Oban, when it had replenished the submarine with its stores.'

'Where did this take place Jim,' Scot asked.

'The reds said it was in the Barents Sea, near Iceland, before retuning for Murmansk. I've got some agents going there to investigate the ship as we speak.'

'I also found after the submarine took on supplies, it took on a British agent off the Greenland coast. Then it sunk our ship and has now disappeared without trace. Incidentally, the captain of the submarine is very skilful and made of steel,' Jim said to the group of men.

'So gentlemen, where do we go from here? For this evil thug has not given us much time, to hand over the gold. I suggest we find the submarine and Tabor quickly, before they can inflict damage on us,' Scot added before finally calling the meeting to an end.

'Jim, Frank, can you stay a while longer,' Scot said as the other officers began to file out of the room.

'Thanks for staying,' Scot said as he approached them. 'Jim I understand you have some additional information.'

'Yes that's right, Moscow gave me a dossier on the submarines Captain and his crew,' Jim replied.

'Really that's very obliging of them, how come you didn't bring it up at the meeting?'

'I thought we should keep this to ourselves for a little longer, I didn't want to put any of our guys in further danger if it was to get leaked out to this scum Tabor. The skipper of the submarine is Krabava and commanded submarines for the last 25 Years in the Russian navy, although now he has retired. Moscow has also stated he's very good in what he does, in fact he was one of their best captain's, even though he did not see any action, however; I cannot imagine he would sink one of our ships without a direct command from someone higher up.'

'I can vouch he's good, for he could have taken me out at anytime, but waited for the right moment, and then sunk my ship with so much ease,' Frank said with a bitter taste in his mouth and with the memory of his men still embedded in his mind.

'How about the rest of the submarines crew, are they as good as the skipper?' Scot enquired.

'They are a mixed bunch by all accounts, only the engineer, his name is Yuri, who had been with Krabava throughout their lives and with the same keenness in the navy.
Both of them had lived in the same village and had travelled to the same school, for they lived in the same street. Moscow also stated they played together as boys, so it would have been natural for them to be together. Tabor was different, as he evidently lived on the other side of the village in the wealthier side of Zhuralev, which by the way, is the name of the village, in Kazakhstan.
The two joined the navy on the same day, except Tabor; both had an excellent records by all accounts.'

'So how come this Yuri fellow never became a captain of a ship,' asked Frank.

'Again according to the files he did not want the responsibility.'

'So are you telling me, the captain is the driving force behind our predicament we find ourselves in?' Scot questioningly stated, thinking that at last they maybe onto the primary course of this saga.

'No, I don't think so,' Jim added.

'Oh,' said Scot and Frank in unison.

'As I mentioned, Tabor came from the same village and it is my belief he plotted this scam at what he is doing, but that's all I know.'

'So Moscow thinks he's the one,' Scot said pursuing further to gain as much information as possible.

'I agree to a point, but the bloke we really need is on that submarine. Take a look at these photos,' said Jim pulling out the photos from his brief case and began spreading them across the table.

'What are we looking for?' Scot asked.

'Look at these three figures, the man in the centre of the photo is Tabor, the chap next to him is called Leshin and on his right, is a bloke called Pozvizd, by the way he is now dead.' Jim then showed the next photo of the same three men, plus three other men in a group. 'Those three you have seen, but who are these three guys, and where are they at this moment, and more to the question what concoction of events are they planning for us? I believe they maybe on that submarine. Another thing we were able to find, Tabor has an assortment of factories, so he can administer his deadly deed. Although I don't think he could muster the amount of finance, for his project, so he must be getting cash from another source to put this kind of operation together, but who?' Jim said taking in a deep breath, after making his final assessment to Scot. He pulled out a third photo showing all six men standing together on the deck of a submarine, looking as if they were celebrating some success.

'I would say he's the skipper of the submarine, you can see by the way he's dressed,' Jim added.

Scot then broke the silence, for it had gone very quiet in the room after Jim gave them the news of the crooks.

'Jim can you contact Interpol and the Brit's, see if they know anything about the other unknown guys, keep me posted,' Scot said straightening his heavy body and signifying that the meeting was finally at an end, but before they left Scot asked Frank to stay a little longer.

'Frank I have got you another ship, as you were cleared of any miss judgement to the sinking of your last one, I am afraid it is not a Frigate but a Corvette, it is the best I could do. She is in Boston with a full crew and ready to sail, she is the Panda. I believe you should have another chance, to get a crack at him.'

'I appreciate it and thank you for all you have done,' Frank said now with a grin on his face, and then turning to face the door after shaking hands with Johnson he left to attend to his next appointment.

Chapter 18

'Jeff, here's a surprise,' Dave said entering his hotel room.

'Oh, what could that be?' Jeff asked feeling better and more contented with the capture of Leshin, and was now about to have something to eat.

'I've been told the Oban has returned.'

'Returned where? Jeff said trying to eat a sandwich.

'To Murmansk of course,' Dave said with excitement.

'Murmansk! How did it end up there? And what about Tabor and his miserable men,' Jeff said shattered at hearing the news, for he could do without this hassle.

'I cannot answer for Tabor, but the crew is still on the ship, I think they are waiting for further instructions from the police, to see if they can leave or not. I dare say they will all be questioned about their involvement in Tabor's affairs.'

'Well we will have to pay them a visit as well. You want to arrange the transport back Harvey,' Jeff said with a mouthful of food. 'What about the plane we came in.'

'I'll check if it's still at the airport,' Harvey replied hurriedly leaving the room immediately to make the arrangements.

'Sorry Jeff but we can't leave until tomorrow, midday; they said something about the ground crew but I didn't understand what. So what shall we do now?' Harvey mentioned when entering the room again to tell Jeff.

'Well it's too late to do anything until tomorrow morning. Dave, you and Harvey go back to Severomorsk, ascertain the score and see what you can dig up, but for Christ sake keep out of trouble. While Jamie and I will head back to Murmansk, as I want to take a good look at that ship. So I'll see you all in the morning.'

When they disappeared from his room, Jeff undressed and jumped into bed and waited for Jamie to knock on his door. Not realising he must have dosed off, for he abruptly awoke thinking something was wrong with the Oban being in Murmansk.

'Come on answer the phone, where are you,' Jeff said to himself, as if the person on the other end of the line could hear him, and then a gruff voice answered.

'Hi Jim, it's me Jeff, I need you to find out about a bloke called Schmitt, if you recall, he went on the submarine with the Walkers. I have a hunch he is one of the men in the photos I sent to you. See if you can find a profile on him, I've got a shrewd idea he's involved in all this in some way or other, I'll explain more to you later.' Jeff then cut the conversation and hung up, satisfied that he may have a possible lead when Jamie came wondering into his room without knocking.

'What's the time?' he said surprised at seeing her as he stood by the phone.

'Time you and I got out of this place and started moving.'

'What already! I feel as if I had not slept a wink, where's Dave and Harvey?'

'Gone, took an earlier flight, it's a good job you didn't have to catch it, as you would not have made it,' she said laughing gently, which somehow seemed to take the pressure off the both of them.

'Once arriving back in Murmansk he hired a car and negotiating the potholes in the streets they made their way towards the docks.

'Jeff,' Jamie began to say, 'she can hold her own you know, she will be all right, trust me, you will see her again and very soon,' Jamie whispered in a soft voice, breaking the silence as they drove along.

'I'm sure you are saying this in the best interest but it doesn't help matters,' he answered back as they approached the Oban secured by ropes along the quayside.

159

On stopping the car by the ship, Jamie then looked around the area in the hope the Russian detective was there as requested.

The docks was still as he remembered, with the miserable bleak sea with a grey film of oil floating on its surface, contaminated by chemicals solidifying into a thick deadly mass.

'I reckon that must be the copper, by the gang plank, Jamie,' Jeff said getting out of the car as he saw the detective.

'Jamie you have a saunter round and see what information you can find, we'll meet back here in a while.'

Jamie went on her way, while Jeff made his way over to the detective to introduce himself.

'Hello I'm Jeff Morgan, glad to meet you,' Jeff said holding his hand out to shake hers.

'Morning,' she answered in a cold voice and not responding to his hand shake. 'My names Nadezhda Dostoevskaya, my boss said we are to go over the ship together.'

'Have you a problem Mr Morgan?' She said noting Jeff taken back by her reluctance to hold his hand.

'No not at all, only I was under the impression a guy was to meet me here, although; I'm sure you are as experienced as any of your colleagues.'

'That my friend, time will tell, you will have to wait and see.'

'That's true. Have you been briefed on what we are looking for on the ship.'

'I got the gist of it, so shall we make ourselves known,' she said already making a move for the gangway, to go on board the ship. They approached a seaman stationed at the end of the gangway and escorted them to the wardroom, where the first officer was waiting for their arrival.

'How can I be of service to you both?' Habart the 1st officer asked as they entered the room.

'Perhaps you can tell us where Tabor and your skipper are,' she beamed with authority, at having the whole Murmansk police behind her so there could be no misinterpretations as to the outcome.

'Mr Tabor I have not the faintest idea, but as for my skipper, he went with an officer from the customs department, said he would be a while.'

Although Jeff was not convinced, he was telling the truth, he produced the photos of the three guys from his inside pocket and pushed it under the officer's nose.

'Can you identify these blokes?'

'No, never seen any of them in my life before,' Habart spat with a vibrant shake in his voice, indicating to Jeff he was hiding something of value.

'Have you a list of all the crew?' the slim 5 foot 4 inch detective asked standing in front of Habart. Her features were very smooth, and her dark eyes sparkled with enthusiasm.

'Yes we have, but the captain took it with him for the customs men, as they needed to see the list.

'Ok, she added, 'we will check them out later,' quickly changing the subject back to the photos.

'You sure you have never seen any of these men before,' Jeff repeated pushing the photos under Habart's nose again.'

'Na, never,' he blurted out but being twitchy.

'Alright show us down the holds,' she ordered.

'Okay follow me, but it will take a while,' he said as they left the wardroom to head into the depths of the ship. Passing through the narrow corridors and gangways and then at length entering the cargo room, which they thought carried the illegal cargo.

'We had a fire down here at sea, that's why we returned to port,' he added to Nadezhda, as she went into the charred room that still had a pungent smell from the fire.

Jeff decided to slip away and have a closer look at the wooden crates, which were still stacked in rows from the time they were first loaded. But as he moved to enter the first row, he saw Habart

161

was about to follow, when the police officer stopped him. Jeff letting the Nadezhda to investigate the burnt paint room, he continued his way amongst the cargo to walk down the first aisle. Finding nothing abnormal with the crates, he then carried onto the next aisle, but halfway down he noticed some odd looking letters on a crate that appeared to be the same style as he saw in the warehouse with Charley. This he thought confirmed of any suspicions he had, about the cargo the ship was carrying.

'I think we have finished here,' Nadezhda said when Jeff returned to the paint room.

'I think there is much more going on that we have seen,' Jeff said and then began telling her about finding the torpedo in the warehouse, when he was there last.

'We'll have to wait for my boss, before we can do anything else. But at least we can make sure no one gets on or off the ship,' she stated dialling a number on her phone, to make contact with her boss. They both leaned against her car watching for any movements on the ship and waited patiently for her boss to arrive.

'Are you married Jeff?' she said surprising him.

'No not now, my wife died a couple of years ago in an accident. She suffered terribly before finally passing away; it was the worst time of my life. I can tell you, I've seen a few deaths in my time doing this kind of work, but somehow hers has haunted me the most. Since then I've devoted all my energy into the job at hand. What about an attractive girl like you?'

'Me, I have no fellows, I like what I am doing and have no time for them.
I have been in the force for 5 years now. At first, I was in a small town some 150 miles north of Moscow, but then transferred here when my mum and dad died. Unfortunately for them, they were in the wrong place at the wrong time and were caught in a cross fire in a gunfight between two gangs. It was then I decided I would hunt the killers down and bring them to justice.'

'Have you found any of them?' Jeff said looking at her rosy red face and noticed how bright her green eyes sparkled.

She was going to add something further, but stopped abruptly when the sound of sirens began approaching them along the quayside, finally coming to a screaming halt by the side of the ship.

'What have you found Nadezhda?' A short stocky man dressed in a smart black suit asked, jumping out of his car with a gun in his hand that was primed and ready in the event of trouble.

'I believe, we have found evidence to what we have been hunting, she said to her boss Gibisi. 'Jeff this is our Police chief off Murmansk.'

'How do you do,' Jeff said acknowledging the police officer.

'Well I hope your right; we are going to look bloody stupid otherwise. The customs men are now on their way with a search warrant, and an officer from the submarine base at Severomorsk will be arriving very shortly to ascertain the weapons, that of course if they are on the ship. I don't need a warrant, but it will add extra weight in searching the ship, if they try to hold us up,' the chief added.

Therefore, with the police chief and the customs men, who had now arrived, they went straight onto the ship, to confront the first officer Habart.

Looking very worried at what may happen, if the police found any weapons, he stood aside and made no argument to them as they went about the task of searching through the ship.

'Do you want to join me, while the cargo is being unloaded?' Jeff said moving in the direction of his car and at the same time noticing one of the cranes carrying the first container from the hold and lowering onto a trailer on the quayside.

'No I'll stay here and watch them putting the crates in that building,' she said, pointing towards the building where they were taking the shipment of crates.

163

Jeff leaving her began to wander back to his car, while at the same time removing his mobile from his inside pocket, as it started to ring.

'Hello Morgan,' a strange voice said, taking Jeff by surprise as he expected to hear Jamie's voice.

'Who are you and what are you doing with my colleague's phone?' Put her on and let me speak to her.'

'Tut-tut, Morgan, you are in no position to tell me, what I can or cannot do,' the voice said with sarcasm and menace, that made Jeff's flesh crawl. 'For the record, my name is Tabor. I know doubt you have heard of me, so listen to what I have to say. You have been a thorn in my side and have caused me countless problems, nevertheless; it has not discouraged me from doing what I have set out to do, even though you have put the police onto me, but alas, that is futile, for many of them do as I command. You will never know who is on my side or not. So here is the deal, call off the cops and no one will get hurt; it would be such a pity, in spoiling the ladies looks, you get what I mean.' As Tabor spoke out his demands, Jeff could hear the sound of a ships siren and a clock striking the time of day.

'Give me sometime, I can't do it on the spur of the moment, I will need an excuse and have to make them believe me,' Jeff responded with a wobbly voice, as the rage built up inside him over this evil barbarian.

'Morgan I agree, but of course I want to hear it on the radio, if there is nothing within the hour, well, I will not be responsible to what happens to her, you understand me Morgan,' he hissed and then broke the link between them to leave Jeff holding his phone in silence.

'Who was that Jeff? You look terrible,' Nadezhda said watching him dialling a number with a shaky hand.

'Harvey where are you?'

'Just heading on to the airport again but this time we have plenty of reinforcements.' However, before he could utter another word, Jeff quickly explained with an agitated voice about his conversation with Tabor, and that he had kidnapped her, and he would not hesitate to kill her.

'I believe he may have taken her near the old submarine pens, as I heard a clock chiming in the back ground, when I was talking with him and recognised it from the last time I was there.'

'Fine Jeff, leave it with us, I'll tell the police and with their help we'll get that scum.'

'That's the last container from the ship,' Nadezhda said ignoring Jeff's conversation with Harvey, noticing the crate loading onto the lorry. 'We better get inside with Gibisi and see what's going on.'

'Get a means to open this box,' the chief said ordering one of his men. The police officer returned a little later with a tool and gave it to Gibisi who instantly jammed it in the lid, and then putting his entire weight on it until a loud tearing noise came from the wooden lid, particles of splintering wood flew in all directions with some of them landing on the floor.

'Goodness me---,' the chief stated looking at the object wrapped in polystyrene inside the crate. 'Let's get this covering out,' he said grabbing at the covering and slinging it to the floor.

'Good afternoon gentlemen, I'm commander Pakienas,' he announced as he entered the building, and moved smartly over to them to come along side them and see for himself what was inside the box. 'Moscow has sent me to help you with a few problems that they said you were having, but I had no idea we are dealing with this,' he said looking astonished by the object in the crate.

'Thank you for your help and we hope that you will be most useful,' Gibisi acknowledged.

'Blimey---,' he gasped in amazement. 'Where in hell did you get this from?' he stuttered.

'What's the problem with it?' Gibisi questioned.

165

'That there my friend is a nuclear torpedo and I'm flabbergasted it has found its way here,' he said spluttering with the same lungful of air.

'I'm sorry to say commander, we've found three more crates, but have yet not seen what's in them,' Gibisi mentioned with alarm. 'That's why you're here; we need you to identify what types they are.'

Pakienas took a closer investigation at the one they had exposed, and then turning round, he face them with a grim look on his face and stared at them in silence.

'So what damage can it do?' Jeff asked.

'A lot, let me show you,' he said pointing at the torpedo. 'This particular kind of torpedo fits a standard 21inch tube,' he began. 'But the rear of this one is most important, as you can see, the twin propellers are shielded by this casing, which greatly reduces its noise, and therefore makes detection less likely, until it's too late. We found it very efficient, as it travels around 30 knots and has a capability range of at least 105 miles.'

'What---,' Jeff Exclaimed.

'Yes 105 miles, and its explosive power would be something in the region of 10 bombs, that you lot dropped on one of Japan's cities during the Second World War, therefore you can see how lethal this weapon is. They designed this particular torpedo for the *Fox-Trot Mark III* submarines, but they have now been decommissioned, scrapped or put in mothballs. The torpedoes were also supposed to be dismantled; well at least that is what I was led to believe,' he said with Jeff and the chief shaking their heads in amazement.

'How could these thugs get their grimy hands on such deadly hardware?' Jeff said disgusted by the lack of security that the Russian authorities had over their army.

'Don't forget, that when the Soviet Union broke up, all this and more was up for grabs. I remember the submarine in question going through a complete refit over two-years ago. Take a look at these plans,' Pakienas said revealing them from his black-bag and began unfolding it to show the diagram of the submarine in question, 'look here,' Pakienas said again placing a finger on the sketch, where the engines would be. 'This shows the original *Fox-Trot III*. You notice the design of the hull and the fixings of its engines.'

'So, what does it mean?' Gibisi added, alarmed as well as Jeff.

'I'm sorry, let's compare the designs of the two submarines, the new engines are fitted with a spring coil and are coated in a kind of heavy plastic between the outer hull and inner skin, plus the engine mountings are constructed of a very hard compound rubber, this in turn, helps to reduce vibration and therefore noise. In addition, the submarine coated with a substance that we are unable to identify. I'm afraid to admit it fellows, but that boat out on the high seas is unique and with Krabava at the helm, you have what I might call, a nightmare on your hands.'

'Are you aware of any weak spots on the boat?' Nadezhda enquired.

'Frankly no,' Pakienas remarked.

'I just cannot believe the stupidity of Moscow, letting these boats and weapons get into the hands of such an evil mob,' Jeff squawked in anger and was about to add more when his phone buzzed again and breaking the conversation that defused the atmosphere that befell them.

Chapter 19

A heavy damp fog lingered across the submarines deck as it drifted idly on the calm sea that late chilly evening; and for the Captain, luck was still on his side although he reasoned that it could not last; it was a matter of time before his adversaries cottoned on to where he was. He scratched his bearded chin with his left hand, as if it would help him think well, for instead of being in the Atlantic they had sailed into the Davis Straits. To add to his troubles he had no idea as to what he should do, as the Oban was out of commission. The task ahead for him was daunting, for he wondered how long it would take Tabor to get his much-needed supplies to him for the rest of the journey.

So in the meantime, it was up to him to outwit his opponents and save his crew from what could be certain death, furthermore; to add to his troubles, what should he do with his prisoners?

The compass still worried him, even though they repaired it and would soon be able to get under way now they had established their new position. Standing in the conning tower peering into the gloom of the wet mist, he listened to the water lapping against the hull of his boat and rubbed his eyes, for he was sleepy but knew that sleep would have to wait, at least until he was entirely satisfied nobody was lurking near by in the horrible gloom.

'I thought you may need some nourishment, to help you concentrate, for we would not want you to fade away, my Captain,' Rachko said chuckling as he joined the captain on the conning tower, holding a ham sandwich and mug of coffee for him.

'You always knew when to come at the right moment Rachko, I'm glad you're here.

You are aware of the struggle we have encountered to date; we are in the Davis Strait's and it will be trying times as we continue through, now that I have decided to go this way,' Krabava said at Rachko with a grim looking expression written over his face.

'Are you afraid my Captain?'

'Not for me Rachko, but for you and the rest of the crew, for we have a saboteur on board, which I must find out who is responsible, before they attempt something else, for he or she has been exceptionally clever.

'Yes you are correct Captain.'

'I find myself in a dilemma, for I have no doubt the saboteur does not care if he or she dies or not, so Rachko we have to be extra vigilant to catch the doer, who wants to destroy us.
I will need to check the files of everyman on board again, only this time more thoroughly, to see if I missed something in what they may have not told me. Will you tell Mianlia to come and take over on your way down?'

'Yes sir,' Rachko said acknowledging him and then descended into the bowels of the submarine.

'Mianlia head north through the Straits, we'll be under cover of this fog for a while as far as I know, as the forecast is predicted it would last for at least the next 24 hours, so keep me informed of any new developments, run with our decks awash with our diesel engines.'

'At what speed, do you recommend sir?'

'Start at 8 knots, we'll reduce speed if need be.'

'Very well sir.'

'Oh incidentally, apart from the helm and planes-man, no one, I say nobody must know which course we are heading.'

'I understand Captain,' the Officer said realising it was extremely important to obey him.

Moving quietly on a northerly heading and at a speed of 8 knots, they eventually dropped to snorkel depth so as not to breach the calm waves and cause a wake behind them.

'This is going to be no mean feat,' Captain Krabava mused as he pondered over the chart table, checking to see how deep they could go, if an emergency emerged. As the boat slowly sailed through the Straits towards the Nares Straits and into the Artic Ocean, Krabava spoke silently to his officers.

'Mianlia, I've estimated that it should take us some 60 hours at an average of 6 knots through the straits, that's assuming nothing shows to stop us,' the skipper added resting his index finger on the route that he had decided to take.

'It's going to be a laborious journey,' Mianlia stated to his skipper.

'Skipper we are there, we've clearing the Straits and now entering the Artic Ocean,' Sakhakov announced sitting at the radio.

'Good take us nearer to the coast of Ellesmere Island, and stop about 1 mile off shore, Sakhakov keep your eyes on the sonar and depth below our keel.'

'Very well sir,' he grunted noticing the skipper moving through to the Walker's cabin.

'I'm sorry to break up the party but I've decided for the good of the boat and for the both of you, which you are to leave our company. A couple of my men will assist you in going ashore, as there is no need for you to stay on board any further as I have aborted our operations,' the Skipper said looking at them to see their reaction to what he was saying. Instead, saw they were aghast and unable to comprehend to what he had just told them.

'What are you talking about?' Mark said baffled by this sudden wickedly act, that he may be playing with them.

'You have no need to be concerned, I have decided to set you free.'

170

'Letting us go, why the change of compassion? I thought we were indispensable to your evil operations.'

'On the contrary, it seems it would be better for us to let you go, as the Americans are everywhere, and you will be a lot safer on dry land, I can assure you. So please get your belongings together, oh forgive me I am afraid this only applies to you two, as Miss Blackstoke must stay with us a bit longer. You are aware she is an agent employed by the British secret service, so in fact she is therefore a spy. It is with most regret she must stay with us, I am sure she will behave herself; if she obeys us, everything will be all right. You can say your fair wells here, we will call you when it is ready for you to go,' Krabava said twisting on his heels and left them to contemplate what he had just said.

With the engines stopped, the boat drifted idly with the tide, as two sailors lowered a dingy into the water for the trip ashore for Ann and Mark.

'Mianlia call the Walker's for it is time for them to depart.'

'Good-bye my dear,' Ann whispered to Charley with a tremble in her voice as the sailors pushed the dingy away from the submarine.

'Right now let's get out of here,' the skipper ordered, when the sailors returned and stowed the dingy in its secure place.

'I want a speed of 24 knots,' he called out locking the hatch cover and checking the seal for visible signs of water, before giving the command to submerge. 'Head away from the coast on a route towards the Bering Straits,' Krabava announced making a shifting move towards the chart table.

'How long before we get to the Straits?' Schmitt enquired to Krabava aloud for all the control room to hear, as he slouched against the bulkhead at the forward part of the control room looking completely at ease, as if he had nothing in the world to worry about.

'I've estimated somewhere around 3 days. Why are you in so much of a hurry?' Krabava said sensing Schmitt was conjuring up an event, which was bound to be of no good.

'What happens when we arrive?' Hans asked clasping his sweating hands together.

'You will know when I do,' he barked at him with irritation to the sudden questions. Schmitt smiled and then departed to return to the forward torpedo room and leaving a nasty taste in the air, which the crew felt. Though Krabava took it in his stride and shrugged it off without a second thought for he did not want Schmitt to get the better of him, and then he left the control room leaving Mianlia in charge, so he could pay Charley a visit in her cabin.

'What do you want?' Charley asked swearing at him and encroaching on her peace.

'Just to see you are all right, and if there is anything I can do for you.'

'Yes as a matter of fact there is, you can let me off this ruddy tub of yours,' she said spitting out the words with disgust and showing her dislike with him as each day went by.

'I'm sorry but I cannot do that yet, for one thing there's no land anywhere near, plus you must realise, wherever we go from now on they will be hostile to us.
Tell me Miss Blackstoke, how did a lovely woman like you; get into this ugly business of spying?' Krabava said changing the subject.

'It's a long story and you wouldn't like to hear, anyway I'm not a spy.'

'Try me, start by telling me where you live in England?'

'You trying to size me up and make me talk well it won't work.'

'Is that want you think, please give me more credit than that. I can tell you this, that friend of yours, what's his name, oh yes Morgan, is very much alive and active.' Her eyes sparkled in hearing the news and showed how much she cared for Jeff learning he was alive.

'How do I know you are telling me the truth, for you could be saying this to try and get information I cannot tell you?'

'Well it's a fact, I am not feeding you duff info, but it's true and you may think I have no compassion, but I have. I have been through a terrible experience my dear.' He faulted with his words as the scene from the past came rushing back to him, although; it was, brief and his emotions showed it was gone in a flash, except she noticed his mood had changed.

'Why do you hate me so much?'

'I don't hate you my dear. But when this is all over, you may understand.'

'You are a very evil person and I hate you. I expect that my fate will be the same as the Walker's, so when do you intend to kill me?'

'Oh Miss Blackstoke, is that what you really believe that has happened to them, well let me try to assure you, the Walker's will be safe and well, all they have to do, is walk a short distance to a place called Alert. Once they arrive, the Canadians will take good care of them. It is only 20 miles from where we dropped them, the terrain will be hard going for them and they would have to wait until daybreak until they can make a move. Nevertheless, I have given them enough supplies for them to reach safety; of course, I have aloud enough time for us to get a good start to get away. I presume now that the authorities are at this moment as we speak preparing to search for us. Alas, I hope in the wrong area.'

'Don't undervalue your opponents Captain.'

'Please give me a little credit, for I am well aware the west are extremely organised in such matters and that we have to be even more vigilant, brain against brain, it will be a challenge I look forward too.'

173

'You really are indescribable; you people baffle me that you can murder indiscriminately without any emotion. I would if you don't mind, prefer you to leave now, I have nothing more to add.' Quietly Krabava departed leaving her with the thoughts of her friend Jeff Morgan.

'Sonar room to skipper,' the voice of Andrei called this time to alert him to the radar screen.

'I've detected a target on our starboard bow, it's about 15 miles, and I reckon it's a merchant ship.'

'Where's it heading for?' he asked leaning over the operators shoulder observing the green dot on the radar screen.

'On the same course as us, she is going to go through the Straits.'

'Good,' he mumbled with aspiration and with a grin across his face. 'Helm bring us round to get behind her, we will stay about 100 yards distance behind her and slow to match her speed.'

'Are we going to be her shadow,' Mianlia said looking astonished, realising what his captain was up to, knowing at the same time he was taking a big chance.

'Do not be amazed, we have practiced this movement on several occasions, have we not, also we have the element of surprise on our side. That ship won't expect us to be behind them.'

As the merchant ship entered the narrow Straits and passed the island Big Diomede, they continued behind for a further 18 miles, anxiously praying the Americans would not detect them with their electronic equipment along the border between them and Russia.

'Captain,' Andrei whispered, 'the ship is turning towards Nunyaho.'

'Blast,' the captain hissed blowing air out through his lips to the annoyance of the ship-changing course.

'I've got another contact sir, this time approaching from the American side.'

'Got any ideas to what it could be?'

'Yes sir, it's a patrol boat and bearing down on the ship at 30 knots, for we must be on the American side of the Straits.'

'There is no time to manoeuvre away, so we will have to stay where we are and hope they don't spot us,' Krabava stated in a low tone that was barely audible to the crew.

They all listened intently in the control room to the small American patrol boat, equipped with its heavy machine guns on its bow and stern. It circled round the ship a couple of times then came to a halt along side her. Luck was with the Zhuralev that no-one noticed them under the keel of the freighter, as the commander of the small navel vessel decided everything was in order and finally sped away in the direction it had came from.

'Reckon they must have been satisfied with what they saw?' Mianlia stated breathing out a sigh of relief.

'I imagine so, by the time they stayed looking over the ship,' Krabava announced flexing his muscles to relax. 'Ok let's get moving, as it will be dark soon and I want to get to Penkigney in one piece and slip into the harbour, before anyone discovers us.

At midnight, he secretly entered the harbour and tying his boat at the key point; with great relief they had finally arrived, although; he had never been to Penkigney.

For years, it had been an old fishing port, but like most places on that part of the coastline, it had changed to furnish the Russian war machine and this place proved to be a favourite for the submarines to hide. The submarines were without doubt, the best tools to use against the west, so they concealed the boats in the bunkers, which gave them an advantage over the Americans during the days of the cold war. It was an exceptionally good location for his men as they could now get some fresh air and celebrate, not that there was anywhere of interest to go in that run down place, as the town had long gone, along with the navy that was stationed there.

'Now listen this is the captain speaking,' he began speaking unhitching the mike from its cradle with his left hand and bringing it close to his lips. 'You have a few hours on land, so I say enjoy yourselves, for it will be another long hard journey ahead of you,' he chuckled. 'Now my fellow men, you go and have the benefit of a rest, for you have earned it and there is not much time,' he finally added grinning, for he was aware they would not see anybody in the town.

Krabava along with Sakhakov escorted Charley from the submarine, to an old run down dirty brick three-story building, with the paint flaking from its wooden window frames and walls.

Pushing her into a small room with nothing but a chair to sit on and locking the door behind her.

For a while all went calm and then she heard the mumble of voices from the other side of the door, then as it swung open it made her jump back, as she stood with her ear to the door trying to hear what was being said and not expecting them to return so soon. The same old woman who had dealt with her in Murmansk and on the plane stood in the doorway.

'I have the rest of your clothes here for you and they have been cleaned, so you can freshen up. There is a bath in the room across the landing; I thought you might like a hot bath, so I have it ready for you. Follow me,' she stated in a blunt voice, for this woman was not for small talk, though it seemed she had some compassion for her being restricted in the submarine.

Charley entered the room with the old woman and instantly saw in the middle of the room an old metal bath, with steam rising from it. Along side the metal bath, stool an old chair, for her to place her clean clothes. The only other piece of furniture was another chair that lay on its side under a small window.

'You'll find some more hot and cold water in the corner,' the old woman said pointing to the left of the room. 'I'll be waiting outside, so when you have finished here give me a call,' then spinning round, she left Charley to shed the submarines smelly oily clothes.

After undressing and throwing the clothes across the room, she lowered her body into the hot water, allowing the bubbles to flow over the rim onto the floor. Closing her eyes, she began to indulge in the foamy hot tub, absorbing the freshness and bliss of the moment. So immersed in the pleasure she did not hear anybody enter the room.

'Ms Blackstoke we meet at last,' he said in his calm soft voice.

'What the bleeding hell! She uttered surprised in hearing the voice. 'Can't you bloody well knock before entering and give a girl a chance to cover?

'That is a privilege my dear that has to be earned,' he stated smiling down at her as she tried to cover herself with the bubbles. 'We have a bit of old business to attend to,' he said pulling the chair over from the window and placing it closer to the bath to sit beside her. 'You are a charming and a very beautiful lady and with a body like yours, any man would die for, so it would be such a pity for anything to happen to it, especially after all this time and trouble we have taken to keep you alive.'

'If that's a threat you'll have to do better than that,' she said observing him and noticing his cold evil eyes.

'I'll come straight to the point. I need to know what information you found from that American agent Jack and your husband.' Charley then instantly realised as he spoke, that he and his thugs did not know Dennis was her brother.

'Well, we didn't find a thing, for nothing was in his room or on him and I never got the opportunity to meet my husband,' she cried carrying on with the scam. 'You remember you got one of your horrible thugs to kill him.

'So you say my dear, but I think you're lying,' he said with a harsh voice and slowly bent so close she could smell his fowl breath on her face.

'If you don't mind I'm not your dear,' she stated ignoring his remark.

'What about that friend of yours Morgan? You both went to the Americans agent's apartment,' he said spitting in her face and catching her of guard, he ruthlessly grabbed her by the throat with his right hand, to force the information from her.

'You really must get your facts right Tabor,' she stuttered and then trying to regain her composure once he released his grip on her.

'How astute you are my dear at having no fear, but alas you cannot impress me with the strong act approach,' he said straitening to his full height.

'Let me refresh your memory, Charley began to say. 'Yes, Jeff and I went to Jack's flat and as I stated, we found nothing, so if anything had been stolen from you, it would have gone to their graves, so I can't help,' Charley responded with assertiveness and hoped it would make him give up this senseless questioning. 'Therefore if you don't mind I would like to continue with my bath and in private before the water freezers over,' she said scornfully, but secretly quivering with fear in the event he may decide to kill her.

'We'll see, we'll see my dear,' he alleged, and then deliberately walking slowly round the bath as if he was going to strike her, but instead moved towards the door and disappeared from the room.
She swore silently under her breath, biting her lip and shaking with the knowledge he could do anything to her and that she was helpless to stop him.

'You will be here for a little while yet,' the old woman stated after Charley had got dressed and had escorted her to another room, this time on the third floor.
After entering the new room, Charley twisted round to say something to the woman, but she had already vanished and fastened the door firmly behind her. Charley once again confined alone, decided to take the occasion on eyeing up her new abode; and directly noticed the room was clean and tidy with a bed under

the only window with blankets neatly laid on it. In addition, a couple of old chairs were by a small wooden table. She went over to the window to see what was beyond the house. Looking out she could see across a wide-open space, where hills rose in the far distance. Her captives had taken the precaution in locking the window, so as she would not be able to make a break for it, not that she could escape anywhere, for the countryside was sparse and barren from any shelter.

'So my friend's, do you think she's telling the truth? And what if she is not,' Tabor announced to his colleague Krabava and Leshin as they sat at a table in the room, which was on the ground floor.

'I would say so, but I think it's up to Sakhakov if she stays on the submarine, as you know we have had problems on board, so if it was my decision I'd dump her here and now,' Krabava stated.

'What makes you so sure he will let her off, after all it was his idea, to have her with him for the duration of this trip, and at least until he decides to come clean and tell her who he really is,' Leshin remarked.

'She could create a load of mischief for you once you're at sea and remember there is still a spy on board, although; it's possible she knows who it is, and may even lead us to him,' Tabor continued.

'Krabava are you prepared to take a chance on having her destroy what we have been working for.'

'Do not fret my friend, all will be fine,' Sakhakov said hearing the discontented men as he entered the room, and endorsed the captains assurance with the girls presence on board the boat.

'I expect you to say that, for you have got a gender of your own,' Tabor retorted as he looked at Sakhakov with displeasure at the arrangements.

'Anyway we have lot's to do, so if there's no more business, I say lets get on our way, and let me deal with the operation,' Krabava said getting up from the chair to make a move.

179

'Where's Schmitt?' Tabor queried.

'I've got him attending to the stores; it's about time he earned his keep.'

'Good, and by the way, he will continue to be with you on your journey to the cape, when he will depart from you and that will be the last you'll see of him for quite a while.'

'Why does he have to be on board, he's no good, he just takes up valuable space and supplies,' Sakhakov said with a hostile voice.

'I understand how you all feel, but that's how it has to be, so try and get along for the rest of the way,' Tabor finally said conceding to their problem.

'I've got some news Mr Tabor.'

'What is it Leshin?

'My friends have told me the American agents have found out about this place; consequently they will be on there way here.' Tabor eyed him with a squint, but at the same time thinking at what action he should take with this latest information.

'Very well Leshin, notify your associates to pickup this Morgan, and arrange for him to be brought here, as the Zhuralev will be ready to sail soon, so the place will be deserted. So Krabava under this new information to what is happening, we will have to change our plans, so check that you have all the supplies for the next part of the journey are on board and get going.'

Chapter 20

Dave and Harvey moved like ghosts through the stinking oily puddles that dotted the area, but somehow managed to avoid the leaking drums, which were stacked three high and placed in long rows on the quayside a waiting for disposal. An old crane stood rusting away from age and bent low over them, as if watching every move they made. Crouching low behind the drums nearest to the single-storey brick house, they tried to figure away of capturing the thugs without anybody getting hurt.

'How we going to get in that house and get them Dave?' Harvey said as he scanned the area round the house for activity, and saw the place had been used for the workforce, when the dock was in its dynamic days, although; it was crumbling through lack of repair with its plaster peeling from the walls.

The agents had responded to Jeff's call quickly and told the police, who had found the crooks in the old building.

The thick oily puddles round the vicinity made the ground very slippery where they needed to make a stand in capturing the crooks.

'It's impossible to see through the window, as they've partly boarded them,' Dave said peering between the drums.

'Can you absolutely say Tabor is in there?'

'Yes we are very sure; he was seen going in with a woman only few hours ago,' one of the police officers stated.

'Brilliant, now at last we have him; this is the beginning of the end to his capers.' Harvey said smiling at the thought of capturing him.

It began drizzling of rain and a mist started to curl its way across the bay and began affecting their visibility, making it even more difficult for them to make any judgement on the area before them.

They slowly crept nearer to the house through the maze of drums, stopped a few yards away, and squatted in the damp to wait for any signs of movement.

'What a miserable place this is,' Dave remarked that was obvious for the others to ignore. He pulled the collar of his coat tighter round his neck in an attempt from stopping the rain from running down the inside.

'That's an understatement of the year mate,' Harvey replied prodding his pal in fun. 'I hope we're not going to be here long in this filth, as I'm getting rather uncomfortable and I'll catch me a death of cold.'

'What's going on, someone's coming out of the door,' Dave said quietly lowering himself further behind the drums so as not to be seen by one of them, who now had came out of the house and stood in the doorway.

He was a tall tattered man with a dark black bushy beard and bedraggled hair that hung below his shoulders, around his torso a thick fir coat stretched down just above his knees. His baggy trousers tucked into his high length boots showed they had seen a lot of wear. He held an automatic rifle across his arms and carried his large bulky weight evenly on both feet, enabling him to use his weapon at a moment's notice, along with the rifle; he had a pistol tucked into his waist. Observing him from their hiding place, they scrutinised the area, to find the best way they could disable this crook without alerting those in side.

As Dave and Harvey along with the police, crouched together monitoring the thug, they heard a volley of shots from their left. Thinking for a split second the crook had seen them, but discovered one of the police officers had started shooting towards the thug. Screams and shouts soon followed amongst the din that followed, and then a cry came as a bullet hit a police officer.

'Dave stay here and when I ask give me cover fire, I'm going to try and get to those drums over there, they'll help me get closer to the thug and perhaps I can nail him,' Harvey said showing his mate to his right where he was heading for. 'As I try to get closer, keep that guy well occupied. Okay, after three, one, two, three.' As Harvey made a dash for the new cover, Dave fired several shots towards the doorway to draw attention towards him. In doing so, it also alerted another crook who appeared from the building, to give his mate assistance to what was now a head on confrontation with the authorities.

Dave expected the thugs to return fire from their position, and was not disappointed as a hail of lead whistled low over his head, missing him by inches.

'Bloody hell,' Dave cried out. 'That was too close for comfort,' he announced to no one in particular and ducking down quickly so as not to be hit by the flying bullets.

Checking his aim, Harvey fired two shots in quick succession in response to the incoming fire and noticed instantly two other men joining the battle. Dropping even lower behind the oil drums for better protection, but all he could do now was to hold on. As hell broke loose with the sound of whining bullets smashing into the drums and brickwork of the house and knocking great chips of splinters from it, while more bullets crashed through what remained of the glass that was still in the window frame. Then above the loud racket, he heard another police officer scream out that he had been hurt and was in desperate need of help.

'Hay Dave,' Harvey shouted to his friend. 'I need more protection as I need to get into the house.' Dave promptly responded by letting go, firing with his gun as fast as the bullets would fly, this time more accurately than before, as one of his bullets hit one of the villains, who keeled over slithering down the wall by the door and ended in a heap on the ground. This action distracted the other guy and gave his mate a better chance of getting closer to the house. The bearded thug then doubled over as a bullet this time from Harvey's gun hit him in the abdomen, his screams of pain were heard high above the commotion of the police officers, who were shouting as they ran scurrying about to miss the flying bullets and shrapnel that ricocheted off the building and drums. Harvey carefully moved to another drum for a better position and then pausing for a brief second at which time he realised he had hit the crook He sprinted as fast as his legs would take him towards the door, shooting wildly as he went, passing the two remaining guys, who were engrossed with Dave and fled inside the building. One of the two stood up to challenge him but was not fast enough for Harvey shot the guy in the chest as he passed and the crook collapsed dying holding his bleeding wound and hit the ground. The third bloke dropped his weapon in panic and put his hands high above his head to surrender, crying out so no one would shoot him. Dave as well as the police sprang to their feet and headed in the direction of the house to make sure he did not try any further tricks.

Harvey moved carefully inside the building, with his gun poised to shoot anyone who showed to be hostile and finding nobody inside, he gradually moving across the room to the next room, he again cautiously swung open the door and prepared himself to challenge any unfriendly foe that maybe waiting for him. As he looked round the room fearful a trap was waiting for him, his eyes circled the place until satisfied it was clear. It was then he noticed a body, lying under a pile of blankets in the far left corner of the room. Progressively he closed on the body, tense and constantly prepared for what maybe in store. Finally standing along side the body and aiming his gun towards the figure, he warily knelt down beside it to take a closer look and to ascertain who it might be.

'Hells bells---!' he screamed with despair at seeing the figure lying helpless in the blankets. 'Someone get an ambulance and fast! He screamed again, this time even louder.

'Dave come in here at once, its Jamie, and she's hurt real bad,' Harvey said barely holding back the shaking of his voice from the emotion as he gazed at her bruised and battered body. He could see her clothes had been torn from her body and scattered across the room as she lay naked bleeding from the deep cuts, that somebody had given her. Dark patches of her bruised skin remained visible with dried blood splattered on her, as she lay unconscious.

'Where's that ambulance?' Harvey yelled, in desperation to get her to a hospital for treatment. Tears began forming in his eyes and made them sting, but unaware of any discomfort he could only see his lovely friend and colleague suffering in agony on the floor. Hardly seeing what he was doing, he covered her torn body with another blanket, in an attempt to make her more comfortable, and praying she would not die.

'Dave I'm going with her to the hospital to make sure she gets proper attention. Will you contact Jeff and inform him of what has happened to her,' Harvey said not waiting for a reply, as he was already entering the ambulance holding on to her left hand, so if she stirred from her forced sleep he would be there to console her.
It started raining heavier as Dave stood watching the ambulance take her away.

'Hi it's me,' Dave said pulling the phone from his inside pocket to make contact with Jeff and then explained to him what had taken place.

'How is she Harvey?' Jeff asked when he arrived at the hospital and saw her lying in the bed.

'Given time she'll get better once her wounds have healed, the fact is, she may become traumatic when realising she's been raped,' Harvey said silently to Jeff as he stood motionless over

Jamie and showing his concern for her at what had happened and hearing her groan from her wounds.

'How you doing babe, are you feeling any better?' Jeff said standing at her bedside along with his other two friends.

'I hurt all over, and feel I've been hit by a steamroller,' she uttered with a whisper.

'No not quite but close, you lay still and take it easy. We are preparing to have you moved back home, as Jim insisted we get you back as fast as possible; he also sends his love which is a marvel in its self. He must be getting soft in his old age,' Jeff added laughing to her to try to soften the impact of the treatment she had suffered by her bullies. 'Anyway he said you will be looked after much better and will make sure you get the right treatment,' Jeff said relaying the message as he faced her swollen face.

'You have a couple of broken ribs, so don't move too much.'

'I'm not going back till I get my hands on the scum that's done this to me,' she added wincing and wheezing as she tried to breathe, while at the same time placing her arms across her chest, hoping to relieve the pain through her body.

'Sorry my girl, no deal its orders from the top, so no arguments you're going home and that's final,' the agent stated as they all tried to comfort her.

As they talked freely amongst themselves, a doctor approached and taking hold of Jeff's arm steered him across the room and away from earshot of the others.

'I hope you are going to say, when she can be moved back to the States doc?'

'I am afraid not, I suggest we keep her for at least a couple of days, for you must realise she has taken a hell of a beating.'

'Are you saying they did more than bash her about?'

'In a nutshell Mr Morgan, more than being kicked and punched, unfortunately for her she had been constantly raped, and in a brutal

186

manner at that, it maybe she will not be able to have children, although; I will still need to make further tests before confirming it.'

'Are these people animals or what? Wait until I get my hands on them, I'll tear them apart with my own bear hands,' Jeff hissed with rage and shaking with this horrible news.

'Two of the thugs you won't have to worry about, as they were killed in the shooting.'

'Damn it, now that's a real shame, I would have enjoyed teaching them a lesson or two, what about the others who were involved?'

'I wish I could say who were responsible, but it appears several of them had taken part in the detestable act. I am very sorry Mr Morgan.'

'Not your fault Doc, but I guarantee you this, their lives won't be worth a nickel, when I get hold of them,' Jeff said looking at Jamie from a distance and then shuffled back to her bedside with his head low to hide his anger that was boiling in him to nearly breaking.

'Excuse me is one of you gentlemen a Mr Morgan?' A young looking nurse asked as she came over to the bedside.

'Yes that's me,' Jeff said turning to face the nurse.

'There is a telephone call for you Mr Morgan.'

'A telephone call, who is it?'

'I do not know, the caller did not reveal his name, you will find the phone in the room on the left just outside the ward,' she said pointing in the general direction of the wards office.

'Morgan speaking,' Jeff answered in anticipation to the caller as he picked up the phone.

'I have details of the person you would like to catch,' a voice said down the line in a distorted way for he was trying to disguise it. 'Meet me at the corner cafe in the main street in one hour, its next to the bank, and come alone,' he said hanging up before Jeff was able to ask anything further.

'Guys I got an errand to make. Harvey I need you to come with me, I'll explain what it is as we go. Dave you stay and keep an eye on here, as these crooks may want to finish Jamie off.
Harvey I desire you to be my shadow, but keep a good distance from me, so wait across the road from the corner cafe and keep out of view. I'll call if I need you to come, as I'm going to meet a chap in the café but have no idea who he might be,' Jeff said as they drove towards the town and the cafe in question.

'Jeff you sure you want to go in alone mate,' Harvey added convinced it could be a trap.

'I will be ok, just you keep your eyes wide open and alert, don't forget to call me, if you see any sigh of trouble,' Jeff said leaving Harvey at the corner of the street and made his way slowly to the cafe as instructed by the caller.

The lights hung low from the ceiling and cast dim shadows across the tables that were down one side of the room; wooden partitions separated them from each other so the occupants could be private whilst having their food and drinks. The owner had placed candles on the centre of each table, which gave the place a seductive atmosphere.

Jeff found an empty partition and plonked himself into it, which had been reserved for him, not that it mattered for there were few people in the cafe. After ordering a beer from the waiter, he gazed round the room to see, if he could identify any dubious candidates in the place. Time appeared to stand still as he waited for the person to show, he started to get agitated when a young woman approached him and sat on the seat across the table opposite.

'I'll have what you're drinking,' she said in a husky voice. She was dressed as far as Jeff could see, in a long navy coat that hid her figure, but still he noticed the sparkling diamond earrings and mascara that she wore and how it enhanced her facial features. Over the glass of beer that she held in her right hand, she studied Jeff's eyes for a full minute before saying a word.

'Mr Morgan,' she began gradually. 'My partner who phoned you was not able to meet you, so he asked me to take his place. I must apologise for his absence. So Mr Morgan may I propose we go elsewhere? perhaps to my flat, for the walls in this building are thin and tend to have ears and prying eyes, you can't trust anyone,' she said hastily swallowing all of her beer and making a move for the exit. Jeff half-heartedly followed thinking what kind of trouble maybe in store for him.

They turned right out side the cafe and walked a little way before turning down a narrow street and into a narrow alleyway, and then halfway along it they took another left and then a right, ultimately arriving at a dark wooden door of an apartment.

Jeff was concerned Harvey could not possibly have followed him, for he would have surely been seen and blown his cover, so deciding to take a gamble with this woman, whoever she was, Jeff went along with her.

'Well,' Jeff said breaking the silence. 'I seem to be at a disadvantage, for you know who I am but I don't know who you are, so how about it, who are you and what do I call you?'

'I'm so sorry Mr Morgan. My name is Yevgeniya but you can call me Zhenya.'

'Ok Zhenya what gives, what's this all about and who are you and your contemporaries?' Jeff said trying not to show her how he felt about the situation he found himself.

'Coffee?' she asked with a smile when entering the apartment. He nodded accepting the offer, and waited for her to continue and make the next move. 'Take a seat please,' she said pointing to the two seated couch that was against the only free wall, as one end of the room consisted of a large patio window, while the other had a cabinet, which was filled with books. Making her way over to the books, she returned to drop a bible on a small coffee table sited in front of the couch and proceeded to deal with the coffee.

'I'm not religious,' Jeff scoffed.

'Open the book,' she said harshly coming back to him with a hot cup of coffee. He looked at the bible on the table before picking it up and then gently resting it in his hands he turned to the first page, stopping abruptly when he saw the photo of Tabor and Leshin standing side by side outside the travel agents that he had visited. His eyes lit up brightly at the same time he sat back in the couch.

'How did you arrive at possessing this?'

'Oh we have our sources,' she acknowledged.

'You still have not told me who you are.'

'I'm sorry Jeff, I and along with my partner work for the Russian Security service. I would like to have told you before now, but when we first met I wasn't sure of you and there are some individuals who would have notified Tabor and his mob, so it's the best way I thought of getting you here.'

'How about the guy I spoke to on the phone at the hospital then, is he an agent as well?'

'Yes, we decided that if I came, no one would get suspicious as the place is used for picking up girls, it has quite a reputation and as you would expect, it satisfies some undesirables,' she said looking more relieved at having told Jeff about her situation and the involvement of Tabor.

On further examination Jeff saw further photos of the six men; he identified them from the computer memory card, only this time they were sitting on chairs on what appeared to be the deck of a submarine, holding a glass of what looked like wine in their hands.

'Do you know these three?' Jeff pointed to the trio in one of the photos.

'Yes they are Pushkin the captain of the Oban, incidentally he has disappeared, which confirms he's either working for Tabor or is one of the main participants; however we are working very hard to find him. The next chap is Captain Krabava of the submarine that is in question, we have a dossier you might like to read on him, the third person is called Leshin, he's Tabor's gopher and does all the dirty work. He's the one to watch out for as he has no scruples at all, and of course you may remember Pozvizd, he was dragged out of the sea.'

'Yes I heard about him. They sure are a nasty bunch, even to kill one of their own, I wouldn't like to knock around with them,' Jeff responded as he looked at her young face. This man on the far right holds the purse strings; well that's what we believe, as we found his name with the aid of Interpol. His name is Hans Schmitt, and a German; unfortunately, we cannot get a direct connection to how he fits in with the mob. Regrettably this chap on the left of Schmitt we have no idea to who he is, or even where he comes from,' she finally added as Jeff flicked through the remainder of the photos and pondered over them as he saw the submarine in various stages of its building program.

So immersed with what he was looking at he never heard the phone ring until she started speaking.

'Ok I'll tell him,' she said down the phone line. 'I've just been informed the submarine in question is at Penkigney.'

'Where the hell is Penkigney?'

'It's on the pacific coast line near Alaska.'

'You must be joking, what's it doing there? You mean to tell me this Krabava filtered through the Bering Strait between the American and Russian defence systems, how could he have possibly achieved that?'

'Can't help you there, but he did and it's believed he's going to head into the Pacific Ocean, what for, that's the big question?' The Russian agent responded grimly.

'I need to get to Penkigney before he sails and capture this submarine, before he vanishes again. Can you organise some assistance for me?'

'Yes I agree with you, you will also need help, so in the meantime I'll get my partner organising some help for us, as well

191

as arranging a flight to get there, but I expect he's got that in order
as I speak.'

Chapter 21

Stepping out of the aircraft, after landing at Penkigney's the airfield, Jeff with Zhenya quickly knelt down on one leg and scanned the area for any signs of life, but seeing or hearing nothing apart from the rain, that fell in abundance from the heavy dark clouds that had filled the large potholes that lay riddled across the airfield.

'What a depressing place this is, how did they get people up here to work?' Jeff questioned.

'No problem really, as they used the local people, but you must remember at the time Russia was in an arms race with the west and if you resisted they sent you to jail, however; that was then and we are now. Things have improved since those days and are still improving, except in these places. No one comes here apart from the fishermen, who live in the village along the coast, so this place just rots away.'

'Well someone must like it here,' Jeff stated walking from the plane across the wet muddy field towards a stone concrete bunker.

As there were no doors to the entrance of the bunker, they carefully entered it, descended a flight of concrete stairs, and reached the bottom, which opened out in a large cavern that somebody carved out of the rock. Carefully surveying the area further, it became apparent to Jeff its use was to hide submarines in and was an ideal location to refuel and replenish their stores without anybody realising they were there. He noticed there were some old submarines all in a state of decay. A couple of them tied at the dockside had sunk with their turrets protruding from the filthy oily water.

Immediately on his right, a submarine secured fast to the quayside seemed not to be in a bad condition. Turning away from that submarine, he looked on the corresponding side and saw rubbish was scattered over the quayside, which they discarded in haste. So drifting over to that side and bending over to pick up a canister for a closer analysis, he noticed the freshness and dates on them.

'Hadn't been long in leaving this god forsaken place by all accounts that's for sure, can't say I blame them, for I wouldn't want to stay here a moment longer than is necessary either.

Tell me about Captain Krabava, Zhenya. How come he got involved in all this?' Jeff asked.

She explained briefly as they began to make their way back towards the stairs and taking particular attention around them in case any crooks showed. Climbing out of the bunker they headed towards a three-story house, and began wandering through the lower floor, stopping now and again for any sounds, but hearing nothing as they continued, he picked up an empty bottle of wine from the table that had been discarded. Satisfied there was nothing further of use they proceeded to climb the flight of stairs to the next floor, which was no better to the one they had just left, as the paint was flaking off the walls in large chucks and had the same dampness about it. Progressing across the landing, he entered the room, where Charley had her bath, although; the water in the bath was stone cold and with scum congealing around its brim.

'No doubt about it she was here,' he stated. 'It appears by the looks of things she must be still on that boat, for what reason I just can't imagine,' he said.

'I'm so sorry,' she replied noticing the distress in his eyes at how he must be feeling.

'Shall we continue,' he said and then began moving up the last flight of stairs to the third floor, where she turned to her left to go into another room, while Jeff entered the one on his right. Not expecting anybody or anything for the place had been exceedingly quiet, he went straight into the room without hesitating, but abruptly stopped on the spot in a split second and kicked himself for being so brainless and careless, at having Charley continuously on his mind.

'Morgan come right in, and make no sound, or you will force me to kill you,' Tabor announced standing in the middle of the room. Jeff moved slowly as ordered to where Tabor had told him to, but kept his eyes focused on the scum he had been pursuing for days, nevertheless; his attention directed to the far right hand corner of the room, where he saw his colleague Harvey, tied and gagged to a chair. Behind him were two more of Tabors thugs both armed with snub-nosed machine guns at the ready, in the event Jeff may try something stupid. Jeff stood not moving a muscle, for he realised it would be futile to attempt to attack any of them, for he was out numbered.

'That's better Morgan. Take his gun,' Tabor uttered quietly but firm to one of his gang.

They now waited to what seemed an eternity for Zhenya to emerge from the other room. Then hearing her footsteps approaching and calling to Jeff, she crossed the landing towards the room where Jeff had entered, not knowing he was in there captured by Tabor.

'Jeff the place appears to be empty and they have taken off, once again eluding us,' she uttered entering through the doorway, and then without any warning they grabbed her by the arm and slung her to the floor. Stunned and completely taken by surprise to what was unfolding before her, and without waiting for her to recover from the sudden attack, one of the gunmen fired three shots into her chest. The sound of the gun exploding in the confined area echoed loudly, followed by the smell of cordite that hung heavily in their nostrils. Her body twitched violently for a few seconds before becoming still. Her blood quickly seeped through her coat, crossing her chest and began to spread onto the bare wooden floorboards. Two more of the men who also belonged to Tabor

195

dived on Jeff pinning him to the floor, before he could react to the attack of killing her, for he was seething with rage and madness to the needless slaughter of the young officer.

'Take it real easy my friend or you will end up the same way,' Tabor barked.

'You're all bloody insane, that's what you are---!' Jeff screamed aloud.

'What the hell had she done to you, she didn't deserve to die and she was just a young girl doing her job.'

'She's a copper that's what and we've no time for coppers, whatever their sex, anyway it's better this way for we saved her far more anguish than she would have cared for. Do I need to draw you a picture,' Tabor said calmly, but with a nasty slur, that Jeff had heard over the phone, only now he could see the slimy smirk on this mans face.

'If I ever get the chance I'll eradicate you from this world, for you don't belong here, I'll tear you apart with my own bare hands that's a promise,' Jeff said still scathing with anger.

'Oh that would be worth waiting for, but I don't think that will be at all achievable. Now stand up. Leshin undo the other one,' Tabor commanded with venom. It left Jeff in no doubt this hooligan ruled with a very unyielding hard hand and that nobody would defy him, for fear of what would happen.

They were hustled from the room and pushed down the stairs at gunpoint, and then herded like sheep towards the submarine pen where Jeff had been a little while earlier. Pushed along outside into the open airfield, Jeff could see it had now stopped raining, although; the mist was a lot thicker than previously.

He wondered how Tabor was going to get away from this place, knowing it would not be long before the authorities would arrive. As the agents descended the steps, the thugs shoved them along to the submarine where Jeff had seen it tied to the dockside. However, as Tabors, killers stood watching Jeff and Harvey at

196

gunpoint, Tabor boarded the submarine and opened the hatch cover to the conning tower.

'Ok you two, get below in the submarine,' Tabor said as the two thugs moved closer to them to stand either side of the hatch cover, in the event the agents may try to make a sudden dash for freedom, or any other unnecessary move. One of them poked his gun into Jeff's ribs for him to move inside the submarine, and as it was pointless to think off escaping, he obeyed and proceeded down the iron steps into the submarine.

Clambering down through the opening they found themselves facing each other at the bottom wondering what next bestowed their destiny. The lid slammed fast behind them and the clatter of heavy boots receded away from the submarine, leaving them in the stillness of the boat.

'I would say we're in a bit of a fix to say the least, so got any ideas as to what they're going to do to us Jeff?' Harvey said breaking the deadly silence as they stood by the ladder.

Dimly lit bulbs inside of the submarine cast shadows here and there, but apart from the creaking of pipes and other parts of the boat all was very still.

'Not at this moment in time mate, I'm as wise as you are, but one thing's for sure; if they were going to kill us, they would have done it back there, when they shot the copper. I can only assume they did not want our bodies discovered, or perhaps they have something else in store for us. So my friend let's not waste anytime talking and see if we can find a way out of here, maybe one of them has conveniently left open one of the hatches. You go and look round the stern end and I'll check the bow,' Jeff said to his friend and then moved away from the ladder in different directions. Jeff progressively made his way through one compartment after another, until finally arriving in the forward torpedo room. Once there, he peered round to seek out the hatches he expected would be there.

Like Harvey, Jeff tried and heaved in vain at one of the hatch covers but to no avail, for they had sealed the hatch fast. So giving up on that one he attempted to try the other hatch, which he assumed they used to load the torpedoes into the compartment, only to find it also would not budge. They had became truly trapped and at the mercy of their captives. Though not giving way to them, he continued once again to try and turn the wheel of the hatch cover with all his strength, but realised it was useless, the lids had been sealed from the outside, which neither of them had noticed, when they had been forced down into the boat.

After further attempts and failing, Jeff rejoined Harvey in the control room, slumped on the deck dejected, and disillusioned by the event.

'This is going to be tough mate, I can't help wondering just how long it will be before they finish us off, for surely they can't leave us here to die of starvation.

Can you think of anyway we can escape from this tub? As I'm completely out of ideas mate,' Jeff said.

'Sorry, but at the moment I seem to be in short supply of ideas as well,' Harvey replied.

'Harvey don't be to disenchant by what's taken place, it's a setback I know, and I'm sure we'll discover an answer to get free. So in the meantime, why I'm thinking a way out of here, tell me how you ended up here, for as far as I knew you were supposed to be keep an eye out for me, what the hell went wrong?'

'When you left the café, I was about to follow you realising you could be walking into a trap, but before I could do anything I was grabbed by Tabors thugs who tied me up and gagged me so I was not able to call out for you. They must have been watching me watching the cafe and then seeing you leave and that I was about to follow you, they quickly jumped me, I didn't stand a chance, for they threw me into a car and then some joker hit me with a needle,

198

well I think it was a needle? For the next thing I remember I was in that house.'

'Is that all Harvey?'

'Yeah I'm afraid so mate, I am so sorry, I have not done us any favours have I,' Harvey replied.

'Not to worry,' Jeff said sitting on the cold grey steel floor of the submarine, with his legs hunched into his chest pondering as to what they could do. When suddenly on impulse, he dragged his body from the deck and made his way back through the compartments to the forward torpedo room.

'Hey Harvey, come on here,' he shouted entering the compartment. Harvey realising Jeff may have found a way out, rapidly jumped to his feet and hurriedly ran down the narrow passage after his mate.

'What's up mate?' Harvey inquired.

'Have you noticed anything in here that may help us get out?'

'Can't say I have, why?' Harvey said looking at his mates face in surprise to his question.

'Take a good look round the place, especially the fittings; you see they haven't been removed.'

'So what---, what are you driving at Jeff?'

'You reckon the same as me, that they will be back soon to kill us, but in my estimation they'll want to make it look like an accident, so what a better way to do it, than in this metal coffin, after all we shouldn't be in here. We would just disappear into thin air and no one would find our bodies, so consequently they would not expect foul play.'

'Well that's a comforting thought to know, that we have a little longer to live to contemplate our navels, how thoughtful of them,' Harvey said not impressed by such a conclusion his friend had came too.

'Come on cheer up mate and think, the submarines on the surface correct?'

'Yeah I saw that, so what?' Harvey said with a harsh tone to his voice.

'And the torpedo tubes are just beneath the water line right.'

'I suppose so, what are you getting at,' Harvey stated with a shrug. 'Ay hang on, wait a just a cotton minute, are you thinking of getting into one of them to get out,' Harvey uttered with a look of shock in his eyes.

'Glad to see you're thinking at last,' Jeff said walking over to the tubes doors, and then spinning round to face his friend, he uttered in excitement.

'We'll have to check the control valves and see which ones operate the torpedo tubes and see if they are operational, ok. So let's do it,' Jeff added enthusiastically, but knowing deep down it was a long shot and a terrible risk, all the same, he set to work on the best course of action that would be possible for them to escape.

'It seems we have no choice, so Harvey, how long do think you can hold your breath for?'

'Not very long, why do you ask,' Harvey answered, when it suddenly dawned on him what Jeff was asking, and then the horrible thought entered his head, that he may have to get in one of the tubes to escape.

'I thought so, you never were much good as a scuba diver, I can hold my breath a great deal longer than you, so I'll try escape through one of them, but remember we can't afford a foul up.'

Time went by as they operated the controls, shutting and opening the inner tubes top door to make sure it would not fail. Once satisfied with its success he then concentrated with the final checking of the tubes valves, only then when contented with them that they worked, Jeff began flooding the bottom left tube, while at the same time holding his breath, to see how long it took to fill.

'Harvey, are you ready for this?'

'No, I don't like it at all mate, I'm afraid I will be responsible for your death.'

'Well if that's all you are worried about, it won't matter, for you will not survive either. So do not be concerned, as it will be all right, trust me, okay, let's do it,' Jeff said taking hold of his friend's hand and shaking it hard at the same time looking into his eyes, fearing it could be the last time they would see each other alive.

'Good-bye Jeff,' Harvey croaked as Jeff climbed into the top left tube.

'Ay mate, not goodbye, for that means forever; I'll see you topside in a jiff,' he said turning to face the outer door and then swiftly scrambled towards it, getting as close as possible to the door, for he needed to be able to push it open once Harvey had operated the valves.

He waited patiently, for Harvey to close the inner door, which seamed to last an eternity, and then hearing it slam hard against its seals with a loud bang that made his ears pop. Harvey fastened and locked the mechanism securely, so the door was tight against its seals.

Jeff's heart began thumping rapidly in anticipation to what was to come, as he lay in the restricted tube for Harvey to open the valves, so the water would flood in and engulf him.

He had never experienced anything like it in his life before and what made things worse, he was totally unprepared for the outcome. Then without any warning, water suddenly gushed into the chamber swallowing him in seconds and took him completely by surprise, even though he thought he was ready and was just able to take a lung full of air as he submerged into the oily cold liquid. He now waited for the outer door to release, for he had expected it to open straight away, except nothing happened and immediately, he started to feel uneasy, so much so that pangs of panic started to rise inside him, yet he knew he had to fight it and keep his self-control. He heard the sounds of groaning and scraping of metal against metal as the door tried to wrench from its rusty seals. Jeff clung on in that narrow tomb in desperation hoping and hopping that that door would spring open. He began to feel the signs of claustrophobia coming over him despite the fact he had never suffered from it in the past and then he sensed the walls closing in on him. He was no longer aware of the time he had been in that tube holding his breath, but swore it must have been time without end, for his lungs had started to succumb to the lack of fresh air and he was now straining to keep his mouth shut, feeling all the time his lungs would burst. When unexpected the outer door abruptly sprang open with such force it bounced back on its hinges hitting Jeff, as he quickly took the initiative, to struggle through the opening. Desperately he pushed hard against the door in an attempt to keep it open, while at the same time, twisting his body fall circle to wriggle out of that small opening. He tugged at whatever he could grab hold of to get to the surface before the air in his lungs finally spent. Pushing against the boat he sprang from that hellhole and shot to the surface at the same time taking huge gulps of the oily salt-water, then once on the surface he grabbed and struggled to free himself from the greasy cold black filth that represented it self as sea water. Now with deteriorating strength he managed pulling himself on a rope from the dockside and heaved himself onto the dockside gasping for breath.

He lay motionless on his back, feeling if his chest would burst with the strain. With the tension of the past occurrence, he slowly rolled onto his stomach and with his body throbbing hard against the effort he pushed himself onto his feet, and began staggering about as if he was a drunk. Gathering his senses at last, he made a beeline for the submarines deck and to the hatch cover he could not open. Kneeling down beside the lid, he understood why it would not open, as he could see a long steel tube wedged through the outer wheel preventing them from moving it inside. He began wrenching at the tube, tugging and pulling with all his might, but he could not budge it. He waited for a second or two and then began pulling once more on it, wriggling it about franticly, but still without success. Sitting by the hatch, he pondered to himself quietly, as to how and why the lid would not release, and then at length once he had relaxed a little to regain his strength, praying that no one would come back to the submarine and catch them trying to escape. He set about with another attempt, and as before, tugging, pulling and twisting the tube again with all the strength he could muster. Only this time he heard the distinctive crack of the seal giving way as it was freed from the constant hammering, that Jeff had given it, and now completely exhausted with the physical force from the exercise he used to open the lid he waited for his mate, to emerge from what they thought would their grave.

'Hi mate, what kept ya,' Harvey said with a smile as he clambered from his nightmare waiting for Jeff to rescue him. 'You look somewhat bushed mate, been out running have you,' he said light heartedly as possible, and making fun of what was a nerve-racking experience, although; Jeff was incapable of speaking he smiled at his friend thinking at how it might have been for the two of them encased in the submarine.

'How can you have such wit at this time? When I bloody nearly drowned in that bloody tube in the process of bloody well getting out,' Jeff finally said spitting out the words with added scorn, while shutting the hatch cover. 'Listen I hear voices approaching,' he said not forgetting to replace the metal tube, so no one would know anyone had tampered with it.

They ran for cover behind some boxes, which were stacked on top of each other beside the submarine.

'Jeff can you see from your position?' his mate inquired.

'Yeah there are five men coming down the steps and are approaching the submarine, though Tabor or Leshin is not one of them,' he said quietly. 'I surmise they have left this bunch of thugs to do his dirty work of killing us.

'What do we do, if they open up the hatch and find we're not at home Jeff? It's not the address I want to go back to and live in again.'

'Be quiet they'll hear you,' Jeff whispered. 'Lets wait and see what they are up to, we're going to have to play it by ear,' he added noticing the crooks were now jumping and thumping on the deck and making a horrendous noise. It would have been impossible for anyone to hear anybody banging and shouting from inside the boat. The two agents watched spellbound by what the thugs were doing and then they noticed a tug entering the pen. Two of the men had grabbed some ropes and were preparing to tie the tug to the side of the submarine as it came along side. Singing and shouting to each other for they were in a very jovial mood, they pursued to unravel the ropes from a capstan on the quayside and were completely oblivious to the fact the American agents had freed themselves and were watching everything in progress. The men in the tug revved the engines and then gradually at first it began to move, increasing in power it started to pull the submarine from its moorings and shifted towards the opening of the shelter of the submarines pen. They headed in the direction of the open bay but stopped short of the exit to the open sea. As the agents looked on, they were flabbergasted by the laughing and the way these guys were joking, for they seemed to have no guilt in the deed they were undertaking and had no idea that their fugitives were free from the oncoming tomb and watching everything, they were doing.

Jeff continued to scrutinize the bay, but could hardly see what the gang was up to, however; it soon became apparent to him, when he heard the first muffled explosion from under the boat, for he had heard those noises far too often.

'Good heavens,' Harvey said. 'They're sinking the submarine; we only just got out in time, for if we hadn't, blimey it doesn't bear thinking about.'

'Come on Harvey its time to make a move, while they're still enjoying their fun and before we are spotted.'

Silently but swiftly they moved to the other end of the dock and crept up the concrete steps, checking all the time in the event one of the thugs may spot them. Continuing through the mist, which drifted idly across the airstrip they made their way back towards the house, moving from one hiding place to another. Harvey nudged at Jeff's arm and pointed to where the plane was still standing as they progressed along.

'Yeah, I've seen it, but we need to find the pilot, so you go on round the back, while I'll try the front, let's hope they haven't killed him also.' But luck was on their side, for the pilot was in the ground floor room which Jeff had been in earlier and chatting freely with the guard and totally at ease with each other as they passed the time of day waiting for the other crooks to return.

As Jeff looked through the window of the room he could see nobody else who could prevent them from escaping, so taking a big gamble, Jeff barged into the room catching the guard by surprise, for he would have expected them killed by now.

Jeff crashed through the doorway entering the room screaming at the top of his head, so much, so he caught the guard completely by surprise. Rapidly lashing out with a good right fist and knocking the guard to the floor, he then followed through by pouncing on him before the crook could regain to fight back and then for good measure, Jeff struck him again with another hard blow to the chin, this time knocking him out. Satisfied he was not going to give them any further problems he dragged the crook to a chair, tied, and gagged him to it. Approaching the pilot Jeff quickly explained what the crooks tried to do to them. Luckily, it did not take much of an argument saying what would happen to them, when the other crooks returned from sinking the boat. Jeff quickly persuaded the pilot and Harvey's argument, for he now joined them and made a mad dash for the plane, running across the muddy grass at a fast sprint to the end of the runway, where the pilot had positioned it earlier for ready to take off. Jeff howled loud to Harvey for them to be out of there fast, for Harvey had stumbled on a bundle in the wet greasy dirt and looking down at what he had tripped over he saw instantly it was Zhenya the young police officer. One of the crooks had dumped her body in a shallow hollow in the slimy ground to rot.

Her body lay stained with oil and mud and she was soaked through with the constant rain, her blood now dried from the injury, and she seemed to be in a deep sleep. Picking her up, Harvey placed her very carefully over his shoulder in a firefighter's hold and proceeded to carry her at a gaunt to the aircraft and then placing her in the plane he climbed in behind her. By this time, the pilot was at his controls and starting the engines. Jeff helped Harvey push the young officer's body further on board and he too scrambled into the plane.

'We're just in the nick of time as I think they're on to us, must have been on their way back to the house and saw us,' Harvey yelled above the noise of the engines.

'Yeah your right mate. Let's hope those bullets don't hit anything important on this aircraft, for we'll know all about it once we're in the air,' Jeff said looking at the crooks as they dashed about firing indiscriminately at the aircraft.

As they tore along the runway at high speed the crooks from the submarines pen, were now in full pursuit for they heard the engines of the aircraft start-up; unfortunately, for them, it was too late and useless for they were on foot and were no match for the speeding plane.

The plane finally leaving the pot-holed runway behind headed into the dismal cloudy sky and out of sight of Tabors evil men. Once in the air and safely on their way, Jeff then began to relax and made his way to a seat behind the pilot. Closing his eyes and with the knowledge they had a narrow escape and that they were on their way to civilisation.

'I think we need to take stock on what's happening so far and where we should go from here,' Jeff said to Harvey as the plane climbed even higher into the sky.

'That's a fact mate, we were extremely lucky to get away with our lives back there,' Harvey agreed.

'Yeah that's a bleeding fact, which tells me we must be getting pretty close to catching them, now that we have met Tabor and have some idea to what he's up too. It all makes sense now, the nuke torpedoes in the warehouse and the missing submarine. The missing link is where and what they are going to destroy. Perhaps the Russian authorities can catch him and send him to jail, before he can implement what he has set out to do. Anyway when we get back to Murmansk we'll check on Jamie and see if she has been sent home, I do hope she has recovered from her trauma?'

'It's a shame what had happened to her, how do think Jim will react when she gets home?' Harvey uttered.

'I should say very much the same as us I suppose, I do think it will be the end of her career with the force though; for I cannot imagine Jim sending her out on any more field assignments. Anyway I recommend we return to Washington, as talking to Jim on the horn is one thing, but I think we need to get our brains a little closer together, apart from that, this Tabor fellow is more slippery than we think and I wouldn't be surprised that he gets away scot free.'

Arriving back in Severomorsk Jeff went straight to the police headquarters and with the assistant of the pilot, he explained exactly what had taken place at the submarines pen. They also delivered the unfortunate Zhenya to them and made it known how very sorry that they could not help her from being killed. Then arriving back at the hotel Dave listened to Jeff and Harvey with amazement as their drama unfolded, whistling through his teeth as he heard the dangerous escapade that they underwent to get away from the thugs. He showed his feelings by pulling his face and cringing to the shooting of the police officer, when Jeff mentioned that part of it.

'Blimey,' he gasped at length. 'You two certainly know how to live it up,' he said astonished at what his friends had done, and especially having the nerve of escaping through a torpedo tube. 'At this end I made sure Jamie got on a plane for home, by the way she sends her love and can't wait to see you both again.'

'How was she feeling Dave?' Jeff said remembering only to well how she looked.

'Not so bad considering, although; I could tell she was in a lot of pain, even though they had pumped loads of drugs into her.'
Harvey then began to reminisce at how he been kidnapped and taken to the same place as Jeff.

'That was a bit of luck, for you two to end up at the same place,' Dave said showing a wiry smile. 'So mates what are we going to do now?'

'We're going back home to the States and as soon as possible,' Jeff stated. 'I'll try and arrange it for the day after tomorrow; in the meantime I think the best thing is to keep our heads down low.'

'Are you going to leave this mess with Tabor to the Russian authorities Jeff? And can you trust them, for they haven't got the best record on earth in catching their thieves,' Dave responded feeling tight at what they had accomplished so far and nearly getting Jamie killed and knowing deep down that when they go back home nothing would happen with Tabor.

Chapter 22

Once on the island of Alert, Mark set about finding shelter for his wife to keep her warm during the night, so she would be fresh and ready for the long hike ahead of them in the morning.

'How far have we got to walk across this rugged country side?' Ann asked, for she was not looking forward to the arduous trek across the barren hills and small creeks.

'I believe we will have to travel at least 20 miles over this bleak land,' Mark said as they trudged on endlessly. 'We'll take a short break so that we can get our bearings, no good wearing ourselves out completely in one go,' he added already feeling exhausted by the few miles they had covered. He was also concerned about his wife, fearing she may not make the journey to the village. So he scanned the countryside ahead of them in the hope he could identify landmarks to follow, but there was nothing but hills and the sound of running water that came from the small streams that oozed from the soggy ground and eventually made their way to the open sea. He sat down on a large rock waiting alarmed for his wife's breathing to subside, and then after a short space of time they started walking, in an attempt to reach shelter before the light faded. Nevertheless, after eight hours of stumbling over rocks and ditches, and on more than one occasion falling down, they at last with great relief spotted a person on a hilltop some way in front of them.

'Are you telling me you were dropped on this coastline by the missing submarine that everybody is searching for and left to fend for yourselves?' The Canadian police officer said having found them and escorting them to his office. He listened intently to their story with some big misgivings as he sat across his desk writing down every word Mark said, making sure he had all the information, before submitting it to his sergeant in Hunavut, which was his head quarters.

He was exceptionally keen to have everything precise, as he looked for any opportunity for promotion, and hoped this may help him get it.

The officer smartly dressed, sat at his desk, which hid his strong slim figure, his dark tanned face that was smooth, while his contrasting white hair revealed his grey-green eyes. His fitness enabled him to tackle all kinds of problems in the area, from bears to people breaking their bones as well as arranging to have them sent to hospital. He was also the local news, as he had made many friends with in the area where he worked.

While Ann tried to sleep, Mark continued trying to describe their adventure over the past weeks.

'Wow, what a story,' the officer announced listening intently to Mark. 'By the way my names Phillip,' he said at length to Mark. 'I can assure you everything will be fine, once my department has verified your story. It shouldn't take very long, before we get the information back; I've made it a priority, so why don't you have a rest, I will give you a call once I hear something.'

'Thank you,' Mark said, but as he made a move towards the room, where Ann was sleeping, the sound of the printer made him twist round.

'Well I will be darned, never in my life did I expect this,' Phillip exclaimed in amazement as he read the paper spewing from the machine that revealed its contents. 'I've read some tales in my time, but this one beats the cake,' he added mystified, that any person could go through such an ordeal as they had.

'Are you telling me you think we are not telling you the truth?' Mark announced above the unexpected noise of the machine and not relishing the thought of being in jail as an illegal immigrant.

'On the contrary Mr Walker, my boss is amazed you have survived at all,' he stated with a huge grin that spread across his face.

'Has he found it's all true?' Ann remarked as she came from the room and hearing the noise of the printer.

'It appears that way, they are astounded you two are still alive and well and that the thugs had let you loose,' Phillip announced with a huge smile that beamed across the room.

'I must confess, I think it's amazing we have made it, what's more we are alive and I hope we can get back home to England. What will happen to us now Phillip? 'For we are penniless and have the only clothes you see.'

'Not to worry Mark, you don't mind me calling you Mark?

'No not at all, that's of course you don't mind me calling you Phillip,' Mark replied with relief.

'Transport is on its way as I speak and will take you to Washington DC, where they will help you to acquire some new clothes. You will meet a Jim Edwards who is head of the CIA and is very keen to speak to you and no doubt will inundate you with many questions about your ordeal. For it is now out of my hands,' he said going over to them to shake them both by the hand and congratulate them at getting into safe hands.

'You are a couple of heroes you know; and the papers are already after you, they have been ringing the department trying to find out about you. Like more coffee?' Phillip said suddenly changing the subject, while putting a pot on the stove and then slumping into his chair with that big grin still on his face. When the phone rang again it made them all jump, for a silence had descended over the office. Picking up the phone the officer listened briefly and then in a quiet voice said. 'Yes sergeant.' He then replaced the receiver back on its cradle and then turning to Mark. 'That's Nunavut police on the line. My sergeant has just mentioned the aircraft that is taking you to Washington is on its way;

211

although; I'm afraid, it won't arrive until tomorrow morning. So in the meantime I've been told to make you as comfortable as possible, so what I suggest we do first is get you some food, and while you're eating I'll contact the local hotel and organize a room for the night,' he said picking up the phone as he spoke to Mark. 'I'll escort you to the hotel in question, where you can have a shower and rest and then in the morning I will fetch you to take you to the plane, additionally I will make sure no reporters disturb you,' The officer said. Ann never heard the officer's comments for she did not entirely follow the conversation but was happy to know they were safe and alive.

The next day as arranged, the plane arrived to take them to Washington as promised and after saying their good-byes; they flew to the capital of America.

'Please be seated,' Jim Edwards said showing them into his office with a warm hearty handshake and patting Mark on the back that instantly put Mark at ease. 'I'm sure it must have been a very terrifying experience for the both of you being confined on that submarine and not knowing what was to become of you.'

'That's an understatement,' Mark said as they approached a soft leather sofa and making themselves comfortable on it, for they were feeling a little apprehensive, as they had never been to Washington before.

'First things first,' Jim began. 'I have organised new documents for the both of you, i.e. passports, travel documents, etc, so you will be able to get home to England without any further hassle. In addition, I have organised for you to purchase some new clothes. An escort will help you round the capital in achieving it; I hope this will soothe some of the pain you have gone through Mrs Walker.

Mark we have a problem I hope you can help us with, that's of course if you don't mind, for we need an insight in that submarine, as we have little information about it. Plus we are having difficulty in locating it, it's been rather elusive to say the least,' Jim remarked.

He crossed the other side of the room and then facing them, he noticed how tired they were looking.

'I'll try to do my best and put you both at ease to alleviate your stress. Would you care for some coffee?' Jim added already pouring the hot liquid into three cups.

'What do you need to know about our ordeal?' Mark replied coming straight to the point, for the sooner the interview was over the quicker they could get back home to England.

'Perhaps you could explain how the submarine was able to be so silent; we have no one as yet to detect it,' Jim exclaimed with a worried frown.

'Well where do you want me to begin?' Mark said rubbing his hand through his greying hair and trying to think of a suitable place to start.

He shuddered at the very thought of being back on board that submarine as he looked at this fellow on the other side of the room, that was asking questions about his experience on the submarine.

'Are you a marine engineer Jim? Mark enquired.

'No I've no such experience in such things, although; I'm a good listener and a very fast learner. Why don't you start, let's say with the diesel motors.'

'Have you a pen and paper as I can draw an outline of them, perhaps you'll understand the running of them a little better,' Mark assured.

Then crossing over to the desk which was at the opposite end of the room, Jim produced a diagram of the submarine from a drawer in his desk, while Ann stayed on the sofa looking forlorn for there

213

was nothing to keep her occupied and didn't want to hear anything, that was related to her ordeal.

A knock on the door, brought the attention to all of them as a woman entered without Jim having asked her to come in.

'Jim, sorry to interrupt you but I have been told a lady in here is in need of rescuing from your clutches, so I thought I'd pop in and see if I can assist with anything.'

Jim introduced his PA secretary Pat to the Walkers, before progressing with his discussion with Mark.

She was a pretty woman in her early fifties, held herself upright, and dressed in a tight navy skirt that hung below her knees and with a light pink blouse, which enhanced her curvy figure that aided her looks and sent a friendly gesture to Ann that she would be pleasant company.

'Yes you can, will you look after Mrs Walker and see she has everything she needs and you know what I mean Pat. Ann, I won't keep your husband very long, I promise.'

'Is that alright by you Mark?' Jim said hoping Mark would agree to his wife going with his secretary and prayed he would not have any further interruptions, well at least until they had finished.

When they left, Mark peered at the diagram on the desk and started to drawer a rough line along the submarines two big engines. He then went into detail telling Jim the way Tabor had installed the equipment; spelling out the design as clearly as possible so Jim was under no elusion to the problem he was facing.

'See the base where the feet of the motor connects to the deck,' Mark said pointing his finger at the place and marking where he wanted Jim to follow. 'They stand on thick plastic coated springs and are attached by huge rubber blocks; this gives the engines some movement and also reduces the noise greatly at the same time. In addition, they enclosed the engines with a soundproof material making them exceptionally quiet, but we did feel some vibration for a time when they started the engines, because they

214

were new and had not bedded in. The drive shaft and bearings ran in a hard plastic case as well and filled with some kind of oil, I did not find out which type. In addition, I could not see what material they made the bearings from, but it made a remarkable improvement to reduce the rumble, therefore reducing unnecessary clatter.

You must understand the sailors in that tub would be very uneasy about any shipping, which may have heard them, so whoever tracks this submarine will have to be extremely good at detecting underwater sounds and distinguishing the difference between submarine and fish. Believe me they have not spared the cost on that boat, I can tell you.

The skipper Krabava is also superb at his job and he's very aware at just how far he can push his crew and his submarine. I know his men will die for him, that's for sure,' Mark uttered looking at Jim for a reaction.

'Yes we have experienced his ability to that. I'm sure you must have gone through hell in that attack.'

Mark made no further comment on the sinking of the frigate and waited for Jim to speak. 'Do you know what his intentions are?'

'Only it's something to do with New York.'

Jim took a pace back away from the desk with his mouth wide open and stunned at what Mark said.

'New York, New York!' he repeated in astonishment. 'How is he going to attack New York?'

'I'm afraid I cannot help you on that, for I have no idea how he intends to do it, he's hell bent on destruction and his aim is to inflict as much suffering as possible on you.

When we left he had at his disposal 14 torpedoes albeit, two of them were nukes. I noticed they had an extensive range; he's prepared for anything you can sling at him and will use whatever force it takes to reach his target, that I can assure you. If your boys take their eyes of the ball he will take them out for sure, as he's anticipating further attacks from your ships at anytime. I repeat he's well and truly ready,' Mark remarked with a stern voice.

'Well that is something to deliberate on,' Jim added and concerned he may release the nukes. 'Do you realise of the consequences, if he's allowed to get away with it. He must have anticipated, you would tell us what he has available to use against us on his boat. I don't understand why he let you two go?'

'You're puzzled, so am I. he didn't even flick an eye lid when one of his own chaps by the name of Pozvizd got shot for fighting on board.'

'Yeah his body was dragged out of the sea by some fishermen. Well that's how he died. Is there anything else you can think of Mark?'

'No I am afraid not, hang on, oh yes, I nearly forgot they still have an English agent on board, unless of course she has been killed by now.'

'One other thing,' Jim added remembering to pull the photos from a top drawer of his desk, where he had kept them for protection. He then handed them over to Mark to view.

'I can identify these guys,' Mark alleged pointing at a photo. These men are Leshin, Krabava, Pushkin, Tabor and Sakhakov and that man there is Schmitt, he is the money behind their scheme, and if you are able to catch him, you may be able to destroy their plans.' Mark concluded giving the photos back to Jim.

I'm sorry I could not be more useful, but if I remember anything further that may be of importance, I won't hesitate to tell you. Oh yes, there was another thing the captain mentioned as he released us, it was that he was going to abort the mission, he didn't enlighten us any further than that. But maybe he was trying to hide his real intent, to divert your ships and aircraft from hunting him in that location.'

'He may have told you that; but we know for sure he's sailed through the Bering straits and replenished his supplies at a place called Penkigney. And now has entered into the North Pacific, after that we lost contact of him again.'

'Do you think he's going to hit one of the west coast cities instead?'

'You could be right, although I think it unlikely, no I reckon he's playing with us and will try to sneak back into the Artic and proceed as before. Whatever he decides to do, we will be waiting for him in the event he tries to go that way. In the meantime, it gives us some time, in trying to identify who this Sakhakov is and his purpose on board. Hopefully it will all fit into place and we can then crush them,' Jim said as a hard knock sounded on the door and stopped them abruptly from any further discussion.

'Come in,' Jim called to the person who had knocked.

'Excuse me sir, I am sorry to interrupt but a message has come in from Jeff Morgan,' the orderly said entering and holding a piece of paper in his left hand to give to Jim.

'What's he up to now?' Jim blurted as if this member of staff would know what was going on in Russia or wherever they were.

'He and his two partners are returning and will be arriving shortly. He stated he is up against a brick wall and as he's receiving not much help from the Russians, as he would have liked, he decided to return. Anyway, he assures he will explain everything to you when he arrives, and he also mentioned the well fair of Jamie and could you confirm she is all right.

'Very good thank you for telling me, I will follow up on Jamie's condition,' Jim acknowledged.

'Another thought,' Mark began after the messenger had gone. Have you considered that Krabava may stay in the Pacific and go south by the cape and head into the Atlantic from there?' Mark claimed by making a calculated guess to what Krabava might do.

'Well that is a thought, you could be right, but why do you think he will try going that way? It's a long journey to take and we would have a better chance of spotting him. And how would he get his supplies and who from?' Jim questioned not knowing the Zhuralev was heading for a secret location.

'Just a hunch Jim that's all. Only this chap Schmitt may possibly have connections in Chilli or even Argentina.'

'I'll better get on to the navy and get someone in that area in case you are right, I will also get in touch with the Chilean authorities and see if they have heard anything to the contrary; I just hope they will cooperate with us. Mark there is another question I need to ask you, would you like to help us a little further?'

Mark eyed Jim with some caution with concern at helping him further.

'What have you got in mind?'

'Well I was wondering if you would like to go with Jeff and sail on board the Panda. It is a Corvette; the skipper is Captain Frank Johnson, he was the captain in charge of the ship that Krabava sank,' Jim announced expecting the worse and ready for a no answer.

'I can't say I would like it, I'll have to think about it a little and mention it to Ann. I know she won't be very happy about it. Anyway what would you want me to do on board the ship, and how about my wife what would she do here?'

'I'll make sure she's taken very good care of. She can stay at my house with my wife Mary. Mary will love to look after her and see she gets everything she needs; you will not have to worry about a thing.'

'Fine so how about the Corvette of yours?'

'Its one of our best new ships, you will not even know you are on board a warship, and before you ask, Jeff is one of our best agents, but do not tell him that I said so, as he is likely to get big headed. He has been following your progress along with us; he's a good man that's for sure, and I'm confidant you two will get on well together, so what do you say?'

Mark went back to the soft seat of the sofa and slumped down on it to think about what he had to offer, he would certainly like to cut even with Krabava for holding them against their will.

'Got any brandy on that Corvette?'

'I'll see to it you'll get the best,' Jim said smiling at Mark and taking he was offering his help.

Chapter 23

Late that evening the Zhuralev slipped her moorings, shifted into the bay, and made for the deep blue waters of the Pacific Ocean. It was a dark night although the stars shone in the black moonless sky. The skipper had decided to sail on the surface, for it was very calm and milky, he knew he could make much better headway on the surface and could cover many miles before daylight, as he was aware his enemies would be after him as soon as they realised which direction he had gone.

Since they had left Penkigney two days earlier, everybody now had adjusted to the routine of sailing the boat, following the heavy party on land, but now they concentrated on what lie before them.

The weather forecast continued to show it would stay clear and bright as they headed on a southerly direction. Krabava was glad, as it would relieve the stress of his crew with the many miles they had to travel before their next stop; for he feared, it would be a very repetitive journey.

Charley decided she would keep herself amused passing the time chatting to her guards. The sailors knew of her predicament and had some sympathy for her, but could do nothing to relieve her constant worry

'What do I call you my ship mate,' she said soothingly expressing her amusement at the quandary the crewman found himself.'

'I'm Valja. And my age is twenty six,' he volunteered wanting to speak to her, as much as she did him.

'Are you married Valja?'

'Yes I am and miss her very much, and would like to be back home with her,' he said soberly.

'You really think you'll get back then? I'm sorry but I don't have your confidence,' she stated kindly, not meaning to put him on edge more then was necessary, but she was aware she had hit a sore point. 'How did you get on this tug then Valja?'

'Once I had completed my service in the navy,' he began nervously to say twiddling with his fingers and showing her how on edge he was. 'I had nothing, and no job to go to when I saw this job advertised. Of course, I jumped at it for the money was very attractive and I need to help my Mother and farther as well as my wife, for you see, we're living with my parents. Well at least until I return, then I'll be able to get our own home with the cash I make from this trip.' He began to speak more freely now about his circumstances as if he needed to tell all the world of his problems.

'Did you have to go for an interview for this job Valja?' Charley pressed him.

'Oh yes, they seemed to be very impressed with me with what at having served quite a few years on submarines.'

'Who interviewed you, Krabava?'

'Yes he was one of three, Krabava, Captain Pushkin and the third bloke, let me see what was his name, oh yes I remember Tabor, yes that's his name Tabor. He was a sleek and extremely well spoken man, dressed very smart as well.'

'Do you realise Valja they would expect you to die for their course.'

'Yes I know, we all have to take a gamble at sometime in our life, and I recognise only to well that we have to work hard, if you want to get on. You must remember also that in my country we were suppressed for years.'

Charley was about to add further but Krabava entered the compartment with Sakhakov.

'You must excuse me,' the captain said being unusually polite and bringing Valja instantly to his feet by Charley and in front of his skipper.

'Valja take a rest, as Sakhakov will relieve you here, but before you take a rest, look at the batteries, it appears they are not performing as they should, check them and keep me informed,' Krabava said ending the conversation abruptly to him.

'Yes sir, right away sir,' he said saluting his skipper and departing smartly from the room.

'You know Mr Sakhakov. He will divert your mind to better things, for I expect you must be fed up with hearing Valja and his troubles,' Krabava said showing no concern to the seaman and any disruption he may have caused and then he quickly retired leaving her alone with Sakhakov.

'Oh well I suppose I will have to start all over again,' she added to Sakhakov.

'Where do you come from?' she said feeling uncomfortable with this associate of the skippers, for he did not seem to have the same sense of humour as the other members of the boat. Before he could utter a word, she heard an almighty upheaval coming from further down the boat, followed by all hell braking loose, with men shouting orders aloud. Then some of the sailors started running through the narrow compartments closing the watertight doors behind.

She then smelt burning plastic and rubber that hung heavily throughout the boats narrow passageway.

'What the hells going on?' she called anxiously to someone who would tell her what was happening.

Then the worst possible thing happened on the tiny boat, which frightened everybody. The power suddenly failed and plunged them into pitch-darkness. Unable to see at a hands length, she began to panic even more when the humming of the engines stopped, the only thing she could hear and make out was the men screaming for torches, and showing signs of distraught, she turned to face Sakhakov in the darkness and asked.

'Can you please tell me, if this is some kind of joke? For if it is I am not at all amused.'

'No it is not an exercise or a joke, but do not be alarmed they will have it fixed in no time at all,' he said in the darkness of the compartment.

She began to shiver, not of the cold, but the very thought of being alone in the same room with this foreigner, who she did not know and it made her nervous with what he might do to her.

She heard the door open to reveal Kazan who was holding a flashlight in his right hand. Its bright beam of light blinded her as he shone it around the room and fixed it on them.

'Take this torch as we have plenty. I'm afraid we have developed a slight problem with electrics but we'll soon have it restored,' he said leaving the torch with them and then quickly disappeared into the darkness to attend to the fault.

She felt the motion of the boat slowly rocking from one side to the other, as the current caught the boat drifting helpless towards the oceans bottom.

'I ask again, can you tell me what's taking place?' She said contemptuously asking her new roommate Sakhakov more sternly.

Sakhakov rose to his feet without saying a word and probing the darkness he made his way to the door, steadying himself against the wall he went into the gangway. She heard him call to one of the crew, although not hearing the conversation but feared it was not good news. After a few moments, he returned and sat down beside her and quietly whispered.

'My dear you must not be frightened, as the engineers are trying to fix the problem and are doing their hardest to find the fault. They are trying everything to ascertain how the system died and getting it restored again. It seems we have lost power on everything on board, but I repeat do not worry, they will find out what it is and have it fixed in no time at all.'

Krabava stood in the dark control room with his thoughts, thinking once again they may have been sabotaged, but at present there was no way he could even begin to find out, if it was an attempt too disrupt his campaign of vengeance.

As the boat lay helplessly sinking in the deep Oceans depths with nothing to prevent it, the skipper thought he was in a precarious situation with the loss of power, for also affected was the air circulation system that cleaned the stale air and critical to their survival.

'What's going to happen to us?' Charley questioned once more sitting in the pitch-black with Sakhakov.

'We will be ok Charley; you don't mind me calling you Charley do you?' She heard him say but still ignored his question with calling her by name. 'Ok Charley I will be candid with you, if they don't fix what has happened and soon, we'll sink to the bottom of the ocean, that's of course if we reach the bottom, for we may be crushed by the extreme pressure of water that will be put upon the boat. Then if we manage to reach the bottom and still cannot fix the trouble, the air will become stale, which as you can guess, will affect our breathing. It will be difficult at first and then become harder with the increase off carbon monoxide as it slowly poisons you. You will become sleepy at first until ultimately you die.

'Have you got any good news to report and how do you know it can be repaired, or are you just trying to pacify me Mr Sakhakov and what are the chances of our surviving or more to the point how long before we perish?

'We will be fine, trust me I'm sure of it.' He said hoping for all their sakes that they would be right.

Do you know anyone on this submarine who wants to die anymore than you,' he said politely, while pulling a blanket from the bed to cover her.

'It may take sometime, so we'll better stay still as not to consume up unnecessarily air, it will be uncomfortable for a while but be rest assured we won't suffocate, I'm convinced of it.'

'This boats a load of junk and I wish to god I could get off it,' she uttered. 'Sakhakov is that what you are called?' she said.

'Yes it is and I'm extremely glad to be here with you at this moment to help you,' he said smelling the fragrance of her perfume and the warmth of her body as he cuddled closer to her.

Then abruptly as someone had turned off the lights, they came back on, flickering on and off a couple of times, before staying on and settling down to a dull glow. Then at last, she heard the motors starting to hum again.

Krabava moved from the chart-table to the bank of dials that showed their depth of 800 feet, and with a grim face he tapped the gauge, to see if it was reading correctly, noticing the needle hover a few times before finally coming to a rest he returned back to his charts.

'Well that's extremely lucky.' He murmured softly to nobody in particular in the compartment. Then swiftly facing Kazan who was watching every move he made, he said. 'We have reached a depth of 800 feet it's not as bad as I expected, for this boat can go deeper. Then reacting fast, he called for the boat to surface.

Life on board the boat became a buzz as the crew resumed their duties now they were back on the move, and they were in a jubilant mood for fixing the problem so quickly and securing the crisis they had encountered earlier.

They started to rise slowly towards the surface, so as not to disturb water as they breached the waves.

Krabava as always, checked everything was clear of any intending prey that would be trying to seek them before finally letting any crewmember on deck. Once satisfied he gave the order for the lookouts to go up and then for his officers to follow.

The boat handled sluggishly as it drifted on the surface, the waves creating a steady rhythm as they rolled with the motion of the sea.

'Open the hatch covers and secure a post at each of them,' the skipper ordered as he went out into the conning tower.

Once on deck he leaned against the bulkhead and sucked in gulps of fresh air, to relieve the stress flowing within him. He then motioned to Sakhakov, to bring the girl on deck for her to get some fresh clean air.

'Mianlia, organise a roster for the men to come up and inform Valja I wish to speak to him, ask him to report right away.

'Yes Sir,' Mianlia said departing swiftly down the hatch.

'You need me,' Valja asked rapidly arriving on deck as ordered.

'Yes I want to know exactly what happen with this latest break down,' he said unsympathetically to Valja.

'Well the main cable from the batteries and relays had been severed.'

'How was it done deliberately and how come you did you not notice it before?' The Skipper hissed with venom in his voice for he was fuming with another annoying stoppage.

'As far as I can tell, the problem lies with the cables, as they are weak and not up to the job, for when they were installed during the refit, I fear someone or even the contractor had tried to cut corners to make extra money. No one could have notice the cables as they are fixed under the floor, so I believe the contractor or whoever assumed they would be safe and not be found out. There was a device attached to the negative lead; I think the idea was for it to operate when we dived below 500 feet.'

'So you are saying this was sabotage?'

'Both captain.'

'I have not had the time to examine the device but it seems likely it would operate on pressure, the deeper you go it switches on to create a short circuit across both the positive and negative terminals. It was a brilliant idea for the person who installed it, for he or she need not have been on board when it operated.'

'Jesus Christ! Whoever did it must be determined to have us killed? So we will have to find out who the perpetrator or perpetrators is and catch them before another attempt is made on us,' Krabava said looking at Valja astounded at what the consequences could have been for them all.

'Yes I agree sir, but who do we start with.'

'Let me deal with that Valja, the question is what can we do to stop this happening again?' The captain said looking out to sea, as if it would give him the answer.

'I'll have to check the entire cables for fear of other parts of wiring on this boat could also be at risk.'

'Really, that puts me in a dilemma as to what action to take; can you determine how bad the other cables are?'

'Not without ripping up all the decking and tracing the wiring.'

'How long will it take?'

'Sorry sir, as yet I cannot tell you that either, I will need plenty of help in doing it and even then there's no guarantee.'

'Very well do what you can, but do not leave the boat compromised for we may have to dive in a big hurry,' he said motioning Valja to get started on the work.

As Charley lay basking on the submarines deck recuperating from the warm rays of the sun, she recapped what could have been a disaster. She listened to the gentle slapping of the waves on the hull, and the slight dull throb of the engines as they now began to move steadily along in a southerly direction. It lulled her into a false sense of security as she gazed at the beautiful blue clear sky, with not a cloud hindering the splendour of the day. She at first thought she heard a small plane droning from their starboard side and then reality came back to her like a bullet scything through her brain, she suddenly realised where she was and that she had heard an aircraft high in the sky, heading she presumed for land and freedom. She glanced towards the conning tower to observe the skipper and wondered whether he had noticed, but unknown to her he had already spotted the aeroplane.

'What do you think skip? Mianlia stated joining him on deck and seeing the craft as it flew high above them. 'Do you think it has spotted us,' making his own observation as to where it may be going.

'We're some two hundred miles from shore; all the same he may put in a radio message to have us checked, that of course if he has seen us. I would hazard a guest it would take a few hours before any ship would be able to get here to explore us and find out who we are. They may send a fighter plane, especially if the plane gives our description,' Krabava said with a worried look drifting over his face, for he did not want to return to the depths as the repairs had not been completed. 'We'll give it another hour and then take her down unless I'm wrong, which we'll be in trouble,' he murmured and then called down the hatch opening to the control room, to see how things were progressing and if they had seen anything on the radar.

For the next hour he would feel very vulnerable on the surface, so he waited for another half an hour running at full power before asking Valja again what progress was being made and could he dive safely, reasoning he would be a lot safer under the waves than on the top.

'I'm afraid you have to go below as we need to dive again,' Kazan said to Charley as he approached her lying on the deck.'

Unhappy about going below, for she would miss the lovely sunshine and would very soon become bored again in the enclosed space of the compartment, but reluctant to go, she did as ordered and slowly getting up she made her way to the hatch and descended below deck.

After 24 hours had passed and without a sighting of any craft, Krabava was beginning to think perhaps the plane had never sent a message about them, but then a call came from Andrei who was reading the radar.

'Target bearing 30.76° south and 86.62° west at 75 miles distance. I'm not able to identify target as yet sir,' he said calmly.

'When do you expect the vessel to be in range?' Krabava asked.

'I estimate about 3 and a half hours sir.'

Krabava began pacing round the conning tower trying to think what action he should take, but his thoughts became interrupted yet again.

'Two more targets on same location and coming in our direction,' Andrei's voice echoed, loud and clear over the speaker but still showing no effect of nerves.

'Very well, we'll have to dive.' He mentioned to Mianlia who was peering through the telescope in the direction of the ships. 'Clear the bridge, helm dive and take the boat down to 250 feet,' Krabava shouted.

Once again, they had to endure the noise of the ballast tanks and to adjust their hearing, as the ships worked their way towards them.

The three ships circled the area where Krabava dived and began carrying on avertedly with their work to seek them.

'Take her deeper, to 800 feet.'

The bow planes turned at the hands of the helmsman, which sent the boat racing for the oceans depths. Mianlia held on to whatever he could, as the boat sank racing for the deep waters. He saw his skipper's stern face with beads of sweat running from his forehead, he forced a glance round the control room to see his fellow men, but decided to keep his thoughts to himself, for he was not convinced going deeper was the answer to avoid the warships.

'Stop engines, rig for silent running,' Krabava commanded through the microphone.

All became still, as the boat levelled at the given depth in that quiet ocean and with the crew waiting for what imagined to be the inevitable sounds of explosions, but nothing happened as the three

229

ships circled the area. They continued for several hours trying desperately to seek them but were unable to establish any contact, so without any results they gradually moved further away to a new location and to perform the same exercise. Still again, to no avail, until eventually they gave up the search and left the area.

More days unrelentingly dragged by, and still she could not understand where they were actually heading, although she remembered Leshin mentioning New York at the time of her capture, but that was ages ago and they now had been in the pacific for days. She became in the doldrums with nothing to do, even though she volunteered to help in the galley or elsewhere on the boat, but the skipper always refused her to do anything. So the long days and nights, which she could not detect whether it was day or night dragged on. After reading endless books and having exhausted them all, she lay on her bunk restless to the fact no one now trusted her.

'Any ideas where we are?' she at length asked Sakhakov one day trying to make conversation with him, for he had been the only one who would talk to her and be helpful.

'I estimate we are about 500 miles from the cape; I am led to believe we are to meet with the Oban again for provisions?'

'The Oban, I thought that vessel was out of commission and impounded in Severomorsk docks?'

'It was, but once they had discharged its cargo it was released to carry on doing its business, for Pushkin who owned and ran the ship had convinced the authorities any wrong doing with Tabor. So as the authorities could not connect him he was able to carry on sailing, mind you they had no idea where it went.

If you're beginning to think, we are going to meet it, the answer is yes and I calculate it would be in about 33 hours. I will of course make sure you have a shower on board her, so you can freshen up, that is of course if you wish, as it will take a little time for our stores to be loaded.' Sakhakov said, then left as Valja entered again to replace him temporary.

When he sat down beside her he helped to make her feel more comfortable than Sakhakov had done, although she could not understand why it affected her feelings.

'Valja did you know Sakhakov, before you joined the boat?'

'Sakhakov, oh no I never saw him, come to that I didn't know most of the crew until we got together and started training, why do you ask my dear?'

'He's been asking a lot of strange questions and I feel a bit uneasy at what he's asking me.'

'Like what kind of questions?' Valja asked her wondering just where this type of talk was leading.'

'Well first of all he asked me about my mother and father and did they live in London. Why would he want to know that?'

'I really have no idea Charley; perhaps it was just idle chat to make you feel better after what had taken place during the last few weeks.'

'That's as maybe but I have a very uncomfortable feeling to what his motives maybe. Is there anyway you can find out what he's up to Valja.'

'I will try but don't hold your breath as it may be nothing at all, I would not get so concerned about it Charley.'

Dropping the subject, she sat back on her bunk in silence once more and listened to the sounds coming from around the submarine. She knew the boat had surfaced for she had adjusted to the movements it made, as it moved through the water, for the boat rolled with the waves listing from one side to the other, although; not in anyway making it uncomfortable for those on board.

They opened all the hatch covers to allow the cool fresh air of the morning to circulate through the boat and replace the stale smelly pungent air.

'Do you want to go on board the Oban to clean up?' Sakhakov called down to her. Despite the fact she did not relish going on the ship with more of Tabors thugs, she surrendered to the thought of getting clean, for it would be heaven to have fresh warm water running down her body again to take away the pain and torment from her metal prison, she made a move to board the Oban.

'Krabava what was the result with that last incident you had, did you find out how it happened?' Tabor asked as they sat round the small polished wooden table in the boardroom of the Oban. Schmitt and Pushkin the skipper of the Oban sat at each end of the table, while Krabava and Sakhakov sat directly opposite Tabor.

'Yes I have ideas to who may be responsible, Krabava acknowledged.'

'So what do you propose to do about it?'

'I think that will be up to you as Valja claims the contractors are partly responsible for they went short on the right materials.'

'Is that so, is he sure about it for I don't want to go blaming anyone who could be innocent?'

'I'm surprised Tabor you even think like that, I would have sworn you would kill whoever it was responsible straight away,' Pushkin added with a sly dig at him.

'Valja would not make that mistake; he has checked the circuits thoroughly.'

'You can't trust anyone these days; ok I'll follow it up. What else is there to report?'

'As I said, we know who the saboteur is so Mianlia and myself are going to set a trap once we arrive at Puerto Harberton, so he will not be able to destroy the boat and our mission, that I can promise you; there will be no more mishaps,' Krabava fumed with a hostile voice.

'That's good to hear, for we are way behind on our schedule, so what else is there to report. Oh yes Sakhakov, what about you and that girl, have you got your affairs in order yet?' Tabor asked staring at him with cold unruffled body language.

'I'm going to tell her before we dock, she can then decide what she wants to do, whether she wants to stay with me or return to her mother in England.'

'Well make sure you get it sorted, as we do not want anymore snags in that direction, now that we are getting close to our target,' Tabor said glaring at Sakhakov with wild looking eyes that made it obvious what he had to do.

'There'll be no more problems on board, be re-assured of that,' Krabava added intercepting the conversation between the two of them. 'Ok back to the other business, have you entertainment arranged for my crew when we dock. I want them rested and if they see I'm looking after them, they will work harder without questioning my orders, moreover they have earned it,' Krabava said.

'Yes it's all been arranged, everyone will be paid and will not want for anything,' Schmitt added since they had sat down round the table. 'Incidentally, I won't be with you on the remainder of your journey as I need to go to Switzerland, to re-adjust our assets for the future,' Schmitt said but not going into any detail as to what the plans would be for the future.

'Very well, I must admit I can't say the crew will miss you,' Krabava commented with a smile and now knowing he would not have to look at him again for sometime.

'If any of you have anything to add to our project, say so now. Ok, right we can now eat and take it easy for a while,' Tabor managed to say in a calm voice and ringing a bell to alert the waiters.

'I will check to see how the loadings taking place on board the boat and then we'll be on our way,' Krabava stated once they had their fill of fresh food and along with Sakhakov they stood up to go, when Krabava looked at Tabor and said in a low voice. 'I look forward to our meeting at our prearranged location that you suggested.' Krabava then turned to leave but stopped when Tabor called to him.

'First before you leave we must toast to our success. To hell with the evil Americans and what they did to our people, for it's now pay-back time,' Tabor hissed between clenched teeth, and then holding his glass high he clinked his glass against theirs before drinking the liquid.

Once the formalities were, completed Krabava along with Sakhakov departed company and left the Oban to set sail. Gathering speed to put as much distance between them, they headed for the cape and beyond. The Oban proceeded on a northerly course while the Zhuralev made for the Beagle Channel and Puerto-Harberton, where they intended to rest for a few nights and party, before continuing onto the last leg of their journey.

Sakhakov knew that this part of the journey would be the only time he would have to mention to his daughter about his circumstances.

'Now tell me have you some good news?' Charley said with frustration once again as Sakhakov entered her compartment.

'On the contrary my dear I have plenty of news for you, only what I have to say you might find it hard to except.'

'What could you add that hasn't been said before?' she said with scorn that cut the air with a knife.

'Please be patient and take a seat, I think you will need to brace yourself, for I feel it will come as a huge shock to you.' He paused before continuing, allowing time for her to except what he was about to say, he also knew it was going to be hard to explain everything to her. He would have preferred a better location than the confines of the submarine and its conditions.

'You see,' he began then hesitated once more. 'I don't know how to put this to you, so I will come straight to the point,' pausing yet again before speaking. 'Charley you are my daughter,' he finally spat out, as if it would make it easier for her to understand. 'Your real name is Svetlana. Well I have told you now and it is the reason I have had you stay on board for so long. I have been trying to find the right moment to tell you, but it's been impossible what with all that has happened over the past few weeks.'

She stared blankly open mouthed at him, as if he had gone raving mad and in utter disbelief to what he had just stated.

'You must be insane, how dare you suggest I am part of you,' she added with a growl that cut through the atmosphere like a knife.

'I can prove it,' Sakhakov said pulling out some photographs from a brief case, which consisted of her as a young child.

At first, he showed a picture with her mother holding her in her arms, while a good-looking sailor was standing by watching them. They were smiling as they sat on the riverbank close to a destroyed road bridge. Across the other side of the river, a church dome was clearly visible in the distance and stood high above some trees.

Mystified, bewildered, and stunned all at once for she could not take her eyes away from the photos before her. Minutes past without her saying a word and then at long last she lifted her eyes to focus on him, albeit still not attempting to speak, for she was in total disarray and could not utter a sound even with her mouth wide open. She sat mulling over the photos, first looking at one then another; then she closed her eyes trying to soak up this unbelievable information.

'I think I can remember a little, I believe I was five years old. But I still don't understand,' she said finally speaking softy, for she could not speak aloud, even if she wanted too.

'Let me help you a bit more,' he came closer to her and sat down beside her. 'Briefly I thought your mother and I were very much in love, when we met in St Petersburg. We lived there for a while and then when you came along we moved to a village called Volzhskiy, where I purchased a house on the Volga. It is a lovely place. Then after four years of living there, I went into the national service as a conscript, where I entered the navy. It was about 9 months later when she must have decided to take off with you for some unknown reason and without a word. I was guttered and desperate and could do nothing to stop her from taking you. I got compassionate leave to see where she had disappeared; I discovered she had taken you out of the country. I cried for hours unable to follow you and bring you back. I was out of my mind and then later I found you went to England, evidently she had waited for the opportunity to take you,' Sakhakov said closing his eyes and picturing the time it had taken place.

'You keep saying my mother but not your wife.'

'That is correct, for we never did get married, for one thing she was English and I'm a Russian, the authorities would not authorize it, well not at that time.'

'So how about Dennis, is he not your son and my brother?' she asked.

'No he's not, I never knew he existed, even to this day I haven't found out who his real father was. I thought perhaps your mother may have explained everything to you, but that does not seem to be the case.'

'So why did you have Dennis killed is it because he would tell the authorities about this escapade of yours?

'I cannot say sorry enough for his death Charley. I had no idea until Pozvizd spouted he had killed him. I was glad I had the chance to kill Pozvizd when he was on the boat and when he had the fight with that sailor, for it gave me the opportunity I was looking for. I wasn't sorry for him, I was glad in fact.'

Charley once again closed her eyes, as if she was living a nightmare and hoped when she opened them the nightmare would have vanished and everything had returned to be normal, but it was not so, as nothing had changed.

'Will you please leave me on my own?' She said with tears forming in the corner of her eyes and then they started to flow in thin streaks down her cheeks. Desperately trying to stop her body from shaking in front of Sakhakov, as he looked at her for she did not want him to get close to her, for fearing she may give him the wrong signs that she maybe forgiving him for what he was doing on board the boat. Instead, without saying a word he backed away and left her to contemplate her newfound news.

It was incredible news Charley reasoned as she lay on her bunk and mortified by the fact that this man had been with her for weeks and had now just informed her he was her true father and had the photos to testify it. Surely, she thought they did not lie, for what other reason had he to tell her of this astounding information. However, her feelings remained with her mother even though she no longer lived with her, as she had moved from her mother's country cottage into a flat in West Kensington, London.

Even to this day, her mother had not said a word about the circumstances about where she had been born and lived for the first 5 years of her life.

Her problem now was what should she do? Remembering the man who has stated to be her father, was prepared to kill thousands of people, and for what? She must have fallen to sleep thinking constantly at nothing else, for she suddenly woke to the noise of the crew trudging by her room.

'We are going into town,' Valja said popping his head into her compartment and telling her they had reached Harberton. 'Are you ok?' He asked noticing she had been crying, as the tears had left streaks down her face and then realising Sakhakov must have told her about being her father.

'Valja you go, have some fun, I'll still be here when you return,' she said in a light-heartedly way as she heard the crew leaving the boat and to jump into the trucks that were waiting for them. Once they were on board the trucks, and leaving a few sailors on board the submarine to get it ready for sea again, they drove a short distance towards a small town singing joyfully aloud.

Stillness descended through out the submarine as she sat alone, hearing the metal bulkheads creaking as they settled.

She considered if her father was going to join her or if he had departed with the crew, but hoped inwardly he would appear to tell her what was going to happen in the future.

'Can I come in and join you?' Sakhakov asked peering through the doorway at her somewhat gingerly. 'Do you need anything?' He asked very nervously to what her reply might be. Having no idea to the fact she would accept him or completely shut him out of his life, which he dreaded.

'I'm fine apart from staying in this place, what is going to happen to me now? Surely you have some idea to what you've got in store for me, now that you have told me who you are,' she uttered demoralized by everything that had taken place, and now not caring for the future.

'You have to stay here for a while longer I'm afraid, as Tabor expects you to go running to the authorities. When we have decided what we are going to do and make sure you're not implicated with the project, we can then discuss where and what to do.' However, before she could reply to what he further had to say, they suddenly heard the voice of Krabava speaking harshly.

'Put the radio hand set down,' Krabava ordered Andrei who was sitting at the radio. He spun round rapidly to Krabava's voice and found he was looking directly down the barrel of a gun, that Mianlia menacingly held pointing it unswervingly at his head.

'Did you really think we would not eventually find out what you've been up to with sabotaging this boat, it was just a matter of time,' the skipper added, his words cracking like a whip in the still quietness of the compartment and echoing throughout the control room. 'I'm sorry to say my friend it's all over for you, as you are a traitor and have to be punished for what you have been doing. I must admit though, tampering with the compass was a masterpiece although a pity for you, it worked to our advantage for instead of heading further South into the North Atlantic and closer to the American war ships, we steered North towards the Artic. Then you tried to destroy the boat with that device of yours by cutting the battery leads. I don't understand how you managed it, but that's all in the past now. So stand and make your way to the hatch. Remember no sudden moves, as Mianlia will not hesitate to shoot you where you stand.'

'So why don't you do it here? You killed Pozvizd quickly enough, do you think it would be better to kill me on deck, or is it you just don't want a mess in here Krabava,' Andrei said as his brain began working in overdrive in finding a solution, to how he could get out of the circumstance he now found himself. For once on deck, they would certainly kill him.

'Come on move it,' Mianlia screamed.

Reluctantly Andrei got slowly from his seat and unhurriedly made his way towards the iron ladder and hatch cover that led to the deck above. Making is way to the ladder his brain raced at a rapid pace thinking how he could stay alive. On arriving at the bottom rung, he paused and looked up through the opening hoping to see the blue sky, but instead he saw Yuri peering down at him with an evil grin and aiming a revolver directly at him in his right hand.

These guys, Andrei thought was taking no chances as it seemed impossible for him to escape. So slowly, he moved on the first rung of the ladder and with deliberation, he carried on upwards breathing deeply as he went to accept his destiny. He knew the risks when he volunteered, as an agent for the Russian secret service was aware that he could be killed; and now he had been caught he waited for the inevitable to happen to him.

'Keep him well covered,' Mianlia called up the ladder to Yuri and seeing him straddling with both legs over the hole waving his gun at Andrei. 'He may try something, so be careful,' Mianlia said noticing Yuri moving his feet from the exit for Andrei to climb out on deck, but also acknowledging Mianlia at the same time. But as

Yuri looked passed Andrei towards Mianlia as he climbed out of the opening, Andrei saw his only chance for freedom and lunged for the gun, knocking it from his opponent's hand. It fell through the hatch opening and hit Mianlia on the head and stunned him, which made him release his hold on the rung, he then fell back into the control room below crashing to the floor and falling on Krabava who was in turn waiting to go up.

Andrei taking the initiative crashed a hard right fist to Yuri's chin, which made him loose his balance and then striking him with another solid punch, only this time Yuri fell across the hatch cover and partly blocked it. Andrei stole a quick glance at him and noticed he was dazed by the blow he had received, he did not waste any further valuable time and took to his heels at high-speed, jumping from the boat on to dry land he fled for the near by trees.

Mianlia groggily got to his feet and staggered for the ladder, this time he climbed to the top, but found he had to move Yuri from the exit, as he was unable to get on deck.

Yuri dazed by the unexpected attack on him soon restored his composure; and unsteadily getting to his feet, he ran for the trees behind Mianlia in an attempt to catch Andrei.

In a blinding rage, Andrei fled for his life. Smashing through the woods and undergrowth with the branches tearing at his clothes and slashing his face and arms. The sweat mixed with his blood as it ran down his cheeks, into his mouth and hindered his breathing as he desperately scrambled for freedom. Fatigue began to affect his legs as they became weaker by the extreme exertion as he stumbled on and on to get away from his pursuers and then at last he broke from the woods to enter a clearing near the waters edge. In a fraught attempt, he looked round for a place he could hide from those who wished him dead. He could now hear his pursuers approaching fast as they got closer and closer and so starting to panic and not knowing which way to turn, he accidentally stumbled on a suitable concealment along the riverbank. Wading into the water carefully so as not to disturb the sediment that would give his new position away, he squeezed through a small hole above the water line at the base of the tree and clambered inside to wait for what he thought, might be the predictable outcome.

His breathing became hard and with the loud pounding from his heart, he was sure they would hear him as they closed in on the area. His body taught as the sound of footsteps came close to his hiding place, nearer and nearer they moved around the area, pushing at the undergrowth and hammering the ground in a frantic endeavour to discover him.

He started perspiring profusely with the sweat running from his forehead down onto his cheeks and into his mouth. Wanting to sneeze but in a frantic bid he fended off the urge, sensing the anger in his enemy's movements as they thrashed past his hiding position. Andrei tried bitterly to control his already overwrought breathing as he listened to their raised voices, shouting at each other as they moved slowly away from his location.

Finally, it became quiet and motionless, relaxing a little he stayed in the hollow for several more hours in the fear they may possibly be nearby and waiting for him to appear.

'Captain I'm afraid we've lost him,' Mianlia stated.

'What do you mean you lost him? He couldn't have got very far away?' Krabava stated when hearing the news.

'He just vanished, one moment we had him in our sights and the next he disappeared,' Yuri acknowledged helping Mianlia out of the situation seeing his captain was mad at them for letting it happen. 'I'm sorry captain it was my fault, I let him get the better of me when he emerged from the entrance.'

'Don't concern yourselves now, just get on board and prepare to sail, as I've called the crew back. I'll have to assume Andrei will find help very soon and give us away so we need to be underway and fast,' the skipper added with a concern tone in his voice.

'What's all the commotion?' Charley asked as the sailors started to arrive back.

'It's not for you to get alarmed about, it's just that we have discovered the spy and he got away from us, so now we have to set sail,' Mianlia said.

As the last sailor made his way on board the submarine, Krabava had already ordered the release of the guy-ropes, so they were able to get underway. As they moved along the channel towards the open sea in the late afternoon, the lookouts searched the horizon for any possible sightings of any approaching boats.

'Captain a fast boat on the port bow approaching,' one of the lookouts shouted from his position.

'Action stations, gun crew stand by.' Two machine gunners smartly positioned themselves at the ready on the conning tower, as well as another two sailors did with the main cannon on the forward deck.

As the patrol boat got within shouting distance, Krabava ordered his gunners to be ready to fire.

'Ahoy there on the submarine, heave too and identify yourself. We are the Argentine navy,' the commander of the small boat called to Krabava.

'Hold your fire, but line up on the target,' Krabava said to his gunners who stood at the ready to operate the big gun.

'Captain we again ask you to stop,' the leading officer on the patrol boat said but this time more harshly.

'We are unable to heed to your request and if you persist in following us I cannot be responsible for what may occur, so you on the patrol boat we'll be on our way and nothing untoward will take place here today,' Krabava announced in a firm voice.

'Skipper on the submarine, I insist you stop. You are in infringement of our territory and must comply with my command.'

'I'm very sorry commander, you must give us some distance and all will be well,' Krabava repeated. 'Stand by to open fire, gunners ready to put a round across their bow. Fire---!'

The loud bang from the decks gun shattered the still air and echoed across the muddy water, bouncing from one hill to another hill that sent birds flying high into the sky in fright. The spent cartridge flew out of the breech of the gun and clattered on the deck as the shell whistled high above, racing over the bow of the small vessel and exploding on its far side in a big plume of water that rose high to reach the blue clear sky. It was adequate, for the Argentine, craft was no match for the submarines arsenal and turned to speed away in the opposite direction, to get away from the submarines guns. But as they started to widen the gap between them and with Krabava in no mood with the officer, for he knew they would report him to the Argentine navy, he would then have to engage them in a fight he could not afford.

'Sink them!' The skipper roared.

More shots rang from the submarine's huge gun but this time far more accurately, hitting the patrol boat on its stern, causing it to come abruptly to a halt. Smoke billowed from its superstructure as several more shells hit the boat, an explosion inside sent fragments of wood and metal flying into the air and then all at once, the boat rolled over and started to sink. The crew frightened at not wanting to go down with the boat, jumped into the water in a bid to flee the flames and the prospect of dying.

The machine gunners from the submarine fired again, this time spraying bullets at the men who tried to escape. Blood mixed with the oil began spreading over a large area of the surface around the stricken vessel and bodies, as they lay floating on the river.

'It appears we've finished them off,' Mianlia said satisfied his gunners had done a good job.

'Ok take her down,' the call came from the captain once they had reached the open sea and had verified the depth below their hull.

'All below,' Mianlia repeated. 'Steer 0100E, take her down to 550 feet,' he continued to say as the crew responded as one in a jubilant mood of their kill, and now unrelenting they journeyed towards the last leg of the trip as they could see the end in sight.

Back in the room where Charley stayed with Sakhakov during the attack, she witnessed his expression as they both heard the sounds of gunfire, pertaining to the killing of the men from the patrol boat.

'Don't you have any guilt about who you kill? It's amazing and with such vigour you complete the destruction in such short time, I can hardly believe it,' she said astounded at the speed it had taken place and staggered at how effective they had been.

'If someone had told me about this, I would have thought it was all from a fiction book.'

'As I have said before, I am not responsible for what Krabava does, I cannot control him. He is what he is, brutal I admit, however; he thinks it is for the better,' Sakhakov responded in a low pitch but also knew, whatever he would say, could not alter the horrible destruction of life which had taken place; not only that she knew further death and destruction would eventually follow, if they carried on with this madness.

For the last affray would do him no good to their relationship which he desperately wanted to improve.

'I cannot imagine the destruction Krabava has achieved makes everything right. It certainly won't bring back his wife and child, or the life he once had, if that's what he's hoping for,' she said to Sakhakov feeling the submarine turning direction once again and guessing they now were heading on a northerly direction along the South American coastline for the last leg of their journey.

Soon they would take on the deadly action, that of course if they are not discovered and destroyed on route, which was possible for the closer they got to their target the more probable they were likely to be discovered.

Chapter 24

'Mr Walker and Mr Morgan, I welcome you on board my ship,' Frank Johnson said holding a hand in friendship as they arrived on the bridge.

'Good evening Captain,' Jeff said acknowledging him with a hearty handshake. 'Mark and I have been asked to come on board and help your sonar team track that raider of yours.'

'Well I jolly hope he can, as I want to settle an old score with that rogue.'

'Yes we heard about that and we are terribly sorry about what happened to you and your men Frank. You do not mind me calling you Frank do you?

'No not at all, but please not in front of my crew, as they are not use to me and I need to build a relationship with them. I'm sure you understand,' Johnson stated though not pleased with Jeff's out spoken attitude, but knew he had to live with it; anyway it would be only for a short stay, for once this Walker fellow identified the sounds of the submarine for his men, they could then leave. As he did not want them on the ship any longer than was necessary.

'If you don't mind I have to see about getting the ship ready to sail, as we are slightly running behind schedule, my first officer will take you to your cabins and see to it you are comfortable.'

'Yes of course,' Mark said as he left the bridge and escorted below deck to their cabins.

Mark sat on his bunk listening to the throb of the mighty diesel engines and could feel the power in them as they pushed the ship from its moorings and out of its holding bay, to head for the deep Atlantic Ocean.

'Mark this is Lieutenant Gibbs,' Johnson uttered as they sat around a big table in the boardroom. Mark sat opposite the radio officer Gibbs, while Johnson sat beside his leading officer and waited to hear what they had to say about the submarine. Jeff stayed out of the meeting thinking about how they could capture Krabava. Mark also thought it was the best thing to do at this stage, for he could deal with whatever was required with the aid of Gibbs.

'Very well Captain, what is it exactly would you like me to do?' Mark started to say, but before he could finish speaking Frank butted in.

'I would like you to give Lieutenant Gibbs here as much information as possible with regards to the operations of that submarine, and in particular to its sonar equipment.'

'I'm sorry Captain I know nothing about its sonar or radar, in fact I no nothing about any of the tracking devices on that submarine.'

'Oh, I was to understand you could identify the noises the boat and its engines made and possibly any other sound as well.'

'I am sure I can do that, I was on it long enough, anyhow, and I will do my best.'

'That's brilliant Mark,' Gibbs said with a strong Texas drawl. He was a tall fellow with muscles that pushed through his tunic as if he wore two a sizes to small. 'I'll be pressing all the buttons so all you have to do is tell me when to stop as we close in on the sounds.'

'Ok when shall we make a move?' Mark said, in a hurry to get it finished as he wanted to be back with his wife, so they could go back home to England. He needed to be with his wife even more, for he misses her warm lovely smile and sensuous voice every time she speaks. He felt very lonely on this ship, even though he was with friends, but was not so sure she felt the same as he.

'First, what can you tell me about the skipper and crew on that submarine, it would be very helpful for me to ascertain what he had on his mind,' Frank Johnson muttered to Mark not wanting to experience another episode like the last time he had dealing with Krabava.

'No time like the present,' Gibbs responded standing, as Mark had finished sipping a hot cup of coffee.

'If you do not mind sir, we'll go below to my sanctuary. Ok Mark, shall we make a start,' Gibbs said leaving the skipper and the boardroom to head for the sonar room.

'The last we heard of the submarine, it disappeared into the South Atlantic after leaving Beagle Channel, but not before sinking an Argentine patrol boat. Two Argentine warships went to give chase; neither of them had any luck in finding her. Christ knows where it is now,' Johnson stated as Jeff entered the room and sat down opposite him. 'He is excellent at evading warships, whatever class they are. It's unbelievable really that with all the modern electrics we have at our disposal, that no one can find her, but I'm sure Mark will rectify it and this time equal the balance, before she does anymore harm. I will tell you this, I will not be caught with my trousers down again, for I have the advantage of better hardware, which I did not have on board my last ship and now with Mark helping us I should say we should have him and soon.'

'You're taking it a bit personal captain?' Jeff replied with a calm voice.

'You may think so, but I've not forgiven him for killing my old crew.'

'Can you identify anything yet?' Gibbs asked Mark as he peered at the radar screen hunting for the crooks.

'Don't get impatient,' Mark remarked as he glared at the screen and listening to the sounds of the underwater world.

'You know it will be marvel if I discover him at all, there's so much noise I can't distinguish one sound from another,' Mark said beginning to sound desponded as the sailors twiddled with the knobs and dials on the console before them.

'Mark this info is magnificent; you have been terrific and very helpful so be rest assured, I'll get that sucker picked out from all the sounds that you had identified as soon as he shows around here. We'll blast him out of the water,' Gibbs remarked with excitement at Mark, at having told him what to listen for.

'I give you credit mate you have bags of confidence,' Mark said marvelling how good this chap really was following the completion of the day, for it had taken several hours working in that room with its glow of flashing lights and instruments.
Mark finally completed had became tired from staring at the radar screens and with hurting eyes as they smarted from the endless glare of lights he left Gibbs and his friends to sort out the rest of the data, hoping that it would be adequate. He moved through the grey metal passageways off ship and soon found himself in the mess deck where he saw Jeff mulling over a steaming mug of coffee.

'What kept you; I thought you said it wouldn't take long?' Jeff grunted whilst still looking at his coffee.

'I'll be blinking glad when I'm back with my wife,' Mark said.

'I don't like Johnson, he's to bloody cocksure of himself, I tell you this for nothing, I believe his judgments foggy from his last encounter, and he will I'm sure if he manages to run into the Zhuralev be in trouble again. I cannot help wondering how he received his command so early, for surely they would have waited a few months before obtaining another ship. All can say is he must have very good friends in high places,' Jeff said venting his feelings with frustration at Mark.

'Yes I would agree with you Jeff, he certainly has not had the time to grieve. 'Jeff changing the subject, are you in love with that girl on board that submarine?' Marked remarked lifting his coffee to his lips and hoping he had not hit a sensitive nerve.

'I suppose I must be for we kinder clicked at first sight, if you know what I mean. She told me she wanted to come to Washington with me when all this mess was ironed out but god only knows when that would have been, and who knows what would have happened if she did. We had a few good laughs together and worked well with one another and for me in particular that meant a lot, for I had always worked on my own since my wife died. I have not felt this way about another woman in a long time'

'That could take a lot longer than anticipated by the way things are at the moment, the question is how are you going to get her off the submarine with Johnson hell bent on destroy it,' Mark said as an officer entered the mess and seeing them sitting in the far corner of the room approached them.

'Excuse me Mr Morgan there's a message for you on the bridge,' the officer stated and not waiting for a reply turned on his heels and left through the same door as he had entered.

On the bridge, the two men approached the captain with apprehension.

'You have a message I understand captain,' Jeff replied to what the messenger had said.

'Yes I have,' he said handing Jeff a piece of paper with the message on it.

'It's from my beloved Jim, he wants us to return to Washington right away, or when you have finished here, he states that my other two colleagues have returned from Argentina and it appears they have some disturbing news, but he doesn't say what.'

'Must be serious then, how's he proposing to get us back?' Mark said curious as to what type of transport they had at their disposal to travel back, as they were now quite away from land.

'No problem Mark we'll have you going back by helicopter, one is on its way and will be here in about an hour or so,' Johnson said.

'Wow looks as if you've already had enough of us on your ship captain,' Mark stated truly amazed at the speed of events that were taking place.

'I take it you have concluded with that Gibbs fellow,' Jeff mentioned as they left the captains bridge to return to their cabins to pack the few clothes they had brought with them.

'Yeah I had done just about as much as I could, although they haven't given us a lot of time.

The chopper landed as predicted on the flight deck on schedule of the ship and with its rotor blades turning slowly, the pilot stayed at his controls to wait for his guests Jeff and Mark to appear after saying a speedy farewell to Johnson and his ship. Mark having no illusion as to the tricky task Johnson had before him, the chopper lifted from the deck and climbing to a height of 4000 feet with its rotor blades cutting through the air to give it maximum lift, they departing from the ship and turned west for land.

'You would think the ship we have just left was a toy,' Mark claimed as he watched the ship diminish in size.

'Pretty cool I must confess,' Jeff said responding to what Mark said but still considering the urgency of the message he had received so was not really taking much notice to what Mark was talking about.

'How long before we get there?' Jeff inquired to the pilot.

'No more than a couple of hour's sir,' he replied speaking in a loud voice above the sound of the rotor blades.

'I will be glad as well as I am on leave once I get this thing booked in.'

'Going anywhere nice?' Mark asked having to raise his voice above the noise of the helicopters props.

'Going home to Kentucky, my folks have a farm and they want me to run it when I leave the service,' the pilot continued.

'How long have you got to go in the service? Mark said continuing with the conversation to pass the time so he did not have to concentrate on the helicopter.

'What's that sound?' Jeff mentioned with a voice that alerted Mark to see if he could identify it as well, but before the pilot could establish the sound the engine spluttered and then abruptly with a grinding and screeching racket it came to a halt. Instantly as the chopper lost power it rapidly commenced to loose altitude and headed at an ever-increasing speed towards the ocean. The pilot holding on tight to the controls tried to glide the craft safely down towards the sea. However, with everything happening so quickly the helicopter pitched into the water and started straight away to sink as it broke apart.

Fumbling to remove their seat belts, they scrambled in desperation from the stricken machine, Mark jumping from the left hand side of the chopper while Jeff struggled to get out of the right hand side, in doing so noticed the pilot had been knockout and had not released his belt. Jeff did not hesitate to help the pilot in releasing his straps, and holding his breath as the craft sank beneath the waves he managed to pull the pilot from the wreck before he drowned.

Surfacing Jeff set about climbing in the life raft that had inflated when they had hit the water and pulled the stricken man on the craft after him. Successfully achieving in getting into the dingy Jeff put his back against its side to regain his breath.

'Where's your buddy?' the pilot questioned speaking whilst gasping for breath and spitting out water yet noticed that Mark was not with them.

'Good god---,' Jeff yelled at the top of his voice and promptly standing up in the dingy to search for Mark.

'I can't see him, Mark---! Mark---! Mark----!' He continued shouted as loud as his vocals would allow, but still there was no response from the vast waters. 'Christ all bloody mighty---! He's gone and drowned---! oh my god it can't happen to him, not now, it's impossible we were together a minute or so ago,' Jeff said with frustration as he searched the horizon, but being obstructed by the waves as a heavy swell hindered his view to see Mark.

He felt answerable for Marks well being and to the fact he had survived the crash and he had not, it was too terrible to contemplate.

'What am I going to tell his wife and how am I going to console her for the loss of her husband?' Jeff said trying to stand up right in the dingy screaming Marks name until he could hardly speak. It was hopeless, for he could only hear the waves as they reached the peek of their crest and then broke to form yet again.

'Did you manage to get out a rescue call?'

'No, I'm sorry everything went dead on me, no one will know of our plight for sometime,' the pilot announced with gloom.

'Surely you have to check in on arrival?

'That's true, but nobody would take much notice as the chopper won't be needed, as I was to take it to the maintenance sheds and log it off there, so it would be sometime, before anybody realises we are in trouble.'

'Christ, bloody-Christ-sake what a muddle this has become. How about the radar, surely that would have plotted our course, there is a tracking signal on the copper I presume?' Jeff continued hoping to arrive at some kind of sense to this insanity.

'Yes there's radar on it, but that does not mean anybody took notice of us on the ship, as we would have come under ground radar from Washington. They were supposed to fit a homing signal on the chopper but none were ever fitted.'

'It gets worse and worse,' Jeff mumbled and slumping back against the dinghies side with his head between his knees, for he had became disillusioned with everything and now expected the worse.

'I don't expect them to look for us until tomorrow morning,' the pilot mentioned with glum frustration and showing signs of pain from the knock on his head that he received from the control panel.

Chapter 25

'Gregg, what's the situation with Jeff and Mark as I never heard from them last night, so I presumed they had arrived back very late for us to meet.'

'I don't know I will give him a buzz Jim, but I did say yesterday they may be delayed in leaving the ship, due to Mark completing in helping them,' Gregg said then swiftly leaving Jims office.

'Hi this is Gregg from ops, can you put a call through to Jeff Morgan, yeah that's right he is staying at the Florida hotel. Ok I will hang on.' He fumbled around with papers on his desk waiting for the connection to Jeff's hotel room and then after several moments elapsed, a voice answered.

'Oh I see.' Alarms bells instantly ringing in his head, although not quite understanding why, he just felt that something was wrong. Already expecting something disturbing had taken place, as Jeff usually contacted him to his whereabouts Gregg replaced the receiver and went to tell Jim about the lack of information he had received.

'Don't get concerned there's bound to be a plausible explanation,' Jim told Gregg.

'Patch me through to the Panda right away, yes that's right, the Panda, Captain Johnson's ship, now---.! You know Gregg that bunch on the switchboard must be thick as two planks,' Jim added with irritation.

'You're getting worried.'

'Yes I am, for it's not like Jeff not to call in like this and so close to home. Have you spoken to Mrs Walker yet?'

'No not at the moment, I thought we should wait till we speak to Jeff and find out exactly what the hold up was,' Gregg stated as

Jim continued to talk about why Jeff had not called. Then the phone rang again interrupting his conversation with Gregg, promptly grabbing for the phone and stumbling he picked it up.

'Hello sorry to bother you, its Jim Edwards speaking,' he calmly said to the hotel manager, and then explained about the two men he was seeking.

'The manager states they did not check in last night, but added he would inform me, when they have arrived at the hotel.'

'What about the ship, reckon they can fill us in with what has happened?'

'We'll soon find out,' Jim said picking up the phone once again.

'Put me through to the station commanding officer,' Jim uttered with a shaky voice. 'Jim Edwards here, can you verify Mr Morgan and Walker have arrived back from the Panda.' Again, he spoke in a calm collected voice, this time to the commanding officer.

'I am sorry to inform you, I have no news of them returning, but have been notified they left the ship ok, but apart from that there is no news of them, it also appears the helicopter has not signed in.'

'We've lost them,' responded Jim trying to hold back his concern. 'The Panda confirms they left, so they must have crashed somewhere,' Jim cried and hitting the panic button to call the emergency services and set them in motion for a sea rescue.

Jim was so intense and concentrating what he was doing he had not noticed who was standing in the doorway looking at him and hearing what he was saying to Gregg.

'Is there something wrong Jim?' Ann said uneasily to the fact something bad had taken place and implicating her husband.

Jim not expecting her to be in his office, was caught off guard with his mouth wide open as he listened on the phone, as the caller explained what had taken place. Dropping the phone back on its cradle his face turning ashen in colour he looked towards Ann.

'I'm sorry to tell you Ann, the chopper has not reported in, we know it left the ship and can only assume it has crashed into the sea. As far as I can tell you the ships radar lost it last night, the operator thought it was due to thick cloud cover and never paid much attention to it.'

She stood listening to Jim telling her quietly that her husband Mark might be lost at sea and even drowned.

Not able to move she stood frozen on the spot trying to suck in the horrible news and the thought of her husband lost. She shook her head from side to side, trying desperately to see how it could happen.

'I promise you Ann we will find him,' Gregg alleged making contact with her and hoping to comfort her by saying everything would turn out for the best.

She wandered across to the couch on the other side of the office and sat down on it. Closing her eyes she placed her hands over them to hide her tears that streamed down her rosy cheeks then staring at the ceiling incapable to make any sense of it, for trauma was visible in her face, as she could no longer control her emotions until finally bursting out crying. Her body shook with the hurt of the news that probably she was never ever going to see her fellow again.

'Why---, why---, why---?' she repeated whispering through her quivering lips.

'Why Ann, I'm so sorry I can't answer that, these things seem to happen without any explanation,' Jim said feeling dismal about the consequences that had bestowed on Mark and feeling very guilty for asking him to help with the submarine.

After what seemed a very long agonising time the phone rang, sounding so loud in the stillness of the room they jumped from the suddenness of it, as you could hear a pin drop on the floor.

They could only hear the suppressed sobs of Ann crying in the office, as she could no longer refrain from holding her emotions.

'Yeah,' Jim said speaking down the phone again expecting the worst. 'I see, ok, I will inform everybody,' he said with a placid voice hoping to break the news gently to her. 'Ann they have pulled two men from the sea alive, as yet there is no identification as to who they are, they will let me know soon as they know,' he said looking into her red eyes, streaked with tear lines that ran down her cheeks.

'He is very strong and he will come back to me,' she responded sniffing and wiping the tears from her face.

'Jeff your safe and well, what happened, is Mark with you?' Gregg asked the questions in succession as he grabbed the phone, before his boss could catch it.

'It's Jeff,' he told the other two in the office, 'he's back on the Panda,' Gregg said delighted in telling this news to his boss.

'Tell them to get back here immediately, they can fill us in with what happened then,' Jim grumbled as he tried to hide his feeling to how he actually felt.

'Jeff stated Mark is not with him, only the pilot and himself,' Gregg said relaying the message to Jim as he listened to the message be relayed to him.

Ann not wanting to hear anymore bad news about her husband, walked out of the office, but bumped into Pat who was very quick to establish a huge problem was afoot.

'Hello Ann,' Pat whispered trying to stop her from passing in the corridor. 'Hang on Ann where do you think you are going,' she asked softly.

'Anywhere that's out of here, I can't stay here any longer, I need to get away,' she cried trembling with despair.

'Do you mind if I string along with you?'

'If you so wish.'

'Give me a second I'll inform Jim to what we are doing,' she added moving swiftly to the office doorway to mention to Jim, if he needed her to call her on her mobile.

'Jim,' Jeff said after finally arriving at the office some hours later with a very concerned uneasy look on his face.

He unsteadily crossed the room slumping onto the same sofa Ann had sat on earlier and waited for his boss to speak.

'How are you feeling?' is all Jim could muster with surprise, for Jeff expected a first degree on what had happened and why they could not find Mark. Jeff slowly went through in detail as to what had taken place with the crashing of the helicopter.

'Honest Jim I tried everything in my power to find Mark, but he just eluded me, I can only assume he must have drowned straight away or had drifted too far away so as not to hear me calling him.'

'Don't feel so cut up about it; it's not your fault the helicopter broke down. If it helps you, I feel very bitter talking to him in going with you.

'Good morning boss, Jeff,' Dave and Harvey said in unison as they entered the open door, and unaware of the crisis which was taking place. It did not take them long realising that something bad had happened, and waited for the details to unfold.
Jeff explained briefly to them quickly at what had taken place and that he done everything possible to find Mark.

'Well there's no shortage of bad news,' Dave said looking at Jeff in particular.

'Why what have you got to add?' Jim added turning his attention to Dave for the new change of venue, but preparing himself also for the news.

'She's a Russian that's what,' Harvey uttered interrupting his colleague Dave as he faced his boss to speak to him.

'A Russian, who is a Russian, what are you talking about mate?' Jeff said throwing the question back in Harvey's face.

'Charley that's who, her real name is Sakhakov, Svetlana Sakhakov and she was born in Russia, well Kazakhstan actually, its some 826 miles from Moscow,' Dave announced surprising Jeff with the news by his abrupt manner.

'Charley, are you saying she's a Russian spy?'

'No not at all, on the contrary she is half Russian and half English; she was born in Russia, apparently not aware that her father is a Russian. In addition and to the point, she has found him unexpectedly on board the submarine, for it was he with the aid of Tabor kept her on the boat. Well that is what Andrei the radioman told us.

'How close would you think they have got?' Jeff said trying hard to soak in this uncomfortable report and yet trying to put the question of Charley at the back of his mind.

'I can't say for sure, but it appears they are getting very close to New York, Andrei said after we found him hiding in Harberton.'

'So what happens now, is she on our side or has she gone over to Tabors side?' Jeff said worried that he may now lose her for good, but was convinced she would not betray him.

'Jeff it's difficult to say for I just don't know, although in my opinion I don't think she would work with those evil creatures and be like them,' Dave stated.

'Maybe Ann can enlighten us a little further as she had spent some time with her on board,' Jim said looking at Ann as she rejoined them all in his office, to check if there had been any further developments about her husband.

'Did this Andrei say how they intended to hit New York and when?' Jim asked showing his concern for the actions of Krabava than of Jeff's love life, for time was ticking against him to find that boat.

'No not at all it was kept very secret, only a few of the gang knew what was actually going on, as the crew thought they were going to New York to enjoy themselves. For they were only interested in earning the money and by all accounts a lot of cash they would get when it was over,' Dave remarked turning to face Jim. 'Anyhow that's what Andrei could only tell us.'

'How about the submarine, where is it now?' Jim asked interrupting them again.

'He could not tell us where it is, only that it's heading north up the coast.'

'I would determine Krabava would be somewhere in the vicinity of Washington by now, by the speed the boat was travelling, of course we only have Andrei's word for this and we don't know how accurate he is with his assumption in his import.

'What do you reckon then Harvey?' Jim said trying to get an accurate answer from him.

'Come over here,' Harvey called as he moved across the floor to the other side of the room towards a large map of America pinned on the wall. 'Look, the submarine was spotted here two weeks ago,' Harvey said pointing at the spot where he wanted them all to see. 'So in my estimation that would bring him about here at 36.36 North by 66.98 West,' Harvey said again stamping his finger on the new location on the map. 'Of course that is not a specific position. Now I would envisage the Panda to be in that area searching and hoping to find Mark.' All eyes focused on Harvey as he made his assumption with the Panda.

'Do you believe they may clash?' Jim gasped suddenly looking disturbed at the thought of Johnson and his ship being-sunk.

'That is a prospect I wouldn't like to contemplate, however; I doubt if Krabava would want to get involved with Johnson again if he could possibly help it, what with being so close to his objective, that's of course New York is his intended target,' Jeff mentioned optimistically hearing what was being said around him.

'Jim do you think we should alert Johnson that Krabava maybe in the area,' Gregg mentioned.

'Yeah Gregg that's a good idea, do it right away will you, the last thing we want, is a repeat performance like last time, what with a psychopathic skipper that's in charge and running loose with a submarine that's carrying deadly weapons of a huge magnitude, there's know telling what he will do next.

260

Now guys, have you anything else to add before we move on to the next part?' Not that Jim had any other action for he was relying on his team to come up with some new answers.

Chapter 26

'Mianlia, steady as she goes, prepare to surface. Surface,' Krabava called with a voice sounding stressed with the problems they had encountered avoiding their enemies from one Ocean to another, to his first officer.

During their long voyage, which had taken much longer than had predicted, they now closed on their target, and he could no longer afford to make any further mistakes.

So swinging the scope in a 180° movement for the second time, ascertaining everything was clear on the surface and assuring himself there were no ships lurking in their vicinity, he gave the order to surface. Only then was he pleased he stood away from the scope as it descended into its slot underneath the deck and stopped as it reached the bottom. He listened to the familiar sound of air as it pushed the seawater from the ballast tank, to lighten the boat for it to rise to the surface.

At first, the conning tower broke through the calm waters of the ocean only to drain away from its deck as the boat emerged from the deep depths.

'I want a man on every hatch cover,' Krabava called as Kazan began to climb up the ladder into the fresh cool air, it swept passed him down the hatch and raced along the entire length of the boat as all the water tight doors had been left open.

'Lookouts up top, and be extra vigilant for our survival depends on your observation,' Mianlia ordered following his skipper and Kazan to the conning tower.

As soon as one of the lookouts had taken up his position, he cried out seeing an object lying on the deck towards the boats bow.

'Sir, I think you better come over and see this,' he called to Kazan who instantly responded jumping down the outer ladder of the conning tower to the deck, and immediately seeing the image laying on the forward deck where the sailor was pointing. Kazan carefully went over to it and bent down to investigate the bundle and cautiously turning it over by its life coat and then stood motionless on the spot for what seemed to be an astonishing moment, as he witnessed the incredible figure at his feet.

'Get the Captain---,' he said to the sailor, 'tell him it's Mr Walker.'

'Walker---, how can that be? It's impossible, for we got rid of him a long time ago,' Krabava stated.

'Sir it is Mark Walker and he's very much alive, well just about that is, what do you want me to do with him? Shall I sling him back into the sea,' Mianlia said truly amazed seeing Mark lying on the deck.

'No take him below,' Krabava responded quickly to Mianlia.

'Yes sir,' Kazan said, stepping in front of Mianlia to strip Mark Walker's orange life coat from him, and then slinging it over the portside of the boat thinking it would plummet to the bottom of the ocean, but instead it drifted away from them on the surface with the current.

Kazan with the help from Mianlia and the sailor lifted Mark from the deck and took him below for Charley to take of him.

'Who's this?' Charley asked as they entered her compartment and infringing on her solitude of peace.

'I think you would like to take care of him,' Kazan said for her to attend to him. 'I would estimate he's been in the water for quite a while, and he's in a bad way,' Kazan continued to say as he laid Mark on the lower bunk.

Her mouth opened wide in surprise, in recognising Mark was back on board the boat.

'Where did he come from? She asked dazed and dumfounded by his sudden appearance.

'We have no idea, so it's up to you to get answers from him when he recovers,' Mianlia said with authority concerned it may be a trap.

So stretching Mark comfortably on the bunk to care for him, they left her to attend to his needs and help him recover from his suffering.

'I predict they will be searching for him, which could put us in a very precarious position,' Mianlia mentioned to his captain on returning to the conning tower.

'That's a fair assumption, to say the least Mianlia, but we still have an advantage, for if we carry on as we are on the surface and head due East out to sea, where I think they won't expect us to go, we can charge our batteries at the same time. For I believe they will be expecting us to hug the coastline to get closer to our target; apart from that if we did go north we'll run smack into the rescue fleet, and that wouldn't do us any good would it.'

'How far out do you intend going sir?'

'In my calculations I would say approximately 250 miles, that should be sufficed and being optimistically it should shake off our pursuers, hopefully take away from the crew any anxiety they may dispel. I predict, if we travel sailing at 23 knots on the surface, it would put us around 100 miles in some four to five hours, given that we don't have any more problems, for time is now on our side. Three hours had passed without a sign of any ship or aircraft until a voice from below in the control room cried out.

'Captain---,' Sakhakov called with a voice sounding anxious to what he had seen on his radar.

'Yes what is it,' Krabava responded calmly.

'I have a ship bearing on 38.05 North and 71.41 West at 25 miles, I also think it has a fix on us sir,' the voice shrieked with apprehension to what was going to happen when the ship finally caught up with them.

'Very well, what speed is it doing?' Krabava added puzzled by the way, the ship had sighted them so easily.

'Its travelling at 35 knots and closing fast,' came back the discerning voice.

'Lookouts below, take her down, go to 250 feet, reduce speed to 10 knots, but maintain course 080°,' Krabava instructed and swearing under his breath for this was the last thing he wanted to happen.

'How could this American ship find us so easy?'

'Sir I may have the answer,' Kazan said then explained quickly to his skipper what he had on his mind.

'Are you saying you threw overboard Mark Walkers life jacket, do you realise it was probably sending out a signal, and that's why they have found us as well.'

'Yes sir.'

'That is a prospect of course; did anybody check the jacket, to see if there was a signal finder attached?' Blank faces told him what he did not want to know. 'Very well, what is done is done, we will now have to make sure he cannot out wit us.'

'Contact now 15 miles and is still closing,' Sakhakov called from the radio room, as he had replaced Andrei since his escape.

'Mianlia surface the boat, take us up so only part of the conning tower is protruding above the waves.' The crew looked with surprise faces at their skipper, as if he had gone mad, but still obeyed to carry out his orders knowing he could out smart this war ship, as he had done it before.

'Kazan as you can speak good English dig out the union jack, take Valja and Yuri on top and tell that American you saw a yellow life jacket floating to our port and that you gave it a look over and seeing nothing unusual you chucked it back into the ocean. Make it credible or we are all dead,' Krabava remarked, but not convinced the story would succeed and then he remembered what Tabor told him what he did on the Oban.

Once they had surfaced, Krabava listened intently in the control room, to the conversation between the American and Kazan.

'You say you slung it back into the ocean?' The first officer called from the warship Panda.

'Yes that's correct, it was something like 30 miles over to the Northeast,' Kazan stated in perfect English.

'How come you didn't keep it and report it to the coast guard, Mr Phillips?' Howard asked surprised at the action of this English officer who had not taken the appropriate procedure, in notifying the coast guard.

'As I have said sir the jacket seemed to have been in the water for a very long time and what with it being torn and no markings suggesting it belonged to anybody of recent days. So I disposed of it,' Kazan stated to the American officer with crossed fingers behind his back, hoping that the story was plausible for this American, but knowing undoubtedly he would find out within the next few moments.

'Very well Lieutenant Phillips we'll check it out.'

'Are you looking for anyone in particular Mr Howard,' Kazan called gaining confidence with his English as he spoke to the guy that was on the warship.

'A chap called Walker went missing yesterday and hasn't been found, so if you spot any other jackets please call in.'

'I am sorry to hear it, how did he end up in the ocean?'

'Involved in a helicopter crash by all accounts,' Howard said as he made to depart from the submarine.

Kazan and the two other sailors in the conning tower breathed a sigh of relief as the Corvette steered away from them, to explore where roughly he said he had slung the jacket. Meanwhile Krabava was getting impatient and thinking Kazan was pushing his luck talking so much to the American.

'We'll let you know, if we come across him,' Kazan said finishing the conversation as the corvette moved further away from them and changing its direction in pursuit of the said jacket.

'How did I do speaking to the American?' Kazan said feeling very proud speaking to the American in English.

'I thought you took a big risk getting into that little chit-chat with them, but I am glad you did it, for it will give us time to get out of here.

Take her down Mianlia, this time to 500 feet and continue on same course, speed 18 knots.

As Sakhakov viewed the radar screen watching closely seeing what the ship was doing as they silently went in their different directions, he wondered how much the American had believed them. The answer was not long coming as he noticed the ship turning on its last heading and coming back towards them.

'Damn,' Sakhakov grunted for all to hear. 'He's rumbled us and returning, reckon he hadn't bought it after all.' 'He's had time to suss out our story about the jacket, and I think he probably would have sent a message to the coast guard, which they have returned with a negative answer,' the captain said now focusing on the Americans next move.

The Panda pounding back approached with its screws increasing at full ferocity began to sweeping the area overhead, as the Texas did; pressing on relentlessly above them, Sakhakov heard the familiar sounds of splashes as objects entered the water.

'Splashes in the water---' he yelled to his team, removing his headphones from his ears at the same time.

Yet again they began to endure the terrifying explosions as the depth charges ignited close by them, this time the crew more alerted and now knew what to expect, although still apprehensive to what may happen to them they feared the worst. The ship passed over them and travelled a little way only to turn and come in for another attack, dropping more depth charges into the water for them to endure.

Johnson recalling his last encounter with Krabava was now more prepared this time and turned his ship faster so Krabava could not execute the same manoeuvre as he did the last time.

This time the charges dropped much closer to the Zhuralev, exploding with more force than the crew had ever experienced, for Johnson was desperately aiming to finish them off.

A salvo of six charges exploded directly above the submarine, shaking the small boat so violently that it put a huge strain upon its superstructure.

'Go to 800ft Mianlia--- and fast. 5° on the right rudder slow to 5 knots,' the skipper shouted above the increasing din.

Deeper they sank towards the ocean's seabed but still they could not get away from the maniac in charge of the ship above them.

The warship once again after repeating its last run over the stricken submarine, turned in circular movements and sent even more charges after them. One of the charges pounced off the small boat and exploded with a piecing noise that coursed the sailors in the stern torpedo compartment to scream out in fright.

'Report damage,' the Skipper announced through the microphone in the control room.

'Waters entering through the right lower tube sir, plus the right drive shaft seal flange is split,' said one of the sailors speaking back on the internal phone.

Suddenly more loud explosions silenced him as the ship above was still tracking their movements as they went deeper.

Shouting and hollering came from the men in the submarine for panic was now beginning to set in.

Then a huge crash rocked the boat that made it veer up steeply by the bow and sway violently from side to side.

'What on earth is happening back there,' the captain roared.

'Kazan will you go and see what is happening back there, and rectify it at once.'

Pushing open the watertight door of the control room he instantly bumped into Mark, who by now had improved and was making his way to lend a hand in the rear torpedo room yet again. On entering the compartment, they saw straight away that the inner tube door was leaking as water was spraying in at a fast rate. Mayhem ran riot, as water was now knee deep and still slowly rising.

'Shut the watertight door---,' Kazan screamed above the turmoil of his men who were panicking and feared they would drown. 'We need to stop the rest of the boat from getting flooded, so let's try and contain the water in this compartment,' he continued to say. Quickly isolating the room from the rest of the boat, he could now deal with the drive shaft, which was still spinning, as well as the leaking tube.

'Captain I need to stop the starboard engine. Get that torpedo from that tube,' cried Kazan not waiting for a reply from his captain. Three sailors scrambled to do as ordered and began pulling it from the tube when its motor started. Its screw caught one of the sailors and threw him across the confined space of the compartment with blood gushing from a severe head wound; he landed in the knee high water in a heap under the bottom torpedo rack and remained. The torpedo slipped even further from its tube and this time it pinned another of the men to the cradle to which he had been struggling with to lash around the cylinder. Gasping in pain he fell to the floor and died on impact as the weight of the torpedo crushed his ribs when it fell out off the tube on top of him.

Mark kneeling down beside the first chap to inspect him also found that he had died, and then leaving him there, he directly returned his attention to the loose torpedo. Finally managing to stabilise a strap around it they pulled it off the deck and secured it to its holding rack. Now with all the torpedoes tightly tied in their respective racks he turned his attention to concentrate on the leaking door.

'What are you up to?' roared Mark seeing Kazan leaning over the cylinder of the torpedo that they had rescued from the tube and back on its rack in relative safety.

'I'm removing these nuts to expose the defusing mechanism, I have to dismantle it and disarm it, or else we'll all go sky high,' he added looking very grim at the prospects of undertaking such a task. Delicately he undid the six nuts that held the plate in place and removed them to show the detonator, and then with trembling fingers he slowly but cautiously removed it.

'Christ that was a near thing,' he said holding the detonator in his right hand whilst holding his other hand to the rack.

'Ok let's stop the water coming in from the tube door,' Mark responded after witnessing Kazan fumbling with the detonator. Wading through the water that was now above knee depth they pushing and shoved against the door until eventually managing to get it closed, only to find it distorted and was still letting a fine mist of water enter.

'Switch the pump on so we can stem the water from rising,' Krabava shouted above more explosions as they continued to seek them out. 'There's only one thing to do to get him of our tail,' Krabava said.

'This is wrong,' Mark added, and alarmed at hearing what they proposed to do but knew in his mind it was the only way to survive.

'It's the only way to get that ship from sinking us,' responded Kazan to Mark sensing what he was thinking.

'I'm not so keen myself, but if it gets that ship away from us then so be it,' he said, as he pushed one of the dead sailors into an empty torpedo tube.

'Here put some of this rubbish in as well. We are ready captain when you are.'

'Mianlia release some oil and pump out the waste,' Krabava ordered hearing the bubbles roar out of the boat at the same time as they had fired the two dead sailors out of the torpedo tubes.

'Mark, how long will this go on for before they kill us all?' Charley questioned exhausted with the thought they were all going to end up at the bottom of the ocean again. 'It just goes on and on, there seems to be no let up,' she cried.

'I know how you are feeling Charley but have strength, we'll see this out despite the difficult situation we are in,' Mark said also showing signs of stress and fatigue, for he had not fully recovered from his ordeal from his watery grave. Slowly the boat moved forward in the dark gloomy waters with a trail of small air bubbles escaping from the damaged rear tube.

'Take her down deeper, perhaps we can persuade that captain he has destroyed us,' the skipper garbled to Mianlia with a dry mouth and preparing for more charges to drop. The pressure of water around the boat began to build against its hull as they slowly edged their way deeper to the unknown depths.

'Jettison more oil and gas. I hope it will convince them for the last time, let us hope it does the trick,' Krabava announced to Mianlia.

'Sir we are still taking on water,' Kazan said concerned with the water still entering the rear compartment.

'It will have to wait, as they may hear our pumps running,' he said lowering his boat gently on the seabed's sandy bottom.

After two hours of waiting and continually hearing the ships screws above them, who was urgently trying to locate them, they finally started to hear it depart.

Satisfied it was now safe to act Krabava brought his attention to the flooding torpedo room, as there was no let up of the water coming from the inner tube's door, which could prevent them from travelling on at an even keel.

'Kazan, you can now activate the pumps, so we can block that leak. Sakhakov if you hear the slightest sound of them coming back, or any other ship I what to know about it immediately.' Both nodded to the instructions and put about getting on with the tasks.

When they removed most of the water, Krabava decided to run for a while on the same path as before, to make sure no one could spot him, once satisfied he then returned his boat to periscope depth to convince him there was nothing lurking to kill them.

'Helm give it 5° on the port rudder, hoist up the main scope,' he said grabbing hold of the handles as it rose from the well, to view through the lens and see if it was safe to surface. Looking through the lens, he saw daylight was diminishing and clouds gathering from the West; this would make it perfect for him to run on the surface.

'It could not be better, we will surface with decks partly awash to pump out the water from the stern compartment and check the damage once it is empty.'

With the dark clouds that had now gathered low over the sky, rain began filtering down on the partly surfaced submarine as the crew set about making repairs, adding to their task the sea was stimulated by the winds that grew in strength, making it impossible for Krabava to fix the tubes door properly. The only thing possible was to maintain running the pumps and recharging the batteries to replenish their dwindling power.

He set out on a precise course, which would take them to be their most affective position to his target.

A shout of joy went out from the Corvette as the lookout spotted rubbish amongst the oil and then another sailor called that he had spotted two bodies in the water. On board the ship, it became manic with shouts of excitement at their first kill.

'At last sir we've got rid of the menace, now we'll be a lot safer from now on and will all sleep better tonight,' Howard said to his skipper, although; having only two dead men to confirm it.

Johnson knew Howard wanted to reassure himself they had sunk the boat, but he was not so sure.

'You know Howard I've been conned before, by that evil skipper on the submarine and I have a nagging feeling I have been tricked once more. Anyway, we will stay for a while longer in the area, as I am not convinced we have sunk him. Still, send a dispatch to command and tell them what we are doing. Tell them I have made contact with the rogue submarine and can confirm we either have killed, or damaged it, say we will have better knowledge after we have established that we have definitely sunk it,' Johnson said sitting deep in his chair on the bridge to wait for the submarine to emerge. Even so, he was totally convinced it was on the bottom of the seabed waiting to escape.

'Gibbs here sir, I'm sorry but we are unable to trace her, I believe we have sunk her, as more oil has been spotted coming to the surface.'

'Thank you Mr Gibbs, report the loss and that we are now heading back to base via New York. If you require me, I will be in my cabin,' Johnson said pulling his tired body out of the chair and departed from the bridge thinking it was not a very happy day's work at sinking the submarine and killing those men, but remembering that Krabava had been a huge threat to them all.

'Mark you have not told me how you ended up in the sea,' Charley said.

'No, I'm sorry, for I've been a little tied up with one thing or another.

Well Jeff and I,' Mark stopped speaking abruptly as he mentioned his name and saw her body stiffen to Jeff's name.

'Jeff is he alive and ok?' she asked startled by the mention of his name.

'Well he was, before our helicopter crashed, can't say now, but knowing him he's a survivor. When I jumped out, I must have hit my head, for the next thing I remember I was floating up and down dazed and confused with the waves.

While in the water, I began thinking of Ann and what a wonderful time we had spent together and realising I would not see her again. I remembered seeing her sitting across the patio table looking so radiant in her green shirt and white T-Shirt,' he said calmly but in a hesitating voice to her, while looking at the floor trying to hide his real feelings from Charley. 'The waves kept hitting my face every time I dropped into the troughs before rising back onto each the crest again. I looked in vain for Jeff but it was useless for there was no sign of him, he had disappeared from sight. A little while later I began to drowse and I must have passed out, well the rest you know.'

'All I can say Mark is you have been extremely lucky, albeit ending here and may even die yet,' she said with sadness in her eyes.

'Sakhakov what is our position? As I think we are at our location,' Krabava said in a whisper for he did not want the crew to know what his real intentions were.

'Yes sir that is correct we are where you asked,' Sakhakov replied without hesitation.

'Very well, Mianlia will do what's necessary with the weapons in forward torpedo room, by the way do it on your own,' Krabava announced with a slight slur to his voice. Kazan, bring the boat round on true course to target and then tell Yuri to make ready the engine for our get away.'

Chapter 27

With a heavy burden on his shoulders, Johnson poured a stiff drink in his cabin for he felt guilty at killing so many men, good or bad and they would be a loss to someone's mother or wife.

As a huge spray of water crossed the bow of his ship as it cut through the rising sea, only to cascade over the sides they carried on with not so much of a blip on the radar screen. Johnson realising there was nothing he could have done to save the unfortunate men on the submarine, returned to the bridge and sat back in his chair. Frustrated by the fact they had made no further contact with the submarine and with a nagging hunch that he may only have had damaged the boat, and that it was waiting for an opportunity to do it's deadly deed.

Two destroyers had appeared at his rear in aiding him in patrolling the waters as they drew nearer to New York, then after 24 hours his command ordered him to return to Boston for the other two ships would still prolong the search.

He returned to his cabin in an attempt to put pen to paper to fill out a full report of the exercise, while contemplating at the same time about his future, for he had now decided to relinquish his command of this ship and instead of taking an office job, he would retire from the navy.

'Captain we have received a signal from the Eclipse, she is passing to our starboard and just below periscope depth.'

'Very well Howard,' he acknowledged with a grunt. 'Let me know of any change,' he said returning back to his letter and imagining leaving the navy.

'Yes sir,' Howard remarked and then swiftly departed from the cabin.

'Bridge what the hell is going on---,' Johnson said, infuriated by the intrusion for he was so engrossed with his thoughts that he never felt the slight thud to ship, but reacting in instance when he heard the sirens sounding.

'Sir,' a sailor said and then pausing before commencing to tell his skipper what had taken place. 'We have been torpedoed.'

'What---! What are you talking about, torpedo, what torpedo?' Johnson roared slamming his pen on the desk, and jumping out of his chair he ran from the cabin to see what was happing on the bridge, pushing sailors out of the way, as he went. 'Well, what's this about a torpedo and where did it come from---?' he yelled in anger to the officers on the bridge.

'Sir I don't know, I can only ascertain for the moment it's from that submarine. It's struck us in the engine room,' Howard spluttered desperately trying to tell his angry skipper. 'Gibbs is speaking to the Eclipse right now for they also have had some kind of contact and are surfacing to examine any damage. She will confirm to us if she has a problem.'

'Very well, engine room, this is the captain, are there any casualties?'

'No sir,' the officer quickly responded.

'Fine I'm on my way down,' he said. Then telling Howard to take over on the bridge, he vanished as fast as possible to the engine room to ascertain the damage.

'What is it?' he stated on arriving to the engineer.

'That there sir,' the engineer said with a startled looking face.

'Christ almighty it's a bloody nuke---!' the chief said exploding with horror as he approached the cylinder and saw the markings on its long slim body.

'A nuke,' Johnson cried in horror at what could have happened if it had exploded. 'Can you make it safe chief?'

'Don't fancy trying to defuse it on the move skipper,' the chief muttered solemnly as he made his way alongside the missile.

'Bridge stop the engines and hold the ship steady as possible,' he said down the internal phone, realising that any sudden movement would spell out disaster for them all.

As the chief moved in closer to the missile he leaned over to get a better look at it and it was then he saw a screw unwinding down the length off its thread at the rear of the torpedo between the two propellers. He froze on the spot in utter amazement, watching the movement and unable to do or say anything to rectify the situation, until finally he shouted with a distraught voice.

'Captain---!' was the only word he uttered, for as the screw reached the end of its thread, the torpedo ignited in a blinding fierce light, ripping fire throughout the ship in a split of a second, vaporising everything in a hot searing fireball of smoke and steam and ripped apart its superstructure. Disintegrating it into tiny fragments then dispersed with the twisting smoke and flames of the inferno, that turned and rolled over endlessly round in a frenzy into the atmosphere.

As the skipper of the Eclipse surfaced his boat, he stood in the conning tower waiting for a report from his engineers with regards about any damage, which they may have sustained with respect to his submarine and then to ascertain what kind of damage he had to deal with. He glanced over his right shoulder to where the Panda would be and facing the bright glare of light and fireball before he too was engulfed in the high temperature from the blast. His tanned skin and dark brown hair melted with the extreme heat that quickly reached him. His boat exploded into microscopic fragments that were heaved high into the reddening sky from the fireball as it weaved its way upwards. The remains of the boat fell back towards the sea and sank to the bottom of the ocean without leaving any trace of survivors.

Then one of the two destroyers at the Panda's stern caught a broadside by a huge mountain of water, which cascaded over their superstructure and then rolled the ship repeatedly until it met her fatal end and sank with all hands on board.

The captain of the second ship watched in revulsion at what had taken place and with the atrociousness of the disaster with the three vessels. He tried in vain to steer head on into the coming danger of the huge mountain of water, but as he plunged the bow into the wall of water to try to scale the wave and ride over it, he found the colossal strength of water too much and it tossed his ship over and backwards. As if, it was a stick thrown away, again meeting the same fate as the others and ending at the bottom of the Ocean without any survivors. A few particles of debris lay floating on the Oceans surface, showing the only evidence that ships had once been there.

Krabava having discharged his lethal weapons turned his boat round as fast as possible in the opposite direction and then at full speed made for the open ocean.

'Give me full power and close all water tight doors,' Krabava ordered disturbed by the event at not hitting his intended target. 'Hang on to whatever you can,' he bellowed once more to his crew. Knowing he could not outrun the shock waves that were bearing down from the explosion; it caught up with them in no time and spun his boat and crew in all directions. Some of the men were able to hold onto the superstructure, while others slung against the fittings of the boat. Finally, as the turbulence subsided, they managed to get the boat back under control and with the stern tube leaking they set about to evade any possible pursuers that would be after them. So ploughing deeper to the depths of the ocean, they struggled with the one engine intact to sail as fast as possible for the open sea.

Three hours after the catastrophic explosion Krabava contemplated whether he should stay below the surface, or raise it above the surface, for he needed to contact Tabor and verify he was close to their position. He also tried pumping water out from the leaking stern compartment, which by now was making the boat sluggish and difficult to handle.

'I hope Tabor is on time, as we arranged,' he said to Mianlia as he peered through the periscope and saw the carnage he left behind, which had been caused by his torpedoes. 'What happened sir?' Mianlia asked bemused by the sudden impact of their weapons.

'Well, it looks as if the American ships got hit by our missiles; they must have gone a stray from its intended target. Only one exploded so I can guess its imbedded it self into the sea bed, while the second torpedo veered off from its path and smashed into the Corvette. 'Ok, Mianlia take us back up to periscope depth, but maintain the same speed. Up scope,' Krabava said. This time holding the handles as the scope rose from its well, he began instantly searching the horizon for any unsuspecting adversary, before deciding to take a chance on surfacing. 'Brilliant Tabor's on our port side and has just landed his sea plane, oh what a sight to see, he's about 2 miles north of us,' Krabava announced quietly to Mianlia. 'Sakhakov, see if you can make contact with Tabor, but keep it short.'

'Hang on a minute, he's sending us a message,' Sakhakov announced while writing down the message on a notebook as it was relayed through his headphones and then once the message was completed he handed over the encrypted message to his skipper.

'I will be in the conning tower, send Yuri up to see me for I want to talk to him about the engine shaft. Oh yes Mianlia you come up as well, Kazan can look after everything in here,' Krabava said hastily climbing the ladder to see Tabor.

Tabor's seaplane showed clearly in the bright blue calm sea, only the plume of smoke from the nuclear explosion in the distance, blotted out the horizon as it hung in the atmosphere. Krabava witnessed Tabor's plane heading smoothly over the surface of the water to meet him and then he began to prepare for him to come along side.

'Ok release the dingy Yuri. Mianlia jump in as we can now leave,' Krabava said with a smug smile deepening over his face.

'Kazan crash dive quickly---!' Krabava screamed into the microphone on the conning tower. Without hesitation, the crew below hit the leaves and dials for the submarine to dive as fast as it was possible, not aware the conning towers hatch cover was open.

As they made their way to the aircraft Krabava glanced over his shoulder to see what was happening, for he thought they might have responded faster than he hoped; all he could see were huge air bubbles bursting on the surface and spreading over a wide area.

'Come on, get in,' Tabor demanded revving the twin turboprop engines to get moving. They soon were skimming across the water at high speed and climb gently into the brilliant blue sky, Tabor banking his plane to port for them to see where Krabava had scuttled his submarine, leaving his men to their fate. Then witnessing no survivors was alive in the water, they headed in a northerly direction towards Russia and for their new hiding place, which was well out of reach from their enemy the Americans.

Chapter 28

'You guys must have found it very a musing with me bobbing up and down in that bloody water,' Jeff said whilst trying to hide his smile.

'No not at all, we just thought you may have decided to swim the Atlantic to good old England,' Harvey added looking at Jeff with a huge grin in his face, for in truth he was thankful he had made it, but knowing also, Jeff was thinking of Mark and had given him up for dead.

'You know, I can hardly believe Charley would go over to the crooks side,' he mentioned to Harvey in a husky voice.

'Ok you guys,' Jim began speaking and trying to regain their attention to settle them down. 'I'll come to the point,' he said once he had their interest.' But before he could utter a word, Gregg rushed into the office shouting words no one could comprehend.

'Turn on the TV, quick---!' he called pushing past them in panic, so as to switch on the TV, to reveal the devastating news which was now unfolding on the screen as the news-caster read his report, they gasped with horror and transfixed on the spot with open mouths at the atrocity before their eyes.

'Christ almighty---!' Dave uttered swearing aloud.

'What on earth's going on?' remarked Jeff.

'I'll tell you what's going on,' commander Billings stated barging into the office, without letting on to anyone. 'That is the result of a catastrophic nuclear explosion, caused by the result of that evil demon Krabava and his henchmen.' Billings spoke with a voice that shook with revulsion, as if he was about to cry. 'Three ships and one submarine has been destroyed and were vaporised in a fraction of a second, with at least thirty-two hundred men and women have been killed in a flicker of an eye,' he said as they watched the smoke still rising into the atmosphere.

'Do you know what ships got caught?' Jim said finally breaking the silence in the room as repulsion began to register.

'The only information we have at present is what we received from the Eclipse, which was one of our submarines passing the Panda at the time. A torpedo had hit then and veered off them without exploding and ran into the Panda's path, although; we are unable to ascertain if this actually happened, for the Eclipse was then destroyed by the blast as well, so there has been no one to confer this statement fully. We are aware, only two torpedoes were used and had travelled some 100 miles distant or so before making contact and exploding, though I hasten to add only one went off.'

'Did you say the Panda?' Jeff said questioning Billings and sensing the anger bubbling inside him, for he could see the distraught look on his face, at losing so many men and women.

'Yes, I did and I am also acquainted that Captain Johnson was in command of it.'

'I wonder,' Jeff muttered turning away from the television-set to walk across the other side of the room, where a large map hung on the wall.

'What's on your mind, Jeff?' Jim asked. 'Think you may know where Krabava is heading for?' Jim added trying to read Jeff's mind, for he understood how his mind worked; in fact, he knew all his team very well.

'Maybe, maybe not, but you said he fired those torpedoes some 100 miles out and east of the Panda. Are you sure of that?'

'Yes we recorded the Panda on 40.30° north and 71.83° west,' Billings stated still not understanding where Jeff's questioning was coming from.

'So if that's the case I reckon he will be about here, are you with me so far?' Jeff added putting his finger at a point on the map, then turned his head to check they were watching. 'You with me,' he said.

'All the way,' they said in unison. Billings voice echoing above the rest of them for he was now showing a lot more interest by what was beginning to formulate. Still it did not change his mind at how he felt about the CIA and their entire goings on behind closed doors.

'In my reckoning I guess he is somewhere in this location,' Jeff continued thumping his finger against the point where he wanted his colleagues to see.

'How do you come to that conclusion Jeff,' Billings asked, but not admitting he thought the same as Jeff.

'Realistically speaking and taking into account how far he would have travelled from the scene and remembering how fast he would have been able to go. For you stated Johnson thought he had sunk him, so in my conclusion he may be damaged enough to prevent him carrying on to his home destination, but if he's not damaged in any way as to prevent his escape. Mark had stated, when I last spoke to him that the submarine could travel at 18 knots below the waves, and at least 23 knots or so on the surface. So let's assume he's sailing at 18 knots. In 5 hours, he would have reached approximately 90 miles from the sinking of the Panda. So that's where I believe we should start the search Mr Billings,' Jeff concluded.

'Sticking your neck out a bit aren't you Jeff!' Jim said in a solemn voice.

'Perhaps I am, nonetheless; Sakhakov wants to save Charley, and of course himself, as well, so they must make for deep water to be able to hide from us.'

'There is something puzzling me?' Billings stated and needing to find as much as he could to inform the white house before any search could take place, as he would need to get clearance for the search.

'We are all ears,' Jeff said as they waited for him to speak.

'Where's he heading for? For we have asked the Russians to cover the ports, in the event the submarine turns up at one of them, they will then detain them and I expect trial them all for murder. We have of course asked for them to be extradited back here to stand trial,' Billings said gravely.

'Commander, I'm sorry to be a drag, but in my view of thinking I believe they won't head back to Russia, at least not on that submarine, as it will take far to long and risky for them,' Jeff assured.

'I suppose you could be right, so how do you think they will vanish then?' Billings stated with a touch of sarcasm in his voice towards Jeff in his approach to solving the problem, while making his way towards the door to leave.

'That I can't say as yet, but they will try that's for sure.'

'Well gentlemen, there's nothing further we can do at the moment till we find out where they are, and find them we will and destroy them that you can be certain,' Billings concluded, and then twisting round sharply on his heels he disappeared out of view, leaving a vacuum of silence behind him.

'Whew mates ain't he a pig headed son of a gun,' Dave said breaking the stillness in the room to explain briefly, that he also disliked the commander's attitude.

'Maybe you are right Dave. Although, I think we should concentrate at what Krabava options are. So while your thinking I'm going to see the girls and see how Ann's coping with all this with regards to her husbands disappearance, for we owe her big time,' Jeff muttered leaving the others to talk amongst themselves.

'When do you think you'll head home,' Pat asked, approaching Ann from another office, where she was staying.

'As soon as possible, anyway after they can definitely confirm that Marks gone. I have already contacted my son and daughter and told them the news and have requested them to stay in England for there is nothing they can do here, as I will be returning home to see them.' Even though, she still had a nagging feeling inside her that her Mark was alive some place.'

'I'm certain Jeff won't rest till he's positive Mark has gone, he will not give up looking for you, for he knows how much you must be feeling. He's also awful about what had taken place, and somehow feels responsible,' Pat declared.

'Yes I'm sure he does, but that doesn't make me feel any better.'

'I will do my very best,' Jeff said over hearing the conversation between the women as he entered the room and without being offered he sat down beside them hoping to comfort Ann.

Harvey and Dave, who had followed Jeff, grabbed a couple of chairs that were opposite Ann and waited for somebody to speak.

'Where's Jim?' Ann said noting he was not with them.

'He's been side tracked, evidently he needs to find out what's happening about the search, he did say he would be along a little later on,' Dave volunteered.

'How would you lot like to go out for a game of bowls and a meal?' Jeff asked desperately hoping to lighten the mood and give them all a break, to what had happened over the last few hours.

The atmosphere lightened somewhat as they mustered in the restaurant after playing bowels and they sat round a large table with its clean white cloth and decorative silverware that had been set at each place for them all.

'I don't want to spoil this evening Jeff, but something has occurred to me.'

'Oh that's ok Ann, fire ahead if you think it will help catch those responsible.'

'Well it's what Krabava said, when we first got on board that rotten boat,' she began to say hovering on what to say further. 'He told us it was his first and last voyage, then he carried on by stating he intended returning to his old home, emphasising old home where ever that may be.'

285

'Did he indicate where it might be Ann?'

'No not exactly, but mentioned something about horses his farther had owned and that they were now being looked after for him. I tackled Sakhakov; if he knew where Krabava's horses might be, but he only told me a place near Terenkol, which is in Kazakhstan, and then he carried on to say he didn't see any horses at the time he was there. But it was a large farm and had plenty of open fields.'

'So it could be big enough to carry horses?' Jeff injected.

'Oh yes, the way Sakhakov spoke about it, it most likely would have been,' she said looking at Jeff taking a sip of wine, that Dave had produced from nowhere.

'Have I said anything that makes sense Jeff,' Ann said hoping not to have spoilt the evening.

'Yes you have Ann and thinking if I was in his shoes, would I have planned the same.'

'I cannot help you with anything else; it was what he said at the time I spent on that boat and until now had for gotten about it.'

'Do not worry Ann,' Jeff said turning his attention to what he might do, if he was in Krabava's position as to how he would escape. 'Let's enjoy ourselves tonight, I'll ask more questions tomorrow, if that's ok with you Ann.'

'Yes, yes of course, if I can help catch them, I'll be glad if only to appease the death of my husband Mark.
You know it's my fault really, his eyes lit up when I told I had booked a surprise break, not realising what the future was in store.'
She remarked with a solemn tone to her voice.

286

Chapter 29

'Somebody get up that ladder and shut the hatch cover, before we all drown,' Sakhakov shrieked in despair at seeing water gushing through the opening and with everybody running round in a blind panic, unable to cope with the sudden event.

'Close the watertight doors,' he bellowed again trying to get some order in the control room.

Kazan realising the danger, made a mad dive for the ladder and proceeded to climb up it in a desperate attempt to reach the opening, but thrown to the floor by the force of the water, which surged through the opening. Quickly getting back on his feet he made another terrific dash for the top, only failing once more, this time the force of the water slung him off the ladder against the control room's console and knocked him unconscious when landing in the knee-deep water. He tumbled over onto his side and sank beneath the water to the cold steel floor.

As the water poured through the hatch at a furious pace, it swiftly began to fill the room, adding further weight to the boat it could not sustain. The boat began to sink more rapidly towards the seabed and creating more problems for those on board as the pressure started to increase against the hull.

Sakhakov was trying to send a message in the radio room, when he first heard the commotion about Kazan trying to stop the flow of water, and then looking to what had happened to Kazan, he instantly ran for the ladder. Having no time to help him he began to fight his way to the hatch opening. Holding his breath and gripping the runs tightly he crawled unyieldingly up it only to find the lid secured by a clap. He knew he had no time to lose, for if he could not reach the latch and release it; they would all die in the next few seconds. Finally grasping his fingers round the latch with all his strength, he heaved at it with all his might and with determination and frantically trying not to swallow any water; he made a last attempt to move it. This time he was able to pull the lid down far enough, so the pressure of water could close the lid and make it secure.

Now with air running out of his lungs, he dreaded the worse as he choked with the searing pain in his chest while holding onto the wheel of the hatch cover. Keeping his head above the water line, for water had filled within a couple of inches of the boats metal ceiling; he turned the wheel to fix it tight.

He looked around the compartment in the bitter cold water, and now was aware he needed to get rid of the water before the pressure killed him. He needed to act fast to survive and save the rest of the crew from this peril as well.

As he hung, holding onto the wheel of the hatch his thoughts began drifting to why Krabava had betrayed them, but found there was no answer as he held on to the wheel, he could not understand the reason, as to why he had done this despicable act on them. Then suddenly something triggered his mind and spurred him into action making him more determined to be free from the chaos.

The Zhuralev slowly sank to the bottom of the Atlantic, and gently it settled to rest amongst the green undergrowth that helped cushion its impact. It rocked from one side to the other for a few moments, before lying quite still, sediment disturbed by the boats arrival, filtered like a fine mist over the boat and sluggishly dropped to the decks floor.

Yelling and screaming from the crew began to subside and only a whimper was audible and that ultimately came to a halt.

'We've been in this situation before?' Charley declared whispering, as if she did not want anybody to hear her.

'Yes I recall. It was when we attacked the warship and I must admit it was a bit daunting to say the least,' Mark replied hearing the creaking, groaning and banging of the boats metal structure caused by the differentiating weight of water that was bearing down on them.

'Yes we have, not only when you were on board, but when we were in the Pacific as well.'

'Really what was that all about,' Mark asked her.

'I'll explain later, if and when we get out of this mess,' she said in a disconcerting voice.

'Ok Charley, now you'll have to be brave and believe me, when I say we will get out of here,' Mark said not entirely convinced they would get free as he spoke to her in the darkness, for the lights had been extinguished when reaching the seabed.

Frightened and disorientated by what had taken place in so quick a time, the only thing he could think of was the past. Recalling when he was in the navy, he never endured the kind of situation, that now represented it self. 'Come on Charley let's find out who's in the other compartments, keep that flash light shining straight ahead so we don't trip over anything,' Mark stated beginning to move from their room and heading towards the rear of the boat.

Reaching the closed door of the next compartment, he stopped to listen for any life, before thumping twice at the door with a wrench he had picked up along the way and then stood back waiting for the reaction he hoped he would receive.

'Anybody in there,' he shouted, then hearing a reply he set about to open the door.

'Give me a hand to open the door,' Mark yelled back as someone started yelling back to him. Spinning the metal wheel fast till it released the catch, he heaved with some help in anticipation to what lay beyond, although; he need not have worried, as it swung open wide to reveal a friendly face staring at him.

'Greetings my friend,' a smiling Valja said to him as he entered through the access and stood just in front of Mark with a brightly lit torch in his right hand.

289

'Greetings---, what---, what do you mean greetings what have you to smile about?' Mark urged.

'At least we are alive and I trust we are able to put this boat back on the surface.'

'I have no idea, we will need to see exactly what went wrong, before we could even think of trying to surface it,' Mark said cynically, for he was thinking this seaman had gone mad.

'Success is not far away,' Valja continued to say as Mark made his way to the next door, which led into the engine room, and once again proceeded to repeat the same exercise as he did earlier.

'Are you four men ok,' he said as they scrabbled out with relief they were not the only ones alive and well.

'It's no good trying the torpedo room,' one of them said to Mark. Mark immediately understood what he meant and returned through the compartments to the control room door and began tapping on it, while Valja feeling the door with his hands and putting his ear against the metal in the hope it would also be fruitful for them all to go in.

'That's not the same sound as the others; I think it's full of water?' Mark grunted on hearing the dull thud each time he banged at the door and with no response from the other side.

'Now Valja, are you still confident that we will get out?' Mark added now beginning to anticipate the worse. 'Anyone else got any ideas as to how we are going to get out of this mess and remember how deep we could be. The last time I recollected I noticed the gauge reading, it was something like 900 feet, and must be very well near the boats crush depth, so I would say there is no hope of exiting from any of the escape hatches with approx 500lbs per sq inch pressing on them.

'Certainly someone would hear us, if we make a lot of noise?' Charley calmly said leaning against the bulkhead near the door to the control room.

'Maybe, maybe not, we can listen for ships overhead and then create hell,' Mark injected, but I have no doubt at the outcome of anyone rescuing us from this metal tomb.

He squatted on the cold floor with his head in his hands unable to think clearly at what they should do next, while hearing ideas the crew passed around, but none had any credence of succeeding.

'How do you think it could have happened Valja?' This time Charley spoke gaining composure and trying to restore her courage and despair.

'It is only a hunch,' Valja put in. 'but by the sound of the amount of water entering the control room, it had come through the conning towers hatch cover, which tells me it must have been left open when we dived.'

'How could it be left open?' This time Mark put the question to Valja.

'I'm afraid we'll never no the answer to that, unless we can get in there and find out what went wrong. But remember if the hatch is open, we'll have to try to close it before we can do anything.'

'Ok, what if it's closed can we empty it from here?'

'No, there are only two places we can empty the water that's in there, one is in the control room and the other is in the engine department. But as I said if the hatch has been left open, and there's no way of telling from here, we are up the gum tree so to speak and are unable to do anything about our situation,' he finally concluded as Mark rose to his feet to listen at the door once again. Then picking up the wrench, he banged even harder this time on the door as if it would cure there problems. The terrific noise echoed throughout the submarine instantly returning a response from a crewmember who hammered back to them from the forward compartment.

'Christ there's more of us alive,' one of the other sailors cried with joy.

'Do any of you understand Morse code? Mark asked as another sailor had already begun tapping a message; his reply soon came to say there were thirty of them at that end of the boat.

'That's makes 55 of us alive,' Mark said knowing those in the rear torpedo room would have perished; for they would have not stood a chance as it was completely flooded.

'I would say we are in a bit of a fix,' Mark grunted solemnly.

'Ask those in the other compartment, if they have any ideas as to getting out; if not our only hope is with a ship hearing us.
We need to conserve power in our torch batteries, so switch off all but two. I just hope the air supplies hold out,' he said with a sullen voice and sitting down to fall silent.

'What's happening now---?' Charley screamed loudly in hearing the sudden sound that was coming from the control room, which made them all jump to attention to what was taking place in there. 'What is it, what's happening? Tell me someone,' she yelled again above the piercing blast of noise that echoed through out the boat.

'Its air escaping from the pressure tanks,' Valja retorted with a stern voice and then starting to laugh with joy.

'What is there to laugh about?' she urged not understanding what was taking place.

'Don't you see,' he said. 'I told you the hatch cover had to be closed to get rid of the water, and the only place apart from the engine compartment was in there, which means someone has to be pulling the leaver manually for the water to escape.'
The noise hit a higher pitch whistle and became unbearable with air screaming along the pipes that sort to tear them from their brackets. Holding there hands to their ears to reduce the sound, but still could not help observing Valja laughing with excitement, Mark wondered if he was correct on his assumption, and that there was in deed somebody in the control room trying to save them.
Air bubbles hit the bulkhead that divided them from the control room as the horrendous racket continued and then the boat began

rocking under the new buoyancy, however it having no effect on attempting to move the submarine from the thick muddy slime, which held it tight on the bottom of the sea bed.

As the screaming air subsided within the confined quarters, silence closed in over the subdued sailors once more, while Mark stood by the door listening for any kind of life from the other side, as he reasoned, that if the air valves were opened to pump out the water then there must be somebody in there alive. He began tapping again, this time more harshly on the door, so whoever was in there would be well aware others were working to free him. Endlessly he moved his way down from the top of the door to the bottom, to ascertain where the water level maybe, then on hearing a hollow echo vibrating from the door he felt encouraged, that the control room was now empty of water, which he knew would hamper any attempt of escaping and leave them to the unforgiving depths.

'I reckon its safe to open, how do you feel about it Valja?'

'What---!' Charley bawled out, we will all drown if you open the door.'

'If we don't open the door we will all die anyway, is that what you want Charley, I think I'll take my chances and get it over with. Valja, I'm ready when you are mate, keep your fingers crossed. But before we open it, you lot better get in the engine room and out of the way if things should go wrong, it's just a precaution.'

Hearing what Mark just said to them, they stood transfixed where they stood, for they had decided silently it was now or never. Charley stood at Marks side in utter bewilderment as to what to expect as they proceeded to open the door.

Her mind started racing back in time, seeing herself as a child and wanting the adventure. She now suddenly thought about Jeff and realised she had truly fallen in love with him and wanted to have him by her side to comfort her. She imagined them living together by the sea where it would be nice and warm rapped in his arms. She shuddered to think of what was to happen, tears crept down her cheeks and she put her hands over her eyes so as not to see the sea rush into engulf her as they pulled at the door.

'If it's full of water we will know sooner than later,' Mark said talking rationally to Valja as he prepared to open the door.

'Very well, it's up to you, go on go for it,' Valja added after expressing his view over their situation. 'Mark you ready, after three we open, one, two, three.' Mark spun the wheel hard and fast releasing the doors mechanism in one quick movement and then with a quick pull at the door while anticipating the worse, it slid open with ease. For a pressing moment, they held their breath, when they saw a small quantity of water that was ankle deep pouring into their compartment, but exhaling with a great sigh of relief that there was only a small amount of water in the control room, Mark without wavering entered into the room.

Shining his torch round in the dark to establish it was safe to enter and why there was no water; he first shone the beam from the floor towards the hatch cover and noticed water spraying in round its seal. He then moved his beam of light across the roof and stopped when he saw Sakhakov strapped by a length of cable to his wrists and his hands gripped tightly around an air valve leaver. Mark made his way towards him, seeing that he hung motionless from the pipes with his eyes closed.

'Help me Valja,' Mark shouted astonished Sakhakov was only unconscious.

'Is he a live Mark?'

'Yeah but he looks bad though, help me get him into Charley's cabin, where she can take care of him.

Charley, his breathings shallow and he has a slow heartbeat, see what you can do for him,' Mark stated as they carried him carefully by torchlight to her room and laid him gently on a bunk.

Charley could hardly believe her eyes seeing her father, for she thought he had died.

'Can someone check the power; see if we can get some light in here?' Valja called to no one in particular.

'Valentine here, I will do my best,' he said responding to the request.

'Kazan's dead, as well as the helmsman and the other two that operated the helm and trimming mechanism. Take them to the rear compartment next to the torpedo room,' Mark said giving the order to another crewmember. 'If we get this tub operational, can we get it to the surface?' Mark questioned to some of the other sailors who had come from the forward end of the boat, and now crammed into the confined space of the control room.

'That's better,' Valja stated when the safety lights eventually came back on, although; dimmer than the main lights but at least it gave them enough light for them to work in.

'At last we can at least see what we are doing,' Valja admitted again.

They continued to keep busy to take their minds of the big problems they had somehow to overcome.

Abruptly the sound of the main pumps sprang into life and began circulating fresh air throughout the boat.

'Perhaps we can sort our way out of this appalling mess,' Valja said while assisting Mark in the preparation for them to escape.

'Valentine what's the state of the batteries? How long do we have, before they give out on us?' Mark said.

'About 72 hours,' Valentine bluntly answered, 'and that's if we turn off the pumps to conserve energy.'

'Not exactly what I wanted to hear mate,' Rachko said, speaking since returning from the bow section.

'I'll endeavour to fix us all a meal, albeit it won't be hot, as I know we have to be careful on the electric,' he grunted trying to smile and then turning away from the scene, he moved from the control room whistling to head for the galley and prepare something to eat.

295

'Can't for the life of me see what he's got to smile about at a time like this?' Valja remarked. 'But I suppose it won't do any of us any harm, if we all tried to look on the bright side. If you need me, I'll be in the engine room, to see if I can get the engine running.'

'What's that banging?' Sakhakov said to Charley, now that he had became conscious and able to take notice to what was happening around him. Charley quickly brought him to speed on events that happened as far as she knew and mentioning the radio had been broken.

'You say it's broke.'

'I'm afraid yes.'

'Help me get up my dear; I need to find out what I can do.'

'Sorry but you are to stay in here for a while longer, there's nothing you can do that is not already being done. Anyhow you can tell me what the hell happened in the control room,' Charley said sitting down beside him for the first time since he told her that he was her father, and waited for him to start talking. Slowly he began to recall to her the actions in the control room why the water flooded the room.

'Krabava and his cronies have done a runner and left us for dead, one of them put the clamp on the hatch cover when they opened it and left it there when we dived, although I have my suspicions as to who it was and why. Consequently, as we submerged the sea plunged through the hatch opening. Kazan tried desperately to shut the hatch but was pushed off the ladder and hitting his head on the console which must have killed him. I know one thing for certain when I get out of this tub, I'll be after them to kill them with my bare hands,' Sakhakov scorned.

'That will be a tall order on your own, what is more you do not know where they are going.'

'Oh I think I do, you must remember I worked and stayed with them for the last two years and leant a lot about there movements.'

296

'You will still need help. Where do you reckon they will head for?'

'A place near Urasa it's in the state of JAKUTIA.' He was about to continue further when Mark entered to check on his well-being.

'How's it going, feeling any better?'

'Yes thank you Mark, what's the position with the boat can we get back to the surface?'

'Maybe, maybe not, one thing is for sure it won't be with the diesels, as Yuri contaminated the fuel before he left, so we'll have to pray that the batteries hold out.'

Sakhakov then swiftly told him about the location where Tabor and the rest of his gang would head for when they got away from the submarine.

'Excuse me Mr Walker.'

'Yes what is it Rachko.'

'I'm afraid to say that the leaking seal is getting worse.'

'Where,' Mark said following Rachko back into the control room.

'It's now spreading right round the hatch cover and looks as if it has been warped by the pressure of water that's bearing down on us.' Mark looked up at the hatch noticing the fine mist that indeed was getting worse round the joint.

'Think it'll stay like that?' Rachko announced looking vexed.

'Hope so buddy, I do feel we should try and get the boat up to a respectable depth, so as to alleviate the pressure around that seal and as quickly as possible,' Mark added to him for he was concerned that the lid may give way.

'How are we going to achieve it Mark?' Mark not responding to his question closed his eyes to think of what may be possible and what may not be possible to achieve them to get the boat moving.

'I suggested to Valja about the problem with the contaminated fuel, so lets wait and see if he has any luck with sorting it out,' he said to Valja as Charley and Sakhakov entered.

'Mark I have managed to filter out some of the fuel, I'll try it if you are ready for this?' Valja called through the mike and sounding very confident of success in getting the engine started. He began to prime the fuel pump so the flow of fuel reached the injectors and pressing the starter button the big diesel engine spun a few revolutions, coughing and spluttering before it roared into life. Transfixed at watching the moving parts, nobody spoke at first as they all stood by the engine watching Valja working with his hands on the machine.

'You're a good man Mark; I could not have done it with out your help, thank you we now have a chance to live,' Valja exclaimed with delight.

'How long will it run for?' Mark said ignoring the complement and trying to hear above the noise of the engine.

'Only half an hour at the moment as that's all the air I've got to use, as you see I've got the men cleaning the fuel system, it will I hope give us a fighting chance to get free.'

'Ok let's take advantage of what we got, start the pump in the stern compartment; see if we can lighten the boat to get it moving,' Mark said before making his way back to the control room.

'You guys, lets get busy,' Mark announced. 'We are going to try and get underway. 'Blow the main ballast tanks.'

'That will be the only time we can do it,' Sakhakov stated as the crew began operating the leavers that would the boat in motion. As the leavers moved to their designated positions, they gave a harsh sound clanging in the confined area of the control room.

'Half ahead, make trim to compensate for drag, helm come steer 280°, steady as she goes,' Mark ordered for the first time in taking charge of the men and boat, while at the same time feeling apprehensive as the boat shook and roll like an old drunk before settling down to a reasonable smoothness.

'We will have a go at reaching the surface straight away,' Mark added noting the men in the control room looking at him with drawn faces, and thinking the same as he with mixed feeling, at getting out safe and alive.

The submarines bow slowly but indisputably proceeded to climb in an upward motion towards the waves above as the water began to increase through the overhead hatch cover, while the pump in the rear torpedo room held back the water in the damaged tube door. With unremitting noises that persisted all over, the submarine the water pressure eased as they ascended to the surface.

'How are we going Valja?' Mark said with his fingers crossed behind his back.

'Carry on boss,' was all Valja could muster.

'Have you considered that if the Americans make contact with us they'll sink us?' Sakhakov questioned with an unbelievable a cynical attitude to his voice, for a touch of jealousy was showing slightly at the way mark had responded with the predicament that they had found themselves.

'I must admit my friend I agree with you, the sixty-four dollar question is, what can we do about it? What with no radio and radar to go by, we are running a little bit on the blind side. Can you ask Valentine if he's free and if he would like to have a glance at it,' Mark said realising the problem and knowing that he needed to save their necks.

'We are now 100 feet below the surface Mark,' Sakhakov said pointing to the depth gauge. Mark heaved a sigh of appreciation that things now were heading in the right direction.

'Good, let's try to see if this thing will surface.'

'We can't get the boat on an even keel the sterns to heavy---,' the helmsman called in frustration. Mark looked at the dials and saw for himself that the stern had become progressively heavier and was beginning to drag them back down again. Water was also spraying through the conning tower seal with increased quantity.

'Mark the stern pump can't control the leak any further and the compartment beginning to fill again,' Valja announced in agitation.

'Sakhakov have another go at the controls for we must get this heap closer to the surface so we can at least get some of us out,' Mark said showing his unease at what was happening to the boat.

Twice more they attempted at getting the boat to the surface but failing on both occasions. Mark then went into the radio room and sat with his hands against his face to hide the despair that he had for Charley and the rest of the crew although not concerned with his own life, he didn't want her to die on his account but felt he was helpless and could not save any of them.

'What on earth is going on Valja?' Mark called to him again.

'I'm so sorry the engine is finished, there is too much contamination in the fuel, I just cannot do anything with it,' he said with a shaky voice.

'Sakhakov, can we get out through to the forward escape hatch at this depth?' Mark asked.

'No it will be impossible, for by the time we get the escape apparatus ready we'll be to deep, also before you ask the batteries are getting too low to run the motors. We're condemned to this metal coffin,' he said shouting out the last word so everybody heard then.

The sailors dropped their tools on the floor in hearing what Sakhakov had said and moved away to their own separate locations within the submarine to be with their own thoughts.

'Turn off all the pumps and lights that we don't need,' Mark called.

'If we stop the stern pump it will flood completely that's for sure,' Valja remarked with a very worried look on his face in the subdued lighting.

'We need time Valja, time to think what we can do to get this boat back up,' Mark said while at the same time sensing the boat sinking back down to the depths far below.

'Have we travelled very far from our last position?' Sakhakov asked seeming exceptionally alarmed.

'No I don't think so, a few miles that's all, why do you ask,' Mark replied.

'It's that we are not far from a cliff face, and as I recall the ledge drops away to infinity, I remember Krabava saying something to the effect that the ocean drops away to a miscible depth in excess of 6000 feet and that we should be very careful in this area.'

'Well if that's the case it won't matter will it?' Mark scoffed shifting his tired weight away from Sakhakov to go to the captain's cabin and asking Charley to join him there as he passed her in the aisle by the galley.

'Charley the news is not good, in fact it's lousy and I think we should move to the forward compartments.'

'Why?'

'Well I reckon when we hit the bottom this time, what with the rear torpedo room full of water that door it won't take the impact and well,' pausing to look into her grimy face and then without adding anything further he shrugged and stared at the floor.

'That's it then, is that all you've got to say, there's no way out of this hunk of junk,' she said inaudibly looking at him with dismay.

'No nothing, we'll have to sit and wait until somebody finds us. I'm sure they will for I can't imagine Jeff letting you die without putting up some kind of struggle,' he said, then moving away from the galley he began to make his way forward to the room where they had occupied earlier when Ann was with him and ignoring Sakhakov with regards to the leaking seal of the hatch.

He nodded to Sakhakov that he was aware that the boat was doomed but continued on his way into the forward compartment followed by the rest of the men who had decided to join him, the last man closing the control room's watertight door behind him.

Chapter 30

'What do you think of the news; they have found debris and two dead bodies floating in the sea which are believed to be the sailor's, from that submarine,' Jeff announced to his colleagues as they gathered in a local bar to discuss the program for the future.

'Well it seems that most of our problems have been solved, and now we can focus on finding Tabor and his gooneys,' Harvey said with a smug look across his face.

'I'm sorry Harvey I don't see it the same as you,' Dave said.

'What's troubling you then Dave, are you conscious of something that we're not aware of,' Jeff asked taking note of his reaction.

'Maybe, but look at it this way,' Dave began, only braking off to take a sip of his beer and then seeing Jim coming into the bar at the end of the lounge and walking straight towards them.

'Carry on Dave we are all ears,' he said hearing Dave's first sentence and encouraging him to carry with what he was about to say.

'Blimey how long have you been there,' Jeff said surprised at not hearing him arrive and by his sudden appearance.

'Long enough, and interested to what you all have to say.'

'Ok you may not agree with this but I think the submarine is still local, whether to strike again, that I doubt or just waiting for the heat to die down before heading home,' Dave said.

'You for real Dave,' Harvey retorted.

'Yeah and furthermore I will put my career on the line that she's at the bottom of the Atlantic probably crippled I guess,' Dave added.

'So where do you propose we find it?' Jim said grinning for he believed that Dave might be correct on his assumption.

'It makes sense; I looked at the data on the Ocean currents and winds in that area for the last 24 hours after the disaster. The wind and current had been running at 1 knot, so on that assumption she will be either where they picked up those bodies or at least in close proximity,' Dave added and having their attention, but nervous for had never been in the lime light like this before with his boss.

'Of course it's only your gut feeling Dave,' Jim replied.

'Not my gut feeling boss, I'm very confident.'

'Ok you sold me but you will have to sell it to Billings before he'll act.' Jim waved his arm to gesture for Dave to follow him out of the bar and to Billing's office.

Neither Jim nor Dave spoke in the corridor as they waited patiently for an answer. Dave paced up and down the corridor in anticipation to whether he had stuck his neck out on this occasion but before he could withdraw from saying what he did to his boss, Billings came out of his office with his hands in his pockets and a stern look.

'I put your idea to the president and I must say I feel the same as him,' he began and then pausing briefly before speaking further, that made Dave feel uneasy. 'We believe that you should go ahead and locate that submarine, if only to put us all at rest that it has been destroyed so they won't be able to strike again. I have already put the wheels in motion and I want you and the others to go to Boston and board the rescue ship where it is taking on supplies. Bring them up to speed and if you have any problems with them refer them to me.' Not waiting for a reply, he twisted on his heels and fled back into his office shutting the door hard behind him.

'I'm glad you're are taking Jeff with you Dave, it will keep him busy and out of my hair, at least until we are certain what needs to be done in Russia with Tabor and the rest of them when they are caught,' Jim said responding to Dave with regards to the submarine.

On board the rescue ship, they discovered three destroyers had to escort them in the event of them making contact with the submarine and threatened by it.

'Captain what do think the chances are of finding her?' Jeff asked once they were on board the ship.

'You are of course aware of the magnitude of this extensive search; however we will undertake to do our best for you CIA boffins.'

'How deep do you reckon we will have to go to find her?' Jeff asked when they had reached the located spot that Dave had mentioned.

They began to lower the two rescue vessels into the water on that mid afternoon to begin their extensive search for the Zhuralev.

'It's hard to say, for I don't know how deep the submarine can go for one thing. Anyhow the sea bottom drops away from 800 feet to in excess of 6000 feet, but one thing is for sure I don't reckon it will go below the 1300 feet mark unless she is made of steel that I am not aware off.'

The ships crew were becoming excited with the activity as the divers adjusted their equipment to engage the depths of the Atlantic Ocean.

'Not much light down here,' Jeff said making his observation with the pilot as he peered into the gloomy waters from the porthole.

There were six portholes across the front and three on each side, plus a further four were at the rear, giving them maxim vision around. The capsule was able to carry twenty persons in all including the pilot and Jeff albeit cramped.

Jeff continued to look through the porthole as they descended into the murky water but still he felt uneasy, for it brought back the memory when he escaped from the submarines tube, although it seemed months ago when it happened.

At 800 feet, they reached the seabed, and the pilot switched on the powerful lights to see through the murky waters only to discover nothing except thin objects that glittered in the powerful ray of light.

'We've searched around this area for the last two hours and only seen plankton and small fish,' the pilot said manoeuvring the mini sub along gravel the seabed.

Jeff started to get inpatient and needed to prove to Jim that Dave was correct in his assumption when he saw him peering through his porthole in his mini submarine.

'We need to surface as we need to take on more air,' Dave called over the intercom.

'Are you positive that you have the figures right?' The leader of the party said sceptical about the whole operation. Dave ignoring him bent over the chart again thinking that he may be wrong but could not see how.

'There is one thing I may have over looked,' Dave mentioned looking up at the leaders face and seeing his frustration.

'Ok enlighten, me I'm all ears,' he spoke with an antagonistic voice.

'Right, If those guys had been dumped over the side when the boat surfaced, we would know where to find it, but what if they got out though an escape hatch when the boat went down. I'm betting that we'll find it a little more to the East.'

'How far do you calculate that to be?' The leader grunted not seeing Dave's logic and having no confidence in his predictions.

'Can we go down again?' Jeff asked responding to the tension between the two of them.

'Let's get to it though I feel this may be the last; we will have to acknowledge the fact that the submarine has been destroyed and gone much deeper than we thought.

Back down in the gloom of the dark waters, both mini submarines descended again and put themselves a little way from each other to

305

be on the safe side in the event that they may have to manoeuvre quickly. They started to scan the seabed once more pushing along the seabed as they went ever deeper all the time, until reaching 1000 feet, their lights penetrating down and ahead through the gloom.

'What's that over there Tony?' Jeff said feeling a lump developing in his throat, for it was all so strange at the bottom and such a different world.

'I'll take a look see,' Dave's pilot acknowledged and proceeded to steer in the direction of the hump in the ground.

'I've found it; it's the submarine all right and doesn't look as if it's very active the way it's sunk in the mud.'

'You reckon they've camouflaged it to make it look derelict,' Jeff called back to his mate.

'No mate, they could not possibly have done that what with the dirt across the deck; no they must have plummeted into the bottom by the looks of things.

'Let's check it for damage,' Jeff remarked to his pilot as they moved closer to the stricken submarine and crossed the stern inches from the deck. Moving some of the silt by their propellers, they headed towards the conning tower.

'You see those bubbles coming from the hatch, seems it still could be flooding,' Jeff's pilot called to his mate. 'You get a fix on the rear hatch cover and take a look inside to ascertain whether there is any water in it. We'll connect to the conning towers hatch and do the same.'

When both mini subs were secured to the Zhuralev hatch covers Jeff steadily released the securing mechanism to undo the lid, his hands shaking with the thought he may see his girl inside.

'Ay mate the control room is flooded, so I'm unable to get in the boat through there, so we are moving to the forward hatch to try there,' Jeff explained to the mini sub.

Lowering his little boat onto the hatch at the bow end of the Zhuralev, he made a positive seal over the cover and waited for Jeff to acknowledge that he ready to open it.

'Did you feel the submarine move Jeff,' the pilot stated as they attached themselves to the hatch.

'Yeah we will have to go very easy,' Jeff replied with concern as he focused on the hatch cover.

'Ok Jeff ready to undo the cover,' Tony the pilot said calling to Jeff again from his steering control.

Slowly Jeff began turning the wheel to free the cover as instructed by the pilot and once having turned the mini-subs wheel fully anticlockwise, he opened it to reveal the submarines main hatch.

'Alright Tony I'm now ready to release the submarines cover,' Jeff said his voice shaking with anxiety remembering that he had been in a lot of difficult situations in the past but, this one were worse than he had ever encountered. His thoughts automatically went to his girl again fearing that she was probably lying inside the boat somewhere dead.

He again began to centre his attention on the wheel and started turning the submarines hatch cover to disengage it; he then lifted it slowly to obtain access to the inside of the submarine and wavered at the outset not knowing what lay in store ahead.

'I've opened the cover and now proceeding to go in,' Jeff called holding on to the hatch as he pressed on through with hesitation, for the feeling inside him gave him the jitters, nevertheless he needed to know whether anybody in there was alive or dead.

'Ok Jeff you be careful,' called the pilot.

'Jeff I'm letting you know there is water in the stern torpedo room, it's completely flooded so we can't try there,' Dave called just before Jeff entered the submarines hatch and started to climb-down the iron ladder into the bowels of the submarine.

'I hear you Dave, its not looking very good in here either,' Jeff' yelled back.

His heart began to beat faster as he climbed onto the first rung of the ladder after hearing the news about the stern he bit his lip and braced himself to expect the worse. Not holding back anymore he commenced to descend to the deck below, his heart thumping and pounded more rapidly when he saw a dim light glowing ahead and was very relieved when he saw no water had entered the compartment.

'It's empty of water; I'm going in further Tony. Shut the lid behind me in the event of any trouble,' Jeff said to him as he let go of the ladder when he reached the bottom. Then carefully with the aid of his torchlight he shone it round the compartment, for only a single bulb glowed dimly that cast a yellow shadow across the whole area, preventing him from see clearly. He scanned the room rapidly at first to see what lay before him as he progressed through the compartment and reacted when the stench of bodies and oil hit him, making him feel nauseous. Repelling the need to be sick he focused on what was there and instantly noticed several sailors lying crumpled on the torpedo racks. Going to each in turn to check if they were alive but it soon became apparent that they had died.

Systematically carrying on through to the next compartment he discovered more bodies laying in all kinds of obscure angles across the deck and sitting against the cold grey metal walls, again going from one sailor to another in turn to verify that if any were alive, and after ascertaining the position, he called to Tony for assistance.

'What have you found down there Jeff?' Tony the pilot called.

'You won't believe this but most are still alive Tony, although they are in need of oxygen, I'm sure they will be ok. I'm carrying on; there must be others here that we can save.'

Jeff shifted on gingerly to enter the next cabin but as he stepped through the doorway, he stood transfixed and immobile for he was utterly astounded. Realising instantly who he was looking at, he swiftly went into action, first going to Charley. For she lay curled up like a ball on the cold floor; he started to give her air from an air tank that he carried with him, until what seemed to be a lifetime he noticed she was beginning to breathe more freely and started to regain consciousness. Then without hesitating, he turned his attention to Mark who was slumped in a chair, with his head in his arms across the small table that they had fixed to the hull of the boat. On Ministering oxygen to him the same as he had done to the others he then darting back and forth to make sure that they were all ok.

'Where did you come from?' Mark said finally, when he regained his senses and the first to speak.

'It's a story that will have to wait my friend for we have to get you out of here before it's too late.'

'Jeff is it really you---!' Charley exclaimed in utter astonishment while holding the wall after recovering.

'Yes my darling it really is me and the formalities will have to wait,' Jeff said abruptly turning back into the other room to see how Tony was progressing with the other sailors.

'Tony we will have to move fast to escape this hellhole,' Jeff said.

'Yeah mate I know, I'm on my way right now, can you rig up a roster for them to leave,' Tony added pulling one of the sailors from the floor to help him to the ladder.

'Will do, but first take those three as they are the worst, I will stay and wait for the RSV to return.' Carrying the first three sailors through the hatch one at a time into the mini submarine and then followed by another 15. Jeff then closed the lid and waited for the sound of the mini submarine as it detached it self from them to depart to the surface.

'How on earth did you endure this place for so long, it must have been hell?' Jeff said to Mark and Charley while waiting for the RSV to return.

'Not the best hotel in the world I must admit,' Mark stated answering with a slight grin as he heard the sound of clanging, which came from the lid as it opened. This time a sailor poked his head through the opening, to retrieve some more men from the stricken vessel.

'Good day you lot anyone for a ride to the top of the world,' he mused as if it was a normal thing for him to do. Twenty or so sailors left the doomed submarine and taken to the surface, which left a total of a few for the next and last run.

'How long are they going to take before they return?' Charley queried looking at Jeff's grimy face with concern.

'It shouldn't be long I guess, I just hope we've got time.'

'Would you care to explain what you mean?' Valja hissed.

'This boat is on the move and slowly sliding towards the edge of the cliff, which has a drop, we won't ever recover from.'

'What do you mean we won't recover?' Charley gasped with a horrified expression written across her face.

'Simply this Charley, if we go over the top this boat as well as us will be crushed to death by the tremendous pressure that will be put on us.'

'Can't we do anything at all to stop it Jeff?'

'No we have to just sit tight and wait I'm afraid.'

'Mark will you give this to Charley,' Sakhakov said handing a parcel to him discreetly and speaking at length for the first time since recovering.

'Why can't you give it to her now?' Mark said beginning to question his motives.

'I think it's best, if you do it Mark, I'm sure she will understand one day, please do not ask me any further questions,' he stated handing the parcel with her name printed on it and c/o Mark Walker.

'It looks as if you had prearranged this sometime ago.'

'Well look at it this way, whatever happens I will not survive, the Americans will endeavour to have me executed,' Sakhakov gestured with a shrug of his shoulders as he faced Mark and knowing he was not going to go free, whatever happens once out of the submarine.

Without warning, another harsh sound came from above, and again the hatch opened to show the same sailor.

'Ok you guys I've got room for twenty, so who's coming with me, I can't stay long as I've got another engagement,' he stated with a wide smirk that showed a mouthful of yellow teeth.

'Mark will you take Charley on this run, I'll take the next trip,' Sakhakov mentioned holding his arms out for Charley to except his embrace, but was ready to respond if she declined. Heading for the ladder Charley stopped and reluctantly took hold of his arms with a sad expression in her eyes and looked at him quickly, and then turning away, she made her way towards the ladder only to glance back quickly to see him standing alone sad in the dim light.

'I'll see you up top in an hour or so,' she said before finally climbing out of sight of Sakhakov into the rescue ship. Mark then also shook hands with Valja and Sakhakov, knowing somehow that he would never see either of these men again alive. Twisting round he then followed Charley up the ladder and being the twentieth to go, in fact he was the last to leave that perilous submarine.

Closing the hatch behind him, it felt very heart-rending it was now all over, but also glad at the same time, for it had been an experience he would never forget. He could now look forward to being with his wife again, and thought she must have been in despair at not knowing whether he had perished or not.

As the motors of the mini sub churned through the water, the rescue submarine disengaged from the deck of the submarines deck and drifted steadily to the surface and to the world above.

Hardly had they freed themselves, when a terrible rumble came from below them and peering through the small portholes, they watched in absolute dismay as the Zhuralev began to edge its way towards the cliff and to the deep depths of the bottomless pit of the Ocean. They could hear the sound of the hull as it scraped along the muddy bottom, shifting clouds of silt and thick sludge as it went which crossed the deck and began to engulf the submarine. It became so thick and dense they were not able to see through the murky haze to witness the bow dipping towards the cliffs edge. Only realising it when they saw the stern rear up to slide towards the edge, and releasing trapped air bubbles that quickly roared towards the surface generating further havoc before the submarine disappeared majestically from view.

Charley wiped her eyes as they filled with tears and ran down her dirty face, as she witnessed the remnants of oil coming from where the boat had once been, and knowing her newfound father had perished with the few sailors that remained on board the boat. She sobbed hard; her body shook violently to the fact she never really knew him and realised she would never discover if he was working for Tabor, or just seeking her to live with.

Chapter 31

'I am so pleased to see you are all alive and well, and Mark I'm very surprised to hear you were on that submarine. It must have been agony for you and Charley as you were on it such a long time,' Jim said as they gathered in the bar of the hotel for a celebration of their success.

'Yes you can say that again, it's been far too long and I thought it would never end,' Charley remarked while stealing a glance towards Jeff, as she held his hand tightly which made her feel even more secure, now her ordeal had came to an end.

'Just to bring you all up to speed,' Jim went on to say. 'The Russian authorities have not as yet caught Tabor and his filthy bunch of crooks, but they were last seen to be crossing the border into Kazakhstan where its believed they have a hiding place and what is more important, we have them tagged so tracking them down should be relatively easy. I realise your ordeal must have been traumatic and I can assure you, they won't get away once we find out where they are. We will catch them Ann, Mark. We have asked the Russians to extradite them back here to stand trial. You may know of course, we have detained the men on the submarine and are questioning them as I speak. I hope they will lead us to the rest of the rotten beggars, so I surmise it will be a better and safer world, when all of them who have been responsible for such a wicked act will be safely behind bars,' Jim said at length.

'Mark tell me, how did you end up on that submarine and what made the skipper bolt like he did and leaving you all to die?' Jeff asked realising it was now the only time he would get to ask him.

'I'll tell you one day Jeff, it's quite a story to tell. But may I suggest we all have a big well-earned party, as Ann and I are heading for home in the morning,' Mark replied and relieved he could put it all behind him.

'Yes, yes of course what a good idea,' responded Jeff.

'Charley what are you going to do with yourself now it's all over?' Jim asked looking at them with a slight smirk across his face.

'That my friend you will have to wait and see,' Charley replied while taking another glance in Jeff's direction to witness his reaction.

'I'll have to say goodbye for now, for unlike you lot some people still have a load of paper work to fill in. Mark, Ann, once again, many, many thanks for your co-operation, for with out your help we may never have solved this mess and that unpleasant business you had gone through. I am so sorry for what you had regrettably found yourself in, I cannot think how both of you endured it for so long. I wish you well for the future, and I repeat if it was not for your help, it would not have been possible to apprehend those thugs. You have been really a big help and if you need any assistance in the future. Please, please don't hesitate to ask me, anything,' Jim said holding out both hands to shake theirs.

'That is nice of you Jim, I am glad I could have helped you but it's a pity I could not help further with catching Tabor and more of his men,' Mark alleged.

'Yes it's a pity but as I mentioned earlier it is only a matter of time, before we have them behind bars,' Jim said and then releasing his grasp on their hands he turned to make his way to the door to leave.

'Oh yes I forgot to tell you guys, Jamie sends her love. She's looking forward to meeting you all again very soon as I can tell you this as she is on the mend, but between you and me, I am sorry to say she will not be going on any further field assignments again.'

'Jim, sorry to detain you, but before you leave, whatever happened about the blackmail tape that you received?' Jeff asked.

'Oh that, I must confess it was a bit of a mystery at first, we never heard from him again, the only conclusion we all came to, was that he wanted to throw us away from our search of Krabava.' He then said nothing further on the subject and swiftly spun on his heels and left the room leaving a vacuum in his wake.

'Ok you guys let's go paint the town red and send Ann and Mark back home with a really big celebration,' Dave cried out with elation.

'Charley, before we go, I've got a parcel your father handed me before we left the boat and asked me to give it to you, when it was convenient, so I suppose this would register as being a likely time. He stated to Charley. He also said you would understand once you have read the contents. I'm sorry I didn't say anything before now as it was his last instructions,' Mark said handing the small brown package to her that Sakhakov had gave him before escaping the boat.

Now with their troubles finally at an end, they left the bar to enjoy the last night with their friends.

www.ingramcontent.com/pod-product-compliance
Lightning Source LLC
Chambersburg PA
CBHW032207030726
47494CB00020B/647